T.M. SMITH

EVERNIGHT PUBLISHING ®

www.evernightpublishing.com

T.M. Smith

Editor: Jessica Ruth

Cover Artist: Jay Aheer

ISBN: 978-0-3695-0890-4

This is a work of fiction. All names, characters, and places are fictitious. Any resemblance to actual events, locales, organizations, or persons, living or dead, is entirely coincidental.

T.M. SMITH

DEDICATION

To you, readers, for traveling with me to book four of the Blood Coven Series, sighing and chuckling in the right places. To you, my critique group, for reading the graphic sex scenes and making sure the characters didn't need to be contortionists. To you, friends, for wanting print copies to display, I hope on a large coffee table in front of the living room sofa. To you Evernight Publishing for making it so.

T.M. SMITH

Terms and Places for the Blood Coven Series

Aerilon
The ylve region of Scath.

Aeternals
A species made up of various breeds who pre-date *Homo sapiens* on Earth. Their creator is the Genitrix Gahya, an immortal who resides in The Vast. After centuries, they grew more cruel and violent, feeding from humans, threatening the continued existence of mankind.

The Alliance Security Agency
A human agency where employees have a distant Aeternal ancestor in their family trees. Once travel between the realms of Scath and Earth became possible, these descendants created an organization to assist Aeternals. Their organization provides Aeternals with access to trade on Earth and assistance in policing Aeternals who enter Earth illegally. They operate a successful cover business, hiring out as bodyguards, private security, and soldiers of fortune. The internal structure includes the Legal Division, Human Resources, Information Services Division, Security Division, and Finance. A board of directors oversees the company.

Amanita Muscaria
A drug used by berserkers before battle. It whips them into a frenzy.

Amori
The incubus and succubus region of Scath.

Angor
A dimension of dark storms and unpredictable weather where immortals are tortured and punished. It is also the final destination of unworthy Aeternals after they die.

Arisen Dawn
A rebel group led by Cerberus. Their beliefs include purity of the breeds and the domination of mankind.

The Assembly
The local government elected by mages.

The Awakening
A ceremony marking an Aeternal's attainment of full power, usually in their early to mid-twenties. The event is different for each breed.

BCA Variant Test
A test developed by Eliphias, Alarik's science lead, to determine if the subject is a Blood Coven descendant.

Blood Coven
Led by the Cambion from Wales, these powerful mages created the realms of Darque, Earth, and Scath in AD 452 where only one world had been before. Aeternals went to Scath, mystical creatures to Darque, and humans remained on Earth. It was the only way the two sentient species would survive.

Bludclan
Vampires are identified by their Bludclan, a social/family group.

Blud Den

A place which specializes in feeding all Aeternal breeds, not just vampires. An Aeternal feeds on the host's blood, soul, fear, energy for magic, lifeforce, orgasm, power, or arousal. O blud dens are more specialized. Here a host takes a drug (most notably opium). The feeding from the host provides a high but is not as addictive as taking the drug itself.

Bludfrenzy
When a vampire is controlled by the need for blood. It becomes the sole reason for living, an addiction.

Bludhaven
The vampire region of Scath.

The Bludhunt
A violent ceremony marking the mating of two vampires.

Breeds
Amazons, berserkers, demons (seven tribes within their breed), djinn, incubi and succubi, mages (or witches and warlocks), satyrs and nymphs, vampires, and ylves. Though each breed has distinct gifts, or powers, all are stronger than *Homo sapiens* and possess better sight, hearing, and smell. Like humans, breeds eat food, but they must supplement it with other nourishment—blood, soul, lifeforce, flesh, fear, arousal, orgasm, or energy for magic.

Camp Follower
An Aeternal who makes himself or herself available as food or sex for Jarek's Firebrands.

The Cede
The Aeternals' funeral ceremony.

The Coalition
The alliance of Firebrands, loyal Scath citizens, loyal members of Scath's government, and humans to defeat Cerberus.

Covenkirk
The seat of Scath's government, the mage region, and the location of the Eastern Stronghold.

The Cubes
Run by gaffers, holding cells for Scath prisoners awaiting trial or interrogation.

Custodes Templii
Formed on Earth by the Cambion before he died. Through the centuries, the group keeps track of Blood Coven descendants, the offspring of the mages who stayed on Earth after the Karmic Schism.

Darque
The realm of mystical creatures, home to harpies, questing beasts, Kalli, Spriggans, Yeti, gagans, polar rats, hellhounds, and more.

D-chip
Digital Implant Communication Chronometer. It is an amazing device embedded into the wrist of each Firebrand warrior and wired to their brains. Its functions are many–telepathic communicator, shadowflasher, GPS locator, emergency portal creator as long as the Firebrand is out-of-doors, a more efficient version of a portal jumper to allow travel through established gateways, temporary cell for captured offenders, and more.

Dionysia
Local government of nymphs and satyrs.

Directorate of Seven
The local ruling body of demons. Each member represents a tribe—animus, avarice, carnal, envy, hedon, pride, sloth. They are chosen by combat.

Elysian Isle
The nymph and satyr region of Scath.

The Encampment
The Amazon, berserker, and djinn region and location of the Southern Stronghold on Scath.

Evermore
A dimension of serenity where worthy Aeternals go when they meet true death.

Freron
A term used by Firebrands to denote another brother- or sister-in-arms.

Gaffers
Like police, the managers of the day-to-day minor crimes on Scath.

Genesis Rite
An ancient ritual where demons fought in combat. The winner spent the night with the ceremony's guest of honor.

Gold Dust
An addictive drug, making users fanatic followers of Arisen Dawn.

Humans First
A paramilitary unit organized by Dante to gather intel on and expose Aeternals.

Isolationists
A group originally organized by Simonis, an ylve, to protest Scath's involvement in affairs outside the realm. He was shoved out as the group became more radical, espousing breed purity and displaying a rising nationalism set on conquering humans. It became the foundation for Cerberus's Arisen Dawn.

Karmic Schism
The splitting of the world into three realms. In AD 452, the Blood Coven cast spells to create Scath and send Aeternals there. At that time, they also created the realm of Darque for magical creatures and Earth for humans.

Knife's Edge
The demon region of Scath.

Lawgivers
Elected drafters of the laws for Scath. A member is chosen from each breed.

Outcast Keep
An area on Darque where Aeternal prisoners are kept.

Ministry of Compliance
Governmental office which regulates travel. Boden is the current director.

Ministry of Coin
Governmental office which regulates finance and drafts

the realm's budget.

Ministry of Culture
Governmental office which regulates education, schools of magic, and Awakening ceremonies.

Ministry of Death
Governmental office which operates prisons, the Cubes, and Outcast Keep on Darque, controls day-to-day crime and gaffers, and regulates the use of explosive weapons.

Ministry of Labor
Governmental office which regulates worker welfare.

Ministry of Prosperity
Governmental office which regulates trade with wildings and humans.

Ministry of the Shield
The only governmental ministry which reports to the Temple of Justice rather than the Lawgivers. The Scion Firebrands are under its auspices. Cadmon is both high commander of the Scion Firebrands and director of this ministry.

Ministry of Well Being
The governmental office responsible for medical facilities, research, science, technology, and history. Alarik is the current director.

Ministry of Wildings and Realm
The governmental office which regulates the wildings and both realms' natural resources, parks, and environments.

Mitakon
A bi-annual Olympics. Winter events are in North Shelters and summer events in the Encampment region.

Monarchy
The king and queen who lead the incubi and succubi.

North Shelters
The shifter region and location of the Northern Stronghold on Scath.

The Path
The words of the warrior Ohngel as recorded by the Cambion from Wales and contained in five-volumes. These books relate tales of the salvation, the betrayal, the creation, the fall and rise, and the destiny of Aeternals.

Pitchblende
A substance which weakens djinn.

Portals
Gateways to and from the realms, created by the Blood Coven at the time of the Karmic Schism but not accessible by all. In the beginning only powerful and approved mages could cast spells for travel. Later, GPS technology allowed for portal jumpers to be distributed to authorized Aeternals.

The Prophecy of Karma
A scroll found by the fire-winged assassin Ohngel, the mentor/guide to the Cambion from Wales, in a cave in the Vakataka Kingdom. The first stanza, though it presaged a dark future for mankind at the hands of Aeternals, it predicted a coven would save them by separating humans and Aeternals. The second stanza

noted the rise of Hades's hound who would lead an army to enslave humans. The last stanza hints at the role of destiny in the prophecy.

The Rage
When a demon loses control of the beast. Usually, they must be put down.

The River Am
A river which defies explanation and natural laws. The witch Indigo, as the Guardian of Time, reads the river. The middle course is the present. Possible futures flow upstream. The lower course, or downstream, shows the just-past to the long-past. No one but Indigo knows the river's location.

Scath
The realm where Aeternals have lived since the Karmic Schism.

Schools of Magic
There are seven schools of magic–Elemental, Conveyance, Forging, Influence, Investigation, Manipulation, Protection. Each mage's powers fall primarily into one category where they are trained in those gifts at the Thaumaturgy Institute. Extremely powerful witches or warlocks may excel in more than one school of magic.

Scion Firebrands
The elite warriors of Scath who follow in the footsteps of an ancestor. Founded soon after the Karmic Schism, they protect Scath and Darque from the most violent Aeternals or creatures. As a side-gig, they also protect humans from the threat of Aeternals who escape to Earth.

When Aeternals are called to join, the initiation begins with the Phoenix brand which burns itself onto the candidates' upper left arms. They experience intense pain until they reach a decision. Join or reject the offer.

The Settling
The demon mating ceremony.

Shadowflash
Old, powerful vampires can trace from shadow to shadow as long as the spot is within sight. It makes travel faster. D-chips give Firebrands this ability also.

Strange But True
The Seattle paranormal tabloid owned by George James, Braelyn's father.

Strigodierna Ceremony
A vampire spiritual ceremony. It is led by the Cruor and his fifty Carnemia.

Supreme Pack Alpha
Chosen through combat to lead the shifters.

Temple of Justice
The body of elected justices who try offenders on Scath. A member is elected from each breed.

Thaumaturgy Institute
Where witches and warlocks are trained in the different schools of magic.

Tribes
The sub-breeds of demons. The inspiration for Christianity's Seven Deadly Sins--animus, avarice,

carnal, envy, hedon, pride, and sloth.

Triumvirate of the Wise
Chosen every fifty years to govern ylves. A chancellor, an imperial secretary, and a grand commandant.

Vampire Conclave
The local rulers of vampires, led by the bludcrown.

Vast
A dimension of clear skies and pleasant weather where immortals, such as Gahya, Gabriel, and the OneCreator reside.

Walkabout
The requirement for influential Aeternals to live on Earth for periods of time to keep current with human activity.

War Council
The governing body for Amazons, berserkers, and djinn, chosen by combat to govern locally.

Watchers
The mages who keep an eye on and maintain the portals and the whorl for Alarik's ministry.

The Whorl
What separates the three realms from each other. Travelers to another realm access it from a portal, travel through it, and reach a portal in the other realm.

Winged Assassins of the OneCreator
Aka The Feard. They or Michael are the only beings who can bring true death to an immortal. Ohngel, the Cambion's mentor and guide, is the fire-winged assassin

of the OneCreator.

LIST OF CHARACTERS IN *THE VAMPIRE'S THIRST*

Abrahm Murdered Kole's parents and is an ancestor of Skyler Maxwell, demon

Aedon Kole's father, Firebrand, animus demon

Adele Lawgiver, ylve

Aisen Silas's half-brother, operated stockades for Cerberus, vampire

Alarik Director of the Ministry of Well Being, Rein's father, Indigo's half brother, warlock-incubus

Alden Maxwell Skyler Maxwell's father, once the CLO of the Alliance

Allias Alarik's employee in Echo's history division who finds evidence of Custodes Templii

Anarai Original Blood Coven, warlock

Anna Skyler Maxwell's administrative assistant at the Alliance

Anthive Jarek's grandfather, djinn

Aras High Justice of the Temple of Justice, eagle shifter

Artha A girl at the group home with Chiara

Bade A Firebrand recruit, vampire

Bahar Lawgiver, djinn (m)

Bett A girl at the group home with Chiara

Boden Director of the Ministry of Compliance, sloth demon

Bounty Kole's executive assistant, vampire

Braelyn James Rein's mate, writer for Strange But True, Blood Coven descendant

Brak A carnal demon, Firebrand

Cage Takes Gold Dust, coyote shifter

Cal The assistant legal officer at the Alliance

Celene Bailey Held captive by Cerberus, heiress, daredevil, adrenalin junkie

Cerberus The hound of Hades who prophecy foretells will destroy the portals and enslave mankind

Chay Full name Chayton, Firebrand, Margo's mate, ylve

Chiara Flores Lives outside Orofino, ID; rescues Dax

Cleatra Works for Alarik at the Ministry of Well Being, witch scryer

D Monz A demon rapper

Daire Lawgiver, incubus

Dania Viktor's mate, vampire

Dante Upper class Englishman who conspires with Cerberus

Darius Jarek's second, Firebrand, djinn

Dax Full name Daxton, Firebrand, vampire

Denim Quinn Ex-military, ex-police, ex-Alliance, Firebrand, Ram's mate, Blood Coven descendant

Dolph Temple of Justice, warlock

Draven Temple of Justice, vampire

Dr. Messenger Dante's scientist/medical doctor

Echo Chief historian at the Ministry of Well Being, a pride demon

Eirene Original Blood Coven, witch

Eliphias Chief scientist at the Ministry of Well Being, a warlock

Ellington Lord, Dante's real name

Engel Original Blood Coven, warlock

Eron Temple of Justice, female demon

Eydris Original Blood Coven, witch

Faelan Original Blood Coven, warlock

Fera Supreme Lawgiver, shifter

Finley Sage Camping in Montana, a caterer

Gabriel The creator of Homo sapiens, an immortal in Vast

Gahya The Genetrix, creator of Aeternals, an immortal in Vast

Galena Firebrand, Amazon

George James Braelyn's father, owner of Strange But True, Alliance board of directors

Gilda Temple of Justice, Amazon

Harry Miller Nash's second, tracker for Custodes Templii

Hestia Kole's mother, Firebrand, animus demon

Horach Kole's uncle, Directorate of Seven, animus demon

Isaac "Lip" Lipton General, US Army

Indigo Guardian of Time, Alarik's half sister, Rein's aunt, witch

Iprix Lawgiver, warlock

Jace de Vries Held captive by Cerberus, worked as vintner in New Paltz, NY, Blood Coven descendant

Jarek Rostamian Firebrand commander of the Southern Stronghold, Lizette's mate, djinn

Jezzi Proper name is Jez, Firebrand, panther shifter

Jonquil Ram's daughter, nymph

Kara One of Jarek's Firebrands, Amazon

Karth Sells Gold Dust, shifter

Kat Full name is Katrina, Firebrand, witch

Kilem One of Jarek's Firebrands, warlock

Kole Firebrand commander of the Eastern Stronghold, Skyler's mate, animus demon

Licia Norah's mother, vampire

Lizette Lee Radio talk show psychologist at WMR radio production studio in New York, Spear's sex slave, Jarek's mate, Blood Coven descendant

Locasta She is the medical examiner at Alarik's ministry, witch

Lort Cerberus's general, vampire

Luka Thorn's brother and pack alpha, wolf shifter

Mara Lawgiver, demon (f)

Margo Hunter Sculpter from Cleveland, OH, Chay's mate, Blood Coven descendant

Mars Dante's general of Humans First paramilitary

Mateo Garcia Colonel, US Army, sometimes called Matty

Masoud Original Blood Coven, warlock

Miller Nash Head of Custodes Templii, Blood Coven descendant, ex British intelligence

Morgana Original Blood Coven, witch

Nace Full name Nacon, commander of the Northern Stronghold, Firebrand, jaguar shifter

Nerina Lawgiver, nymph

Nico Abello Lead agent with the Alliance until he becomes a Firebrand, Blood Coven descendant

Niviane Original Blood Coven, mother of Seraphine, witch

Noor Original Blood Coven, warlock

Norah Captured by Humans First with Varik, vampire

Ohngel The fire-winged assassin of the OneCreator and mentor to the Cambion, an immortal

OneCreator Ruler of Vast and Evermore

Ossar Norah's father, vampire

Ram Firebrand, Denim's mate, satyr

Rein Vampire-Warlock-Incubus mix, Firebrand, Braelyn's mate, Blood Coven descendant

Rike Lawgiver, berserker

Roshan Temple of Justice, djinn

Sabine Celestial nymph, Firebrand, Nico's mate

Sari Luka's mate, wolf shifter

Seraphine The daughter of Niviane and the Cambion, witch

Sig Firebrand recruit, demon

Silas Ran stockades for Cerberus, disgraced Firebrand, vampire

Simonis Founder of the Isolationists, ylve

Skyler Maxwell Chief legal officer of the Alliance, Kole's mate, Blood Coven descendant

Solemnia Original Blood Coven, witch

Spear Keeps Lizette Lee as a sex slave, berserker

Stian Original Blood Coven, warlock

The Cambion The Cambion from Wales is the warlock who gathered the Blood Coven and created three realms of Earth, Scath, and Darque from one world in AD 452

Thorn Firebrand, wolf shifter

Tyr Firebrand, warlock

Uwrick His spell isolated Kole and Skyler on Darque, warlock

Varik Son of Viktor and Dania, captured by Humans First, vampire

Viktor Lawgiver, vampire

Wynnfrith A respected Firebrand killed by a harpy

Xanthe Original Blood Coven, witch

Zora Alarik's executive assistant, succubus

T.M. SMITH

THE VAMPIRE'S THIRST

The Blood Coven Series, 4

T.M. Smith

Prologue

What I hold in my palm is the present, but each grain is the past.
— Ohngel, as he scooped a fistful of sand from the beach

Wales, Fourteen Years After the Karmic Schism of AD 452

In the quivering firelight, the Cambion's shadow danced on the calcite-draped cavern wall, mushrooming, stretching toward the ceiling, an image more haunting than his own dark figure.

The only sounds in the cave were the trickle of an underground stream and the crackle of tinder. Crisp, cool air taunted the warlock's nostrils while a damp breeze from a vent deep within the bowels of darkness feathered across his face.

Fourteen years ago, he and the twelve other

powerful mages of the Blood Coven performed the Karmic Schism to forge the three realms of Earth, Scath, and Darque from one world. Afterward, he ordered the spellcasters to remain hidden on Earth along with their offspring so they could not be used to re-open the portals.

The witch Niviane violated his trust by sending their daughter to Scath. Though a child of his seed, her birth had been unknown to him. Despite being an unwitting partner in the betrayal, his guilt was heavy, his soul drained of light.

Worse yet, Ohngel, his mentor, the fire-winged assassin of the OneCreator, now warned that the progeny of their union could play a deadly role in what was to come.

Though his offspring's destruction would be a simple matter, it was never one the Cambion considered. He was not so iron-hearted. Besides, Ohngel said events must play out as they happen.

To counter Niviane's perfidy, his mentor set new tasks for him. And though the Cambion did not understand the strategy behind these tasks, he trusted the male who had become his friend.

Today, he would perform the most perplexing chore. The hem of the powerful mage's robe traced a spidery pattern in the dirt when he shuffled back and forth, preparing to cast an enchantment. With a twist of a wrist, he ignited wood shavings, twigs, and logs. Once the flames licked high, his weary, trembling fingers dug into his pocket to extract a pouch containing galangal, hazel, jasmine, and lemongrass along with rarities from African tribal elders. He tossed the contents onto the fire.

Murmuring words gleaned from his time in the dark jungles, the Cambion morphed, bones snapping, flesh tearing but re-assembling as feathers. A beak formed. Talons curled from his feet.

He stretched and fluttered, savoring the new shape which would take him to Scath, the realm of Aeternals.

With rich brown wings spread wide, the red-tailed hawk soared over a farm in the Amori region where a young succubus scattered grain for hungry chickens. He swooped down on the maiden to plant his seed, to enfold her in the soft velvet of desire.

With a talon, he slashed his breast, feeding her his lifeblood. In nine months, the succubus Coye would birth an incubus babe.

His task complete, the Cambion returned to the cavern's blazing fire. With his hands raised high, the sleeves of his robe sliding down to reveal thin arms, he summoned Ohngel.

Taller and broader than the mage, his mentor leaned against the cavern wall, his eyes heavy with remorse. "Only one of your two bloodlines will survive."

"Will it be chaos or order? Will it be the child born of Niviane or Coye?" asked the Cambion.

His mentor shook his head. "I do not know the answer, friend."

Wings snapped from Ohngel's back, carrying him to the ceiling. From there, he zeroed downward toward the fire, bursting from the flames as the Phoenix in bright blue, green, yellow, and crimson shards of light. Beating against the air, he soared out the cave entrance.

When he swooped close to the ground, the prophetic bird exploded into a thousand brilliant colors. The multihued debris swirled in a whirlwind before settling into a slow roil which formed a giant red dragon. Opening its dagger-toothed mouth to unfurl a stream of fire, the beast forced the warlock to throw a defensive arm in front of his face while the creature lurched toward destiny.

The stage was set. A new play was in motion.

Chapter One

Scath, Present Day

With two demons and a warlock nipping at his ass, Dax ran faster than a questing beast chased by a squadron of harpies.

No doubt about it, he was shitkicker deep in a sticky mess. He'd been trailing the three males as part of a Scion Firebrand investigation into the drug trade on Scath when they surprised him by doubling back. He hadn't noticed until it was too late. Dumb move. Maybe he needed to get his act together, stop doing time in O blud dens.

Yeah. Not happening.

In the distance a thick stand of trees created a patchwork of light and shade on the forest floor, but he was unable to shadowflash into the dark, canopied shelter to escape. The old and powerful mage on his six must have hit him with a blocking spell. Since Dax was no lightweight in the vampire ability department, he was surprised.

Though he traveled at high speed, stirring dust, his boots thudding on the dirt road, it was time to take it up a notch. He rocketed forward. An eye over his shoulder told him the pursuit team was also double-timing it.

Damn.

Veering into the thicket, he parted tall shrubs when he burst ahead. Dodging fallen tree trunks along with scattered boulders, Dax tried to lose the unwanted traffic. He risked another backward glance. They were still coming strong.

His pursuers must not have spent the night

sucking on some opium strung-out blud whore's throat while pumping off to Imagine Dragons' "Believer." They had probably eaten a nutritious breakfast. Too bad his mother hadn't been the type to nurture him with a hearty bowl of oatmeal and a push onto life's right path.

While he navigated a steep incline, he tapped the D-chip implanted in his wrist to call his partner, Scion Firebrand Tyr.

No response.

Dax messaged him through the link which connected their brains to the chip. *Where are you? I'm being chased by three asshole drug dealers in Arisen Dawn uniforms. I can't trace away because a fucking warlock spelled me.*

With his vampire powers negated, Dax tried his backup. He tapped his wrist. The multifunctional implant allowed him to shadowflash, like his now-useless vamp gift. He chose the top of the hill where he saw the shade beneath a large tree. In an instant, he was there. When he materialized, he rested palms on his knees, gasping for breath. When he twisted his neck to have a look-see, the three pursuers popped out of the mist like tics.

Impossible.

Not only did the warlock block his innate vampire abilities, but he obviously had a top-notch tracking spell in play or a device similar to the Firebrands' chip.

What if I jump to Earth? Unlikely they can follow me there.

Again, he called Tyr. *I'm heading to a portal and Earth. Contact you from there if I get across without my tag team. Over and out.*

Not paying attention, Dax nearly ran into a tree. He wove around it to keep on hustling. His followers had dropped off a bit. Hoping they were wearing out, he plowed through a low bush.

If he reached the portal before Larry, Schmuck, and Curley, he could get to Earth. Where? Somewhere isolated.

In a previous visit Earthside, during one of his required walk-about stints, he'd camped out in Idaho. Good locale. Few humans. A nearby gateway.

Jumping a boulder and running around a tall shrub, he tapped his chip. Still no answer from Tyr. Dax wondered if his warlock *freron* was punishing him for all the calls he'd ignored while distracted by O blud or by just plain being a snarly dickhead.

The portal was ahead. Almost there.

Once through the entrance, he tapped his wrist, somersaulting through the Whorl to Earth, the rough ride scrambling his brains. Vampires weren't meant to travel this way. It was unnatural. After he landed in a cave in the woods as planned, he shook his head to clear it. Outside, he scanned the area. Not a human in sight. So far, so good.

He scrubbed a fist across his jaw, trying to jar his memory. On Scath, Dax had watched his soon-to-be pursuers from cover while they talked to a male peacocking it in a sports car. The guy handed off a package to the warlock. The prick in the sleek auto was familiar, but he couldn't place him. Maybe he should stow the walk down memory lane until he wasn't being chased.

Good idea.

Dax took cover while he eyeballed the gateway. What the…? One demon scrambled out of the cave. The other dealers wouldn't be far behind. With little time to wonder how they'd acquired portal jumpers which could track him, he was sprinting again.

It was all about power and stamina now. So he

really regretted his vices. The drugged blood. The lack of sleep. Not enough food. Too much pussy. Not working out with his *frerons* to build strength. His life was about to take a left turn onto shit road. At least he wasn't leaving anyone behind who would miss him. Maybe his sister Bounty. But she was better off without him.

That's when the demon snagged his shoulders, tackling him to the ground. Big mutherfucker.

From a less-than-auspicious position flat on his back, Dax threw out both legs to spring upright. When the bigger-than-a-Stryker-tank demon charged, the Firebrand landed a scissor kick to the male's chin. Crunch. Bones splintered.

With his fingers moving his jaw back into place, the guy rushed forward only to be taken to the ground by Dax's swift footwork.

Grasping his assailant by the shirt, the vampire Firebrand pulled him up onto wobbly legs where he slammed a fist through the guy's chest. Dax stared at the beating heart before he popped the organ between his fingers. When he shook his hand, crimson goo splattered in the air.

Aeternals could survive most injuries, other than those which left them with no heart or no head. Those were no-goes. Fast trip to the Evermore. Being engulfed in flames didn't work out well either.

Before Dax could enjoy the kill, the second demon wrapped him in a headlock. With an arm thrown behind him, Dax tossed the male overhead. *Whoomph*. His pursuer shot to his feet. The two exchanged fists to noses, jaws, and ribs before the vampire Firebrand planted a side-kick to his opponent's ear.

The demon leapt back, holding his head as if it rattled. Then he came at Dax with the works. A foot to the gut, a jab on the chin, a one-two punch to the face.

The vampire took it all, but bells were ringing with each hit from the giant's meaty knuckles.

Fire shot from his opponent's hand.

Fuck.

He was an animus demon. Dax hated fire. He dodged the blaze. Almost. The skin on his left side sizzled. When he charged, he caught the flame-throwing asshole's neck in his jaws, fangs buried in the jugular.

Dax had handled the first asshole with ease. Number two was about to go down for the count.

Like all Scion Firebrands, Dax was beefed up, bagging an extra dose of power once he accepted the Phoenix's call to serve as a Scath warrior. Always handy when faced with an attack by two demons. But the warlock who exited the portal tipped the scales. One wave of the male's hand as he cast a spell pinned the vampire to the ground, arms to his sides and legs spread.

What a shitty way to exit. Trussed and tied to an anthill. Not my best moment.

A warlock could only create so many spells before he ran out of juice. But Dax didn't have much time and this guy didn't look weary.

When somebody says life passes before your eyes when you're about to croak, believe them.

Dax flashed on a brutal past. His mother. Weak. His stepfather. Evil. The O blud den where he'd been raised. Rat's nest of blood, sex, and more blood. Bounty's face floated into sight. First as a child. Then as a fully grown female, honorable, a thing he hadn't tainted, someone he was proud to call sister.

A spell dug its fingers into Dax's chest while he fought the deadly intrusion. His muscles clenched, trying to form a shield. But the warlock's magic was strong. It broke through.

Large animals charged through the bushes,

howling, attacking. Dax inhaled. Exhaled. Each breath shallower than the last. Faint scents drifted into his nostrils. Crisp air. Honeysuckle. Pine. Moss. Damp soil. Leaves rustled beneath the killer's boots. Dax heard a bird singing, a fucking bird, just before pain shot from his wrist. Next, it was cut-to-fade as a final thought flitted through his brain.

I hate warlocks.

****

The best part of Bounty's job was the action. As Commander Kole's vampire executive assistant at the Firebrands' Eastern Stronghold, she occupied a front-row seat. Disconnecting from a call, she was eager to return to eavesdropping on the heated meeting in her boss's office.

Spit and fury blasted through the walls as Kole and Thorn went shitkicker-to-cowboy-boot. They were pissed. She should have ordered the room soundproofed.

No fun in that.

Tyr was also inside with the excitement, probably enjoying the up-close-and-personal show she tuned into from her desk chair. She could have been unscrupulous, pressing an ear to the door. But she had her good name to consider.

Bounty's eyes rolled right as she caught Kole's booming baritone.

"I'm waiting," he yelled.

The next voice was Thorn's, a wolf shifter. "Luka's my brother. It's my pack. I didn't have a choice."

"Son, choices abound in this world. Problem is you made a shitty one."

Silence.

Then Kole again. "How much did you tell him?"

Thorn's turn. "I didn't really tell him anything. I

asked questions."

"Like what? Don't make me pull this out of your ass."

Bounty pictured flames shooting from her animus demon boss's fingers. She had enough to do this week without arranging for a patch job on the wall. She had fireproofed his office, but sometimes he burned through the protective layer.

Thorn again. "I asked Luka whether the pack was involved with drugs. When he turned furry on me, I shifted to demo who was the better brother. Once I subdued him, my teeth in his neck, he returned to his skin. I told him he was without honor. Our parents would not be proud. I left."

Then Tyr started in on the shifter. "Here's the thing. By the time Dax and I got to Karth, the entire pack had moved out. Whereabouts unknown. We would have been to North Shelters sooner, but we were caught in a situation with a female. We didn't get on the road again until after Ram's rescue. You fucked up our job, buddy."

Honeyed words rolled off the tongue of the sexy Goth warlock. Bounty had to think about Karth for a minute. He was the wolf shifter who'd been doling out the new drug Gold Dust like candy. Thorn and Tyr had been about to corral him for some Firebrand-style questioning when they arrived to find Luka and his pack gone.

"He's my brother."

Tyr said, "So ya said. I told you about Karth because I trusted you. It was a heads-up, not a call to shout out a warning which gave them time to run."

"It was not my intent."

Tyr laid into the wolf shifter once more. "Yeah. Well, best laid plans and the shit which goes with them."

Bounty heard movement.

"Plant your ass back in the chair, shifter. I'm not done with you."

Only Kole owned big enough gonads to speak to Thorn like that.

"I'm through. I can't undo what's been done. The ball's in your court. Do what you need to do."

Somebody got thumped into the plasterboard. Bounty's money was on Thorn with Kole doing the thumping.

"You're suspended until I decide you're not. Get the hell out of my sight. When I'm ready to see your ugly-ass self again, I'll give you a buzz. In the meantime, you're on vacation."

Thorn stormed out the door, slamming it hard enough to jar Bounty's good mood.

"Hey, shifter. Where are you headed?" Her hands paused above the keyboard.

Thorn stopped at her desk, running fingers through his straw-colored shaggy hair, which hung long on the sides. Jagged claw marks on his jaw stood out in bright red when he was angry. For a moment, he looked lost. "My ranch, I guess. Maybe I won't fuck up there."

"He'll cool down. Promise you'll check in with me."

"He might get chill again, but will I?"

"It's okay. I like my wolves a little edgy. I'm waiting for my promise."

Thorn stopped shifting his aimless booted feet long enough to throw Bounty a weak smile. "I'll check in. Cross my heart or some such crap."

"Good wolf. Now, try to have fun on your suspension."

Bounty rested her chin in a palm, sighing as Thorn's snug-jeaned backside and western boots disappeared out the door. She loved her job. Aggressive males who didn't know how to wave a white flag. Warlike females who walked the talk. A boss who could face plant every hot-shot Firebrand until they screamed like sissies. Plenty of excitement. They also protected Aeternals, and humans when necessary.

Sweet gig.

****

"Where is my dickhead partner?" muttered Tyr to the wall at the Ministry of Well Being's med center where Kole sent him after Thorn's ass-kicking. If his big, black-haired, cold-eyed vamp sidekick was in a blood den doing a little feed and fuck, Tyr was going to be pissed. Dax had left several troubling messages. Now, he was practicing his usual disappearing act, not answering his D-chip call.

A healer stepped out of the room where the human female was in a spell-induced coma for her own good while the staff worked on her injuries.

Several days ago, he and Dax had been on a mission to visit Karth about drugs when they found her in the middle of the road. She was a mess. Bruises, cuts, unconscious, clothes torn, covered in stinky shit.

Really.

Tyr elected to bring her here since Dax preferred not to be around a bleeding Earther. Best for the female to avoid the fanged fiend anyway. She sure couldn't fight off the male if he got thirsty and toothy. After dropping her off for care, Tyr swung by for Dax and they headed out for Karth again. When they arrived at his locale, the pack was gone and Thorn was boots deep in shit.

The healer looked left and right. When he spied Tyr, he signaled.

"What's up?" asked the warlock Firebrand.

"She's still in the induced coma but showing signs of awakening soon. She was terribly dehydrated, malnourished. Looks like she got into a fight with thorny bushes in the elements. We have her hooked to nutrients, and we're monitoring her vitals. Witches have been speeding her healing along, but we aren't prepared to treat an Earther."

"She's gonna snap out of this?"

The male in the white coat nodded.

"Do your best. I'm outta."

The healer placed a hand on Tyr's shoulder but snatched it away when the Firebrand dropped a look on him. "What are we supposed to do with her?"

"Dunno. Not my business. I found her, brought her to the ministry, and reported back today by special order. Wait till you hear."

"At least stick around until she awakens."

"Man, she's just a human. I think you can handle her. I'll let Commander Kole know she'll survive. He's likely already contacted Commander Jarek since she's probably one of those slaves his stronghold's been hunting down. Somebody'll come for her."

The healer turned kicked puppy eyes toward the Firebrand.

Tyr threw both arms into the air. "Okay. You win. I'll do bedside duty."

Good to his word, he slumped in a chair near the patient, the leather seat creaking under his weight. She looked better. Someone had cleaned her and washed her hair.

Without warning, the human's lids popped open, and she was peeper-to-peeper with Tyr. Scuttling backward on the bed, she winced. Her eyes flashed a severe-risk alert, but she didn't say a word. Leaning against the headboard, she did a one-eighty of the room, her head swiveling from side to side.

Tyr squirmed in his seat, the leather creaking as

he shot her his most trustworthy grin.

After about five minutes of silent appraisal, laced with a heavy dose of oh-God, she spoke in a harsh, raspy whisper. "Where am I?"

He rose to approach her slowly, trying not to be intimidating. Given his black leathers, face tat, and piercings, it was a hard look to carry off.

Yep, wouldn't you know it, she cowered, shrinking into a small ball to get away from the scary warlock.

He raised a hand, the universal sign of *I come in peace*. "I'm not here to jam you up. I found you on the road and brought you to this medical facility a few days ago. Name's Tyr, by the way."

Her gaze flipped to a glass, her shaky hand reaching for it.

When she snatched her trembling fingers back, Tyr snagged the water. He brought the straw to her lips. "Here. Drink."

She slurped a few times. That's when she glanced at the needles, bags of fluid, and machines.

"For your own good. You were dehydrated. Needed food, too. Can you tell me what happened?"

"Where am I?" she asked, her voice stronger.

"I told you. A med center."

"I mean is this another planet or what?"

"Or what." Tyr stepped away, preparing to sit again.

Her brows furrowed, only assuring him he lacked the patience to explain shit to the female. "I need to talk to somebody in charge right now. They still have my friend, and I promised I would save her. Please, help me." She swung her legs to the side of the bed but collapsed onto the mattress when she tried to sit. Her head bounced on the pillow.

Tyr reached her in three long strides to put her back under the covers. “Whoa, female. You’re way too weak to stand.”

“Then you have to help me save Celene.”

“Was she another human with you?” Now he perked up. Things were finally getting interesting. Someone else needed a rescue. Firebrands loved to play the hero.

“Yes.”

“You were both sex slaves?”

“What?” She pulled the sheet to her waist. “No. Prisoners. The guys who guarded us weren’t human. I know I sound crazy, but it’s true. May I have more water?”

Tyr brought the straw to her lips. “What’s your name?”

“Jace de Vries.”

“Hold on a sec.” Tyr set the glass onto the side table before tapping his D-chip to call Kole. He reported what Jace had told him. Then Kole made him wait. And wait. Finally, the commander returned. *Uh-huh ... Yeah. Fuck you say.* The warlock smacked his forehead. *Sure, I love standing guard at a damn medical facility while everyone decides what to do with an Earther. What’s so special about her? ... Double fuck. I’m on it, Comm. And can somebody find Dax? He’s still MIA.*

Chapter Two

Near Orofino, Idaho, Present Day

Chiara Flores waved her finger around like a divining rod. Hundreds of alphabetized labeled jars filled the shelves in the pantry. Alfalfa to zedoary. Some plants she gathered from the woods to process. Others she grew in her garden or ordered online.

"Ginger root, wild. Ginger root, wild. There it is." She removed the glass container which was parked between garlic and gingko leaf.

In her kitchen, an old man in faded jeans sat at the marred pine table where she consulted with her clients, usually neighbors from the bordering Nez Perce Reservation. He pushed his white waist-length hair behind his ears before resting his head onto elbow-propped palms. When he moaned, his lids closed against the bright light streaming in through the windows.

"How long have you been getting these migraines?" Chiara dumped a few dried stems into a mortar. With a firm grasp on the pestle, she ground the roots until they wore to a fine powder.

"Just a few weeks now."

She poured the pulverized wild ginger into a plastic bag, offering it to the man. "This should last a month, but if your headaches don't disappear by then, you need to go to a doctor in Orofino."

"Sure thing." He crammed the powdered root into his pocket.

"Put about a dime-size portion on a flat surface or plate. Pinch one nostril closed. Sniff through the other. Do the same on each side. No more than four times a day."

With his fingers rubbing his temples, he rose on old, unsteady legs. She placed a palm on his shoulder to guide him out while lending a little sympathy.

While Chiara watched, wondering how the man had managed to walk to her house, a young woman with straight black hair woven into a thick braid stepped onto the porch. She bounced a boy wrapped in a wool blanket on her hip.

Chiara waved her inside. "You're next. What can I do for you?"

"Jake has a cough. He's barely getting any sleep at night. So I'm awake, too. But I gotta work every day."

"I'll fix something for him." Chiara pulled out a chair for the mother while she touched Jake's cheek with the back of her hand. "No fever is a good sign."

Returning from the pantry, she carried a tall jar filled with a thick liquid. "Is he allergic to anything, Angie?"

Cough. Cough.

"No. Nothing."

Cough. Cough.

Before she rattled off directions, two men shoved through the door, the younger with an arm around the older's waist to steady him. "Quick. My dad was chopping wood when he hit the side of his foot with the axe. Not bad enough for a doc, but something for the wound would be good."

The father hopped into the kitchen, his injured foot bobbing with each jump.

Chiara raised a hand, signaling her intent to finish with the mother and son. "This is a syrup made from wild onion. One to two teaspoons per hour. If Jake's cough gets worse, you know what to do. Go to a doctor."

"Thanks." The mother hefted the boy onto her hip, gaping at the man's injury while blood dripped on

Chiara's linoleum.

"Here." She pointed to a seat, moving a stool in front of it for his foot. "I'm Chiara. Nice to meet you … uh."

After he flung himself down, he propped his heel on the offered footrest. "George Tano from over near Kamiah. Son's Edgar. Sit, boy."

"It's okay. I'll just stand out of the way." The man folded his arms across his chest, his denim shirtsleeves rolled to his elbows as he leaned against a cabinet.

Chiara slipped on surgical gloves, fingering the man's dirty toes, wiggling them one by one. The cut was in the fleshy part of his foot, but she'd examine it more carefully once she cleaned away the blood. "I'll be right back." She disappeared into the storage room, reappearing with a jar labeled Yarrow. "I have just the stuff." The glass clinked onto the table.

She removed a small basin from under the sink, ran warm water in it, and brought out a clean cloth to wash around George's wound. He'd sliced some blood vessels but not much damage to bone. When finished, she scooped salve from the jar, smoothing it onto the cut. "This should work, but if you don't see a little improvement each day, you need to go to the doctor. I doubt you chopped into the bone. A miracle." She wrapped the foot with a bandage. When Edgar aided his father out the door, he dug into his pocket to deposit cash in a box by the entrance.

Wiping an errant strand of curly dark hair from her forehead, Chiara sighed. Busy day. More and more people arrived on the doorstep with regularity. The little bit of money they left helped with supplies, but she preferred privacy. Her house was becoming party central for the injured or ill.

She marched to the kitchen, pulled out the tea kettle, and turned on the faucet.

Knock. Knock. Knock.

Her rickety door banged against the jamb.

"Hey, girl. You home?"

It was a familiar voice. "Ernest. I'm over here boiling a pot for tea. Can I get you a cup?"

"Sounds good. How ya been? Your dogs are going a little crazy out here. Something's stirring them." He slammed the door, scooting out a chair as he dropped a bulging plastic bag onto the floor beside it.

Chiara paused to listen. Sure enough. The animals were howling. Could be a coyote. Could be a field mouse. Victor, Boris, Ivan, and Peter didn't care. No prey was too small. They loved to hunt. She turned to the whistling kettle. After extracting two cups from the cabinet, she returned one, replacing it with a bigger mug. Plunking a tea bag in each, she poured in the hot water. Afterward, she carried them to the table. "Help yourself to the sugar and cream. You know where everything is, Ernest."

As always, her neighbor stirred one teaspoon of sugar along with a dash of milk into his tea. He sipped it, aahing before he leaned back in the chair. "Hits the spot. Best drink around."

"It's store-bought chamomile. Anyone can make it."

"Better made by your hands."

Chiara angled her head toward the bag on the floor. "Laundry?" Since several of her neighbors were without power to their cabins, she took in their dirty clothes. The extra income helped.

Ernest slid his gnarled hands onto the table, his knuckles swollen from arthritis. His leathered, mottled skin told the story of a man who labored outdoors most of his hard life. Now he suffered the cruelty of the wear-and-tear disease, his deformed fingers frozen into painful jagged forms which he wrapped around his cup to enjoy another taste.

Ernest must be in so much pain. I could... No. I can't.

"Are you here for your oil?" It was the best she could do.

"Yep. It's time again. I've been using it a lot lately. Ran out." He patted one jacket pocket and then the other, reaching into the last one to extract an empty bottle which he handed to Chiara.

After she set her teacup down, her chair scraped along the linoleum flooring. From the pantry, she called out, "I'm going to have to find more wild mint in the woods come spring. Though the oil's getting low, I have enough to last the winter."

"If you need any help, I can send the grandson along."

Ernest always tried to put Chiara together with the young man. She appreciated the thought but ruled out all relationships. "No, thank you. Besides, its growing season is over."

"You are alone, girl."

"I have four unruly wolfhounds. I don't need a guy."

The dogs yelped and howled louder.

"I'll be on my way." He pocketed the oil, almost dropping it when his fingers struggled to grip it tightly. "You've got some critters to settle. Maybe they're hungry."

"Maybe."

Ernest stared as if he delved into her soul. "What's wrong, girl?"

"I don't know. Life's so complicated."

"You never should have given me the remedy for indigestion. Then I wouldn't have spread word of your miracle cures."

She nodded.

A few years ago, she shared an herbal concoction with Ernest to help his indigestion. Afterward, he sent a hiker limping onto her front porch, bruised from a fall. She administered arnica, known for helping painful contusions. When a visitor complained of congestion a week later, she offered him horseradish root. A client suggested she place a donation box near the door. Eventually, people crowded into Chiara's peaceful life, disturbing her self-imposed isolation.

"But let's put the blame where it belongs. You forage for plants to make your own pantry pharmacy, increasing your supply year after year. What's that say?"

"I'm my own worst enemy?"

Laughter rumbled from Ernest's chest when he made his way out, dropping a few bills into her box. "You need to set prices for your remedies. People should pay for your efforts."

"I don't do this to get rich."

He patted her arm. "No, Chiara. You do it because you're a good person with a big heart."

If he only knew me better, he wouldn't say that.

"Stay warm, Ernest. It'll be chilly soon. A breeze is coming."

"Not as bad as it's gonna get later in the fall and through winter."

She walked Ernest to the porch, watching him limp into the woods, his threadbare shirt flapping in the wind, his hips swinging unevenly as his knees jerked with each step of his disease-riddled body.

Noticing several jars were nearly empty, Chiara took a pen and pad into the pantry to take inventory, but the dogs exploded into feral howls. She dropped the notes onto a shelf before running out to the porch.

"Victor! Boris! Heel now!" The animals barked, fading from view as they scattered into the thick woods. Chiara sighed, fisting her hip. Her toe snapped up and down on the timbered deck. "What's wrong, guys?"

With a disgruntled chuff, she charged into the house where she struggled into a sweater before slipping on her boots to chase through the heavy briars after the dogs who hunted unseen prey. They usually heeled when commanded.

What is wrong with them?

Chiara elbowed aside a branch, releasing it. Pushing through brush, she tracked the wayward wolfhounds. Her hand reached for the next meddlesome limb while she ducked to avoid low-hanging leaves.

Whoosh. Snap.

She shoved more branches aside. When the bracken grew too dense to maneuver, she realized she was in a pickle, retreat no easier than advancing.

The dogs howled, still chasing their game. Whipping in the wind, sharp-edged holly leaves bit her flesh. Most often, the plant was a treatment for heart disease or high blood pressure. Today, it was the enemy.

Chiara's feet and arms tangled in vines, the tendrils manacling her as they snatched, grabbed, restrained her limbs. Yanking at the ropy plants, she broke free to plunge deeper into compact growth.

She picked healing herbs in these woods. The verdant undergrowth would not conspire to imprison her. She slapped another limb away from her face.

"Ivan! Peter!"

The thick foliage of the northern rain forest muffled her shouts. Head-high in gnarled, constraining bushes, she fought to move toward her panicked hounds.

They hear me but are ignoring my calls. No dinner for the beasties tonight.

Chiara tripped over a fallen trunk, an obstacle in the path of her foot. Decayed and fresh leaf bits puffed into the air when she face-planted into pine needles, bark, stems, leaves, and moss.

On unsteady feet, she tweaked her jaw, brushing off her long skirt, frowning at the tear in the hem. Fudge buckets. She loved this outfit.

The cries of the dogs changed. No more frenzied yelps. When she broke through the tree line into a clearing, she spied her animals with their prey.

In the distance, two huge men in dark clothes lumbered into the forest, dragging another between them. Boris and Ivan tracked them.

The intruders didn't strike her as hunters. She had chased enough of them off her property.

She faced Victor and Peter, who paced around an unmoving, bleeding man.

Cautiously, Chiara approached while commanding the dogs to stand down. The stranger lay face down. His tattered and scorched T-shirt exposed contusions and open wounds. Sturdy boots had done a number on his body. She saw the prints.

She struggled to turn the man onto his back, but he was solid muscle with massive shoulders and heavy legs.

Dropping to the ground, she used her feet to flip him.

Ugh. Done.

With the man on his back, Chiara saw his injuries better. Blood poured from a gouge in his wrist. A huge hole was in his chest near his heart. She touched her hand to his cheek. Despite the elements, his skin was warm. The hint of a goatee and mustache didn't hide the bruise on his jaw. She brushed aside the strands of long black hair lying across his strong, angular face. Thick dark lashes feathered on his eyelids.

She noted lacerations on his body. Likely, he had cracked ribs. Internal organ damage. Burns on his left side melted parts of his shirt into the skin. A broken leg gave an unnatural bend to his pants.

Her gaze moved to his upper arm. A tattoo. Colorful feathers. Deadly talons. Chiara jumped away, a gasp escaping her lips.

It can't be.

She studied his face. The dirt and blood hid some of his features. Boris and Ivan rejoined their brothers, all four dogs circling the man, yelping even though she called for them to settle. It was him. What were the odds she would run into the same stranger years apart, states away?

Stop. Focus on the present problem.

Chiara didn't know how she could get him back to her cabin, but she would try. Of course, she planned to take the road rather than the forest route. The man was twice her weight.

First things first. Set his broken leg.

She scoured the ground for two branches to stabilize the limb after she fixed it. Finding what she needed, she returned to her patient.

"Ivan, Boris, this is going to hurt like a sonofabitch." She grasped each side of his ankle, closed her eyes, and whispered words which drifted away on the flurry of wind. As the air shimmered, an icy breeze fluttered her hair. She tugged on his foot, holding it steady. Slowly, the bone popped into place.

The man's body jerked, but he didn't awaken while Chiara tied a branch onto each side of the leg with supple vines. "That's good, Boris. At least he's unconscious. Probably didn't feel the pain too much. Let's make a sled."

She wandered the nearby woods, gathering big and small branches. Tired of her long, unruly hair lashing her face, she pulled a scrunchie out of her sweater pocket. Once she controlled her wild mane in a messy ponytail, she placed two large limbs about three feet apart in the dirt. Across those, she layered shorter ones. Satisfied with the pattern, she wove ivy vines through them to hold them in place.

Grabbing the unconscious man under his arms, Chiara lifted his shoulders. With orchestrated moves, she slipped the contraption underneath him with her foot while dragging him onto it, inch by inch. Once she settled him into the makeshift sled, she stepped away to study her patient.

Hell. I hate being cold.

She blew on her hands, warming them. Chiara pulled her wool sweater over her head and tucked it around the man as best she could. Then she hauled him to her place, her journey slow, laborious.

Her cabin was hidden deep in the forest where she'd run after the foster home. The incident there had freaked her out enough to stay far away from crowded cities. She was too dangerous.

Chiara lived alone, isolated to protect the innocent. Unfortunately, more and more people visited her. Now she had another unwanted guest.

With the door of her cabin open, she lugged the sled through the kitchen and into her bedroom while four dogs watched. "Okay, Boris, ideas? How do I get him onto the bed? Right. If we can't bring Mohammed to the mountain."

She snatched spare blankets from a closet to create a pallet on the floor, rolling the familiar man on top. She fluffed a pillow under his head. Once she removed her bloodied sweater, she covered him with a furry comforter.

"Don't look at me like that, Ivan. It's the best I can do. You're right, though. He may be dangerous, not being human and all. I'll restrain him until we make sure he won't hurt us."

With heavy rope from a kitchen drawer, Chiara tied a length to each wrist, securing the other ends to the sturdy iron bed frame. She was careful to avoid the gaping wound high on his wrist where something had been removed.

While sitting cross-legged on the floor, she observed the results of her labor. "Good God, Boris, I'm Kathy Lee Bates from Misery. Even bloody and injured, he's delectable, but I'm not tying him down to ravage him. I just want him well enough to get on about his business. I owe him."

She had never forgotten the man. Though he was dirty and beaten, he looked nearly as he had fifteen years ago. Inhuman. Her brain warned caution. But Chiara was rarely cautious.

Chapter Three

Perched on a rickety wood chair near the doorway with Ivan and Boris guarding her feet, Chiara prepared to escape if necessary. With an eye on the patient, she rested her elbows on her knees.

The man on the pallet starred in her dreams after the accident. When she was a child, he was her superhero, her champion without cape or tights. As she became a woman, he transformed into an ideal with a haunting otherworldly face, his cold, obsidian eyes seducing her. His muscled body pressing her to the bed. Real men, by comparison, came up short every time.

Sometimes she thought she had imagined the fangs, but she knew better.

Go ahead. Say it, crazy hermit girl. Your hero is a vampire.

"No matter what he is, Boris, the man on my floor deserves to be cleaned a bit and healed."

Chiara pushed off the chair, still eyeballing the patient before she stepped into the kitchen to get the basin from beneath the sink. After she filled it with warm water, she snatched a sponge from the bathroom.

Kneeling beside her injured hero, she brushed his midnight hair off his face, drawing her fingers through the long strands. As she remembered, it was soft, shiny.

When Ivan lifted a sleepy eyelid, Chiara arched a brow. "Don't be so judgmental. Okay. You're right, boy. Rather than ogle the man, I should wash him. First, I need to check for a head injury." With fingers probing his scalp, she found a small orange-size lump. "That could cause a problem."

After gently resting him on the pillow again, she dipped the sponge into water, rung it out, and swiped his forehead. She wiped across his thick-lashed eyelids, hard-angled cheekbones, and wonderfully full lips. She cleaned the sinister goatee which dusted his chin.

After washing away the worst of the gore on his face, she inventoried his wounds. The guys had tried to rearrange his looks. Cuts and a lot of bruising marred his skin. She fingered his jaw. Not broken. The back of her hand caressed the stubble she loved on men in fashion magazines, but this guy was no model. Way too masculine, too wild.

Chiara chewed her lip, glancing at the dogs. "Okay. Off task again. While I'm here should I check out the fangs? Sure." She pinched his upper lip between her thumb and forefinger, lifting it. When he snarled, she jerked, immediately releasing her grip.

The two wolfhounds shot to their feet, growling. "Don't worry. He's still out, but I was right. He's got wicked chompers."

She slid the comforter to his waist. Biting her lower lip, she ripped his tattered T-shirt from hem to neck. She couldn't miss the chain. She bent over him.

Yuck. A string of long pointy teeth. Like fangs.

She flung the gruesome bling over his shoulder.

Squeezing water out of the sponge, she swiped across his muscled chest and abs. She lingered too long, careful to avoid the multiple deep lacerations and the severe burn on his side. The worst gash was over his heart. Almost as if someone had tried to rip it out.

Chiara leaned back on her heels. Her hero was more delicious than she'd remembered. Ripped. Rock solid.

Her gaze hovered on the zipper of his leather pants while she toyed with the snap. She wouldn't be peeking. *No.* He could have wounds there. She would sponge off the blood and check them out. It was the right thing to do. *Zzziiiipp.* When she fisted the waistband to slip them down an inch, she saw he wore nothing underneath. Immediately, she tugged them back into place, re-snapping them with shaky fingers. *Pervy. He'll have to stay as is. Wounds or not.*

Chiara moved on to his arms. With his hands tied overhead, she had trouble washing off the blood. *Damn.* His bicep was bigger than her thigh. Good thing the sturdy ropes were lashed to her bedframe. The feathers on his Phoenix brand seemed to flutter when she wiped the sponge across it. Moving on, she touched the inside of his right wrist where a macabre skeleton with fangs was tattooed.

Finished with the clean-up, she had a better picture of his injuries. Checking out his closed eyelids again, she rose with the washtub in her hands. The wounds needed more than water.

"Watch him, boys. I'll return in a sec."

Ivan grumbled. Boris cracked a weary eye but didn't stir.

After restoring the basin to the cabinet under the sink, Chiara opened the pantry to scan the labeled jars lining the shelves. Oils. Dried herbs. Various concoctions. She pulled down the container marked calendula oil, admiring her creation.

Months ago, she gathered marigolds, plucked off the petals, and mixed them with olive oil. Afterward, she placed the mixture into a glass jar, sticking it into a brown paper bag where she shook it daily. Recently, she strained the concoction before returning the filtered calendula oil to the darkened pantry.

With her patient again, Chiara tucked her skirt beneath her to sit cross-legged beside him. Scooting closer, she dipped her fingers into the healing goop, gently dabbing some onto the wound at his wrist, the deep gash at his heart, and his burns. She moved on to other scrapes sullying an otherwise perfect body. Satisfied with the efforts, she screwed the lid on the jar before setting it on the floor. She ran her hand along his leg. It seemed properly set.

When Chiara re-examined the man's chest, her palm clasped her mouth. *No way.* Small cuts were already knitting together. Even the more serious wounds scabbed over somewhat. Calendula oil was great, but it didn't heal injuries that quickly. She settled her legs to the other side, leaning on a hand. *Amazing.*

"That's not normal. Huh, boys?"

After an hour, he still hadn't awakened. She resumed her vigil from the chair, fearing the head injury was serious. *Did she risk using the curse again? Maybe.* She wiggled fingers in front of her face. When the air shimmered with icy energy, she snatched them back to her side. *No.* Her healing potions would have to do. The other was too unpredictable.

While her eyelids fluttered, her mind filled with memories of her hero on the pallet. In her dreams, he was big enough, bad enough, fierce enough to scare anything or anyone who haunted her nightmares. When monsters came, he was the one who peeked under the bed, opened the closet door, or flipped on the cellar lights. Not really him, of course. Rather, the idea of him. With his courage as an example, Chiara found her own inner strength. Now he needed her.

Chiara's chin bobbed to her chest.

She was reading a book in the backseat, sucking on her lower lip, pouting. The family was in the car, driving to a lake where they told her she could swim, play in the sand, meet other kids.

Early in the morning, they loaded luggage, swimming gear, and fishing poles into their late model station wagon. Before beginning the journey, they stopped at The Hole in the Wall to grab donuts for the road.

Now it was past lunch. She was hungry, telling her father just that, but he wanted to get closer to the lake before they ate. Pulling a face, she whined, grumbled. "Nobody ever does what I want."

Her parents ignored her to argue about directions.

Chiara returned to her book, harrumphing, sighing, making enough noise to let her mom and dad know she wasn't happy.

She was absorbed in the story of the Black Riders who had wounded Frodo with a cursed blade when three things happened at once. Her mother screamed while the car jerked wildly. The brakes screeched, and she whipped forward, unable to hold onto the book. It tore out of her hands. The station wagon rolled. It rolled and rolled and rolled. She lost count.

When it stopped, she was hanging upside down. Hurting, she yelled, "Mommy." No answer. "Daddy." No answer.

Whoosh. Flames shot from the front of the automobile. A loud noise sounded as glass sprayed the backseat. She closed her eyes, but shards stung her cheek. A big hand reached in through the broken window to yank open the door even though it was all smashed. A man's head moved into view before he crawled into the car to wrap an arm around her. He ripped off her seatbelt. He was so strong.

Fire surrounded them, but he ignored it to drag her from the backseat. Before he pulled Chiara free, she snatched her stuffed monkey. Her mother made her promise to keep it close. No matter what.

The man's arm curled around her head while an

explosion blasted her ears, shaking the ground. The man didn't talk. He just nestled her against his chest, holding her tight so she couldn't see anything, jostling her when he ran fast.

His arms were thick. She clung to the one with the painted bird. Its eyes were red, mean-looking, but its feathers were beautiful, colorful blues, greens, and reds. She held onto the wings for comfort as they rippled under her fingers, letting her know she was safe.

Blood trickled into her eyes. The man growled. When she lifted her head, she saw them. Fangs. Real fangs. Not the wax kind for Halloween.

Chiara wasn't frightened. She was fascinated. Her fingers, moist with the blood which leaked from her forehead, reached out to touch his white teeth, but the man gripped her wrist gently while he pulled her away from his mouth. He closed his lips, twisting his neck suddenly, his attention caught by a sound she didn't hear.

She listened. Sirens.

Carrying her further from the burning car, he settled her in the grass off the road. "When they get here, you yell," he said.

"Wait!" She desperately clutched his arm. "Get my mommy and daddy before you go. They need help, too."

Sad, black eyes locked on hers. "They're past help, kid. You're alone now. Do as I say. Yell when the humans get here."

"No. You have to save them."

He pinched her chin between a thumb and forefinger. "They're gone. Nothing you or I can do. Get it? Take care of yourself now." He pried her fingers off, backing away.

"Don't go. Please." She wept, tears running

down her cheeks. Her tiny hands fluttered when she reached out for him.

"Crying doesn't help anything, kid. Get tough, and don't let anybody mess with you. You'll do great."

Turning, he ran toward the woods, looking over his shoulder when he made it to the trees. "Remember. Shout out when they get here." Then he drifted away like smoke.

A deep growl woke her from her reverie. The patient's eyes snapped open. They were as black as a raging, angry storm. When he shifted his arms, or tried to, he snarled, baring fangs.

Oh, shit. They're bigger. They're sharper than I remember.

****

A chill skittered across his body, irritating his nerve endings.

Someone is using a spell. The warlock? No. Somebody else.

Dax drew shallow breaths, careful to keep his chest from expanding. No scent of the demons or mage.

His memory surfaced fragment by fragment. He'd killed one demon and was well on his way to ending the second when the warlock interfered. Lights out. Now he was here.

Where?

He cracked his lids enough to see a sliver of light. Someone was in the room. Out of squint-range. He'd have to take a risk if he wanted to assess the sitch. His lashes fluttered. Up. Down. A female blinked in and out of his vision. He couldn't hold his eyes open.

Dax tried to sit.

Not happening.

His hands were bound with something. *A rope?* He was in a bed. *No.* Not soft enough. A pallet on the ground.

Unbidden, a growl rumbled from his chest as his sandpapery lids scraped open. He flipped his arms a few times, testing the bindings. Then he stopped to glare at his captor.

No challenge.

She perched on a chair, her body tilting forward, poised for a fast escape. Dark curly hair hung to her waist. Plump lips wrapped around her thumb as she chewed on a nail. *Lovely.* Her eyes were bright though jittery. *Good. She should be afraid.*

What was the smell? Witch's concoction? Add it to the spell he sensed earlier. *Strange*. Something was off about the female.

Wiggling his loose bindings, he drew his wrist near his nose. His chip was missing, and the odor of the salve on the wound reeked of a witch's brew.

"What did you do?" With a cough, he cleared his throat. "My D-chip?"

She shuffled her feet, still prepped to run while she wiped sleep from her eyes. "What's that?"

He twisted his wrist toward her as far as the ropes allowed.

"Those guys cut something out," she said, her voice a smooth molasses which clung to his skin.

"What did you put on it?" Dax relaxed into the bindings.

"It's a homemade remedy." She held his gaze.

He didn't know how long he'd been out. Still, the deep gash in his wrist along with the other lacerations should be closing faster. He sensed a couple broken ribs. A bum leg. A hole in his chest. Burns. A whopper of a headache. Pain.

A rhythmic pulse beat in her neck, blood rushing through the vein capable of speeding his healing. He licked his lower lip. His body agreed with the assessment, his belly rumbling from gnawing hunger. Dax needed to feed.

"My leg is broken. Did you set it?"

"Yes."

"Why are my hands tied?" Unblinking, he stared at who he determined would become his meal, never taking his eyes off where he planned to pierce her flesh.

When she maneuvered to her feet, she leaned against the doorjamb, a long skirt wrapped around her legs and a snug T-shirt hugging delicious curves. She was prepped to sprint. Not that it would do her any good.

"Look at me. I'm a five-foot-five girl and you're … well … a lot more. I wanted to help you, but I needed to be certain you wouldn't hurt me."

"And?"

"A-a-and what?"

When she stuttered, Dax sensed she was hiding something. "I don't know. You tell me."

The nervous female's boots tapped on the wood floor as her gaze dropped. "Um. Sure. This might sound crazy. Are you a vampire?"

Interesting question, but she was about to find out the truth anyway. Why not give her a preview of coming attractions?

Dax shot her a toothy grin that exposed his fangs, ones which had grown longer, pointier, her shapely throat a beacon for his thirst.

She flinched and glanced out the doorway, eyeing an escape route.

When she twisted back toward Dax, Chiara stuttered. "You don't remember me."

"Should I?" He growled, his body needing blood to heal.

"No. I've changed."

Had he fucked her? Humans weren't to his taste. Blood too thin, bodies too frail for the workout he liked to give his partners. Still, it wasn't out of the question since she was a tempting little thing.

"I'm sorry. I don't remember when we hooked up. Untie me, let me rest a bit, and we can go at it again. Afterward, I'll hit the road. No harm. No foul."

"What? No. We haven't had sex." Her brows furrowed while she worried her thumb.

She was angry, but hunger shot through his gut once more. He needed a bite soon. Enough chit-chat and making nice. "Okay. I give. How did we meet?"

"You pulled me out of a burning car when I was ten." Sadness veiled her eyes, beautiful orchid eyes the color of a flower on Darque.

Dax let the observation roll around in his somewhat hazy brain for a while. A little girl. A burning car.

Nope. Wait. Yep.

Now he remembered. The kid was strapped in the backseat. The two adults in the front were goners. He yanked her out in the nick of time before the twisted hunk of metal went kablooey.

She'd been such a skinny thing. Cut up from the accident. He pulled her from the station wagon but didn't let her eye the carnage. Her parents had crispied in the front seat. No child should have to see such a scene. Tough kid. Once he heard sirens, he set her in the grass, telling her to scream when help arrived. He hid in the woods, watching until the paramedics found her. Afterward, he shadowflashed to a nearby portal.

The female had filled out in all the right places. She was still small. Then again, most people were small compared to his six-foot-five vampire Firebrand frame.

"Nice to see you again, kid. Looks like life's been

kind. Now, untie me."

She cocked her head to the side. "Not just yet."

"What's your name?"

"Chiara. Yours?"

"Daxton. Dax." With eyes locked onto hers and a hint of a grin on his lips, he jammed his fists forward, snapping the ropes which held him. "Oops. Run, Chiara."

****

Colonel Mateo Garcia leaned over the huge Western US regional map spread across a table in the otherwise bare room inside a shingled, single-story, green-roofed building. His pen tapped a spot. "This is another portal in our zone."

Beside him, General Isaac "Lip" Lipton eyeballed the location. "Looks as if it would be a popular place to slip through." He stood, legs apart and hands clasped behind his back, wearing combat dress, the distinctive tan beret of the Rangers tucked under his arm.

Joint Operations Special Command created a new exercise. Operation Frankenstein. They assigned Lipton to organize one of three Special Mission Units. His SMO was tagged West Bank. Mateo Garcia was in command of two battalions of Rangers. Along for the ride were a Task Force Green unit and a Task Force Blue unit.

Joint Ops also gifted them with Dante's disgraced ex-military man who went by the moniker of General Mars. Lipton and Matty had escaped with the guy and a doctor from the British nobleman's compound in a helicopter just before all hell broke loose. They were armed with proof of the existence of otherworld creatures. The Englishman died that day. But they turned his intel and their hitchhiking companions over to the US Army's High Command.

Unfortunately, they were stuck with Mars, Joint Ops ordering he be involved with the current mission.

The man was an irritant, a braggart, a fool, and without a conscience. As Matty saw it, those were his good points. An investigation revealed his name was not Mars. Following a dishonorable discharge from the British army, he'd led a mercenary unit into Africa where he was rumored to have destroyed an entire village of men, women, and children. Standing next to such a miserable asshole chapped Matty's balls. But orders were orders.

The Dr. Frankenstein scientist disappeared. Matty didn't care. The guy was creepy.

General Lipton's West Bank forces deployed temporarily to an abandoned military base near Monterey, California. Despite having sold off most of the site, the Americans had wisely hung onto selected buildings from which they ran black ops. This mission was the blackest of ops.

"We capture if possible. Kill if necessary." Lipton drummed his fingers on the table, glancing at Matty, a trusted officer and long-time friend. "What do you think, Colonel?"

"From what Dante told us, a snatch and grab may be difficult. I'm opposed to unnecessary risks."

"I have no problem with a kill order," said Mars, his eyes sparking with excitement.

The general drew his lips tight while he studied the disgraced man. "Are there more portals than these in the western sector?"

"It's possible, but Dante only logged these. His source piecemealed the intel to us." To indicate fourteen spots, Mars tapped repeatedly on the map. "His Lordship wasn't aware of others."

Lipton stiffened his military spine, a loud breath escaping his lips. "We have the go-ahead to use extreme measures to interrogate any captured otherworlders. Maybe we can uncover other portals. If we do, we shut down the whole bloody lot of them."

"Devil's advocate here. But have we considered sitting across the table from these guys? Seeing what a little civilized palaver can do?" Matty planted a stiff arm on the map. He had a few military tenets. Settle disagreements with talk or sanctions. If that fails, go to war. If war is the option, win. Simple. Have the baddest attitude and the baddest guns.

"You don't palaver with monsters," said Mars. "Trust me. They will kill us on sight."

The colonel wasn't about to trust this mercenary bastard. He'd rather snuggle up to an otherworlder.

"I understand your thoughts, Matty. But we've been advised against it. Contact is too risky. The long-term mission is clear," said Lipton. "If it's not human, capture it or kill it. Extreme containment."

The general shifted from foot to foot before continuing. "Arm some soldiers with the tranc bullets developed by Dante's research scientists. Their aim will be to capture. Dress the other troops to kill. We possess the Englishman's formula to enhance the physical strength of our men. Not knowing the long-term effects of the drug, I've advised command against using it before more study. So far, they're listening."

"Time for a little shock and awe." Matty folded the map, taking it along as they exited the stark room to walk on a derelict road, grass growing in the cracks of the concrete.

Lipton swiped a hand across his head before slapping his beret into place. They marched to the multi-storied building next door, Mars following the officers like a good pet. *Snake. Rattler.* Crowded into the tactical operation center were four primary officers, all highly capable, all handpicked. A red-headed lieutenant colonel commanded one of Matty's Ranger battalions. A woman officer led the second. A gray-templed colonel was in charge of Task Force Green while a Seal commander steered Task Force Blue. Staffers rounded out the assemblage.

When Lipton and Matty entered, chatter ceased, silence falling across the room like dominoes. Bristling with curiosity, bodies turned in chairs to face the front. The audience sensed something big underway. Of course, it was doubtful, even if given twenty-one questions, they would guess this mission.

Hell. Despite what he had seen, Matty struggled with belief. As a kid, he'd fought mock battles against invading aliens with a blaster strapped to his hip. But he never dreamed Earth contained another realm brimming with non-humans.

Intriguing news really.

When approached by a soldier gripping a microphone, Lipton waved him off. "Thanks, son. I don't need that."

With Matty at his back, the general stepped forward, cleared his throat, and paused for a moment to hold each officer's gaze. Using what Matty thought of as his Patton voice, he said, "I see the best of the best sitting in front of me. You are here to train, to take other men and women into battle against an enemy we have never faced. Damn, most of you haven't even imagined this opponent."

Drawn brows, frowns, and squints met his puzzling words.

"No way to hold your hand and lead you into a gentle waltz. So I'm just going to throw it at you in a big ball." He paused, spreading his legs and clasping hands behind him. "We are not alone. Beings other than humans walk among us. Vampires, demons, satyrs, witches. Fuck! Anything from your nightmares. It will be our job to send them to hell."

First silence. Followed by disbelief. Then a few snickers. Whispers. Finally, full-on jabbering.

Lipton leaned forward, raising a hand for quiet. "Welcome to Operation Frankenstein, West Bank SMO."

Yeah. Hang onto your Flash Gordon blasters, boys and girls. We're in for a bumpy ride.

Chapter Four

The new office on the bottom floor of the Covenkirk stronghold still smelled like fresh paint. Rein slouched in a chair, propping his shitkickers on his commander's desk. "Who was that?"

"Tyr." Kole scrubbed a rough, meaty hand across his buzz-cut hair as he disconnected from the warlock Firebrand.

After hooking his sunglasses onto the neckline of his black T-shirt and swiping fingers across his icy blue eyes, Rein, the vampire-warlock-incubus mix, waited for his commander to break down the conversation.

"Tyr is at the med center with the human female he and Dax found on the road. Says she's Jace de Vries."

"That's a name Miller Nash got from a tracker. She's one of *Custodes Templii's* missing Blood Coven descendants."

"I relayed the intel to Tyr. One more to add to our growing collection. The warlock says she's messed up but on the mend. She's also going on about some female who was with her. Celene. I told him to get more news. Maybe this Jace is the key to finding other descendants."

"We should be so lucky. I expect Miller to contact my mate with additional names soon. Maybe this Celene will be one of them, or maybe she's just a sex slave left over from Silas's ring."

"Is Miller coming in from the cold? I don't feel tight having a fucking Blood Coven guy running around Earth with no backup."

"He's some hotshot ex-British Special Forces asshole. Thinks he's smarter and faster than Cerberus. Personally, I think he's arrogant enough to make it."

Rein kept his gaze on Kole's tented fingers,

sparks leaping from them onto the male's desk. Par for an animus demon, especially one with an extra dose of aggression.

Kole fisted his hands. "I wonder how many descendants Cerberus has stashed somewhere. More good news. Dax is still off the grid."

"A time may come when we need to put him down, Kole. How's that sit?"

"Not well. We're chosen by the damn Phoenix because of some ancestor Firebrand who served. When the scorching tat burns onto our arm, we have a choice. Turn down the offer or accept. If we accept, we're given a jolt of extra power along with more muscle and a shitload of aggression. But here's the kicker as I see it. While we save the world, who saves us? Dax may turn feral, but he's ours to protect as long as possible."

"We aren't all salvageable, Kole, especially vampires with bludfrenzy. Look at Silas. He crossed over. Once it happens, no coming back."

"We're not putting down Dax. Not in the middle of this fucking war. Maybe never. Besides, he's too good at what he does. Sometimes a killer is what we need. Even one with a slippery conscience."

"Good or not, he spends way too much time sucking on O blud whores. It will catch up with him, if it hasn't already."

"You had your bouts with darkness, Rein. Who hasn't?"

"Yeah, but the love of a good woman saved me." Rein chuckled, propping one boot on top of the other.

When he'd come out of the Awakening, he gave over to his vampire side, sinking in a river of unrestrained violence. Truth was, he still walked the edge. Though he held his urges in check, rage was a rope that tugged at him always. Violence at one end. Control holding onto the other. One step from the abyss. The Firebrands, meditation, and his mate Brae were his circuit breakers when negative energy sizzled through him.

Kole *hmphed.* "You assume Braelyn has saved you. Big leap."

"Straight up, but I'm a fighter. Maybe Dax's devils are beating him."

"Don't write the male off too soon. Besides, with Thorn suspended, we need everyone in the game. In the meantime, we're flooded with recruits being called to duty."

"You said the situation is rare."

"Yes. In these numbers. We had an uptick in newbies before the Nymph and Satyr Civil War, the vampire Uprisings, and the Incubus Raids. With so many flocking in, fate has something bad in store for us. How's Ram working with the recruits?"

"Good. He's got a training schedule. Mostly, he and I take on the newbies, but he's also rotating in other Firebrands when they're available."

"Offering all kinds of styles is valuable."

Bounty interrupted with a shout from the outer office. "Grab the landline."

Kole lifted the receiver. "Talk."

The commander was famous for poor phone manners. Still, poor was better than none.

"Can't say we didn't expect it," Kole growled into the speaker.

Rein arched a brow as the commander slammed the phone into its cradle.

In response to the unasked question, he said, "Cadmon. The ylve is calling with bad news. It seems the American military is attacking Aeternals who exit certain portals Earthside."

"I guess the crazy Englishman Dante shared gateway locations with those army guys before they lifted off during the raid on his Louisiana swampland fortress."

Kole pushed a few papers around on his crowded desk. "We pulled out for fifteen hundred years, have been forgotten, spoken about in whispers over a campfire, written into myth. Now, humans know about us again. Once we had to protect them from our savagery. I wonder if the reverse will be true today. Not only do they outnumber us, but their technology may be a match for our gifts."

"Don't forget. The American officers probably escaped not only with gateway sites but with Dante's formulas to turn ordinary soldiers into superhumans as well as his recipe for tranc bullets."

Kole tapped his fingers together to contain the sparks which shot out whenever he was pissed. "Dante conspired with Cerberus to get to Ram, blaming the satyr Firebrand for the death of his daughter. By exposing us, the Englishman may have started a war, an event which will also trigger support for Cerberus's cause. Unfortunately, trade between the realms will be impacted, in addition to other inconveniences. Humans have no idea how tightly entwined our economies and societies are."

The realms were connected thanks to trade agreements drafted by Kole's mate, Skyler, chief legal officer at the Alliance. Because of her, humans unknowingly exchanged services and goods with Aeternals. Scath exported wine, agriculture, tech, the ever-popular he-man motorcycles, and countless other products or inventions. The Aeternals' realm imported an equally staggering amount from Earth.

Today, some of their kind even lived Earthside

where they owned businesses or vacation homes. Lawmakers owned hundreds of thousands of warehouses, empty stores, parking garages, or unpopulated land for portals sites. If Earth caught a cold, Scath sneezed. Likewise, if Aeternals downed too many shots of whiskey, humans got drunk. Their lives were symbiotic, entwined even though most humans remained unaware of the relationship.

"If we are at war with Earth, an added bene for Cerberus is that the Firebrands will be busy fighting their armies. We will have to ignore Arisen Dawn," said Rein.

Kole scribbled a hasty note on his electronic tablet. "We know the descendants of the Blood Coven figure into Cerberus's plans. Our mates aren't safe. The traitor in Skyler's office who sold the portal site locations to Dante may have also given him the Alliance headquarters. I already ordered my mate to pack up in Chicago." He shoved his device to the corner of his desk and leaned back in his armchair.

"How'd that go over?"

"I have as much control over Skyler as you have over Braelyn, asshole."

"The question for now is, how do we persuade an army itching to kill or capture us that we're on the same team?"

"Especially since we'll be standing between them and Cerberus's Arisen Dawn if his intent is to destroy the humans."

"Basically, we watch our sixes and our dicks. Back and front. What's new?"

"This fucking puzzle hurts my head." Kole checked out a button on his landline but obviously opted to shout rather than punch it. Obstinate bastard. "Hey, Bounty, have someone find Dax. Tell him to answer his fucking calls and to join Tyr. Then get someone over to the Ministry's med facility to relieve the warlock until the Blood Coven witch is upright and walking."

"Yes, O bossy one."

"Damn female vampire. If she didn't have such mean computer skills, I would have fired her decades ago."

Rein swung his boots off Kole's desk. "You're not tough enough to fire her. Face it, she'd take you down, fangs buried in your neck before you could lob a fireball."

"Straight up. Nico and Sabine are still running point on the Arisen Dawn watch. They've confirmed Gold Dust drug money funds Cerberus's insurgents. Maybe our Firebrand lovebirds will fetch intel on him and his larger base of operation."

Kole glanced at the stacks of paper on his desk. "Cadmon says he's got a special agent in deep with Cerberus."

"Who?" Rein paused in the doorway.

"Dunno. Claims the male has creds."

****

Dax growled when the female bolted for the outside door, stumbling in her fear.

He shook the remnants of the binding off his wrists, his fangs biting into his lower lip, his feral eyes glowing hot red. She should have used chains. As if they would have held him. Still, it was stupid of her. She should be more careful.

Despite a nagging hunger, he shivered with the anticipation of the chase. Stalking and catching the spry little black-haired gypsy with the long, torn skirt and blouse which dropped seductively off her shoulder would be exciting.

Stalling, he gave her a fighting chance. Even with a head start, she was doomed. He'd catch her with ease, draw her tight against his body while he sank aching fangs into Chiara's delicious pale neck. His cock stiffened just thinking about the game.

She was fragile. He'd have to be careful. Did he have that much control? The O blud was weak in his system now. But years of fulfilling his depraved pleasures still shaped him. He vowed to manage his urges with the little chit. Afterward, he'd leave her in good shape and with no memories of his visit.

With stiff muscles, he ambled through the kitchen, opened the screen door, and stepped onto the porch where he stretched his arms above his head. To test his leg, he shook it out. Though it wasn't fully healed, an infusion of blood would do the trick. He fingered the wounds on his bare chest while he glanced at the raw burned flesh on his side. With no shirt and his favorite leathers torn, he shivered in the chill air.

When dogs charged to the steps, growling and snapping, Dax flipped a savage glare toward them, beast to beast. He snarled. Message received. Whimpering, the animals stilled, perhaps not content to let him chase their mistress but acknowledging him as the most brutal among them. With his hand slicing downward and his teeth gnashing, he said, "Stay." His gaze flipped to the woods while he bent to rub one of the hounds behind an ear.

Dax twisted his head left, right, straight ahead. "Where are you, kid?"

He sniffed the air. *Delicious.* Her scent was a sinful mixture of lavender, honey, and vanilla, laced with fear and adrenaline.

Would she taste the same? How long has it been since I've fed from a clean female? Decades? Centuries?

His hearing was sharp. Bare feet crunched leaves and forest detritus straight ahead. Dax set a comfortable pace, ignoring the pain in his throbbing leg.

No reason to hurry.

He brushed aside a leafy branch hanging across the path, not letting it stop his forward movement.

Splash. Squish.

She had obviously stepped into a puddle of water.

He would make the feeding painless because she deserved the kindness for saving his life. He wasn't a complete monster.

Not yet.

Spying her colorful skirt through the bushes ahead, he jogged toward her. When his hunger cut like a blade through his gut, he broke into a run. If he waited longer, he risked losing control.

Chiara's thick hair swayed with each bouncing step. Her arm tangled in a vine, costing valuable time.

Not that it mattered.

Panic widened her lovely orchid eyes as she glanced over her shoulder.

When he snared the female, he flung an arm around her waist, lifting her off the ground. While Chiara kicked against his shins, her arms flailed like a bird caught in a downdraft. She threw a fist over her shoulder, striking his face.

Dax laughed. "Love pat, kid." He grabbed both of her hands as he shifted her into a horizontal position, squeezing her arms between their bodies. "Now, kick and hit all you want."

With his fangs throbbing while Chiara still fought, he footed it toward the house. Dax's desire ratcheted to the next level. He growled. "Stop or I'll take you right here."

"Just try it. Put me down, fangmouth."

"Is that your version of asshole? If so, I'm offended."

Once he reached the porch, he climbed the three steps to fling open the screen. Her head hit the doorjamb.

"Ouch. Watch it."

Dax's heart throbbed as red drops pooled around a wound on her forehead. "Sorry." Surprisingly, he meant it.

When he threw her onto the bed, she scrambled backward on all fours, planting her spine against the headboard. For all the good it would do her. "I saved your life. Is this my payment?"

He was mesmerized by the rise and fall of her chest with each deep breath.

Dax stared into her vivid orchid eyes. "Beautiful," he whispered. "I won't hurt you. I must heal. Which means I need to feed."

"I was healing you."

"Not fast enough."

"I don't want to die."

"Die?" He brushed his tangled hair away from his face, knowing he must look like a nightmare. She was a blood virgin, not like the females he usually tapped. *Be gentle.* "Nobody said anything about killing. I'll just take a little. If I don't do it now, I could lose control later. It's for the best."

When she flipped a hand up, he grabbed it, brushing a kiss onto her wrist before he bound it along with the other to the bedpost, using the discarded rope on the floor.

She jerked at the bindings, her luscious mouth open. "Does it hurt?"

"No. I can make it pleasant."

"Untie me then. I'll let you bite."

A hollow laugh escaped Dax's throat. "I know you'll let me. You don't have a choice." He licked a fang, his gut clenching from hunger.

"But you'll like it more if I let you." She glanced at her hands.

"Not necessarily. I appreciate a little fight."

"If it's fight you want, vampire, bring it on." Her legs scissored as her arms twisted, her wrists chafing from the movement.

"Stop it, kid. You're hurting yourself."

She flinched when Dax threw himself onto the bed, grabbing her ankle. His hand began a slow glide under her skirt and along her thigh. She stilled, her breath hitching.

Straddling her, he dropped his head to capture her lips with a soft, warm kiss. Electricity sparked through every nerve in his body.

Chiara froze, mute, stunned, but scenting of arousal.

Just feed. No reason to kiss.

Unable to stop himself, he seized her mouth again. Her lips parted in invitation.

Heavenly.

With an urgency he chose not to examine, he plunged his tongue deep as Chiara responded, tangling with him, stroking, sucking. He fisted her shoulders, drawing her near as he thrust in and out, his rhythm slow, seductive.

When Dax withdrew from the welcomed kiss, he nibbled along her chin, not breaking skin. At her neck, he licked the pulsing vein, drawing her flesh into his mouth until it plumped, turning cherry red. "Sweet."

He jerked away, unable to bite. Why was he acting the gentleman vampire? Not his style. He took what he wanted, what he needed. Or, more likely, he paid for it. "I must." His damn eyes pleaded with her.

"You need it to heal?"

He nodded.

"It better not hurt. Go ahead."

Chiara angled her neck. When his fangs slid into her flesh, she cried out his name. Her gasp changed to a moan as the pain inhibitor in his bite hit.

His cock hard, Dax groaned while he rocked against Chiara's thigh. Back and forth. Teasing his groin. His balls were about to explode.

Gahya. Never had anyone tasted so delicious. He was right. Honey, lavender, vanilla. Human but not. He was too euphoric to consider the dilemma. She just was. On his tongue, coating his throat, her blood was an addictive flavor.

Chiara's hips rose off the bed as she arched into his thrusts. "Dax. Please."

He didn't know why she begged. Did she want him to stop? Did she want more?

He withdrew his fangs, stopping before he took too much. When he licked her wound to close it, his hand dropped to squeeze Chiara's breast, his hips still undulating, his cock painfully rubbing against his zipper.

"Yes, Dax." Her breathing was shallow, choppy.

He pulled her peasant blouse far off her shoulders, exposing a sensible white bra. He lifted a warm mound of flesh out of a cup. Bending his head, he sucked her plump nipple into his mouth, nipping it, licking it until it was a pebbled nub.

His arousal painful, Dax unzipped his pants to palm his shaft, stroking. Up. Down. Faster. Again. Once. Twice.

"Damn, Gahya. Yes," he roared. His seed erupted. He froze as it continued to spill. When it finally stopped, he threw a leg off her and collapsed onto the bed beside her, his arms limp at his side.

I humped a little gypsy skirt's leg, shot my wad milking my own cock. I'm no better than some pre-

Awakened randy male vamp. What am I thinking?

"You oaf. I said you could have dinner, not get your rocks off."

Two red punctures marred Chiara's neck where he'd fed. Despite his healing saliva, she carried his mark. His palm flattened on his aching chest. Guilt? *Hell, no.* He was proud.

Chiara wiggled as far away from him as her bound arms allowed.

Dax pushed to the edge of the bed. He tucked himself into his pants and zipped up.

Humiliating. I haven't done that since... Nope. Since never.

And his release had gone on and on. Especially considering his cock's intimate relationship had been with his hand.

"You moaned when I fed," he mumbled. A weak-ass defense.

"What? Is a moan code for you get to diddle yourself until you come all over my bedspread? Well, you've eaten lunch followed by a perverted quickie. Maybe you can untie me, fanghole."

He rose and adjusted his pants, his cock still wanting Chiara. *Amazing*. He was fully sated with her blood, but he still ached for this human female. He snapped the rope from her wrists. "Again with the insults, kid. Watch your mouth."

"Really? My language offends you? That's a laugh. You sucked my blood. Which wasn't a bad experience, by the way. And proceeded to fondle me while you gave yourself a hand job. But my calling you a fanghole is offensive."

She rubbed the rope burns on her skin.

Watching, Dax lifted his finger to his mouth, slicing it across a sharp canine. "Here. Let me."

Chiara pulled her brows tight but allowed him to smear blood over her wounds. They healed instantly. "I'd thank you, but it's your fault it happened."

"I needed the nourishment. It's how I survive. No apology."

"Find another donor next time if you're gonna Jolly your Roger again."

"Your mouth could do with a good soaping." When Dax leaned toward her, Chiara raised a hand.

As she brought it down, the temperature dropped, a chill breeze hitting Dax's face as she drew power from him like a witch. He flew off the bed, and his body slammed into the wall so hard plaster crumbled. Dazed, he pushed off, brushed dust from his chest, and shook his head. "What the hell!"

Chapter Five

"Let the guys handle those." Skyler Maxwell, a Blood Coven descendant and Alliance chief legal officer, patted her administrative assistant's shoulder.

Instead of bending to grab a packed box, Anna straightened. "We have so much to carry out."

"Sit and relax. Kole hired a bunch of oversized Aeternals to load the stuff onto trucks. Our task was to pack. Let them do their jobs."

A demon entered the office at that moment, twisting his body to squeeze enormous shoulders through the doorway. He brushed a boyish lock of brown hair out of his eyes. "What next?"

Anna pointed to the corner, a mischievous grin lighting her face. "Those."

The guy bent over with his tight backside exposed to their view, flashing muscle as he lifted three heavy boxes.

Both women winked at each other.

"You're right, boss. This is much better." Anna sat on a chair, cocked her heels onto a box, and shimmied her skirt up to show more leg. "Did you get a load of those thick arms? Of course, he has nothing on your Kole."

Another mover strode into the room, his eyes scanning Anna's legs. "Those?"

She nodded. Once he left, laden with boxes, the admin assistant clicked her stilettos to the floor. "I might have to help him."

"You do that."

Skyler patted her sleek bun, not a hair out of place. The employees were scattering, some to less well-known Alliance offices on Earth but others to Scath where the Scion Firebrands offered to provide quarters for the human organization which assisted Aeternals. Each Alliance employee's veins contained a smidgeon of nonhuman blood, most of it from the time of the Schism over fifteen hundred years ago. Barely a drop in the old DNA bucket.

Skyler glanced up, sensing her mate before she saw him. His innate power nearly knocked her over as he thundered into her office, his boots pounding on the tile.

"Frisca, what the fuck's taking so long?"

No romantic greetings from her man. Still, he took her breath away, her gladiator with his stony jaw, buzz-cut hair, and blazing red-gold eyes, an animus demon whose fire burned near the surface. And talk about thick muscled arms. No one beat Kole in that department.

He swept those arms around her and, with a hand to the back of her head, pressed her against his solid, mile-wide chest where she was warm and safe.

"You're messing my hair."

He tugged on her once-neat bun. Pulling her head back, he pressed his lips to her mouth. No gentle kiss. His tongue urged entry, and she gave it willingly. After making her heart thump madly, he deserted her. "Now your lipstick's messy, too."

"So are you." She wiped a red smudge from his mouth.

"I'm taking you out now."

Kole excelled at barking orders. But she didn't always obey. "I'll be the last to leave my offices, demon. Don't even think about telling me when to go."

He gave her his lopsided grin which usually got him his way.

Not this time.

"Stubborn female. Then I'll help." He stacked

five heavy boxes, lifted them, and lumbered toward the outer office.

Skyler shoved stray papers into an empty container. Contracts for a new company, trade agreements, things she loved working on every day. She hoped to run her operation from Scath or to find a safe location on Earth.

Kole returned, the air vibrating with his energy. “Anna’s out. Ditto Laura, your paralegals, and your assistants. All the boxes are loaded and headed for a remote portal. All other divisions have vacated. You’re next, Frisca. Am I going to have to carry you?”

Skyler trailed a hand along the familiar wood of the doorway, looking around to say goodbye. Here was where a techy betrayed the Alliance by selling gateway locations to Dante, a human who turned out to be Ram’s father-in-law. The Englishman, a co-conspirator with Cerberus, created his own small army to get back at the satyr Firebrand whom he blamed for his daughter’s death. The greedy mole compromised not only several portals but possibly Alliance headquarters.

Here was where her grandfather and father had worked as chief legal officers. Here was her first job out of college. Here was where the board appointed her as her father’s successor when he died. It may not have been the life she would have chosen, but she had molded it into something good, something worthwhile.

Here she met her mate. The amazing demon whose love became her torch in the darkness. They’d had a child, Kae. Still an infant, but already she had Daddy wrapped around her perfect little finger.

Kole looped an arm over her shoulders, pulling her tight. “It’s just an office. You’ll have grander headquarters someday. I believe in you, in your ability.”

She tilted her head, her mate’s eyes glowing gold

fire. "But I became a woman here. I met you here. I became someone I like. I gave birth to a precious girl."

"You'll always be that woman. She isn't defined by brick and mortar, Frisca. She's defined by what's in here." He tapped her heart.

Skyler wrapped a hand behind her mate's head and pulled him down for a kiss, a hot, meaningful kiss. *What the heck.* Her lipstick was already a mess.

"You're brilliant, demon. Come on. Let's blow the portal."

He shot her a toe-curling smile. "Fireworks are my specialty."

When sparks jumped across Kole's fingers, Skyler touched fingers to his arm. "You won't burn down the whole place, will you? It is a historic building."

"No. I'll let loose a controlled burn. Just enough to get rid of any evidence of us." With a flick of his hand, wildfire shot across the room.

****

Chiara blew on the nails of what she liked to think of as her trigger hand. "Don't try anything with me, fangmouth. Hero or not, I'll cast a spell to wipe the floor with your dead ass. I am not your Big Gulp with a side of ejaculation."

She might have been exaggerating her powers a bit. After a spell, she needed time to regenerate. She could never have done a back-to-back, but he didn't need to know.

Dax shoved his black, snarled hair onto his back while he stared at her with those predatory obsidian eyes. She'd never met a man so seductive. If he weren't so menacing, he'd be her fantasy come to life.

When he'd saved her from the burning car, he became the poster boy for superhero. Through a child's eyes. Once she was older, he'd starred in every dream as the tall, buff romantic lead. Through a woman's eyes. In her nightly fantasies, he was painfully beautiful. Strong but kind. He would come to her bed to seduce her with his sultry mouth and sweet words.

But the man in front of her bordered on malevolent. *Still*... She chewed on the tip of her thumb. Having seen him work his penis—his huge penis—was erotic as hell. She wanted to touch him, stroke his hard flesh, make him come in her hand.

"What are you?" He puzzled his forehead, his long, dark lashes outlining his eyes.

"I imagine a witch."

"What do you mean, 'you imagine?'"

"I haven't met any others. I have no one to compare myself to."

While he inched closer, his nostrils flared as he sniffed the air. "You smell human. Your aura is human. But you cast a spell like a witch. I felt the chill. And you channeled your power from me, feeding like a mage. Have I mentioned I hate witches?"

"Good to know. Did you make me this way when you took me out of the car?"

"What? No. The salve you rubbed on my wounds earlier. How did you come by it?"

"Self-taught. I read books on potions, herbs, healing, the works. If it sounds witchy, I buy it."

"But you can cast spells, too?"

"Sure." *Sometimes. Without much control.* Of course, he didn't need to know the particulars. Chiara shook out her arms, preparing to use her hands again when Dax's lips curled into a snarl. "Stay put, Vlad."

"I'm not Vlad." He cocked his head to the side.

"I'll sizzle your bones if you move closer."

"I can't stand here forever, little witch."

A stare-down commenced, but Chiara broke eye

contact to chew on her thumbnail. "I suppose not. What do you propose?"

"You don't spell me, and I don't…"

"Bite me? And no more tying each other to beds." Her fists popped to her hips.

Dax's gaze tagged her neck. "I'm okay with no binding, but I need blood to survive."

"How often?"

"Daily."

"I'm not a two-legged blood bank. What about sucking on a nice rabbit?"

"I don't do furry animals."

"A snake then. No fur."

He smirked, his hungry eyes far too intense.

"You've had your snack today. Focus. What happens if you don't get your daily donation?"

He brushed a hand through his hair, only drawing attention to his high cheekbones, stubbled chin, and flexed bicep. "I'll weaken, but before that happens, I'll go blood-crazed and attack. Trust me. You don't want that to happen."

"Just go back where you came from to get your blood shake. Leave me alone."

Dax waved his wrist, the wound no more than an angry scar now. "Can't."

Chiara began to pace. "Witch walking here," she said, raising a cautioning hand when he took a step in her direction. "What if I bottle some of my O-pos for you? You can drink me from a glass jar."

A feral grin tugged at his lips. "Where's the pleasure in that?"

"Exactly. That's our compromise. You slurp me from a container. Once you heal, you're out of here even if you can't return home. Now. What's next? Where did you come from? How will you get back?"

Chiara sidestepped Dax to walk into the living room where she slumped into her most comfortable chair.

"You're a witch, but you really don't know about us?" he asked.

Two hundred and fifty pounds of bare-chested gorgeous but dangerous man leaned against the doorframe, his hair hanging mid-back. Without the feral gaze or cruel sneer, he resembled the hero of her dreams. She would have to be careful, though, because he wasn't a fantasy. He was real. He was deadly. It occurred to her she may have glorified him in her dreams. Maybe his heroism had worn off over the years.

"What us?" asked Chiara.

"Scath. Aeternals."

"Not a clue."

"I gotta shower first."

She pointed toward her bedroom. "Sure, but then answers. There's a bathroom through there. The towels are clean."

Chiara listened to the water while she pictured a naked Dax with water sluicing down his shoulders, his arms, his hips, his thighs. What had she gotten herself involved in? He wasn't what she remembered.

Stop fixating on a fairytale.

She was so busy fantasizing, she did not hear Dax slip into the room. Startled, she realized he was wrapped in nothing but a towel, shaking his head, sending water flying.

Holy shit. He isn't a fairytale, but he's a man built for dreams.

"You're not dressed," said Chiara.

"I have no shirt. My pants are dirty and torn."

"Where are they?"

"On the floor in the bathroom."

"Slob. I'm not the maid. Take care of your own crap."

Chiara slapped a hand over her eyes, curling deeper into the comfortable chair when Dax flopped onto the couch. His thighs spread, he tossed an arm across the back cushions. "I'm an Aeternal from Scath. I can't get home easily without my D-chip. That's what they dug out of my wrist. I'll stick around for a bit. Until I figure out a way back."

She peeked through her fingers. "Can you get decent? Close your legs and stop exposing your boy bits."

Dax arched a brow. "Boy bits? Hardly."

He swung his legs onto the sofa and sprawled out. His biceps flexed as he plopped a pillow under his neck and locked his hands behind his head. The towel perched precariously on his hips but covered the essentials. She would ignore his long, powerful legs, slabs of chest muscle, and the trail of dark hair leading from his navel to the towel.

Yikes.

Solution. Ernest's clothes. He was a big guy, too. Of course, everything Dax had was distributed differently. She jumped up, rushing to the laundry room where she had folded her neighbor's clean clothes, having forgotten to give them to him when he'd stopped by for the arthritis concoction.

She flung them at Dax. "Put these on, please."

Standing, he let the towel fall. She spun around on her heel and squeezed her eyes tight. The man had no decency.

He chuckled. "You can look."

Ernest's pants hung low on his hips, but the XX shirt stretched snug across his chest and arms.

Chiara returned to her comfortable chair. Back to

the subject. *Aeternals.* Leaning forward, she rested elbows on her thighs. “You mean you live forever?”

“No. When Gahya created us, we were near immortal. Somewhere in time, we contracted a virus, probably as a punishment. At least, that’s what the myth-tellers say. But who knows the truth?”

“Gahya?”

“Another story. Let me finish with the one about Scath and Aeternals first.”

****

Tyr cranked his bike to top speed, screeched into the parking lot, slamming on the brakes, and hustling into the Ministry of Well Being.

Sabine, a tall female whose breasts Barbie would admire, paced in the hallway. When her head whipped around at his entry, two long blonde braids pitched over her shoulders.

“What’s wrong?” asked the warlock. “Is she worse?”

“No. She just won’t shut up about you. Tyr this. Tyr that. It’s enough to make a grown nymph gag. She’s driving her blood pressure and mine through the roof. The healers ordered me to find you. To muzzle her, I think. Now get in there to take care of the female.”

“What the fuck am I supposed to do?”

“Don’t know. Don’t care.” Sabine flicked her braids over her breasts and tootled goodbye on her way out.

Tyr thundered into the patient’s room, his boots pounding an angry rhythm on the tile. “What gives? Why me?” His expression remained grim despite the vision that greeted him. The female rested against the headboard, long, bare legs stretched out beneath an ugly blue medical gown. Thick strawberry hair curled around her shoulders, large smoky blue eyes veiled by dark lashes looked his way, and a moist tongue flicked out to stroke her plump lips. All of this and an innocent heart-shaped face. Tyr didn't do innocent. Or Blood Coven witches.

The *femme fatale* arched one brow, gave him a barely-there smile, and spoke in a honeyed voice which suggested hot sultry nights and fucking. "Hello. Nice to see you again."

Tyr fought the urge to cup his ears, muffling the siren's song before he crashed onto the rocks like Ulysses. "I'm here."

"Thank you for coming. First, I need out of this place. I'm supposed to go somewhere called the stronghold. Second, we need to find Celene. She counted on me to bring help. That woman … Sabine … said you're a Scion Firebrand, and you guys are looking for humans who were brought to wherever it is we are. Since it's your job anyway, you can help me find Celene and get us home."

She might be sugar-coating the request with politeness, but Tyr sensed a command behind the words. Since he didn't respond well to commands, he did what he did best. He shelled out his Goth-warlock stare which toppled even crazed berserkers. "First, you get out of this place when the healers say you do. Second, I am not your babysitter or one-male rescue team. I will find someone who can help you locate this Celene."

With a tap of his wrist, he explained the situation to Kole.

After he disconnected from the convo, he ran fingers through his spiked black hair. "Keep your ass on the bed while I talk to the healer."

"What's happening?"

"Shush. Just stay."

Tyr thought he heard "I'll be a good puppy" when

he walked out of the room, grabbing the first healer who tried to sneak past him. "When will she be ready to go?" A thumb pointed in Jace's direction made it clear which patient he was talking about.

"She's ready now. As the responsible party, just sign her out of the facility."

Tyr stomped back into the room. "Let's go."

She stroked a hand along her body. "Clothes?"

With the doorjamb in one hand, he swung out into the hallway, shouting at the retreating healer. "She needs clothes."

"We only carry medical gowns."

When Tyr snarled, the nervy guy held his middle finger high.

"Fuck. Do I have to do everything?" He touched his wrist to call his *freron. Sabine. Find her some clothes and get your ass over here with them.*

The human female signaled him from the bed. "What are you doing?"

"Getting you clothes."

"I'm particular about what I wear."

"This should be good." *Hang on, Sabine. The princess is putting in a shopping order.*

"Pants. Size six since I've lost weight."

Tyr relayed the message.

"Sensible shoes. Flats. Ones I can walk in easily."

No fuck me shoes, Sabine. "Size?"

"Eight and a half. Is it cool outside?"

He nodded. Bored with the convo.

"A sweater would be perfect. I'm tall. A medium should do. I like some color, but not too much. Does Sabine have good taste?"

"She's a nymph. She only wears stuff showing nipples." He relayed the information, adding, *Princess wants a sweater. Medium. And tasteful shit.*

Conservative. Nothing like what you wear... How would I know where the fuck you should go? Do I strike you as a designer kind of guy?

Sabine's chuckle came into his head loud and clear thanks to the D-chip.

What's so funny?

Tyr disconnected, flinging himself into the nearby chair.

After Jace settled back against the top of the bed, she crossed her ankles. He was a sucker for long, shapely legs. Despite the formless medical gown, she was wicked shapely.

"Where am I?"

"Didn't anybody let you know anything?"

"Nope."

He drew a deep breath when she shot him with her siren's smile. "You're on Scath."

"And that is?"

"The Blood Coven created Scath and Darque over fifteen hundred years ago. My kind left your realm, taking the wildings with us, to protect your kind. Humans. The Whorl separates us, but trusted Aeternals go back and forth through portals."

"*The Path* is true," she mumbled.

"Huh?"

"Nothing. What's your kind?"

"I'm a warlock. Other breeds are vampires, demons, nymphs. You get the drift. Not human." He glanced at his D-chip. *God.* Could time pass any slower? The female was rapid-firing questions at him as if she were reading from a list. On his best days, he didn't want to be the spokesman for all things Scath.

"Why were Celene and I brought here?"

Tyr slunk deeper into the chair, getting comfortable for what was likely to be a long, painful inquisition. "Not sure. But a bad guy named Cerberus is hunting for descendants of the Blood Coven. You are one. Maybe your Celene is, too."

"I'm human." She bit her lower lip, waiting for his answer.

"Maybe. But fifteen hundred years ago, one of your relatives wasn't."

She waved her hand. "I'll think about this later. Now we need to find Celene. Afterward, you can send us home."

"You might be screwed." Tyr crossed his arms over his chest. "You'll stay at the stronghold until we catch this Cerberus and make things safe for you."

"What's the stronghold?"

He glanced at his chip again. Yep. Slo-mo. "My headquarters. One of the Scion Firebrands' places. Others of your kind are there."

"Other human descendants?"

Tyr nodded. "But some are hardly human anymore." He rolled his eyes up, mentally ticking off the residents. "There's Braelyn, Margo, Skyler, Denim, and Nico. Oh, and Lizette but she stays with Commander Jarek at another stronghold."

Before she could ask another question, Sabine raced into the room. The nymph Firebrand dropped a big shopping bag next to the warlock. She pointed at the human, saying, "You are high maintenance. Please appreciate how hard it is to find … um … tasteful clothes on Scath." She turned on the heel of her boot and left.

"She's not very friendly." Jace leaned forward, sneaking a peek inside the bag.

Like a magician pulling a rabbit out of a hat, Tyr stuck his hands into the sack to drag out two scraps of red lace. Pinching each between a thumb and forefinger, he held them on display. *Nice.* He pictured this female in only the red lacy underwear. "The nymph's got good taste."

Jace blushed, a pretty shade of pink coloring her cheeks. "Don't fondle them. That's really creepy. And juvenile. Just toss them here."

He twirled both undergarments around on his finger before flipping them at Jace. After he peeked into the bag again, he launched it onto the bed. "The rest is boring. While you slip into new duds, you can tell me about Celene." Tyr shifted upright in the chair, waiting.

"I'm not getting dressed while you're in the room. Scram." She pointed at the doorway.

Ignoring the gesture, Tyr held a hand over his eyes. "I won't peek." His digits slipped apart while a grin spread across his face.

"Shoo."

When her eyes lit with a smile, Tyr almost clasped a fist to his heart. Despite wanting to see her in the lace panties and bra, he sauntered into the corridor, shouting over his shoulder. "I'll check you out and be waiting in front."

What a gentleman. No. What a wuss.

Chapter Six

Though Celene Bailey was thrilled Jace escaped, she was lonely without the extra chatter. The house was too quiet. Lort the crazy vampire and his demon sidekicks moved her twice, but she clung to hope, believing her ex-roomie would rescue her.

In the years following her parents' deaths, the newspapers tagged Celene as *The Daredevil Heiress*, but she didn't feel much bravado as she rose from the bed, slipped into her robe, and plodded to the kitchen.

Rule one. Maintain my strength. She prepped a breakfast of scrambled eggs, toast, and tomatoes. Of the two, Jace had been the cook, but with her friend gone, Celene stepped to the plate, fixing basic meals to keep her healthy. Finished eating, she brewed another cup of strong black coffee, carrying it to the couch.

Rule two. Keep occupied. After setting her cup on the old, scratched coffee table, she lit a fire and pulled out a new volume of *The Path: Words of the Warrior Ohngel.*

She and Jace had read about the famous warlock who pieced together the Blood Coven and whipped up a few realms so humans could survive without the savage Aeternals using them as dessert. Another volume recorded how Niviane screwed the guy over by sending their daughter to Scath. The third was about the creation of the Aeternals. Now what?

Weary from a lengthy truth-seeking journey, I, the Cambion from Wales, rested beside a late evening fire after finishing a meager repast. A nightchat flew from the trees, singing. The warbler-like bird trilled, chirped, and whistled, its raspy notes a message from Ohngel, the fire-winged assassin of the OneCreator, the male I would deem prophet and friend in the coming years.

Oft thereafter, Ohngel or the prophet-warrior's emissary, the nightchat, emerged from the thickets to tell a tale of hope, courage, caution, or enlightenment for the Aeternals placed upon this world by the Genitrix Gahya.

She skimmed the descriptions of previous volumes, concentrating on the new book.

As I wrote by candlelight in a large dim chamber of the cave, Ohngel, my enigmatic mentor, ventured inside. He was a male who painted himself not only as an assassin with an easy conscience but also as a grudging rescuer. Tonight, he told a tale of The Fall, an event oft pondered among Aeternals. That story and the rise of Homo sapiens formed the substance of *Volume IV: The Fall and Rise.*

Celene glanced at the wall. No longer allowed outside for exercise and with no windows, she relied on the clock to tell her the passing hours and days. Having no idea whether it was accurate, she chose to believe it was 9:30 in the morning. She planned to read for another hour before showering, dressing, and dwelling on her lonely existence.

With her legs curled beneath her on the couch, Celene wondered if, wherever Jace landed, she was also reading *The Path.* The thought giving her solace, she returned to the book.

Though millennia had passed, Ohngel continued to have an unhealthy obsession with Gahya's Aeternals. At least, that's how he saw it.

Sated after a thorough fucking, he turned on his side toward the Genitrix, broaching a subject which was beginning to bore even him. "They grow more savage."

"Can you not rest in the glow of our pleasure? Why must you always talk of my creatures?" She sat up, pointing toward Earth.

Ohngel looked below to see a male demon laugh, his fiery beast assuaged, having fed on his companion's orgasm.

Gahya fluffed her golden, wavy hair. "His female sighs with contentment. Would that I could do the same without your nattering on about my creations. All is good."

"What is good is not necessarily right."

"Why are you so opposed to my sharing carnal knowledge? It frees us from the boredom of eternity. I gave my Aeternals an extraordinary way to nourish their bodies. I gave them desire. I made them for us, my love. They are perfect, without faults." She scattered the leaves around her with an angry hand, her thighs wet from his release.

Ohngel relaxed despite her show of temper, hands behind his head, his still erect penis twitching against his belly, his need never fully sated. "Be honest with yourself, Gahya. You created them because you could. You thrive on the pride of ownership. But it will be a shame if they are destroyed because of your hubris."

Tears threatened to escape her eyes. "Why can you not revel in my accomplishments?"

"I appreciate your achievement. In fact, I admire your Aeternals. They are sentient beings with hopes, fears, and dreams. They are creatures of will. I see how they love life. But monitor their paths, teach them. Do not simply give them the desire of the gods and set them adrift. Their aggression will destroy them. Give them courage, honor, and loyalty to temper their passions. They are capable of greatness."

Ohngel began to recognize he possessed an irritating protective streak. He did not know where it came from or when it would lift its unwelcome head. Fight as he might, he could not rid himself of it. It peeked over his shoulder, tugging on an earlobe, demanding to be heard. Yes. Irritating.

The Genitrix sniffled. "You do me an injustice, Ohngel. I teach them what I choose. They are satisfied." Her chin jutted out with stubborn pride.

The male and female demon continued to lie side by side, exhausted. The female's hand rested on the male's lower stomach near his semi-erect penis. Before she pleasured him again, a disturbance sounded.

A second male demon crashed through the bushes, roaring, his fists pounding his chest. "Mine," he thundered as he latched onto the female's wrist to pull her from the hard ground and toss her behind him. He crouched, calling forth his clawed beast, challenging her lover.

The sex-glutted male rose to bring forth his own demon. A savage battle ensued, each creature tearing at the other, each coveting the female and gripped by a possessive rage.

But the intruder ripped open the lover's throat, tearing flesh, muscle, tendon, and bone. As the stronger of the two contenders, his last act was to tear off his opponent's head. Dropping the body at his feet, he twisted toward the female, his prize.

She stepped away, her eyes wide, tears staining her cheeks as she gazed upon her dead lover.

The victor was not finished. He lumbered into the bushes to drag forth an earlier kill, an offering to his newly won female. With a lifeless gift at his feet, he thumped his chest with pride.

Gahya gasped, fighting for a breath, a loud wheeze escaping her throat. The victor's offering was a forbidden kill. A Homo erectus. The OneCreator decreed these creatures off limits.

The Genitrix sprang to her feet, her eyes wide

with shock. And, perhaps, fear.

Ohngel propped himself on his elbows, his expression dispassionate. The boss was going to be pissed. He had expressed a future use for Homo erectus.

Celene closed the book, resting her hand on her pulsing heart. *Wow.* Ohngel could certainly tell a simmering tale. She glanced at the clock on the wall. More than an hour had passed. *Oh, well.* What else did she have to do besides shower? Nothing. *The Path* was more interesting.

****

Tyr waited for Jace beside his motorcycle, plugged into Rancour's "Banished."

The door to the Ministry of Well Being opened. The tall strawberry blonde who walked toward him was sexy as hell. A high and tight ponytail tied back with a colorful scarf swished from side to side with her hip movement. Plaid pants stopped mid-calf, showing off flat black shoes. She wore two matching sweaters, the outer one with tons of tiny buttons. Tyr's warlock heart thumped against his chest when he remembered what was hidden under the clothes.

Red skimpy panties and a lacy bra. Oh, baby.

He wanted to unwrap her. Unsnapping her bra, he'd free those luscious breasts. He'd nip on them a while before he hooked a thumb in her panties to slide them down her legs.

Where are these dumb ideas coming from? I'm hardcore. She's definitely not.

She smoothed hands down the snug sweaters and on to her hips. "I'm dressed like a fifty's throwback, sweater set and all. Have you ever seen *Happy Days*?"

"Sure. Brak and I did a TV sitcom marathon once. The Fonz." He combed fingers through the hair on the sides of his head. "Great stuff."

Sabine must be yucking up the clothing choices. But they fit Jace. She was an innocent from the fifties. Off limits.

As Jace drew closer, her eyes widened, bouncing from Tyr to his ride.

"What?" The Firebrand stubbed out his cigarette and removed an earbud.

"A motorcycle?" The female eyed him from boots to spiked hair. "No wonder you're wearing a lot of leather."

Tyr glanced down. Leather pants. Leather jacket. Leather boots. "So?"

"Nothing."

When he tossed her a helmet, he glared. "Put this on."

"I've never ridden on a motorcycle."

"I'm shocked."

"They're not safe."

"They are when I drive. Now zip it and get on. You asked me to take you to the stronghold and here I am. If you want somebody else, I can call." He cocked his head as he waited for an answer.

Jace slipped the helmet over her head. "I'll go with you, but I still think these contraptions are unsafe. They don't call them a surgeon's wet dream for nothing."

"Life's full of bad shit." Tyr grabbed her arm, pulling her forward. He snapped on her headgear and tugged. "Now you're safe." He swung a leg over his machine, motioning for Jace to climb on behind him. "Keep your feet on these. Hang on tight to my waist."

When her hands slipped around him, he shuddered. Which made no sense. The chick was straight out of the fifties. Not only were they opposites, but he didn't even like her type. The don't-rock-the-boat type. Boats should be rocked, and sometimes they should be poked full of holes, capsized, and scuttled. But his only job was to drop her at the stronghold and be on his way. He hoped the taint of home-and-apple-pie didn't stick to him.

Tyr took off with a lurch, squealing into a lane while Jace's fingers dug into his flesh. She let out a little yip as he smiled.

Once traffic grew light, Tyr throttled up, speeding along, hoping to scare Little Miss Priss.

"Faster," she yelled in his ear.

What the fuck? The uptight female likes speed. Let's see how she takes this.

With an open road ahead, he shot forward.

She poked a raised thumb in his face.

Surprise. Surprise.

Tyr took the long way. He planned to humble the princess, but the best laid plans and all that shit. The longer ride was worth it. Her breasts pressed against his back while her hands drifted further down his hips. For a fifty's chick, she squeezed dangerously close to his raging hard-on. When he pulled into the stronghold's underground garage, he stuck out a hand to assist her off the bike. Just like a gentleman.

Her eyes were bright, and a smile lit her face. "Riding your bike was more fun than I thought. Thank you. Maybe we could do it again sometime."

Tyr didn't answer. He unsnapped her helmet, slipped it from her head, and crushed his lips to hers. She gasped but didn't push him away. Not even when he thrust his tongue into her mouth and pulled her against his leathered body. He couldn't help the erection that pressed into her belly. A fast ride and a hot Trixie always did that to him.

Wait a fucking minute.

She tasted sweet, spicy. Tyr couldn't get deep

enough as their tongues tangled. Coming to his senses, he released her lips and stepped away.

She pulled her ponytail tight and straightened her prim sweater, tugging on the bottom. "What was that for?"

"Damned if I know. Let's go." He clasped her hand, dragging the fifty's chick behind him while biting his tongue before he started saying shit like *cool*, *daddy-o*, and *cruisin' for a bruisin'*.

****

From the garage, they walked through a hallway to a set of stairs. Climbing them, they dodged workmen carrying weight equipment down the steps.

In the foyer, Jace peeked around Tyr, hoping she didn't have helmet hair.

The stronghold was bigger than she expected, and a fiery redhead, fists on hips, controlled the commotion, shouting instructions to the workmen.

"That's right. Everything goes. All the mats, the weapons, the machines, the works. It's not like this is a surprise. I told you the stuff was heavy."

Once the men disappeared, the woman spun around. "Hey. You must be Jace. I'm Margo. Forgive the chaos, but we're mid-remodel. The training facility used to be on this floor, but now the new and improved version is downstairs. This level is the gathering area."

She pointed behind her to three over-stuffed leather couches, a huge coffee table, a colorful geometric-patterned rug, and a giant television.

"The kitchen's thataway. A game room for the boys over there. The library. Upstairs are the apartments." She took an exaggerated breath. "I guess I should let you speak. Chay says I'm chatty. He should talk. Anyway, welcome."

The redhead clasped Jace in a strong embrace.

"Nice to meet you, Margo."

"Hey, Tyr. Long time no see." She funneled her hands to her mouth, turned toward the kitchen, and shouted. "Braelyn, we've got company. How about some coffee in here?" With a friendly smile, she latched onto Jace's arm. "Come on. You two sit."

Tyr, obviously at home in the stronghold, flopped onto a couch and planted his boots on the table. Jace chose a different sofa, away from the disturbing but delectable warlock. Sitting primly, she folded her hands and crossed her ankles. Margo sat beside her.

"What's your story?" The redhead plumped a pillow before leaning back on the sofa.

A tall, lithe woman with spiky auburn hair and a freckled nose entered, balancing four cups and a pot of coffee on a tray. Shoving Tyr's boots to the side, she set it on the table. "Don't start till I'm ready." She poured four cups, grabbed one, and, with her legs curled under her bottom, sat on the other side of Jace. "Grab. I'm Braelyn. Okay. Begin."

"Me? I guess you know my name. I was born in Poughkeepsie, New York. At Cornell in Ithaca, I studied viticulture and enology. A winery in New Paltz hired me after graduation. It was a plum job. Anyway, that's probably not what you're interested in knowing."

"Nope," said Margo. "Good info for a job interview, but how did you get here?"

"I was driving to work at the vineyard when a van pulled alongside. Two enormous guys jumped out and snatched me from my car. It was straight out of a movie. A rag to my nose. A bag over my head. I awoke in a jail, surrounded by a bunch of other people. It was hell. Screaming, crying, bodies dragged out."

Braelyn patted her leg. "I've been in that hell, too."

Jace pulled her brows tight. "How did you get out?"

"My mate, Rein, and other Firebrands rescued me. They destroyed Silas and Aisen's operation."

"Were you ever taken to a house?" A spark of hope flashed in Jace's eyes. "Perhaps you were held in the same place Celene and I were."

Braelyn shook her head. "What about you, Margo?"

"Chay and I were in a cell somewhere, but no one else was there." Margo wiggled her fingers. "My wonkiness saved us. What about your prison?"

"One day, I awoke in a house where I met Celene." Jace sniffed, brushing away a tear as it slid down her cheek. "She and I hatched a plan to escape. She does all this extreme sport stuff, like base jumping, but I was a record-holding runner in high school and college. We decided I stood the best chance at escape. I promised to find help and come back for her." Jace sighed, her shoulders slumping as she grabbed onto a cup of coffee. "May I have the cream?"

Braelyn passed a small pitcher. "Here you go. I guess you were moved to a house because you're a verified Blood Coven descendant."

Margo crossed her legs, patting Jace's hand. "I hear Skyler is looking for Celene. She's one of us. A strong scryer."

"She visited the Ministry of Well Being while I was in the med center to tell me about her visions, but she said the process would be better if I had something personal of Celene's. I don't."

Braelyn sipped her coffee. "Try not to worry, Jace. The Firebrands will make sure you keep your promise to Celene."

Margo faced Tyr. "So, warlock. What are the

warriors doing?"

"We're combing the woods near where Dax and I found Jace, searching in grids. Going out farther and farther. Nothing yet. But we won't give up."

"See there. They'll find her." Braelyn wrapped her hands around her coffee cup.

Loud footsteps interrupted the talk as an extremely handsome man with long caramel-streaked hair thundered down the stairs, buttoning a black silk shirt, the tail hanging out of his pants. He skidded to a halt when he spotted the four in the gathering room. "Hey."

"Hey yourself, Ram," said Tyr. "What are you doing here?"

"Uh … lunchtime." He tucked in his shirt and rolled his sleeves.

A door slammed upstairs. Fiddling with her hair, which was drawn into a ponytail revealing a scar on her cheek, an athletically fit woman flew down the steps, almost stumbling into Ram. "Oh. Hi, everyone."

"What did you have for lunch, Denim?" asked Tyr.

Denim blushed. "We don't want to be late, satyr. Let's go." She raced ahead of Ram.

Margo hid a smile behind her hand. "I wish Chay would come home for lunch."

When Jace glanced toward him, Tyr fixed his steamy, purple eyes on her. She clasped a hand to her fast-pounding heart, hoping no one else heard it. *Thump. Thump. Thump.* The tat under his eye, the silver bar piercing his brow, and the jewelry worked for him. Spiked black hair, broad shoulders, tight leather pants. She especially admired the pants. Her previous dates were young upwardly mobile millennials, MUPPIES in three-piece suits, Tag Heuer watches, and manicured nails. She doubted Tyr owned a suit.

What's wrong with me?

He was probably into all kinds of kinky sex Jace only heard about in hushed whispers around the office water cooler. So why was she drawn to him?

And why was she picturing him naked with his arm muscles bunching while his hot, sweaty body pressed down on her?

Tyr glanced at his D-chip. "I have to clock in with Ram. New recruits. I promised to show them a few blade moves."

Jace popped off the couch, following him to the stairs like a lost lamb.

At the last minute, he turned. "See ya."

"Will you? I mean, you have to help me find Celene."

"It's the stronghold. I'm usually around. I'm a Firebrand. We'll all be hunting for your friend."

"When will you be back?"

"Sometime." He shrugged while he started down the steps.

"Sometime," she muttered, returning to the gathering room. God. She sounded desperate. Pathetic. Did she want Tyr for herself, or did she need him to find Celene?

Don't be so melodramatic. Let the man leave. He's not my type.

Wiping her brow, she turned toward Margo and Braelyn. "I have to find Celene and bring her home. Will you help?"

Chapter Seven

Nerves on edge as if nails clawed a chalkboard, suspended, and pissed, Thorn had left Kole's office. He closed his place in Covenkirk last night. Now he was in his truck, kicking up dust.

The commander was right. He was on the fence. Was his loyalty to pack or the Firebrands? No better locale to think than his Montana ranch. But first, he was swinging by to visit his brother.

He suspected where Luka might be hiding. Hence, he and his truck were tooling along a dirt road in North Shelters, heading for a favorite spot they'd often used when their old man was on a binge. Safe in their secret cave, he couldn't use them as punching bags.

Thorn patted the dashboard of the Ford Super-duty F-450 Platinum black beauty, dubbed the She Beast.

A good female. Reliable. Beautiful. What more could I ask for?

When Mickey Lamantia's "Tough Mudder Trucker" came on the radio, he blasted the volume. With the window rolled down, he lit a cigar and sang along to the tune. The wind blew through his hair as his tires hummed on the way to freedom.

When he reached the foothills of the Clawtooth Range, Thorn pulled under a grove of trees. He snubbed out his Blazing Dragon, the most expensive smoke sold on Scath, opening the door before he toed off his boots. He put them on the seat bench after he removed and neatly folded his clothes.

A few easy stretches out of the way, he expanded his chest with a deep breath. Muscles snapped, bones popped, flesh tightened. The air sizzled with magic energy, a touch of pain along with a lot of pleasure.

Thorn pawed the ground, his nose bombarded with scents. Damp earth, old leaves, pine pitch, a rabbit. With a shake of his thick chestnut brown fur, peace settled over him for the first time in a while. He padded up the mountain, unfettered, wild as Gahya intended.

The wolf's steps landed lightly on the forest floor as he leaped scattered boulders or prowled around trees. When he neared the cave, he dropped to the ground, creeping forward on his belly, his animal senses alert.

Head high, he sniffed. Luka was in there with his mate, Sati. And blood. Thorn did not smell any other wolves. *Strange*. He expected the entire pack to be hiding here.

With his nose to the ground, Thorn followed the familiar scent to the entrance where he shifted to human form, nakedness not bothering his kind. Deep inside the cave, someone whimpered.

Still no whiff of anyone other than Luka and Sati. He hunted from one chamber to the next, following the twists and turns the brothers had explored long ago.

In a large domed cavity, Sati, the source of the weeping, sat in human form before a fire. Luka, bloodied, his fur matted, and, at least, one leg broken, rested his head in her lap.

Though she glanced at Thorn when he entered, she did not acknowledge him. He moved closer, eyeing his brother's mate since she could turn feral at any moment.

"What happened, Sati?"

"You happened, Thorn." She growled as she cradled Luka tighter.

"What do you mean?"

"After you came with your talk of drugs, Luka was shamed. He tried to rally the pack, but Karth challenged him for leadership." She nuzzled her mate's fur. "He lost. They left him lying bloody and broken in the dirt. After what he has done for them. For the pack."

"He's my brother, Sati. I love him, but he hasn't had control of the wolves for a long time. You can't lay this problem on me. He let them down, blinded to what was happening. Perhaps he finally tried to straighten shit out. Too little, too late."

Thorn noted some of Luka's wounds had knitted closed, but not all. "How long has he been this way?"

"A day."

He should have healed. "Set the bone in his leg, Sati. He needs to feed."

"Don't tell me what to do. You always wanted to be alpha. You were jealous when the pack chose him, jealous because he was stronger than you."

Thorn ignored her rant, knowing he was more powerful than his brother, also aware the wolves had begged him to defeat their cruel father in a domination match after Luka failed. So he challenged their father.

Afterward, the decision was simple. Luka wanted to be pack leader. Thorn did not. Since he was content to be a Scion Firebrand, he passed the leadership to his brother.

"Set his leg, Sati."

"No. If he heals lame, he can't fight Karth again to take back the pack."

Thorn approached to lift his brother into his arms. Sati snarled, shifting in an explosion of color, attacking with canines bared.

He had no choice. Thorn backhanded the female wolf, sending her flying into the cavern wall. He crouched, growling a warning when she attempted to rise. She mewled, curling into a ball, no longer challenging his right to care for his brother.

"Never provoke me, sister. I am an alpha."

With both hands on his brother's leg, Thorn pulled in opposite directions until the bone popped into place.

Sati shifted, eyeing Thorn cautiously before she returned to the fire. There, the she-wolf nestled her large mate, once again stroking Luka's fur.

As the chilled air of night approached, Thorn added logs to the dying embers. He left the cave to hunt, bagging a fatally injured deer. After he dressed it, he made several trips to bring the meat into the chamber.

In front of Luka, he put a hunk of raw thigh. Over the fire, he grilled steaks for Sati and himself. With the scent of the deer flesh under his nose, Luka lifted his head. After tearing off pieces to eat, he returned to sleep. To heal or survive, a shifter needed just a bite or more.

Two days, he and Sati waited in the cave with the injured wolf. Thorn moved only to get water, cut off meat, or cook. He rested his back against the limestone walls, his chin dropping to his chest, catching sleep when he could.

A snarl woke him. Thorn snapped his lids open. Luka was stalking on his belly, head lowered with his paws pulling him forward.

"Back the fuck off, asshole." Thorn didn't twitch a muscle. He closed his eyes, unconcerned with the threat, his body showing disdain for his brother's power.

When Thorn finally cracked his lids, Luka had shifted. Though caked with dried blood, he looked healed but dispirited. His shoulders slumped and his brows hung heavy. "I lost the pack, brother. Our family has been alpha for centuries. I lost it. What am I going to do?"

"Don't ask him," screamed Sati, jumping onto her feet, hands flying. "It's his fault."

Luka swung toward Sati, his eyes flashing amber. "I know you love me, mate, but right now shut the fuck up. This is my fault. Thorn doesn't want the pack. He never wanted them, even after he defeated Father. It was his by combat, but he gave it to me. So show him respect, something I have failed to do." Despite his harsh words, he stroked her hair.

Sati relaxed her taut muscles, saying no more.

Thorn crossed his ankles, his bare legs stretched out in the dirt. "What you will do is rest, get strong, and think hard about what you want."

With a sigh, Luka flopped down on the ground near his older brother.

"When you decide, act. If the alpha life is not for you, find an honorable pack. Petition to join. On the other hand, if you want the job, ask yourself why. Because of me? Because of Father? No good. If only you can save the pack, can make their lives better, then fight to win them back. Get healthy. Train. Challenge Karth to regain control. That's a hard road, brother."

"You're right. I need to think."

"Whatever you decide, I'll stand by you." Thorn clasped his arms around his sibling and held tight. "Whatever you decide."

Luka's head dropped onto Thorn's shoulder.

Breaking off the embrace, the Firebrand shifter leaned against the wall, the damp chill sinking into his bones. "I'm headed to Montana for a while. If you want to get in shape at my ranch, you and Sati are welcome."

"No, but thanks. I'll stay here for a bit. This was our refuge as kids. It worked wonders for us then. Maybe I can draw on its healing power again."

****

Dax lazed into the couch, stretching his legs onto a worn coffee table. It was becoming his evening routine. Four wolfhounds on the floor. Too comfortable. Too familiar. Too peaceful. But he had an excuse. Since he was stuck here for some time, he'd play nice. Besides, he lacked the will to devise a move-on plan.

He'd even resorted to non-sexual feeding. Not from a fucking cup, mind you. Had he ever drunk that way? If he had, he sure didn't remember. So for the time-being, he took from Chiara's wrist, biting while he blocked all thoughts of fucking her.

A total gentleman.

"Do you have any booze?" Dax threw an arm over the back of the sofa.

Chiara slipped out of her chair, pivoting left. Right. "Yeah. Somewhere." Her finger rested on a tasty plump lip. "I put it in the pantry. I'll look."

"A big glass." Alcohol had a limited effect on Aeternals. Of course, anything was better than nothing.

The little witch clinked a tumbler of golden-brown liquid onto the coffee table. Sniffing the one in her hand, she asked, "Do you think it's spoiled? I've had it for some time."

Dax's eyes narrowed. Then he laughed. "No. It's whiskey, not milk."

He took a long pull, savoring the burn. Where was he? How would he get home? Without a D-chip, he couldn't open a portal or communicate with his *frerons*. He had to locate a friendly to give him a lift to Scath.

Though Dax was physically healed, the warlock had done a number on his vampire powers. They were too polluted to use. He'd need more strength before he could shadowflash. Without that ability, his traveling would be slow. "Where are we?"

"Idaho."

"Near the Nez Perce reservation?"

Chiara nodded.

At least part of the plan worked. He was in a familiar region. "How far from here did you find me?"

"About a half-mile."

"Last I remember is coming through the Whorl with two demons and a warlock on my six. I killed one."

The same portal was too remote to hitch a ride home. Little traffic. Also, the bad guys might be covering it. He needed another gateway where Aeternal travelers passed through frequently.

The female curled her legs beneath her fine ass. "The dogs found you. Some men were hightailing it through the brush, dragging someone between them."

Dax carried his tumbler to a window. When he drew the curtains aside, he threw back the last swallow of his drink. No one was outside. "Did anybody follow you back to your cabin?"

Though Ivan's ear twitched, the dog didn't stir.

"I don't think so. Demons? A warlock? From your place?"

"Yeah." He turned to lean against the windowsill, a bare foot cocked over the other.

"Apparently, sunlight does not bother you."

"Huh?"

"You're standing in it."

"Don't believe all the vampire shit we've fed humans over the years. How close are we to Seattle?" There, he could seek help from Braelyn's father, who owned a tabloid, or from an Alliance office.

"Five or six hours by car. More if it's snowing in the mountain passes. An unseasonable cold spell is on the way. A bad storm, I hear."

"How about Missoula?" That was a well-traveled portal. Someone always coming or going.

"Maybe three-and-a-half hours. Again, more with snow."

"Do you live here alone?"

"Why?"

Dax snarled, his patience thin. Conversation with the little witch was a challenge.

Chiara shivered. "Don't snap, snarl, or growl. Yes."

"Why the boonies by yourself?"

"My business. I don't know you well enough to tell my life story."

"After I saved you from a burning car?"

With an arched brow, she looked over the rim of her untouched glass of booze. When she took a sip, her nose wrinkled. "You're playing that card?"

"Fair enough." He wasn't much of a sharer himself. Dax returned to his relaxed slouch on the sofa. He hadn't been to Missoula. He hadn't visited Seattle either. Both locales were out unless he had wheels. "You have a car?"

"Yes." Chiara's stomach rumbled.

Dax grinned. "Did you growl at me?"

"I'm starving." She uncurled from the chair, her skirt falling to cover her bare feet. "I'll start dinner. You need anything?"

"Nope."

Dax swung his legs onto an arm of the couch, resting his head on the other. The whiskey and logs on the fire warmed him while Chiara banged around in the kitchen, singing a tune he didn't recognize. With eyelids closed, he allowed her voice to slide over him as it soothed his tense muscles, his nerves. Having nodded off for a bit, he awoke to the scents of roast beef, carrots, and potatoes. Biscuits. Pie. Apple, he was sure. His nostrils flared. Apple with cinnamon. *This was nice.* A house in the woods. A beautiful female. Nobody to chase or kill.

Wait. Hell no.

Domesticity was not his gig. He shot upright, his feet thumping onto the floor.

Do not let your guard down, vampire. A mate or picket fence is not your future.

"Dinner's on the table." In the doorway, Chiara blew an unruly lock of hair from her cheek while dusting flour off her apron.

A sharp pain struck his groin. He wanted her. Here. Now. She was enticing with wild black curls to her waist, a long gypsy skirt which hid her legs, and creamy shoulders bared by a peasant blouse.

The female's bright orchid eyes latched onto him. Definitely a witch. Why didn't she have an aura? She was human through and through. Did she learn the craft from a book? Still. The peepers.

"Have these always been the same color, kid?" Dax circled his eye with a finger.

She hesitated, her lips drawing into a pout. "You may call me Chiara. I'm not a kid. I'm a full-grown woman. And no. How did you guess?"

What would make a human's eyes…? *Oh hell no.* Not another one. He tossed back his drink, wishing he could mainline the stuff. Suddenly, feeding from Chiara didn't seem to be a good idea. She had witch peepers. Cast spells. Had no knowledge of Scath. Was human. As if he hadn't had enough bad luck in his life.

Fuck.

If not careful, he could be like the other besotted Firebrands. Mated to a Blood Coven descendant. Impossible. He was black-hearted, too corrupt. No more feeding from her. Even from the wrist. That kind of stupidity could lead to a connection he didn't want.

In the next second, the dilemma of the little witch rocketed to the backseat. Dax bolted upright as he angled an ear toward an unwelcome sound.

"You haven't answered…"

He raised a hand. "Shut up."

She stuttered. "W-h-a..."

He whispered, "I said 'shut the fuck up.'" He rushed to the window, pulling back the drape just a crack. Though the sun had barely set, the thick woods were draped in darkness. Thanks to vampire vision, Dax could see as clearly as if it were day. "No more time. To the car now."

Grabbing her hand, he yanked her into the kitchen. "Forget dinner. Keys? Wheels?"

Chiara's feet skittered on the floor when she planted them to prevent Dax from tugging her along. "The barn."

He halted, giving her elbow a firm yank. "Now, little witch. Assholes coming."

Chiara pointed to keys dangling from a hook. Dax snagged them and his boots while she plucked a raggedy monkey from the counter, her coat from the back of a chair, and stepped into shoes. He resumed dragging her. When the wolfhounds blocked the way, she kneeled and slung her arms around Ivan. "You're the leader. Take the boys to Ernest's."

After he and Chiara raced across the yard, Dax jerked open the barn doors. When he sighted the car, he moaned. "A Prius? Really? They'll outrun us."

As she went for the driver's door, he pushed her away. "No." The keys twirled around his finger.

Chiara grumbled while she slid into the passenger's side. Dax folded himself behind the wheel, chin to his chest and knees scrunched under the steering column. She chuckled, rapidly shoving a fist over her mouth. Then she straightened and pulled her skirt in, slamming the door.

As he punched the gas, the car crunched gravel, rolling along the driveway. "Real funny, huh?" Dax slammed on the brakes, skidding, while he turned the wheel sharply to swing onto the road.

They sailed off with Chiara lurching forward and then to the side, glaring at the driver.

The dogs darted in front of the piece-of-shit Prius before turning off to head through the woods, Dax assumed toward Ernest's place, whoever he was.

"Which way to Missoula?" He fixed his pupils on the rearview mirror as three Aeternals charged down the road after them. A satyr sprinted forward, making good time. He was fast, arms churning and legs chewing up the rock.

Dax floored the accelerator. "Damn pussy car."

The speedy Aeternal got closer and closer until he hopped onto the rear bumper. The Prius jerked from side to side.

As Chiara seesawed with the movement, she gripped the dashboard. "Do something."

Dax swung a feral-eyed glare at her while he pitched the wheel, trying to dislodge the unwanted rider.

The male stuck to the bumper like glue. He catapulted to the roof. The driver's window shattered as a fist crashed through it. When the guy tried to leap into the vehicle, he jacked both feet into Dax's jaw.

While he fought off the satyr, the car zigged and zagged, tossing Chiara against the door.

With a hand grabbing the wheel, Dax punched the attacker's gut hard enough that the male lost his grip on the roof. He toppled backward, his legs the only thing keeping him in the car.

The satyr struggled to hoist himself into the Prius, but Dax had other plans.

"Hold the wheel," he yelled at Chiara. Once she did, he captured a leg in each hand and flipped the attacker out, sending the Aeternal's head bouncing onto the gravel road.

Both hands in business again, Dax grinned. "Thanks, little witch."

She glanced out the back window. "He was really fast."

"Or this shit-for-car is really slow." In the rearview mirror, he saw the two companions scoop the satyr off the road.

"If you can't appreciate the Prius, get out."

"I like my ass. And it's safer here."

She chuckled.

"Do you always laugh so much?"

"Yes. Definitely when I'm nervous."

"Seems strange to find humor in our circumstances." Dax eyed the mirror again. "We lost them."

When Chiara fluffed her skirt and tugged her peasant blouse into place, Dax's attention zeroed in on her breasts.

She tilted her head. "Instead of ogling me, why not tell me what's going on."

"I don't ogle, but your jugs are hard to miss."

She dipped her chin to look at her chest and yanked on the white top so she exposed less skin. "Well?"

"The whole story will have to wait. In a fucking nutshell, we're being chased by males who want to ice me. That's bad news. But there's worse. If they find out what you are, they'll nab you."

"What am I?" she asked.

"A witch."

"So? Nobody has cared before."

He glanced in the rearview mirror. *Nothing*. "I created a shit storm by leading them right to you. You may be a special kind of witch. The kind they'd love to get their hands on. Now my job is to protect you."

"You protect me? Hah! That's good. I saved you from those guys."

Another glance told Dax no Aeternals were in sight, but he didn't doubt they were still following. He turned onto a new gravel road, kicking up so much dust the three blind mice could track them. What he wouldn't give for a nice concrete thoroughfare.

"When do we hit a paved highway?" he asked.

"We would have hit one sooner, but you flew by a turn. In fact, you added about an hour to the trip. So, about twenty miles this way. Also, we'll be climbing and hanging over the edge of a mountain, but don't ask me which direction to go. Oh, no. The little witch doesn't know crap."

"Stop whining. It's better when you laugh. No wait. It's better when you shut the fuck up."

She crossed her arms under her eye-worthy chest, emitting an unlady-like snort. "Have it your way, fangtard."

"You have a mouth, kid."

"Chiara. Not kid. Not little witch. I have a name. Use it. Also, I'll use whatever language I want. Besides, criticizing me is a pot-kettle-black thing. See the irony?"

Dax white-knuckled the steering wheel as he muttered. She was correct. Soon they were chugging up a mountain and crawling along a cliff-hanging edge. Dax wasn't fond of heights, but he would plunge to his death before admitting it to the female thorn in his ass. In one spot, he was fairly sure the right back tire spun on air.

All the time, the little witch faced forward with a smug grin curling her lips, arms crossed, breasts plumped.

Once they descended the curve-hugging road, they came to a paved crossroad.

"Which way?" Dax blew out a relieved breath.

Trying to hold his temper in check, he twisted toward the stubborn female.

After no response, he unfisted the wheel to twist in the seat, opening his mouth to drop fang. "Answer me. To Missoula. Which direction do I turn?"

Silence.

Dax combed fingers through his hair, snarling. "You can talk now."

She arched her brows. "Who? Me? I'm supposed to shut the fuck up."

"Not anymore. Speak, dammit. Which way?"

"The fangs and growls are a wasted effort. Turn right."

Dax spun the wheel in the direction Chiara indicated. "Are you going to dole out information turn by turn?"

"Maybe. It depends on how much you piss me off."

He mumbled under his breath, "Probably a lot."

"What? I didn't hear an apology."

"An apology? What the fuck? I'm not sorry about anything."

"You missed the turn back there."

"Mutherfucker, witch." The tires squealed as Chiara slammed forward when he pounded the brakes into the floor. He spun toward her, his jaw a chunk of cold steel. "This is serious. You have no idea what these males will do to you. Stop making this difficult."

He hung a U-ey, mumbled curses, and turned at the junction.

"It all sounds disturbing, but I'm still waiting before I dole out directions," she said with a smug tilt to her lips.

"Okay. I shouldn't have told you to shut the fuck up. You bring out the worst in me. Now tell me where the hell I turn next."

Chiara dropped her arms to the side. "Apology accepted. About three miles farther, go right."

Dax couldn't stop the growl rumbling from his chest and rolling across his lips.

Chapter Eight

The lights were dim or burned out, but Miller Nash knew his escape route even in the dark. He climbed the chain-link fence and dropped to the other side. His boots hit pavement and kept on trucking as he turned left into another alley. When he opened a battered metal door, he legged it across the empty warehouse, his speed snowballing. He headed for the back. Outside at a nearby building, he jumped to bring down a fire escape ladder. Hand-over-fisting-it to the second floor, he flipped open a window and crawled through, charging out the door into a hallway where he took the stairs to an exit onto the roof. With a spurt, Miller cleared the roof and vaulted onto the next and the next buildings.

He'd planned the route earlier. Just one of the many escape paths to keep an ex-British secret service agent on his toes. Miller was never without a strategy, back-up money, extra ID, and a good pair of trainers. He hoped he wasn't still living like this when he was an old man. He'd be three-legging it with his cane or, hell, maybe wheeling it in a power-driven chair.

Running was tiresome. Being on alert 24-7 was tiresome. Being alone, for the most part, was tiresome. Sure, he occasionally shagged a female. Mostly pros. He was a wham-banger. No time for soft words and gentle ways. *Nope*. Go deep and head home.

Just once, Miller would like to spend the night with a woman in his arms, maybe one who'd ask about his day.

"How was your day, babe?" "Not so bad, luv. I escaped these Aeternals chasing me. How was yours?"

Enough with the sob story. Haul ass.

From the last rooftop, he charged into the

stairwell and exited at street level. The late-nighters crowded the area. He counted on hiding in the foot traffic. Taking off his jacket, Miller turned it inside out. Now instead of plaid, it was black. He took a New York Yankees cap out of a pocket and slammed it onto his head, pulling the bill over his eyes.

In front of his destination, Miller risked a brief backward glance, seeing no one unexpected.

The ex-Royal Marines commando and ex-MI6 operative opened a wide door into Grand Central Station. At this time of day, it wasn't busy. He'd have preferred crowded work traffic. But…

Studying the marquee, he found the next train out of the city. If he hustled, he could catch the Northbound to Poughkeepsie. Wherever the hell that was. It wasn't here. So that was good.

Ticket in hand, Miller jogged toward the platform. As he arrived, the train was loading. He took a window seat in the nearest car so that he could see who came along the walkway.

Pulling the cap tight over his eyes, he covered his jaw with his hand as he stared at the passing people. All looked good.

No supes chasing him. How did they keep finding him? He'd moved on each time, burying his tracks. Changed identification. Laid low.

After a while, the knobhead with fangs would show. The guy was also the same bloke who tried to jack him off the street nearly a year ago and had bitten into his neck. That's when Miller became serious about running. He might as well be starring in a remake of *Butch Cassidy and the Sundance Kid*. "Who are those guys?" But he knew who they were.

Miller was the lead tracker for *Custodes Templii*, the ancient group responsible for the offspring of the creators of the three realms. As such he was aware of Scath, Aeternals, and the descendants of the Blood Coven.

Fifteen hundred years ago after the Karmic Schism, the Cambion from Wales insisted the Blood Coven stay behind on Earth with their families rather than relocate to Scath with their own breed. He ordered them to scatter and hide.

Soon after, fearing a time of danger would come, the Cambion founded *Custodes Templii.* Twelve trackers were chosen from the descendants of the original coven to monitor their own bloodlines, documenting births, deaths, moves, and oddities. Since the powerful mage had no offspring, no one covered his line. It dead-ended with him.

That time was now. Cerberus, identity unknown, was snatching coven descendants from Earth.

As the train chugged out of the station, no strange men hurried along the platform. Safe for now. He was certain no one was tracing him through *Custodes Templii.* His contacts changed out burners all the time. So what was happening?

Maybe he'd question his new best friends. Braelyn and her hulking Aeternal mate.

****

The stranger strode out the back door of Fang's, exiting into an alley ripe with the stench of lost dreams, waste, stale food, and booze. Degenerate Aeternals lined up in front of a shifter, exchanging cash for packets containing amber-colored dust.

Shoving to the front, the visitor new to Covenkirk said, "Karth, my man. I hear you're the male with the Gold Dust."

"Yeah? Who the hell are you?"

"Name's Roark. I'm buying." He held out

rumpled bills and shuffled from foot to foot, anxious.

Karth eyed him. Then he dug into his pocket. “Here. First one’s free. If you like it, come back for more.”

Roark’s hand shook as he snatched the fix and shoved the money back into a pocket. “I need something to take the edge off. Ya know?”

“Don’t we all.” Karth turned his attention to the others in line.

Back inside the bar, Roark ambled over to the nearest crapper. Inside a stall, he took out a paper, ran a line of homegrown, and sprinkled Karth’s shit on top. Rolling it tight, he twisted the ends and lit up.

Taking a long, deep drag, he let his head roll back on the metal door and waited.

Yeah. There it was. The buzz. *Damn, that’s good.*

He took a second hit. Then another and another.

His chest puffed out, and he was ready to take on the whole fucking world. *What to do?* He was loaded with aggression and no outlet in sight.

When Roark strode out to the noisy, crowded bar, he sought the biggest mutherfucker he could find. He tapped a muscle-bound demon on the shoulder. “Hey, asshole, you want a piece of me?”

“Nah, go away.” With a brush-off, the male returned to his beer.

“Hard way, huh?” This time, Roark latched onto the demon’s arm and yanked him off the wooden seat.

Stools clattered to the floor while Aeternals shoved tables aside to clear a path for the fight.

Roark pointed to his own chin. “In the name of fairness, you first.”

The demon obliged with an uppercut that hurt like a bitch. They exchanged punches until the other male stayed ass-planted on the floor.

That was the definition of winning, wasn't it? Just push off the ground one more time than the other guy.

Roark sauntered across the bar and out the back door again.

Pumped, he located Karth still in the alley. He had an urge to tell the Gold-Dust-dealing shifter how he felt. Taking deep breaths to control his surging chest, he snatched the guy's arm. "I want in. Ya hear me? Let's do this. Power to Scath and all that shit."

Karth must have liked Roark's blood-stained shirt and happy face, because he said, "Come with me."

****

Two hours into the trip, Chiara's chin bobbed onto her chest. She stretched, breathing in extra oxygen to stay awake. "I'm starving and tired. It's late. Can't we stop someplace with a bed and food?"

"No. You sleep right there. I can keep going."

"I know. You're Superfang the Vampire. I, on the other hand, am a human who needs food and a nap."

"Got bad news for you, witch. You're not entirely human."

"Say what?"

"I just said it."

"Newsflash. I have a nasty temper and will zap you with a spell. Now, tell me what you meant." She rubbed a fist across her heavy-lidded, gritty eyes.

Dax glanced at Chiara's face. "Okay. We'll stop for food and a few hours' rest, but I want to reach Missoula early morning while it's still dark. Look for a motel with a restaurant."

"Aye, aye, captain." She saluted.

Dax groaned, muttering again.

"You know, you talk to yourself a lot." Chiara sat straighter as she faced the window.

"Only since I met you."

"There," she shouted, pointing to a sign on the right. "Two miles ahead. Home-cooked food with reasonably priced rooms. What could be better?"

"A few ideas pop to mind. Getting rid of your ass. A hit of O blud. Being alone." But Dax pulled into the parking lot when he saw the motel on the right. "You register. Get a room in the back. Only one."

Grabbing her purse, she slipped out of the car and entered the office, stretching her legs, shaking her skirt. "Hey," she said to the clerk, pasting on a smile as she walked inside. Sudden concern for the safety of her dogs made her sad. Had they made it to Ernest's? Did they miss her? "One room, please. My brother would like the back 'cause he has trouble sleeping. Road traffic."

"Sure thing." The guy handed her a key card once she signed in and paid. "Is the one enough?" He leaned forward on his elbows, flashing a flirtatious, dimpled grin.

"It is. What do you recommend at the restaurant?"

"The hamburgers. Also, I recommend you meet me there at about midnight when I get off work. I'll put a coin in the jukebox so we can dance."

Convinced Ivan was taking care of the other boys, she surrendered to the adventure she was on, even though it was a dangerous one. Besides, this kid was innocent and delightful.

It's just as easy to be happy as it is to be sad.

She chucked under his chin. "Sweet. But I've had a long day and plan to crash. Next time, handsome."

Key card in hand, she slid into the passenger seat. "Around back. Room 22."

"Why are you so happy?" Dax snarled, staring through the glass at the clerk who was still leaning on his elbows, wearing a silly-ass grin. "Did you need to flirt with him to get a room? Couldn't you just pay?"

"Sure, but where's the fun in that?"

Another growl from the vampire.

Jealousy?

Let him stew. She'd thought about him for years. Her savior. The man with wild, hungry eyes, hard muscles, long hair, and chiseled good looks. The man who would always keep her safe. Now she was alone with her dream god. But he had a nasty disposition. And that was when he was in a pleasant mood. Still, whenever he touched her, her knees trembled.

Slut. But can I be a loose woman if I only want one man?

Correction. One vampire?

Slut-in-training, maybe. Not full-time yet.

****

Thorn wasn't pleased to leave Luka, but his brother had to travel recovery road by himself. At a Scath portal, the Firebrand shifter tapped his chip, disappearing, truck and all.

He and his black Ford Super Duty F-450 Platinum She Beast rode east out of Bozeman at night, eventually turning south on 89. Along with Ward Davis, he sang "Old Wore Out Cowboys." At least he was free. Free of letting down the Firebrands. Free of letting down his pack and Luka.

With a cigar clamped between his teeth, Thorn scrubbed a fist along his jaw. The childhood scar from before his Awakening ached like a warning. Or maybe a guilty conscience.

After turning onto the gravel road, he traveled across a wide valley. Above an iron gate in the distance was his brand, Claw Ranch, drawn with five straight lines through a horseshoe tilted onto its side to look like a C. The closer he got, the easier it was to breathe. The less his scar ached.

Thorn ran cattle and some horses. His chief ranch hand lived down the road a distance along with a few other hires who took care of his place. They knew little about its owner, but they managed the property well. It was all he needed.

Making time with dust flying behind the She Beast, Thorn spotted his log cabin. He chuckled as he pulled the cigar out of his mouth, a puff of smoke escaping his lips. His dream started out as a small one-bedroom getaway. But it grew until it became a retreat on steroids, a place where fellow Firebrands and packmates could visit to enjoy Montana's wide-open spaces.

Now, it had three bedrooms, a bunkhouse, a giant kitchen with the latest equipment, and a long table cut from a tree on his very own property. The great room boasted a giant stone fireplace, a massive TV, and a long bar for drinking and chatting. Navaho rugs covered polished dark floors while baskets and horse blankets hung on the walls.

Few people had been here yet, but the place was just recently finished. Eventually, laughter, boozing, and a lot of fucking would fill it.

Thorn parked and hopped out, his worn cowboy boots clumping across the porch. His breath caught when he opened the door. "Home," he whispered.

Once he unloaded his small duffel from the truck, he checked the fridge. Full as he had asked. Looking forward to a good run, he left, racing toward the mountains in the distance. His wolf wanted freedom. Like man, like beast. Both had been cooped up too long, caught between pack and Firebrands.

Thorn ran for about five miles until he reached the thicker woods abutting the national forest. He shucked his boots, socks, pants, and shirt, folding and laying them alongside a familiar tree.

He closed his eyelids, preparing for the feeling which accompanied a shift. Some described it as painful with joints popping and bones reforming while fur sprouted. He found it thrilling. *Hell.* He liked a little pain. Good for the soul.

On all fours, he shook his chestnut fur to release the tension. His black and white muzzle near the ground, he scented pine needles, damp earth, and crisp air.

The wolf threw back its head and howled. *Freedom.* And it ran, dodging trees, climbing mountains. No more thoughts plagued it. It was all animal. His beast was in charge, and it knew only pleasure. The thrill of nature. The joy of the hunt. Birds scattered. A deer took off for shelter, but the wolf wasn't ready to kill yet. The speed and feel of the wind ruffling fur was all it wanted.

It skirted a freezing mountain stream for a while until an urge surfaced. He shifted beside a pooled area where he jumped in. The water was so cold it shriveled his balls and chattered his teeth, but the icy chill invigorated him. When he'd had enough, he climbed out, tossed back his wet hair, and shifted into his wolf again. Charging forward. Howling. Stretching his legs in the moonlight.

Hours later, once his limbs quivered with exhaustion, he returned to his tree, curling onto the ground, enjoying the fresh mountain breeze.

When a scream pierced his sleep, the wolf bolted onto all fours. It raced toward the sound, pulling short when a backpacker's campsite came into view. Near the tent lighted with a kerosene lamp, a female struggled between two males.

Thorn shifted to human to better understand the scene playing out in front of him. The attackers wore Arisen Dawn black uniforms with an insignia on a shoulder patch, two mountains with a red sun between them. Each gripped the female's arm. She resisted, twisting and kicking. No way could she shake off a berserker and demon. Thorn recognized their breeds by their unmistakable auras.

Why would two Aeternals hassle a human female?

Thorn debated. Attack as a naked humanoid? Not his favorite. Attack as the wolf? Okay but probably not successful against a berserker and a demon. His best bet was to charge into the fray as a partially shifted wolf, bigger, upright, clawed, and fanged. The half-formed beast might traumatize the female, but it could stop the two males for sure.

Thorn shifted, releasing part of his animal. He barreled out of his cover. Leaping, he wrapped his jaws around the demon's neck, cracking bone and tearing flesh.

The first Aeternal didn't stand a chance against Thorn's surprise attack. The male fell to the forest floor, blood gushing from his neck. With its claws, the near-wolf ripped off the demon's head and tossed it aside.

Surprised, the berserker dropped his hold on the female, lumbered toward the enraged shifter, and halted, his legs spread in an aggressive stance.

Thorn spared a quick glance at the female. Injured, she fell onto the ground, her eyes wide and her mouth open in a silent scream. She scuttled backward against a tree.

The berserker was a big mutherfucker. About seven feet of solid muscle, making Thorn wish he spent more time in the gym, beefing up and absorbing a few tricks for fighting giant-ass behemoths.

Excitement sparked in the big guy's eyes, as if he was enjoying what was about to come. Thorn's feral half-wolf grinned back, the claw marks from his childhood drawing tight on his jaw. He showed no fear since that was food for a berserker, and he didn't need the guy well nourished.

Thorn, claws out and canines bared, dropped into a crouch while he circled the crazed giant. Lunging swiftly and digging his nails deep into the male's gut, Thorn took advantage of the giant's slow-moving size. The stunned berserker glanced down and clutched a hand to his gored stomach. The shifter would need to do more damage to drop this male.

Then the guy's legs crumpled as he sank to the ground. In his place stood the human female with an iron skillet in her hand. She dropped the makeshift weapon to steady her palms on her wobbly knees.

Thorn, though surprised, took advantage of the help to grab the berserker by the neck. He twisted off the male's head, letting it fall beside the body.

Collapsing onto her hands and knees, the human upchucked.

As Thorn shifted to his human form, he glanced at the two fallen males. Pretty gruesome. Two headless Aeternals. Blood and guts everywhere. Good news, they weren't going to resurrect. She should be grateful. Of course, she'd probably never seen a half-shifted wolf before. He might have some explaining to do. A vampire who could erase memories would be handy right about now.

The distressed damsel wore hiking boots and dark pants. In her current position, she showed off a nicely rounded ass.

When she stumbled to her feet, she pivoted toward him, her gaze doing a slow roll up Thorn's naked body. Her wide shoulders tapered to a trim waist, but between the two were luscious, well-proportioned breasts. As she paused at his groin, he realized he was fully aroused. Well, he did love a good fight. And there was nothing better than a beautifully fit female giving him the once-over.

Thorn lifted a finger. “Hold it a sec, darlin’. Wait here.” He sprinted for his clothes at the base of the tree, slipped into his pants, and returned to the campsite. He glanced around to memorize the area so he could return later for the bodies.

The female was in the same spot where he’d left her, lit by the camp lantern and a bright moon.

Her pants were torn, exposing one deeply cut but shapely thigh. Despite her hand pressing on her upper arm, another wound leaked blood. Thorn passed a fist across his chin. Lacerations, likely from the sloth demon. *Not good.* She’d go night-night soon.

“What are you?” she asked, her attention plastered to his bare chest.

With her unwavering gaze on him, he adjusted his pants. He was usually aroused after a fight, but the female’s stares didn’t help. “A rancher.”

“Bullshit.”

When she swayed, Thorn rushed forward, swooping her into his arms. “Steady, darlin’. The demon sedated you. Claws from a sloth demon mean lights out.”

The contact with the female sent an electric jolt through his body while the wolf prowled just under Thorn’s skin, clawing to get free. Man and beast struggled for control. They wanted to bite her. To mark her. And wouldn’t you know, blood sped to his already swollen dick. Talk about harder than rock. Even his balls were on fire. Only one thing did that to a male shifter.

The word *mate* roared in his ears.

Hell no. Not now.

A mate was responsibility. He wasn’t sure he was

ready for more weight on his shoulders. Unfortunately, when a wolf met its mate, it didn't care. And the male would want her no matter what.

"Huh? Demon?" Her lids fluttered open and closed as her head lolled against his arm. Her hand reached out to stroke his scarred jaw.

"So pretty," she slurred as she crumpled against his chest.

When the smooth deep bronze skin of her cheek brushed against him and her tight black curls tickled his pecs, he knew. He would always protect this female, his mate. Life just got more complicated.

Chapter Nine

Dax leaned back in the booth, arms folded behind his head, pupils fixed on Chiara's neck. Despite his having snarfed down two cheeseburgers with the works, an order of fries, onion rings, and a couple strawberry milkshakes, the little witch's pulsating vein was still appetizing. Change in plans. Later in the room he would feed from the Blood Coven witch. Sure, other Firebrands were addicted to the descendants, but he wouldn't do that.

What could one more time hurt?

"Pay the check." Dax's voice grated against his throat like rocks.

"I don't have an unlimited amount of cash. We'll need an ATM soon. Glad to see you have no hang-ups about women paying."

A harsh laugh grated against his throat, painful memories flitting through his mind. Females had paid for him often. And males. He enjoyed them. The bonus was, as long as he fucked for his stepdad, no one fucked with Bounty.

With a slow, sad song playing on the jukebox, Chiara leaned across the table, chin resting on the backs of her hands. "I'll take care of the check right after you dance with me."

"Not my thing."

"It is if you want me to pay."

After unfolding from the booth, Dax sauntered out to the middle of the floor. "Well, why the fuck are you waiting?" He finger-waved the female toward him.

The little witch laughed. Again. The sound beelined for his heart, untangling it, warming it, making it not-so-blackened.

With hips swaying, Chiara sashayed onto the floor. Toe-to-toe with Dax, she wrapped her arms around his waist, sliding in close. Near enough her breasts rubbed against his chest.

Head bent, his loose hair a curtain around her, and his nose buried in her neck, he gripped her waist to pull her in so tight the jut of his arousal twitched against her belly. If that's what the little witch wanted, he would happily oblige. Especially since he was going to taste her tonight.

For the last time.

To the beat of the song, Dax rolled his hips while she ground against the bulge in his jeans. He drew his tongue languidly along her neck as she shivered. His lips followed, one kiss after another.

Once the music ended, Dax pushed her away. "Now pay the hell up and let's leave."

"Your mood flips give me whiplash." She rubbed her neck.

At the register, Chiara opened her purse to take out her wallet. With the bill settled, they returned to the motel in silence, Dax focusing hard on not grabbing her and sinking fang in the parking lot.

The minute the door of the room closed, he body-slammed the little witch against the wall. "I'm still hungry."

She wiggled her wrist in front of his mouth.

"Not tonight. From the neck."

"No. Look what happened the last time. Wrist."

Dax captured her lips, his tongue sweeping across them. When she opened, he flicked inside, licking, stroking. But he forced himself to pull away. "Neck."

"There are conditions."

"Conditions? I don't do conditions."

"You do if you don't want me to turn you into a

toad. No fucking."

"Is everything else legit?"

Her brows scrunched tight. "I guess. No draining me dry. And no feeding from anyone else while we're together."

"What? Are we going steady, too?"

Her tempting lips curled into a smirk. "Them's the rules. Fangs are in your court, vampire." She stroked her pulsating neck with two delicate fingers.

Since he suspected she was a Blood Coven descendant, this was the last time he'd feed from her. Firebrands, drawn to them like moths to light, mated them. Not Dax. He'd step away. Just once more. Then no ball and chain for him.

What did he care about rules once he ruled out long-term with Chiara? He strolled to the bed, balanced on the edge, and beckoned with his hand. When she came, he pointed to his lap. "More comfortable."

She draped herself across his legs, laced an arm around his shoulder, and tossed a strand of hair onto her back. "Happy Meal. Dig in."

When Dax cradled her in his arms, his dick sat up rock hard. He closed his eyes as he nuzzled her neck, drawing in her wild scent before he struck. Sinking his fangs deep, he sucked hard.

Chiara flinched, but the pain inhibitor in his bite kicked in fast. She moaned, grinding her ass into his lap.

With each wiggle, Dax's less-than-solid resolve wavered.

No. I promised not to fuck her. But all else is fair.

Reaching under her skirt, he slid up her shapely leg. At her thigh, the vampire stroked her soft flesh.

"Yes," she whispered, spreading her legs.

Taking her plea not only as consent but also as encouragement, Dax palmed her hot, moist sex through her panties. She thrust against his hand, her hips undulating.

With Chiara's warm blood sliding down Dax's throat, he fingered her panties aside and trailed through the wet lips of her pussy. The delicious female was so ready.

Though only partially satisfied, he stopped to focus on Chiara's needs, licking the two puncture wounds to close them. Mark a first. He never cared much about a sexual partner. If they got off, great. If not, too bad. But he wanted Chiara to take pleasure in the feeding, to know he treasured her gift.

Dax's thumb circled her clit as he plunged a finger deep into her channel.

"Yes, Dax."

He withdrew to throw her onto the bed. She propped herself onto her elbows, her orchid eyes fixed on him as he crawled between her legs. He bunched her skirt at the waist and tore off her panties. Once he buried his head between her thighs, his tongue stroked through her folds, dragging back and forth as she bucked her hips, begging him for release. He pumped two fingers into her, setting a wild rhythm.

"God. Don't stop, Dax." She gripped his shoulders as she trembled, rocking against him, moaning. Faster and faster.

While prodding her sensitive nub, he thrust his tongue in and out of her. His free hand reached for her breast still covered with her blouse. She obliged him by pushing it and the bra cup down. Molding his palm around her bared flesh, he squeezed, pinching the nipple hard enough to make her gasp.

With both hands, she fisted his hair, pressing his mouth harder against her need. A shudder rolled through her body. "Yes. Yes."

Dax continued to suck and lick, prolonging her orgasm until she pushed him away.

Chiara's arms flopped to the side as her chest rose and fell with deep breaths. "Wow." She tugged her bra and blouse into place.

When he jumped off the bed, he planned to head for the shower to jack off. His balls were like boulders with a ton of dynamite about to blast them to bits. He needed relief fast.

Chiara grabbed his arm. "Where are you going? Did I say we were through?"

Dax snapped around to look at her. A growl rumbled from deep in his chest.

"Pull down your zipper and walk back here."

He obliged. Facing Chiara, he pushed his pants to his knees. His cock sprang free. He was so hard his balls ached.

As she scooted to the edge of the bed, she tossed aside her torn panties and pulled her skirt into place. When her lips were level with his arousal, she licked a bead of cum off the crown of his penis. Dax almost lost it, but he locked his knees. He wanted her mouth wrapped around him.

When her hand gripped the root of his cock, Dax shuddered. She stroked up and down.

"You're big." She licked the tip of his dick again. Her tongue wet him from crown to hilt.

"Stop teasing and suck me off." He fisted his shaft and dragged it across her lips. "Open up real nice, little witch."

"Ooh. The fangsucker wants me to get him off with my mouth."

Before she stopped talking, he shoved his dick inside. When she moaned, every muscle in his body tightened.

While Chiara took him deeper, he tangled his fingers in her long curly hair, pushing it aside to watch his dick slip in and out of her sweet lips. He groaned, not knowing if he could keep his knees from buckling.

"Go deep, witch. Take me." With his grip urging her, he was careful not to choke her, but his control was on edge.

She set a slow rhythm, gliding up and down his cock. One of Chiara's hands reached for his balls, caressing them until he was about to explode. They clenched with the need to release.

He tightened the grip on her head and rocked his hips forward, his rhythm faster, each thrust deeper. He was so close.

"I'm coming." He tried to pull out, but she didn't let him. *Holy hell.* She wanted him to spill inside her mouth. That did it. He went off like a rocket. His hips undulating, his seed rushing to fill her while her nails dug into his ass.

"Take it all, witch. That's it." His climax was staggering. Never had he orgasmed so long. What was her effect on him?

When her lips popped off his dick, she backed off and looked him straight in the eyes, wiping her hand across her mouth and smiling. "How was that, vampire?"

He jacked up his pants and strode toward the shower. "Rest. We're on the road in two hours."

She chuckled at his back. "If you need another blowjob, let me know."

Holy shit. She was good. No. Great.

Dax felt an uncharacteristic stab of jealousy. She sucked him like a pro. How many males had she been with? He gripped the walls of the shower, rage washing over him along with a stream of water.

He shut off the shower, slipped into his boxers,

and tossed his wet hair, splattering the mirror.

In the room, Chiara was curled under the covers, sound asleep on her side. Dax slumped into a nearby chair and propped his feet on the bed, trying to relax but keeping his eyes open. He could use some mind-numbing O blud right about now. Something to make him forget the sweet taste of the female and her mouth on his cock.

So what if she'd blown a lot of guys. She could never be as depraved as he was.

Dax's lashes fluttered shut.

Next thing he knew, he jerked awake.

Morning. He'd meant to get going earlier.

Chiara stirred, stretching her arms overhead, jutting out those perfect breasts. She yawned but started yammering at him right away. "Explain why these guys want me."

"We need to get on the road to Missoula. I wanted to arrive there while it was still dark, but that's not happening." Dax yanked on his borrowed jeans and his own worn boots and stalked into the bathroom to splash cold water on his face.

"Not my fault. Answers first or I'm not budging," she yelled.

With a towel in hand, he dried off in the doorway. "Okay. The clipped version. I'll fill in with the rest on the road to the portal. Only one thing turns a human's eyes purple. It's likely you're a Blood Coven descendant. That means extremely dangerous Aeternals from my realm are hunting for you. You don't want them to find you. So we're both on the run. I need to get you to Scath where our healers can test to confirm what I already believe. I don't know how you turned."

"You think I'm going to traipse after you onto another realm 'cause I like your fangdick?"

"Somebody should wash your mouth out with

soap. But no. I expect you to follow me so you don't get kidnapped by these assholes and diddled with as a plaything."

"You just want my blood. I'm a handy supply."

"Vampires can always find blood. And we're not particular."

When she looked crushed, Dax regretted his words, but talking with Chiara was like going ten rounds with a questing beast. "You're coming with, little witch."

"Ask me nicely."

"Okay. You're fucking coming with me. So hurry and get ready. I'm pulling out in five minutes."

She raised a hand to cast a spell. "Really? Breakfast first."

Dax flashed to her side, grabbing her fingers. "Listen. Better hungry than dead. They will find you. If they can, they will kill me, and I don't know what they plan to do with you. I am your best bet."

"God help me then."

"Yeah. I don't think he's going to give a big assist."

****

Lort stood on a mountain peak early morning. On one side, he overlooked the bustling Arisen Dawn garrison. On the other was a view of Narobi Flats in Darque. The muscles around his heart contracted. *Anticipation.* That was the sensation. The time grew near when the army he was putting together for Cerberus would conquer Scath and Earth.

Though the encampment was in a remote region of the wildings' realm, a spell protected the huge site from all but their own foot soldiers and officers. Big enough to quarter the current number of troops, it occupied a small valley nestled among towering mountains.

A strong wind blew Lort's ankle-length leather coat open. His dishwater-blond hair swirled around his face. Below, the garrison was alive with activity, soldiers rotating between barracks, heading to training grounds, the mess, or strategy meetings.

Following Cerberus's order, he recruited two kinds into his army. The dregs of his command were those males and females taking a drug which compelled them to join the cause. Each dose of Gold Dust was laced with a compulsion spell. The perfect cycle. Taking the drug made the user want more, and each hit made the user a stronger convert. Sure, most were crazy from abnormal side effects, but they were perfect front-line fodder. In all skirmishes, they would be sent in first to draw fire. They were expendable.

The other soldiers were the backbone of the army. They joined Arisen Dawn because they were believers. Aeternals were destined to rule all realms. They would once again be the species fate intended them to be before Blood Coven interference.

Lort had directed his officers to keep the soldiers busy. Inactivity was a killer for any army. They trained and marched. Strategy lessons, supplemented with indoctrination, fostered the cause. Below him, sergeants led drills on the practice fields. Others oversaw instruction on the shooting range. Experts conducted sessions to enhance the innate talents of the breeds, whether they were demons, warlocks, or vampires.

A smile pulled tight at the corners of Lort's mouth. Forays Earthside would begin soon. The disposables, those strung out on Gold Dust, would be sacrificed in the name of the greater good. Sent through a portal, they would ravage an unsuspecting population, feeding on them, draining them for nourishment. The goal was to create fear among the Earthers. When others learned of their successes, more supporters would join the cause. Nothing gained true believers like victory in battle. The bloodier the victory the better.

The garrison on Darque could quarter 9,000 soldiers and 2,000 support personnel. A bigger, grander garrison in the same mountains but further south was under construction. Nearly complete.

Using the ancient Macedonian army as a template, Lort organized Arisen Dawn into military units of varying sizes, the smallest group being sixteen foot soldiers. The Aeternals he appointed as officers earned their spots based on skill, cunning, savagery, and most importantly, one simple moral code. Aeternals, the superior species, will rule all realms no matter the cost.

The garrison site was a two-story rectangular structure with barracks on three sides, lower and upper levels. The mess and indoor training facilities were in a center building with offices and meeting rooms on the second floor. Outdoor training occupied all other grounds. The firing range sat at the north end against a cliff. Though mages at the Ministry of Well Being kept guns from the realms, Cerberus created a spell to allow them here. That made Lort certain Cerberus was a warlock of extraordinary power.

As he assessed the strength of the encampment from his observation point, the vampire general shifted his stance, his hand gripping the hilt of the short sword strapped to his waist. The buildings were not shoddy wooden structures. Rather, the rock foundations and walls were impregnable. Even if not cloaked by a spell, the garrison blended into its environment.

A harsh chuckle escaped his dry lips. And all was hidden from the prying eyes of the Scion Firebrands.

****

The director of the Ministry of Compliance kept

Cadmon, Nace, Jarek, Kole, and Skyler waiting in the conference room for thirty minutes.

"I'm gonna fry his ass when he gets here." Kole thrummed his fingers on the table.

Skyler massaged his shoulder, her touch usually calming. "I may let you."

Hands folded, Cadmon was always the patient ylve high commander. "Too bad we need his help."

Nace growled, his jaguar close to the surface, while Jarek rested a bored chin in the palm of his hand, his numerous braids dangling to his waist.

The door pushed open and Director Boden, a bureaucratic smile on his lips, entered the room. "Greetings. So sorry. Other duties occupied me longer than I expected." The smaller-than-average sloth demon gripped the back of a chair to pull it out and slide his smarmy body into it. "What can I help you with?"

Kole released a burst of fire, an ember landing on the director's expensive wool jacket. "Oops."

Boden brushed off the ash, his lips curling into a peevish snarl. "My lateness could not be helped, Commander."

"Yeah. Neither can my temper."

Skyler rubbed her mate's shoulder again, whispering in his ear.

Kole patted her leg. "I'll be good." He didn't like the director of the Ministry of Fuck-All-Incompetence. They had history.

Boden, whose parents led the rebels in the Demon Insurrection of 1451, rode Kole's ass all through school. Most of his breed had joined the rebellion, including Kole's relatives such as his grandparents and Uncle Horach. But his parents, Scion Firebrands Hestia and Aedon, remained loyal, rounded up rebels, and fought against their own.

Abrahm may have been the knife-wielding demon who mutilated and killed Hestia and Aedon, but others, possibly even Boden's parents, condoned him and his team of cutthroats. Kole took his revenge by killing all those who'd had a direct hand in the death of his mother and father. Because no solid evidence against Boden's family existed, he left them alive. But his gut, which was rarely wrong, told him they were complicit.

While most demons' bodies bore runes of their ancestry, Kole's markings did not record a complete lineage. He'd had them painfully removed. *Screw them all.* Except those of his mother and father. Now runes depicting Skyler and Kae were on his chest near his heart. As far as he was concerned, they were his history.

Cadmon cleared his throat, casting a silent message to Jarek and Nace which warned them to stop grinning at Kole's antics. "We want new portals opened to be used only by Firebrands and trusted members of the Alliance."

Boden's lips puckered. "Oh. That will be extremely difficult."

The animus demon commander's fire-gold eyes flashed a message to the director.

"I'm not saying impossible. Just difficult. We would have to build the infrastructure Earthside. Garages, storefronts. Buildings like that. We can't have you popping up in the middle of a crowded street. What would the humans think?"

"We're already outed, you pompous…"

The ylve high commander held up a hand to interrupt Kole. "We don't care about hiding from humans anymore. What I care about is having access to Earth when our other gateways are compromised. So, I suggest you build a shitload of new ones. Screw the infrastructure. And do it now." Cadmon rose to his full height and threw back his shoulders, his military bearing unquestionable, his rare temper on display.

His companions raised their brows, looking shocked at Cadmon's uncharacteristic outburst.

Boden's hands trembled. "Right away, High Commander." He whipped out a tablet. "Would you like to tell me where you want them?"

"No. I'll leave Kole to the task." Cadmon strode from the room.

The director swallowed hard when he twisted toward Kole. "Commander, I am sure we can work together to complete the task."

"I'm sure we can, too. If we can't, I'm gonna toast your balls."

Skyler laughed. "You're incorrigible."

"But you love me, Frisca."

"True."

When they got down to business, Boden was more accommodating.

Chapter Ten

Finley snuggled into the soft mattress, drawing the fluffy pillow to her cheek. This was sure better than the sleeping bag on the hard, cold ground.

Wait.

She shot upright, tugging the clenched blanket up to her neck. Where was the tent? She peeked under the sheet. Naked. She sniffed. Coffee. Biscuits.

A door swung open, and one of the biggest guys Fin had ever seen prowled into the room, a towel wrapped low around narrow hips, a dark goody trail starting below his navel but disappearing before revealing the prize at the end of the rainbow. Droplets clung to his tanned skin, and water splattered the walls as he shook out shaggy chestnut-brown hair. He grinned, no doubt aware of his deliciousness.

The guy approached the bed, and Fin bent her neck to look up and up and up. Claw marks stood out on his jaw. Amber irises, more pronounced because of jet-black pupils, made him feral-looking but sexy.

Wolf.

"Good. You're awake."

Was that a growl?

While the man mesmerized her, the blanket glided down Fin's breasts. Her nipples hardened, exposed to the cool air and a hungry, animal gaze. She snatched the cover up to her chin. "Who are you and where the hell am I?"

Standing over her like a hulking, wild presence, he growled again. A warm, throaty sound. The wolf version of a purr. "You were in the woods fighting off two men last night. Remember?"

Her heart pitter-patted against her chest as she

stared at the tented towel. Fin resisted licking her lips at the evidence of the hunk's erection. Big body. Big cock. Natch. She dipped her chin, closing her eyes to shut out the fully aroused male within touching distance. The scene was coming back to her. "Right. Two guys attacked me. You … killed both of them. Ripped their heads off. One with your teeth and the other with your bare hands. Which, by the way, were clawed."

"Blood loss, darlin'. You imagined it."

"Nuh-uh. You mentioned a demon." The comforter slipped again as she scooted away from the tempting man-wolf.

Brows arched, he sat on the bed, his towel falling slightly open. Fin had no scruples about sneaking a peek. She was right. Huge. Just like last night, he was Big Mac size.

Fin covered herself once more. "Could you back off a little? You make me nervous looming over me."

"I don't loom."

Gazing into his amber eyes, Fin tried to ignore the desire making her sex moist. "Whatever. Besides, I know what I saw. Those two guys were not normal, and neither are you. You're like wolfman or something. Hot. Really hot. But not normal."

His grin went straight to her lady bits. Fin was not a shrinking violet, but she did not react like a teenage girl in heat either. Her response to the guy was explosive.

"Hot, huh? You know what else is hot?"

Other than you?

As his eyes smoldered with promised sex, she wiggled to satisfy the tingle between her legs. "No. What?"

His nostrils flared. "Breakfast. Get dressed. Then come on out." He lobbed another grin and dropped his towel, moving toward a chair.

"Good God." Fin sucked in a breath.

With a tight ass on display, he slid into well-worn jeans. Commando. *Gasp*. He drew on a white T-shirt and topped it with an unbuttoned flannel plaid. Barefooted, he padded out of the room, waving a hand toward a different chair.

Fin sighted the oversized shirt where he indicated. She threw off the blanket to examine her bandaged thigh and arm. Not only had he stripped her, but he'd cleaned her up, too. Obviously, the big guy got a long look at her. Good thing she wasn't shy.

His garment came to her knees. Decent enough.

She found the man in the kitchen, sipping on coffee as he read a book. She couldn't catch the title. Probably something about weightlifting or mixed martial arts.

"Hey." She entered and fingered her snarly mess of tight black curls. Though close to her head, one side was longer, hanging over her eye. Her stylist told her it was a sexy look. "I'm Finley Sage. And you are?"

The hunk looked up with those mesmerizing wolf eyes, swept his shaggy mane off his face, and stuck out a huge, calloused hand. "Thorn."

"Does Thorn have a last name?"

With lips curled into a smile, he held onto her longer than was decent. "Nope."

"Somebody washed me, tended to my wounds, and got an eyeful."

"Yep."

"While I appreciate being saved and bandaged, the rest could be a little creepy."

"I confess. Spent a lot of it admiring your curves and such. From all those muscles, I'd say you work out. Love a female who takes care of her body."

With his brows arched and that sexy grin on his

face, Fin didn't blush. Not her style. Her eyes met and held his. She waved a dismissive hand. "Okay, let's flirt later. Right now, I'm hungry and want answers." She yanked out the chair across from Thorn.

He hopped up to snatch two plates from the cabinet. After piling on scrambled eggs, bacon, and potatoes, he set a basket of biscuits on the table. "Coffee?"

"Strong and black."

Setting it in front of her, he parked and began eating.

With a big spoonful of fried potatoes in her mouth, Fin moaned. "That's great." She shoved in hurried bites before laying down the utensil. "Now. Answers."

"What are the questions, darlin'?" Thorn's rock-hard, huge biceps flexed as he leaned elbows onto the table.

"What are you and why did those men attack me?"

Thorn swiped a hand over his wet hair. "I honestly don't know what they wanted. Did you know them?"

"Hell no. One was like a giant, super strong hulk. The other sported some nasty-ass fingernails. He flickered."

"Flickered?"

"Yeah. One minute he was a man. Big but normal. The next he looked like something from *Hellboy*. Don't get me started on you. You were all clawy and fangy with a bonier face. A werewolf?"

Thorn's eyes narrowed as he studied her. "Werewolf?" He laughed, biting into a biscuit slathered with butter.

"Yes. Talk, dammit. I've kinda known about

weird creatures my whole life. Trouble is, I thought Mom was crazy. Until tonight. Wish I'd listened closer to her mad ramblings."

"Tell me about your mom's … uh … ramblings."

Fin signaled for another biscuit. After he passed the basket, she looked around. "Got any jam?"

Thorn popped out of his chair, opened the fridge, and clunked a jar of apricot jam onto the table.

With her mouth full, Fin mumbled. "You gotta understand, Mom wasn't right in the head. At least that's what I thought. She always said we weren't alone, creatures other than humans sharing our world. Vampires, werewolves, demons."

"First, no such thing as werewolves." He continued with a shrug of his shoulders, "I'm a wolf shifter. One of the guys who attacked you was a sloth demon. His claws contain a sedative. That's why you passed out and slept so late. The other was a berserker. They come from … my place."

She drew a deep breath. *Get your head around this, girl.* "Your place? Not Montana, I take?"

Thorn shook his shaggy-haired head.

"Why me?" Fin shoveled in a spoon of scrambled eggs.

"I really don't know, darlin'. Enough questions for a while. We've got all day."

The self-reported wolf shifter suddenly turned dreamy eyed and heavy-lidded. He crooked a finger. "Come here."

Fin wasn't a virgin, but she didn't hop into any stranger's bed, or lap, either. But this guy was a magnet. He wanted her, and she wanted him. "Why don't I want to say no to you?"

"I'll explain later. It'll be an interesting story." He crooked his finger again, a gesture which would normally piss her off.

After she rested the spoon on the table, she strolled to Thorn. He pushed his chair back. Fin straddled his lap, the borrowed shirt riding up her thighs. She ran fingers over the claw marks on his stubbled jaw. After brushing aside the soft hair which hung in his face, she stroked his wide shoulders. Traveling downward, she touched his enormous biceps. Fin leaned in, her breasts against his chest, as she tongued his ear.

The wolf groaned. "You're giving me a raging hard-on, darlin'."

"I am?"

"You are." His eyes closed.

"All of your parts are like a human's, right?"

A big, firm boner thrust against her.

"Maybe I'm a little more endowed." He shifted beneath her.

"Why do you keep sniffing?"

"Your arousal is scenting the room. My beast is going crazy."

She laughed, scooting back and forth along his groin, savoring the friction. "Bring it on. Wait." She slapped a hand to his chest. "You don't go all wolfy during sex, do you?"

"No."

Believing him, Fin undulated her hips into Thorn's arousal as he growled.

Scooping her into his arms, he lumbered to the master bedroom where he threw her onto the mattress, drawing the shirt over her head. "Let's lose this."

The bed sank as he crawled beside her. Swinging a heavy leg over her thigh, he pulled in for a kiss, his lips brushing hers lightly.

When she opened her mouth, his tongue thrust inside. He was fresh air, mountains, and pine bark. Wild.

She sucked hard on him as he ravaged her with a deeper kiss.

Turned on by his snarls, Fin arched her back, fingers tearing at his shirt. She broke the kiss. "Too many clothes."

Thorn ripped off his plaid and T-shirt as Fin drew his zipper down to free his dick. "Oh, yeah."

His sharp white canines exposed and his amber eyes aglow, he kicked his pants down his legs and off the bed.

The shifter's hands explored Fin's thighs and stomach, pausing to palm a breast. He squeezed, rolling her nipple between his thumb and forefinger until it was a tight bud. When he dropped his head to suck on her, his wolf-like hair tickled her skin.

"Oh, yes." The man's mouth was warm and wet. His lips succulent. She thrust against him, forcing him to take more of her breast. "Thorn."

Fin's hand fumbled as she searched for his cock. *There it is. Oh my.* Big. She stroked up and down his length while Thorn rocked his hips into her palm.

"Darlin', if you keep that up, I'll embarrass myself in a sec. Damn. Can't wait any longer. I promise the next time will be slower."

He flipped her over, hauling her to her knees. With one hand snug around her waist, his other trailed along her backside until his fingers stroked the wet lips of her sex, one sliding into her hot channel.

Fin moaned, bucking into his touch.

"Good girl." He pulled out and returned to her moist heat with two fingers, spreading her, preparing her.

"I want you inside me, Thorn."

"Look at me," he said.

She twisted her neck to gaze into the feral, starving eyes of a gorgeous man while the thick head of his cock nudged at her entrance.

"You are mine."

"Yes." She didn't hesitate, allowing him to lay claim to her.

Fisting his shaft, Thorn inched into her, his steely hard flesh sliding against the walls of her sheath.

Each slow glide filled her more. He was so damn big. She drove her hips back, forcing him to feed her all of himself.

When he was deep, his balls tapping her ass, Thorn stilled until Fin grew accustomed to his glorious thickness. Then he hammered forward.

Oh, God.

In. Out. Deeper. Flesh against flesh. A wild coupling. She fell to her elbows as the friction increased and he thrust deeper. His rhythm grew frantic, and her muscles clenched around his thickness. "Yes. Don't stop."

His fingers found her clit, pinching and circling. Thorn growled, his drive into her savage, as if he knew her body, each erogenous spot, each pleasure point.

One hand clasped her breast, squeezing roughly, hurting with pleasure. She lost all control, pushing against him, taking more of his thick length.

The shifter's groin slapped against her ass when he hammered into her, harder, faster, fighting for his release. His teeth latched onto Fin's shoulder, keeping her immobile, claiming her in a wild, untamed way.

What started as a shiver rolled through her like lightning in a storm. Fin came, calling out, grinding against his cock, wanting to hold him inside forever. "Thorn."

With her release, he howled, his hands bruising her hips as he clutched tight, shooting warm seed into her. Filling her in a way she had never experienced.

"Mine."

"You're mine, too, Thorn. Mine."

They stayed plastered against each other, her back to his chest, for what seemed like an eternity. Then Thorn rolled to his side, taking Fin with him, pulling her in tight, his rough hands running up and down her stomach, gliding to her shoulder where he soothed the skin he'd bitten. "Are you okay?"

"I'm great. But you must think I'm easy, falling into bed with you right after we met."

"No, darlin'. I think you're mine." His words were muffled as he kissed along her spine. "And you feel really good."

She reached behind her head to stroke his hair. "Wolf, you have no idea what you do to me. Now tell me the interesting story about why I can't resist you. And why I think you belong to me."

****

If Dax squeezed the steering wheel any tighter, it would crack.

"What's wrong with you? You've been in a foul mood all morning." In the passenger seat as they drove toward Missoula, Chiara twisted her hands in her lap.

Rather than answer, Dax pounded a fist on the dashboard. He twisted toward her, his sharp fangs exposed. Kudos to her, she didn't cringe.

"Is it me? Did I do something?"

He spit out his concerns. If he didn't, he worried he might explode. And when vampires exploded, bad shit happened. "Exactly how many knobs have you polished?"

"What?" Her voice rose so high it was squeaky. "Speak English."

"How many males have you blown? Sucked? Tromboned?" He fixed his gaze on the road again. "Wait.

Don't answer. I don't care." He stroked a hand through his hair.

"You're serious?"

"Yes. No. You have a way of making me stupid."

"You're my first. How'd I do?"

Dax white-knuckled the wheel, gritting his teeth, mumbling, "Great."

"Online porn is very instructional. I Googled the best recipe for Denver omelets, herbs to relieve headaches, and how to give a blowjob. Do you have any special requests?"

For whatever crazy reason he didn't feel like exploring, her answer soothed his anger. He returned to a silent sulk.

Obviously, Chiara couldn't stand the quiet because she chattered again. "You don't understand. After you saved me from the car, you were my hero. For years, I drew on an image of you to make me brave. You helped me survive when I was alone."

Dax rubbed a hand over his stubbled goatee. "Not me, Chiara. Some fantasy you created. I see how you look at me. Dreamy-eyed. I'm not anyone's hero. I've done bad things. You need to get over me because I'm an asshole."

"Yes, but you're my asshole."

"Never. I belong to no one. Never will. When we get to Scath, you need to forget about me. Plenty of heroes pass through the stronghold. I'm not one of them."

Chiara cocked her head to the side, her gaze a warning. "I'm pretty tough, vampire, but if you push me away long enough and hard enough, you could lose me."

Dax swallowed hard at the thought but pushed it away. "Best thing for you. Stay far away from me because you're a good human."

"You know nothing about me. I wish I were good." She wrung her fingers together in her lap. "I may not go around giving random guys blowjobs, but…"

When Dax opened his mouth as if to stop her, Chiara held up a hand. "But I'm not good either. I've killed."

****

Roark got his wish. Karth took him to the Arisen Dawn garrison. Now, he eyed the next challenger, a wiry ylve with lean muscle. Though inches shorter and pounds lighter, the breed could be dangerous.

While the guy circled around on the mat, he chattered. "So, you're a shifter. What sort? I can't tell from your aura. Nobody here can."

"Yeah? Sorry." Roark pivoted, always facing his opponent.

"You're not sharing? What region in Scath you from? North Shelters?"

"My biz." Roark made a grab for the ylve's legs. *Yep*. He was slippery, easily jumping out of the way.

"Wrong. Arisen Dawn biz. You have to share."

Roark snapped a kick toward his opponent, taking him off his feet and smack onto the mat. He threw an elbow to the guy's throat. "No. I don't. All I have to do is beat your ass. Done."

He rose and backed away, his predatory gaze searching for another challenger. This was turning out to be a great day. He'd top it off with a few shots of whiskey and a soft female later tonight. Not too soft.

A big-ass demon shoved two front-line gawkers out of the way. "You want a piece of me?"

"Not my type. I'm hetero all the way. Unless you want to drop to your knees and suck me. I'm down with that."

The demon sputtered, snarled, and turned red. As

he lumbered forward, flames shot from his hands and ears.

Okay. Maybe I shouldn't have pissed off an animus demon.

Roark rotated to deliver a roundhouse kick. Too angry to block the move, the demon took one to the head. When he staggered backward, Roark laid it on strong while avoiding blasts of fire. He targeted the male's solar plexus, groin, and throat. When the massive beast dropped like an anchor and stayed put, Roark backed off the mat.

A vampire stepped from the shadows where he'd been eyeing the fights.

Glaring, Roark used his deepest, growliest voice. "What the fuck are you looking at? You want to try your luck or are you in love with my ass? If it's my ass, you should know I don't give it away."

A hungry smile curled the vampire's lips, the tips of his sharp fangs glistening. "You might be what I'm looking for."

"Drink, fuck, or fight?" asked Roark.

"Fight." The vamp swaggered into the light. "I'm the general here. Name's Lort. Now answer the ylve's question."

"Which one? He asked a couple."

"What kind of shifter are you?"

"You can't get a bead on me because I'm one of those rare mixes. Generations of my family bred with different kinds. Coyotes, lions, bears, ravens. For all I know, a few hummingbirds."

Must have made sense to the vamp because he nodded. Mixed shifters were rare but possible, their auras confusing.

"A bastard." The general brushed his dishwater-blond hair over his shoulder. "Don't advertise. Cerberus abhors mixed heritage."

No condemnation in his tone. Just a warning.

"Yeah. That's what they call us. Bastard shifters. I'll be sure to keep quiet about it. Nothing to brag about anyway."

"Can you handle weapons?"

"Name it."

Lort glanced around the room. He jerked his head toward the wall with tactical knives.

Roark snatched a couple from the rack, tossing one to the general. "Blade up."

The vampire licked his lips, stepped onto the mat, and crouched. He waved Roark forward.

Obliging, he fronted the general, spreading his legs into a wide stance.

His first move was to size up his opponent with a quick head-to-toe. Lort was all about power, but Roark was an equal opportunity killer. Win by any means necessary. He could dance like a prima ballerina or come out like a tank rolling over a stalled Prius.

Lort tossed his blade from fist to fist.

Roark smiled. *Okay*. The general wasn't only about power. He was into deception. Trying to catch his opponent off guard. Suck him in.

Watch the eyes, though. They never lie.

Still playing catch-the-knife, Lort charged. Roark slipped to the side, arms up, abs tight.

Roark waltzed around the general a few more times.

"Come on, bastard shifter. Fight."

"In good time, General."

They drew a crowd. Males and females gathered around, leaving only enough space for the combatants to go at it. It didn't help Roark's ego that the bystanders cheered for the general.

Lort thrust forward, stabbing into his gut.

"Good one." Roark ignored the pain to circle again. The male was fast.

Roark spun, kicked, and slashed but missed his target.

Yeah. Fast.

When the general lunged, aiming for his gut again, Roark deflected the blade with an arm-elbow move. The maneuver cost the vampire, leaving him open for an assault.

Taking advantage, Roark charged, rotated, kicked, and struck relentlessly. Feinting with his knife, he used his free hand to take the general to the ground.

Once Lort was flat on the mat, Roark kneed his chest, pinching his neck with the blade tip. "Point, game, match."

The victor immediately jumped up, releasing the general, who snapped to his feet seconds later.

"How are you with hand-to-hand? Breed gifts allowed." The vampire general pulled back his lips, revealing fangs as he flashed behind Roark to catch him in a headlock, preparing to rip out his throat.

So, the competition wasn't over yet. This male held a grudge.

Roark half-shifted to eagle, talons punching out. He rotated his body, shoved a shoulder against the vamp's chest, and placed his leg behind Lort's. After flinging the general backward, Roark stepped away, crouching, waiting for the next assault.

"Better than I am with a knife."

Chapter Eleven

When Chiara dropped the I've-killed bomb, the car swerved. Dax righted it but insisted on an explanation.

Once she recovered from the automobile accident, the hospital sent Chiara Bianchi—she hadn't taken the name Flores yet—to a state agency where her life forever changed. In time, they moved her to a foster home.

She spent six years there until…

The agency promised her the family was respectable, a dream placement. Hardly. Nightmare on Elm Street was more like it. Except this was Ellen Grove Avenue.

Chiara possessed two pairs of pants along with two shirts, which her foster parents expected her to launder daily by hand. The washtub was outside. No matter the weather, she scrubbed her few belongings and clipped them onto a line to air dry. Food was scarce, kindness scarcer. Five kids lived in the home, three girls and two boys. The girls were okay. The boys were mean.

Life was an endless routine of hunger, hard work, and strict lessons. The fosters woke the children each morning with a call to come downstairs. Breakfast was a piece of toast with grape jelly. A teaspoon of it. Water. They went to school with a paper lunch sack, its only contents two pieces of white bread, a thin spread of peanut butter, and another level teaspoon of grape jelly. When returning home, the kids got off the bus. They reported to their rooms to do homework. Dinner was promptly at five. If anyone was late, they didn't eat.

After eating, they formed a prayer circle to read passages from the Bible. Often the fosters chose a verse based on one of the children's perceived sins. Impoliteness. Failure to finish a task. Slouching at the table. Ungrateful behavior. Laughing.

The children sometimes selected a passage. Chiara's favorite was Jeremiah 29:11. "For I know the plans I have for you ... plans to prosper you and not to harm you, plans to give you hope and a future." She clung to those words on many a dark night.

After the readings, the children returned to their rooms for lights-out at eight o'clock. Sleep disturbed by nightmares preceded another day just like the others.

The weekends were worse. The morning began with breakfast, followed by silent contemplation. They spent that time in the living room, sitting, hands in laps, eyes downcast, thinking.

Chiara thought mostly about the man who had saved her from a fiery car. He would ride up to the house, usually on a sleek motorcycle, knock on the door, and take her hand. When the fosters refused to release her, he'd pull back his lips to bare his fangs. Once they stopped screaming, they'd shove her outside with him. They were on the road. First stop was Disneyland, where her hero stuffed her with frozen chocolate-covered bananas. With his wallet open, he handed her wads of cash to buy cool clothes. Afterward, they attended a Maroon 5 concert where they had front row seats.

With the end of scheduled contemplation, Chiara re-entered the real world. The kids cleaned their own rooms, followed by pitching in to clean the common areas. The fosters never allowed them to grocery shop or go to malls. Friends never visited. No phone calls came for them. Birthdays or holidays were days like the others. Celebration was a sin. Happiness a cardinal sin.

When the fosters caught a boy sneaking out at night, they called the children to observe his punishment.

He stood defiantly in the middle of the room while the dad ordered him to drop his pants. Chiara still saw his knobby knees and red, faded boxer shorts as he challenged the foster parents to do their best.

Chiara closed her eyes, but a smack to the back of the head warned her to watch. As the boy stood there, pants at his ankles, folded over his torn sneakers, the mom flicked a switch across his buttocks. Over and over until he was bloody. Nobody cried. Nobody defended him. The children watched. When the punishment ended, they returned to their rooms while he cleaned up the mess he had left on the floor. Show over. Lesson learned. Do not leave the home without permission.

The kids shared two bedrooms where the fosters locked them in each night. Despite the punishment, the boys continued to take off once it was dark. At least, they bragged about their exploits. The girls were too scared to try.

Bett was one of Chiara's roomies. Ooh! That girl had a mouth straight from New Jersey. She taught Chiara the finer points of cussing or dishing out insults. Cigarettes, too, but Chiara gave those up.

With only two years until freedom, Chiara would have stayed with the family despite its cold cruelty, but the boys changed. When they broke into the girls' room, the knobby-kneed boy held down Artha, hand over her mouth, while the other raped her. The girl's sobs frightened the young Chiara, who tried to help but was thrown back onto the bed. She was no match for either attacker. She pulled a blanket over her head to muffle the cries.

When the girl complained to the fosters, they were all treated to various passages from the Bible, one being Proverbs 13:5. "The righteous hate what is false, but the wicked make themselves a stench and bring shame on themselves." Following the reading, Artha got the switch. She didn't have to drop her pants. The lashes came to the backs of her legs.

When the boys visited again, Bett willingly offered herself up. She said, "It's time I get laid, even if by two pimply faced pencil dicks."

One day, the taller boy cornered Chiara in the upstairs hall following room cleaning. When he made it known she would be next, she cowered in fear each night. Bett, while telling her being fucked by two ugly pencil-dicked boys hurt, helped her drag a dresser against the door. The girls took turns sleeping fully clothed. Artha wasn't much help since she slept curled up in the closet with the light on after her experience.

After about two weeks, Chiara jolted from her sleep to see the dresser slide aside while the door slowly opened. The boys entered as she and Bett huddled together in a twin bed.

"Oh. Look," said the taller boy. "They're waiting for us." He grabbed his crotch. "You're gonna love this."

He crept closer, his cruel eyes on Chiara. Leaping from the bed, she cringed in a corner, shaking. When he was so close she felt his breath on her hair, she threw her hand into the air. "I wish you were dead."

With a thump, he crumpled to the floor. The teens stared as the taller boy's chest didn't rise and fall.

The knobby-kneed boy bent over his friend as a wide-eyed Chiara clasped a hand to her mouth.

As she hugged Chiara, Bett asked, "What's wrong with the little asshole?"

"He's dead," said the boy. "She killed him."

Bett dropped her arms, staring at her friend, fear in her wide eyes.

Chiara froze. She killed someone by wishing him

dead. How? When her legs worked again, she grabbed her stuffed monkey and pried open the bedroom window, crawling out onto a tree limb. She climbed down the trunk. Running, not stopping until she reached an alley behind a restaurant, she hid on the other side of a dumpster where she fell asleep. When she awoke, it was still night, and she was hungry. Scavenging food from a trash bin, she wept, wondering what to do now.

When a man with rumpled clothes stumbled into the alley, a bottle gripped in his palm, he trapped her between the wall and the dumpster. His fingers pushed into the waistband of her jeans. She raised her hand and wished he'd die. When he fell to the ground, she didn't bother to check for breathing. She knew she'd killed again.

Chiara charged out of the alley, running to the closest ATM, where she removed a card from her monkey. Her mother had crammed several cards, a little cash, and numerous notes inside the stuffed animal. There was also the phone number and address of a man her dad called a fixer.

With money from the ATM, she rented a room in a motel, telling the clerk her mother was in the restaurant next door getting them an early breakfast. She collapsed onto the bed not a moment too soon. Her body quaked with tremors. She couldn't control her arms or legs as they flopped up and down, spasming. A loud buzz obliterated any thought. Finally, she stilled and slept.

That morning, she called the fixer.

He could do anything from creating a new identity to burying bodies. He taught her how to access all the funds in her numerous bank accounts and move them elsewhere. The guy shared tricks for being on the run. How to find cheap but safe lodging. How to obtain odd jobs where no one would check her ID closely. He showed her how to hang on until she was old enough to pass for an adult. The man was good. For a price, he explained how to stay off the grid.

As Chiara Flores, she bought property with a cabin outside Orofino, Idaho, on Nez Perce land. The Native Americans left her alone, almost guessing what she was.

She had no idea how she had killed the boy or the vagrant, but she knew she was dangerous. Too dangerous to live around people. In time, she learned she could heal with the same hand which murdered. She didn't trust her powers, though.

In the early years, Chiara cried often. She was a freak, someone who murdered with no conscience. Part of her said they deserved to die. Another part regretted her actions. She wasn't normal. What was she?

With the story finished, she hung her head. Dax reached across the seat to tip her chin with his fingers. "Those fuckers earned their fate. You did nothing wrong."

They rode in silence for some distance, Chiara accustomed to Dax's long periods of brooding quiet.

Once he spoke, he didn't say what she wanted to hear.

"I'm the most dangerous monster here, but I will never hurt you."

"I know," whispered Chiara, a tear sliding down her cheek.

"But I'm not the male for you." He tapped his head. "It's very dark in here. You are nothing to me. I am nothing to you."

"That's cruel."

"Sometimes to be kind, you have to be cruel. Besides, cruelty's my strength. Why did your mother give you a BOB?"

Chiara wrinkled her brows.

"A bug-out bag. Or in your case, a bug-out monkey."

She shrugged, swiping a hand across her damp cheek. "I don't know. For as long as I can remember, she made me promise to keep the monkey close. I was to use it if something happened to her and Daddy. Mom made me read the notes inside, recite the plan, and memorize bank accounts numbers and info for the fixer. I swear, I think I said the word *monkey* before I said *mama*."

"Why didn't you use the BOB earlier?" asked Dax.

Chiara pursed her lips, thinking. "Dunno. Too young. Fear I couldn't take care of myself. The time wasn't right."

****

"How do you propose we get through two cops and a barricade?" asked Chiara.

Two blocks from the Missoula gateway, a growling Dax pulled to the side of the street. "Quiet. Let me think. If we had left in the dark like I wanted, I could have shadowflashed around the portal to eye what's going on. It'll be harder now."

Chiara patted her skirt, re-arranging the folds. "Not my fault. You were supposed to wake me."

His obsidian glare didn't frighten her. *Fact.* He looked more handsome when he was irritated. The angry crinkles in the corners of his eyes. The way his jaw locked. His full, pouty lips.

"Use your cell to find another street to the portal." He dragged his fingers through his hair.

"Yes, sir." She studied the screen after tapping in their destination. "Take a right up there. Left first block. Five blocks. Then another left."

Scrunched over the steering wheel of the small

car, Dax started the engine as Chiara suppressed a giggle.

Following her directions, they ran into a second barricade manned by three cops. "Okay. Make a U-turn to get back on the last street. Take a left. Go about six blocks. We'll approach from the north."

Damn. Another roadblock.

Chiara consulted her phone. "Only one more road leads to the portal. Should we try it?"

"Why not. We can't be more fucked than we already are."

Finding this street barred also, Dax suggested they sit out the day in a motel. *Oh, goody.* An entire day with a pissed off, morose, brooding vampire.

"Can we shop for some clothes first? In case we're here for a while. Not wearing panties, since you destroyed them, is a bit breezy."

"Fuck." Dax shot a hot glare at her.

Chiara located a Target, where they rolled a shopping cart into the men's section. "What do you like?" she asked.

"Anything." Dax threw pants and shirts into the basket.

"You didn't even check the sizes." Chiara tossed his selections out. From a stack, she read the labels on the men's pants she pulled out. "Black. Right?"

He nodded.

She chose three pair after eyeing his waist and ass a few times. Shopping for a guy's clothes was so exciting.

At the shirts, she paused. Picking out one, she held it up to his shoulders. *Holy shit.* The double X would be quite snug. A win. She tossed three into the cart.

"Briefs or tighty-whities?"

"Huh?"

"Underwear."

"Don't wear the stuff."

Chiara knew already, but she gasped nonetheless.

"Are we done?"

"No. We've just started. We need something to hold our items."

As Chiara took off down the aisle, Dax followed with a grunt.

After loading a large navy-blue duffel into the cart, Chiara eyed a display. "Toiletries. How could I have forgotten? Are you particular about toothpaste brands or deodorant?"

"What do you think?"

"That's a no." She studied the brands, grabbing Crest Complete. Whitening and fresh breath. Twofer. Next, she selected men's and women's deodorant. "Do you need razors? Of course you do." She tossed a pack in the cart.

Muttering something unintelligible, Dax snatched the basket, heading down the aisle with a long, fast stride.

"Where are you going?" Chiara chased him down, an armload of combs, brushes, fingernail polish, moisturizer, and shampoo. "Slow down. We need hair conditioner."

"We're done."

"No. I don't have my stuff. Women's is over there. Stop snarling. Your fangs are showing."

By the time they checked out, Chiara had chosen several skirts, tops, panties, bras, socks, and two nightgowns for herself. Dax tried to escape again when she insisted on trying on bedroom slippers decorated with sleeping bunnies because motel floors were grungy.

After they loaded the bags into the car while Dax still pouted, they found reasonably priced lodgings off the main street. Once settled into the room, they headed to the attached cafe where the vampire said they'd gather intel on the roadblocks.

The waitress poured their coffees while pulling down her off-the-shoulder blouse until Dax had to be blind not to see the swell of her boobs. She snatched a pencil from behind her ear, tapping it on a small notebook.

"So, what's with the blocked-off streets in town?" Chiara frowned at the woman who continued to yank on her top. How much more tit did she want to show? Pretty soon, she'd be lounging across Dax's lap with the blouse at her waist.

Flipping a strand of dyed carrot-colored hair off her face, the woman said, "Dunno. Been that way for days. Whatcha want, honey?" Pencil and pad in hand, gum popping in time to her taps, she eyed Dax as if he were the meat *du jour*.

"I'll have three cheeseburgers, extra fries, a strawberry malt." The fangtard had no problem ordering first.

"You?" The waitress was clearly less enthusiastic about Chiara's order, taking it while she kept her heavily lined and mascara-laden eyes glued to the dark-haired vampire.

Once the waitress walked away, a man in the booth behind them turned and patted Chiara on the shoulder. "I think it might be a carnival. I heard big trucks going by. The kind they keep packed with equipment. I don't like having those carny guys in town. We got a lot of nice girls here, and you know about those rides and games boys. Drinking and carrying on till early morning. Bunch of con artists."

An older white-haired woman at a nearby table threw out her idea. "Nonsense. A movie. They're definitely shooting a film. I bet pretty soon a bunch of actors will arrive in town. I hope one's Brad Pitt. I'd rather spend time with Steve McQueen, but he's dead. So, Brad's my second choice."

"Bullshit," said a cowboy at the table next to her. "Gotta be military maneuvers."

"Why do you say that?" asked Dax.

"I spied some army guys the first day. Those vehicles that rolled into town were green cargo trucks. Seen enough of them when I was on duty to know what they look like. Not carnival equipment."

A kid leaning against the jukebox said, "Aliens."

"What?" Chiara lifted her chin from the palm of her hand.

"A spaceship probably landed, and the government's got aliens there. This is what the guys on my football team are saying. We figure they're cutting them up, dissecting them. Finding out where they're from. What they want with us. Maybe their planet is dying, and they need food. Joe Martin, he's team captain, says we're probably gonna be processed and canned when they invade. He watched some movie where the aliens ate humans. Or they could be carrying some outer space virus. If so, we could all die from a disease. Likely turn into zombies."

When the waitress brought their order, she said, "Well, it could be terrorists with some bioweapon. Those Al-Kinda people from the East Coast are dangerous."

Chiara's mouth fell open. "I think you mean Al-Qaeda. And they're from the Middle East, not the East Coast."

She gave a whatever-wave with her hand while she turned a toothy grin to Dax. She placed the cheeseburgers in front of him.

"Where's my salad?" asked Chiara.

"Coming."

"You're all crazy," said the man in the booth behind them again. "Just a carnival. By tomorrow night, we'll see shooting games, Ferris wheels, food booths. No terrorists. No aliens. No army. No movie-makers. But a lot of good girls are going to have their hearts broken and their dads will be getting out the rifles."

"This has been helpful," muttered Dax, biting into his burger, his pupils eyeing up the waitress like dessert.

Once carrot-top left, Chiara reminded Dax of a promise. "Remember what I said about feeding?"

"What?"

"I'm not seconds." She tapped a finger to the vein in her neck. "You take from this but no one else. Get my drift?" Dax may not be the hero she once thought him, but she was possessive of him. Her blood was a bargaining chip to make him hers. Maybe for only a brief time.

Dax rolled his eyes.

Chiara kicked his shins under the table. "Scary vampires don't do eye-rolls. They show fang, growl, bite. They do not act like a teenage girl."

Dax almost snapped the tabletop when he got out of the booth to clomp off.

Chiara shrugged with an explanation to the patrons. "My boyfriend is very upset because he's having penile-dysfunction issues."

Dax, obviously hearing her, strong-armed the door. The bell on it clanged, shook, and clunked to the floor.

Everybody seemed a little sorry for him.

Chapter Twelve

The satyr waited among the thick trees with a clear line of sight to the log cabin while the witch he was forced to bring along plagued him with endless questions. Why did Lort think he needed her help to investigate the scene?

"So the vampire came through the portal back there, and the two demons and a warlock dug out his D-chip but were distracted before they could kill him?"

He nodded, wondering how many times she was going to ask the same questions.

"You found him as he was escaping in a car with a female?"

The satyr wanted to snatch her by the hair and bitch-slap her. Maybe he'd just fuck her into silence. "For the third time, yes. That's why we're going into the cabin to re-check it."

"Don't get testy with me. I was assigned this task by the general himself. I don't fail."

"I do? Bullshit."

"I didn't see you bring in the target's body. Did I miss something?"

The satyr had almost caught the vampire Firebrand. Then the male flipped him out of the car window. The flesh on his back was still raw from his skin-meets-gravel skid. The hunt was now personal. Besides, the satyr did not intend to wind up on the wrong end of Lort's sword as the demon and warlock had. Just more victims of the vampire's anger. "No, but I was close."

"You know the whole close and horseshoes saying. Anyway, let's go inside."

With a smirk, the witch pushed him aside on her

way to the porch.

Damn cunt.

They stepped quietly onto the steps and knocked. When there was no answer, the satyr twisted the knob. The door swung open. He palmed a gun and crept inside, motioning for the witch to follow. He scented the air. "Empty. They haven't returned."

"We'll split up. I'll take this side." Her booted feet tapped on the wood planks as she headed for the kitchen.

The satyr opened the door into the human's bedroom. The bed was made, the room neat, all drawers closed. In the bathroom, he eyed the makeup left on the counter. Stooping, he picked up a wet towel from the tiled floor. He sniffed. "Vampire."

Once he had cased the rooms, he met the witch in the living room.

"What did you find?" She scanned the area.

"The vampire definitely made himself at home. He showered."

"So, is she a good Samaritan who took the Firebrand in, or is she an accomplice he knew?"

"Why do we give a shit? Let's just find him. Why does Lort want the vamp so much?" The satyr's trigger finger was ready to eliminate the male.

"He saw something he shouldn't. In order to find the vampire and kill him, we need information. Anything could prove useful."

"Okay, I'll play the stupid game."

"The vampire and the human left in a hurry. The kitchen is a mess. Food still out and dishes dirty. I found something else of interest. Come see."

The witch led him to a pantry which was spacious enough for the satyr pushed in behind her. "What's this shit?" His eyes roamed over shelf after shelf of herbs, concoctions, and jars.

Taking one glass container in her hand, she rolled it over, label up. She unscrewed the cap, sniffing. "Healing potions."

The satyr slipped his gun into its holster. "She's definitely human. No witch scent in the house."

"Could be a human with a knack for elixirs." The witch set the jar back on the shelf and examined a few more.

The satyr wandered into the laundry room where he cracked the lid of the washing machine. His nostrils flared. "Vampire blood. Mixed with human. Hey. Check this out."

"Looks like the female was our target's food source." His partner returned to the living room where she examined a photo of a female. "Is this her?"

He pursed his lips. "Dunno. Didn't get a good look. She was riding passenger while I was being tossed from the window."

She pocketed the picture. "Did you find a computer or any papers?"

"Nope." He held up his hands to show her they were empty.

"Where was her car?"

He nodded toward the barn in back. "It was small. A Prius. Didn't catch the plates."

"So the witch-wannabe took off in her car with the Firebrand in the driver's seat. Was she a willing or unwilling accomplice?" She fisted her hips, her head cocked to one side.

"What the fuck difference does it make?"

She bristled. "An unwilling companion will weigh him down. A willing one can help him get to his destination faster. I might ask Lort to take your head just for the fun of it. You're too stupid to live. Your muscles must be squeezing your brain. Is it painful?"

The satyr sneered. "Are you schtupping the general?" It was the only explanation why such a miserable creature continued to survive.

The witch laughed. "You're more his type. Young. Male. And stupid. All we have is a photo, the make of her car, and the road they took out of here. No records tell us where they might go. I'm guessing a portal, but if she is human, how will they get through? She won't have a jumper. He's without his D-chip. I would head for a well-traveled gateway and wait for a lift home, find known Aeternals nearby, or drive to an Alliance office."

"Too many options. We need a scryer to find them. Come on. Let's gather something personal to take to one." The satyr returned to the laundry room, snagging used towels for the journey back to Scath. The clock was ticking, and he was highly motivated to find the vampire. He stroked his neck, liking how it sat on his shoulders.

****

On the couch in the cozy living room, Fin snuggled into his arms, a hot chocolate in her hand. She shivered, wrapping the teal blanket decorated with bison tighter around her.

The wolf shifter clutched her shoulders, gently urging her forward. Untangled from her body, he rose to crank up the fireplace with another log, poking it with an iron rod until it blazed. He was naked and completely at ease with the fact. "You can't resist me because… This is hard to explain."

"Try. I need to know why you're irresistible. I gave in when you crooked a finger." Fin could not understand why being with Thorn felt right, why she wanted him so badly.

"Are you dismissing my more-than-ample

charms?"

Fin snorted, hugging the blanket tighter when Thorn crawled onto the sofa and resettled her into his arms. "No. I am aware of your charms, but there's more. Talk, wolfie."

"You're my mate, darlin'." Thorn's muscles stiffened as if prepared for disbelief or peals of laughter.

She giggled as the hot chocolate sloshed in the cup. "Your mate?"

"Yep. Shifters are close to their beasts. Wolves more than most. Anyway, my beast wants you. Big time. Knows you're its mate. And you are attracted to my beast."

"No doubt, but how can that be?"

"Magical shit just happens with shifters."

"Hmm. And you're okay with that? With me?"

"Happier than a free, wild wolf. My animal is designed to bond. And where my beast goes, I follow. In your case, quite willingly. Seeing you, talking to you, making love to you, it all fits. You're meant for me, Fin. How's it sit with you?"

She nodded, a dreamy smile curving her lips as she twisted her neck to gaze into his amber eyes. She brushed his errant shaggy hair behind his ears. "I don't have a beast inside, but I'm drawn to you, too. 'Drawn' is too pale of a word. Engrossed. Fascinated. Magnetized. Better."

Thorn's lips pressed to hers, hot and promising. Suddenly, he pulled away. "Wait. Why aren't you scared of me? When you first saw me, you should have gone into shock. I had fur, claws, and huge-ass chompers. Most people wouldn't take the sight in stride. Hell, the general pop would faint if they spied my wolf."

Fin leaned her head back onto Thorn's chest. After a moment, she sighed, leaned forward, and set her cup on the table. "The whole story about my mom, who obviously wasn't totally crazy, might explain a lot."

"I'm all ears."

She tugged on a lobe. "I understand wolves have very big ears."

"All the better to hear you with, my dear."

She laughed and began the tale.

"A single mom raised me. She was great. We didn't have a lot of extra money, but we spent time together. Playgrounds, picnics, movies, stories, playing with dolls and trucks, just talking. She was employed at a big company which I think was connected with the government. At least, as a kid I thought so because everything was very hush-hush."

"Where did you live?"

"Denver, until I was ten. Then we moved to Chicago. Anyway, she started slipping. Small things at first. Forgetting to shop for groceries. Forgetting how to find our apartment. Not paying bills. Later came the paranoia."

"What do you mean?" Thorn shifted, getting more comfortable.

"She bought extra locks for the door. Two at the bottom, three in the middle, and one so high I couldn't reach it without standing on a chair. Mom checked out the windows constantly, looking for something or someone."

"Did she talk about her fear?"

"Not at first. She said general stuff like 'They're coming.' Some guys showed up one day. In suits. All business. At least, at eighteen that's how I saw them. They said they were from the Alliance where she worked…"

"Stop." Thorn stiffened beneath her. "She worked for the Alliance?"

"Yes. They told me they checked her into a private hospital. For her own good. A mental hospital. Apparently, she went all psycho at work. Climbing on her desk. Throwing things. Shouting. They said she grabbed a knife and was cutting herself. The suits told me where she was and how to get in touch. Before the men left, they searched the house, removing notebooks, her computer, a few boxes of other stuff. Afterward, they were gone."

"You must have been terrified."

"I wasn't good. I Googled the mental facility to get some information. It was exclusive and very expensive. I was worried since I didn't know anything about her insurance. When I called the Alliance office, they said everything was covered. They would take care of her. Part of me was relieved. Another part was confused."

When Fin shivered, Thorn tugged her closer to wrap his arms tight around her.

"I visited her, but eventually it got hard to do. Some days she was catatonic, unmoving and silent. Other days she was crammed into a corner, shaking, terrified of me. She ranted about demons, vampires, werewolves, witches. You get the drift. Looney tunes."

Fin twisted to look into Thorn's amber eyes below his arched brows. "Or so I thought. When I met with the doctors, they talked about late-onset paranoid schizophrenia and a variety of anxiety disorders. The prognosis was not good. Her medical team kept switching medications, looking for the perfect combination. If they couldn't find a solution, they said Mom would lose complete touch with reality."

"How'd that go?"

"Some days okay. Most not."

"I'm sorry." Thorn's calloused hand rubbed down

her arm, soothing her.

"I asked the doctors if the problem was her hallucinating about fictitious creatures, but they said no. Her extreme paranoia and anxiety along with suicide attempts kept her in the facility."

Fin sniffled, her head tilted to stop the flow of tears. "I attended a few sessions of NAMI—the National Alliance on Mental Illness—where I learned to accept what I could control but to release what I could not. Eventually, I let her go. She died. A heart attack a few years back. I'll cherish the days when she was lucid. She'd call out my name. 'Fin, baby,' she'd say. 'You look so pretty.'"

Thorn nodded. "I understand having to step back from family better than you think."

"When those guys attacked me, her fantasies were front and center in my brain. You turned part wolfie, making me rethink the whole werewolf thing. You didn't scare me because part of me was prepared for you. Besides, you saved my life. Afterward, I wondered. Wondered how much truth my mother spoke even though she was paranoid. Come to find out, Mom was straight on some things. Of course, she was a danger to herself."

Fin rolled over, burrowing into Thorn's chest, nuzzling him. He tipped her chin up with his knuckle. As he was about to take her lips, she slid open her eyelids.

"Holy shit." He almost dropped Fin when he jumped upright with her in his arms. "Your eyes are purple."

"Oh, circles under them? Are they puffy?"

"No. Your irises are pale purple."

"Don't be ridiculous. They're brown."

"They were. I'd have called them sable. But that's old news."

Fin kicked her legs until Thorn set her on the floor. She rushed to a rustic iron mirror on the wall. "Holy shit is right. That's not possible."

"Sure it is." The wolf shifter sighed. "I need to tell you something else about you and your mother."

****

"Darlin', did your mom ever mention the Blood Coven in her ramblings?" asked Thorn.

"No. Not that I remember." Fin curled her legs beneath her on the couch while Thorn threw another log on the fire.

Turning around, he ran a hand through his hair. "It explains why the berserker and the sloth demon were after you. Have you taken a recent blood test?" When she narrowed her eyes, Thorn persisted. "Just go with me here. Have you?"

"Yes. I had a bad infection. The doctor drew blood to see if anything too awful was going on. Turned out to be this season's popular virus."

"That's how they found you."

"Why? Who?"

He chuckled, removing his flannel shirt. Thorn rolled up a sleeve on his tee, showing her his Phoenix brand. "This is the mark of a Scion Firebrand. I am one. We're warriors. I'll explain why that's important in a sec."

"Okay…"

"Bad guys on Scath, that's my realm, led by a male called Cerberus are hunting for descendants of the Blood Coven. These witches and warlocks created Earth, Scath, and Darque from one world about fifteen hundred years ago, basically to save humans. At first Aeternals—that's me and other breeds—couldn't travel through portals. Eventually, technology allowed us through them, but access is controlled. This Cerberus, we think, wants the descendants because he plans to destroy the portals and throw the realms wide open. I don't need to tell you how bad it would be if a hungry bunch of us started pouring onto Earth."

"What does all this have to do with my eyes?"

"Bear with me. He found you because of your blood test. He sent the demon and berserker to get you because you have a drop of witch in you. They wanted to see if you are actually a Blood Coven descendant."

"So?"

"Surprise. As it turns out, Scion Firebrands seem to have a thing for the descendants. Witches eyes are always some shade of purple. Sex with me jumpstarted your powers. It's been happening to other Blood Coven descendants."

Fin's brows scrunched. "Let me see if I have this straight. You're saying I'm a witch."

"A newbie. You need training but yep."

"I'm one of these Blood Coven's offspring. You know this because my eyes turned purple after we had sex."

"Right again."

"This Cerberus guy wants me."

Thorn nodded.

"And I'm in danger?"

Thorn bristled, controlling himself before he popped some claws and fangs. "You're safe with me, darlin'. Always. You're my mate."

****

Later that night, Dax told Chiara he was going out for a walk, to think, to plan.

She chewed on the tip of her thumb. "Sure."

Hiding in the shadows of the café, he watched the lights go out. Darkness didn't bother him. He preferred it to the bright light of day. More at home in the inky night where his vampire vision gave him a distinct advantage over humans.

Soon the waitress with the flaunted breasts and long neck exited the door, turning a key in the lock. Before she could react, Dax was upon her, silencing her. With an arm locked around her waist, bending her slightly backward, he exposed her pulse. His lips kissed where he would bite as his fangs stretched in preparation. But incapable of the task, he sighed and pushed her away.

Damn little witch.

"Fuck." Waving a hand across the female's face, he erased all memories of him and Chiara from her mind.

On his way back to the motel room, Dax muttered, something he did frequently since meeting the human witch. "Damn. Holy Schism. I've been pussified."

He'd sought the waitress as an experiment. It had failed, but he would not allow Chiara to be connected to him, to darken her soul as he had his own. Though they were connected for the moment, he would sever the ties. He didn't need a female attached to him. She didn't need a male who couldn't even take care of himself.

He opened the door to their motel room, not even trying to be quiet. "Wake up, female."

Chiara's eyelids fluttered as she tried to hold them open. "What?"

"I'm hungry. Get the hell over here." If he was a big enough asshole, which was easy for him, she'd see he was no hero. She'd see him for the monster he was.

She stretched and crawled toward Dax, kneeling with her hands on her thighs. "Have you kept our agreement? You didn't go back to snag a quick bite from the waitress, did you?"

"Hell no."

What is she, a mind reader?

He'd wanted to. Wanted to see if the other female made his taste buds pop like the human witch did.

"Okay. Snack time." When he sat on the mattress, Chiara crept onto his lap, stirring an immediate reaction from his cock. He pushed her lush, long, curly hair over her shoulder and sank fang.

Delicious.

Dax's first pulls were strong, fierce. Once he slowed, he savored the taste of Chiara, her blood fresh and wild like the herbs she collected.

When she moaned and ground against his arousal, his hand slipped under her nightgown. He scrunched it to her waist as he rolled her onto the bed. Unzipping his pants, he freed his throbbing shaft. Gripping it, he dragged it through her wet folds while he still clung to her neck, drawing on her nectar.

Chiara bucked her hips, her body reaching for him. Dax forgot about his promise to her. He withdrew his fangs and readied to plunge into her sex. To find release.

"I love you." Chiara's whispered confession was cold water.

"What?" Dax stilled.

Her beautiful orchid eyes glistened with moisture as she stared into his. "I love you, Dax."

He lunged off her, fisting her gown, yanking it down to her ankles. "No, you don't. I'm fucked up. Besides, the feeling's not reciprocated."

Wide-eyed, she stared at him. "That's mean."

"Do you want me to lie? I'll keep you safe until Scath. There, we part ways." When she scooted back to lean against the headboard, he tucked himself into his pants, groaned, and zipped up. Springing off the bed, he paused at the door. "I'm outta here."

Chiara's hands twisted in her lap. "What are you

going to do?"

"I can shadowflash from one dark location to another. Any place I can see. If I take it a step at a time, I'll keep tracing until I'm close to the portal. See what's going on."

Chiara's fingers tugged on a long strand of dark curls. Dax wanted to touch her. He'd like to... *Damn. Don't go there.*

"Be careful, won't you? I mean, I don't want to be left alone."

He rushed outside before he did something stupid. Using vampire speed, he reached the first barricade they'd encountered earlier today. When he saw an empty alleyway two blocks away, he popped into the shadows there. Next, he hid in another unlighted spot. After about five more stops, he was alongside a brick building near the portal. This was no carnival, terrorists, bioweapons, nor movie shoot.

No military war-game maneuver either. Heavily armed men in US Army uniforms gathered on the street, scrutinizing the storefront which housed the portal.

Hidden in the dark, Dax observed the scene for hours. During one of his mandatory stays on Earth, he'd been in a Special Forces unit. He knew enough about warfare to recognize the military's positional advantage.

Off to one side, men sparred and exercised. Their speed, agility, and power demonstrated they were well-trained and physically fit but not jacked up on Dante's superhuman shit. Good news.

Tents were pitched in the streets. Two medical vans waited with personnel standing alongside chatting. Three Apache helicopters sat on the ground. One section held troop carriers.

The army had cordoned off a large area, evacuated the neighborhood, and waited for Aeternals.

Having broken into the storefront housing the portal, they could fire on anyone exiting a gateway. He wondered if they were armed with bullets or tranqs.

Just then, shots rang out. Two men exited the storefront with a slumped body between them. Another two soldiers dragged a dazed but struggling Aeternal out. Dax couldn't make out the breed. Both were males. They were loaded into one of the medical vehicles. Armed escorts stepped inside with them, closing the back end. The vans sped off, probably headed to a nearby larger base of operation.

If Dax tried to help the Aeternals, the military would capture him. Chiara would be alone. But the helplessness rankled.

Two men who looked like high-ranking officers chatted under a bright streetlamp. Each held a confiscated portal jumper. One soldier turned the device over to study it. Scratching his head, he shrugged when the guy next to him asked a question. If the human soldiers figured out how to work the things or how to replicate them, the news was not good. Dax sure could use a device right now, but he was not likely to snag one.

The whole situation was FUBAR. He and Chiara were not going home from a gateway in Missoula. Where now? He had another idea. If it panned out, he could notify the Firebrands as to the clusterfuck Earthside.

Chapter Thirteen

Before daybreak, Lort craned his neck to watch a striker team of harpies fly overhead in combat-box formation. The black-winged creatures flaunted deadly beaks, poisonous claws, and ruby-red lips which curled into sinister smiles as their long hair fanned out in the wind. While the wildings rode prevailing air currents, their thickly lashed eyes scanned the ground, unable to see the Arisen Dawn garrison hidden beneath a cloaking spell. The perfect sentinels, they kept visitors away from the headquarters while they provided an early warning system with their shrieks and cries.

The harpies' nests to the north made them frequent fly-bys. Roaming the area to the west were questing beasts, and gagans hunted in the mountains. All kept Arisen Dawn soldiers close and unwelcome guests distant. The garrison was in an ideal site.

Cerberus called Lort's attention back to *terra firma*. "Continue to concentrate on infiltrating North America through the western portion of the United States. How go the early forays?"

"Excellent. Soldiers are slipping through portals in Los Angeles, San Francisco, and Portland and will next move into Montana, Washington, and Idaho."

"Have you run into heavy opposition yet?" Cerberus paced on the overlook as he questioned his general.

"None, but we're avoiding locations we think Dante shared with the Earth armies before he died. Nevertheless, we could find the military waiting for us at future invasion sites, not knowing exactly what he told them. That's why I send in the drug-compelled Gold Dusters first. We can afford to lose them. If all goes well,

I then dispatch our loyalists. I directed both groups to cause as much havoc as possible. In the wake of dead bodies and Aeternals roving the West, human civilian populations are screaming for information and protection. Since the armies have not yet shared intel about us, the people haven't figured out who we are or where we are coming from."

Cerberus stopped with the back and forth to preach his usual message. "The time will come when they can no longer keep us a secret. Arisen Dawn will bathe in human blood and fear. Once we have tested North America, we move to the rest of the world."

"I prefer to think about the current battleground. One victory at a time. Besides, we can only slip a limited number of our soldiers through at a time with handheld portal jumpers. This fact hampers a quick resolution to our war."

"Is Boden making any progress on creating better devices where we can send more fighters through the portals?"

"Yes. We are up to ten, but the director says that's as much juice as he can get out of the handheld gadgets."

Cerberus paused to stroke his jaw. "Boden was tasked by Firebrands to add gateways. Has he done so?"

"No. Once he openly supported our cause, Alarik removed his support. Without his mages, Boden is unable to complete the task."

"Hmm. New gateways would have been helpful, but the plan is coalescing. When it does, the portals will disappear. The Whorl will cease to exist. We will flood onto Earth to take our rightful place as rulers of the one world."

Lort glanced above to see the last harpies in the striker team disappear. "Though our stable of descendants is increasing, we do not know if we have one from each bloodline yet."

"I may have found someone to help with that problem. Like I said, my plan is progressing on schedule. You do not need all the details. On another note, where is the Firebrand vampire?"

"We don't know. When he jumped to Earth, my people failed to kill him. They have paid for their incompetence. At least they removed his D-chip. I sent in a second team which just missed him. They are searching for leads at a cabin in Idaho."

The dirt at Cerberus's feet swirled, dancing along the peak where they stood. Swirling, the dust enveloped Lort. The dark smoke grew hands, lifted him from the ground, and constricted his breathing. "I detest failure, General."

"My best resources are on him," Lort rasped as his fingers swatted at the black cloud circling his neck.

Cerberus calmed the storm gripping the vampire, allowing his feet to touch rock again. "Because he has seen too much, he could expose one of my allies. I am not ready just yet. Get the Firebrand before he contacts his stronghold."

"We will find him. Right now, he cannot communicate with Scath. Though we suspect he has found help from a human on Earth, the vampire will not evade us forever." Lort winced, not allowing his fangs to punch through his gums. He held his temper, recognizing Cerberus as the superior being, most likely a warlock of advanced years and power who could crush him with a single spell. The vampire would kowtow to that strength while keeping his acerbic thoughts in check.

For now.

"I also understand a Blood Coven descendant escaped capture in Montana. Is this true?"

Lort lowered his lids lest his eyes turn red to betray his anger. “But we are searching the woods for her.” As a skilled warlock, Cerberus obviously plucked thoughts from the general’s mind before he wished to share them. Lort didn’t like his brain invaded.

****

Chiara wiped the sleep from her eyes and stretched her arms overhead. Never much of a morning person, she definitely wasn’t a let’s-get-going-at-4-AM girl.

“Can I have coffee first?” Her eyelids scraped shut. “I know you’re talking, but the words aren’t registering in my caffeine-deprived brain.” She rolled onto her stomach, pulling the blanket over her head.

Dax snarled. “I’ll be right back.”

When he returned, she caught the aroma of coffee. Spurred on by the hope of caffeine, she leaned against the headboard.

The grumpy vampire shoved a cup into her outstretched hand. “Drink.”

“Sugar? Cream?”

He patted his new black cargoes, reached into a pocket, and pulled out her requests.

Chiara’s head lolled to the side while she mumbled, “Thanks.”

When the vampire started to talk again, she held up a hand.

“Shush. Wait.”

Dax growled. He paced one length of the room. Back. To the wall again. He glared at Chiara, who was slowly sipping her coffee.

“Can I shower and dress before you go all snarly vampire on me? I can’t handle the shouting until then.”

“I don’t shout.” A rumble arose from deep in his chest.

"Okay. Substitute growling for shouting." Chiara swung her legs over the edge of the bed, straightening her nightgown. She stood and wobbled into the bathroom. Before she shut the door, she peeked her head around the jamb. "Would you be a dear and get me one more cup?"

Dax's fingers tangled in his hair, but he set his own coffee down before he stomped out of the room.

Chiara brushed her teeth, fingered the puffy bags under her eyes, and stepped into the delightfully warm shower. Letting the water sluice over her, she gradually came alive.

What kind of a man, not man, vampire, gets up this early in the morning? One who has a death wish.

She forgot to bring clothes into the bathroom. *Oops*. Wrapping a towel around her, she peeked out the door. He was back. "Will you toss me my stuff?"

"No. Get it yourself."

All six-foot-too-much of solid male lay on the bed, ankles crossed, arms folded under his head, biceps bulging. He would entice any woman to commit sin, especially one who'd dreamed about him most of her life. Why did he have to be a jerk? In the future, she'd keep her lips zipped. No professions of love.

Instead of sighing, Chiara checked to see she was adequately covered.

Hell. I show more than this in a swimsuit.

"Grouch." She raced into the room and opened the duffel. While she grabbed panties, bra, a long skirt, and a cute, cropped T-shirt, Dax's eyes followed her. "A gentleman would look the other way."

He let out a snarl-laugh, something he did so well and so often, as she hustled back to the bathroom.

Dressed and groomed, she came out for her second cup of coffee along with the vampire's story of last night's exploration.

"I saw an army at the portal. I'm guessing Missoula was a gateway on Dante's share list. While I watched, soldiers captured two Aeternals. We can't get to Scath from here, but a *freron* of mine owns a ranch in Montana near Bozeman. I know where it is."

Chiara was amazed that words she didn't know days ago now made complete sense. Portal. Aeternals. Scath. Except one. "A *freron*?"

"Another Firebrand."

"Okay. I guess we drive to Bozeman. How do you know he's there?"

"I don't. Just a guess he will pass through soon. He was in trouble when I left home. Nothing serious. He's an honorable male. A wolf shifter." Dax drained his coffee and stood.

The vampire's fingers combed through his gorgeous, straight midnight hair. A habit? Or did she make him nervous? She hoped so because he sure as hell tied her in emotional knots.

Dax hefted their newly purchased duffel and unlatched the door. In the parking lot, she reached for the driver's door handle. He yanked on Chiara's elbow. "Think again, little witch."

"My car. My baby to drive."

He shook his head as he forced her to the passenger side. "Are we going to have this argument every time?"

"We will until you get over this alpha thing you got going. Women have been driving for years."

"Not with me."

"Who's Dante?" She snapped on her seatbelt, letting the argument rest for now.

"Breakfast first."

Chiara pointed ahead as they pulled away from

the motel. "Let's do that drive-through. Over there."

Once they stopped in front of the menu board and speaker, Chiara leaned across him to order for both of them.

Dax pulled his brows tight. "I can speak for myself."

"Of course you can. Now you know how I feel about your insisting on driving all the time."

"Not the same thing." His grouchy lips twitched downward.

"It's exactly the same thing."

Dax snarled, driving up to the window. He set two more coffees in the holder, tossing the bag to her.

With the breakfast in hand, she passed a biscuit and egg to Dax. He waved off the hash browns. *Big mistake.* Chiara stuffed the wrapper into the sack. With a yum and a sigh, she opened wide for a huge bite of her McDonald's sandwich.

"How can you scarf down all that grease?" Dax took one bite before tossing his. He pointed at one of the coffees. "Take off the lid." While he sipped, he pulled out of the lot.

"I have a highly active metabolism. Besides, I don't ride you about your preference for blood."

"It's not a preference. It's a necessity. One I happen to enjoy." He blew on his hot drink. "You'll like Thorn. Everyone does. He's honorable. Steady. Mate material."

She chewed until her mouth was empty. "You said that already. And you're not mate material?"

"Right."

"Are you going to fix me up with your friend?"

Growl.

She crammed in another mouthful. "I iss ma ogs."

"What the hell did you say?"

She paused to swallow. "I said, 'I miss my dogs.'"

He relaxed his arm on the center console. "They'll be fine. They're just dogs."

Chiara glared at him. "You're so insensitive." Besides, to her they weren't just animals. They cared about her. They were, maybe, the only ones who did.

Dax shrugged but seemed to rethink his statement. "I'm sure Ivan's taking care of Boris, Victor, and Peter. He's smart."

"You know their names. You're right. Ivan's so smart, I have to watch him. He's sneaky, stealing food from the table, getting the other boys into trouble, crawling into my bed at night without permission."

"Lucky bastard," Dax muttered as he turned the corner.

Her hands fell to her lap, unfinished sandwich and all. A tear trickled from her eye. "I miss them. They're all I've got."

"Eat up. You'll feel better."

She wouldn't. Her childhood hero was rescuing her again because he had to. But he wasn't a man who would be with her tomorrow or the next day. Her dogs were not with her. She was headed off to be with strangers. As always, Chiara was alone.

****

Kole ran a finger over the edge of Queenie's axe, testing it and examining its bevel. With a Japanese stone already lubricated in water, he sharpened the blade using a circular motion, the handle down between his legs. His fire-gold, appraising eyes scanned his efforts. Satisfied, he flipped the axe so the handle was upright, resting against his shoulder. He sharpened the other side. Getting out a piece of leather, he repeated the process several times.

"Must be the anniversary of the Amazon's death." Ram leaned back in a chair across from his commander's desk, an ankle crossed over his knee as Kole stropped the cutting edge of the weapon.

Thwop. Thwop. Thwop.

Annually on the date of a Firebrand's death, he honed and polished the warrior's favorite fighting tool until it gleamed. Today he honored a special warrior. "Did you know she was in line to be the Amazon queen? Hence the moniker that followed her. Instead, the Phoenix called her to service. She could have rejected the call. She didn't. Once she joined the Firebrands, she never looked back. Belinda was her given name. You weren't a gleam in your satyr father's eye when she partnered with me, a green recruit." Kole set the leather strap aside, standing to return the battle axe to its spot on the wall. He stared for some time. "*Frerons* all."

The demon commander returned to his seat, where he tented his fingers. "She taught me everything I know about fighting and honor. Queenie was a warrior who died too young."

"You do right by her, Kole. All of us appreciate how you recognize the fallen."

Bounty sauntered through the doorway. "Get your asses to the gym. Brak and his unit just returned from a mop-up near a portal. Lots of injuries. I called for Alarik's healers."

Ram and Kole's boots ate up the floor as they raced down the hall. A grim sight met them. Wounded males and females leaned against walls. Some were spread out flat being tended to by healers. The coppery scent of blood was ripe in the air.

Kole strolled from *freron* to *freron*. With so many recruits, he couldn't even remember the name of the female ylve who clutched a hand to the gaping hole in her side. One of Alarik's people examined a second deep laceration on her leg. A good commander would know the name of each warrior. Kole vowed to do better. He crouched beside her. "Firebrand, how are you doing?"

"Fine, sir. Just a little flesh wound. Nothing more than a nick."

Kole glanced at the healer who shook his head.

"Once you're better, warrior, report to my office. We'll talk about your future. I think you'll be pleased."

Despite the pain in her eyes, her lips tugged into a smile. "Yes, sir."

Kole moved on to an injured incubus who was gritting his teeth to keep from wincing. "How ya doing, son?"

"Dreaming about the soft healing touch of a female. Looking forward to finding one tonight."

Kole chuckled, tapping the male's shoulder.

His gaze sweeping the room, Kole eyed Ram kneeling beside Brak, the unit's leader. After he moved from Firebrand to Firebrand, chatting them up, he approached the two males.

With a strip of material torn from his shirt, Brak staunched the flow of blood on his upper arm. When a healer walked his way, he waved her on to another injured *freron*. "Take care of him first."

Kole waited until they were alone. "What happened out there?"

"We ran into a shitload of armed Arisen Dawn fighters headed for Earth at that portal near the Strigodierna Shrine in Bludhaven. My unit engaged despite being seriously outnumbered. They fought like warcats. Proud of them, Comm. They're raw but mighty. Anyway, a few sonsabitches escaped through the gateway. We killed most, though. What remained turned tail and scattered."

Ram watched the blood from Brak's wound drip onto the floor. "Did you give chase on Earth?"

"No. I made the decision to return. Not one of us is uninjured. I had no choice."

Kole fell into a crouch, an elbow on his knee. "Wise decision, demon."

Brak waved off another healer, but Kole called him back. "Hold on. See to this Firebrand now."

When Brak shook his head, Kole snarled. "I'm the commander here. I get to say who does what. Your wound is nasty. Can't have one of my best losing an arm."

As the healer worked on Brak, Ram fired questions. "How many insurgents?"

"Maybe a hundred." The demon flinched, snarling at the male who helped him. "That hurts, you know?"

"How many got through?" the satyr asked.

"Only a couple. I should have sent someone after them, but we were ass deep in fighters."

"You did better than anyone could expect. Ram, get a cleanup crew to the site. See if there are any survivors we can interrogate. Destroy the bodies." Kole voiced the question which had to be asked. "Any of ours dead?"

"None, Comm. They done good for kids. I'd have any one of them on my six in the next battle."

Ram nodded and left the training area.

Kole followed the carnal demon's gaze around the room. Soft moans were the most he heard out of the wounded Firebrands, even the ones with serious injuries. Brak was right. These recruits were brave males and females. He hoped they were strong enough for what was coming.

Tap. Tap. Tap. Bounty's footsteps echoed across

the gym floor. "Galena and her unit are headed into the stronghold. She's called for healers. They ran into a bunch of Arisen Dawn assholes trying to get to Earth from North Shelters."

Kole brushed a hand across his buzz-cut hair. Looked like the Firebrands were going to war with a minimal number of experienced warriors and a shitload of green recruits. Battle and bloodshed would test the newbies long before they were ready.

****

While he drank a beer in Poughkeepsie's Icehouse which overlooked the Hudson, Miller's cell buzzed. "Harry. What's happening, mate?"

"Just traveling around checking on my charges. I've been all over the place. I wish my people would move into the same city. I'd settle for the same state. Hell, at this point, maybe the same country. How are you?"

"Been better. Blokes are still on my ass."

"How?"

"I don't know. Our phone system is safe. I ditched everything on me when they tried to nab me. Different clothes, watch, phone, wallet. There's no tracer on me. It's making me barmy." Miller tapped his beer mug on the bar to request a refill.

"Not to be doom and gloom, but what if they catch up. What should I do?"

"Call me three days in a row. If I don't pick up, ditch all the phones. Have our trackers change to new locations. Call Braelyn James. You've got the number. Then forget about me." Miller sighed, resigned. Resigned to disappearing on Scath or being snagged by his pursuers. He didn't like his options. "Have my backup take care of my bloodline. You know her. In fact, have her take over now. I'm too busy running to do a good job for my people."

"Miller, this isn't sitting well with me, man."

"Hey. I'm still here, mate. I'm not easy to catch. Anyway, what's the call about. I know you're not so in love with me you just called to hear my dulcet tones."

"You're right. I've got a list of names. Eirene's tracker called. Celene Bailey has been missing. She's some heiress with a death wish who does all these extreme sports things. He didn't think much about it when she didn't come home for a while. Nothing new. Time has passed. He talked to neighbors. Apparently, she was on her way to Venezuela to base jump over a waterfall. Crazy shit, if you ask me. Anyway, he flew to the site, talked to the outfitters she hired. A guy says she made a successful jump but disappeared after a safe landing."

"He didn't report her missing earlier?"

"Nah. He said these adventurers are unreliable types. She paid upfront. Not unusual for his clients to take off with no goodbyes."

"She could be off on another exploit."

"Could be, but the guy said she shared with some of her fellow crazies how she was headed home after the jump."

"You said you had more names." Miller paused to take a gulp of his brew.

"The other's from Faelan's bloodline. Finley Sage. Apparently, her mom died a while ago. The tracker said she took off a bit of time from work for the funeral. Afterward, she was back to the job, mourning the loss but dedicated. When the catering business had some downtime recently, she took off on a camping trip."

Miller heard the shuffling of pages.

"To Montana. She should have been home a few days ago. We're not talking about a lot of missing time.

She could have extended the vacay. My gal says Fin's employer claims she would not extend her trip without notifying him. Not her style. The boss is worried something happened to her while she was communing with nature. In fact, he's called into missing persons."

Harry rattled off several more missing and their backgrounds.

"I'll give the names to my contacts. Sorry to lay all this management shite on you, mate. Bye for now."

"Miller. You said they told you to come in for them to protect you. You might consider it."

"Not yet. I don't do well in lockup."

Miller enjoyed a good dustup now and again. Keeping one step ahead of predators was different, though. It was exhausting. He needed a good self-talk.

The buggers are cheesing me off. No reason to give up, though. Buck up, mate.

Chapter Fourteen

Dax slid from behind the wheel, jacking his boot on the car's doorframe as he scanned the area. He reached into the backseat to remove the duffel and Chiara's threadbare monkey.

"You drive too fast." Chiara stepped from the vehicle, lifting her arms overhead, stretching left and right, her breasts pushing against the fabric of a thin cropped T-shirt.

Damn. She looked good. His erection punched the front of his pants. He was jonesing for a hit of O blud. *Sure. That was it.* Couldn't be the present company.

She snorted when she rounded the car. "What's in your pants? Did you get a knobgoblin from driving?"

Damn thing was hard as a rock. He needed a female. "You have a mouth. Where do you come up with your shit?"

But Chiara would not do. Delicious taste mixed with Blood Coven descendant was a bad combo. He could not keep sampling her brand. He had to unload the female. *Hell*. She tasted so good if he kept her, he'd probably kill her within a year.

"I had a lot of Google time in Idaho. You'd be surprised what you learn on the net."

Dax sighed. Unload her. Thorn was good looking, he supposed. She'd be attracted to him. Most females liked shifters. *Yep*. The wolf was a good solution. They would all return to Scath where Thorn could step in to take care of Chiara. The solution pleased him and pissed him off.

Fuck.

Peals of laughter sounded from behind the ranch house. "This way." Dax dragged her toward the giggles.

"This place is incredible." Chiara twisted her neck, glancing around as he clutched her hand. Her feet stumbled to keep up the pace.

In the corral, a female perched atop a big appaloosa. She swung both legs to one side of the saddle, laughing as Thorn grabbed her hips and drew her down his body. Her arms clasped around his neck while he brought her in for a kiss. When she was on the ground, he squeezed her ass, his hips rocking into her. Their actions were clear.

Chiara eyed Dax with a grin curving her lips. "You're right. Your friend is likable, but if I'm going to hook up with him, I think it'll be a threesome. You could join us. We'll have a foursome."

"Mouth. Can you keep it shut?" With Chiara still in tow, Dax called out to Thorn. "Hey. Shifter."

When his *freron* turned around, his claws pushed through his fingers. Auto-fight reflex. "Vampire. What the hell are you doing here?"

With the female locked to his side, a wary Thorn approached.

Dax combed fingers through his hair. "I need your help."

The shifter, decked out in his signature boots and a sweat-stained cowboy hat, gave Chiara the once-over. He missed nothing. "Intros would be good, vampire. This lovely is Fin." He kissed the female's palm as she blushed.

Dax bobbed his head toward Thorn's companion. "She's Chiara. Let's finish inside." He had no intention of holding a long confab in the open.

Leading them through a rear door, Thorn shucked his hat, leaving it on the back porch.

"Coffee? Tea?" asked Fin, hanging a heavy, too-big sweater on a hook. Probably Thorn's.

"No. We've had enough." Dax was eager to get talking about the problem. Interesting, though, the female seemed at home in Thorn's place.

"Don't speak for me, vampire. I'd love some tea, Fin." Chiara followed the other human into the kitchen. "Dax, don't start without me."

He *hmphed* but waited till the females returned with a tray. Fin took a cup for herself and handed one to Thorn. Chiara lifted hers, closing her eyes as if savoring the smell. When all parties were settled, he began the story.

****

Rein leaned over Braelyn's shoulder to glance at the caller ID on her cell. His lip curled into a smirk. "One of my favorite humans is reaching out to you."

"Play nice, mate. Hey, Miller."

"Luv."

"She's not your love, asshole." Rein's enhanced hearing let him listen in on the conversation.

"Tell me, luv. Is the bugger plugged into your phone line?"

Braelyn walked away from Rein before his macho aggression tied him in knots. "No. He's just a vamp mix. Super hearing. What's up?"

"I've got several names for you." He went through the list, ending with Celene Bailey and Finley Sage. "None of these were on the list of descendants you're protecting."

"We don't have them. Just a sec." She held the phone away from her ear. "Honey, do you know anything about these women or men? Celene sounds familiar."

"Celene is the name Jace keeps mentioning." Rein crossed his thick, solid arms over his chest.

"You're right." Braelyn held the cell out so Miller could eavesdrop on the conversation.

Rein filled him in on the latest attempts to locate Jace's fellow captive. "Firebrands are scouring the area where Tyr and Dax found Jace. The better noses have been sniffing to find a trail. But because she disguised her scent in pine needles and scat, they're having trouble backtracking her."

"What about the other names?" asked Miller.

"I'll check, but I haven't heard them before." Rein reached into a pocket to retrieve a small notebook and pen.

"Did you catch all that, Miller? We do have Jace. You gave us her name the last time we talked. We have a line on Celene but haven't found her. We don't know about the others."

"I have a question for the enormous fanged one, luv."

Braelyn smiled while she handed over her phone. "He wants you."

Rein snarled but put the cell near his ear as Braelyn leaned close to listen. "Yeah. I'd love to chat with ya."

"Every time I settle in for a bit, the bad guys show up. I'm a careful bloke. It's not like I'm leaving a trail of breadcrumbs. At first, I thought it was coincidence. Bad luck. Whatever. Now I'm not so sure."

Rein was silent.

"You still there?" Miller sighed into the phone.

"Thinking."

"Think fast. I hate staying on too long."

"A powerful mage could scry. With your hopping all over the place, though, that gets dicey."

"Any other way? There's no tracer on me. I'm sure of that. I change places, names, use cash. I'm a pro at covering my trail."

"When you were almost nabbed, did a vamp bite

you?"

Braelyn arched a brow when she stared at her mate.

"One did. Sonofabitchin' bloke left a real mess on my neck. I snatched myself away from his choppers but almost bled out. Why?"

"If he was old and powerful, he could be tracking your blood. How much did he take?"

"Enough to make me know pain and pleasure. And I'm not into guys."

"That's how they're tracking you, then."

"Are there a lot of chaps out there who can do that sort of thing?" Miller sounded a little worried. He should be.

"Too many to identify."

"Anything I can do to counter it?"

"Have a mage spell your blood."

"I'd have to come in for that?"

Rein shrugged. "It's no simple thing."

"Can lots of your people do this spell?"

"I'm one."

"Is there anything you can't do, mate?"

"Yeah. Tolerate talking to you, asshole." Rein sneered into the phone, sorry Miller couldn't see his expression.

"Same. Tell luv I said ta."

"I'm all over that."

Braelyn snatched the phone before he could pop more shit. "Ta, Miller. Stay safe."

****

Celene pulled the bedspread up to her neck, sniveling, feeling sorry for herself, and tossing wet Kleenexes into a growing pile. No one to talk to. At least no one who was human or sane. Jace hadn't rescued her yet. What did that mean? Had she been caught? Could she find the new digs? Had she found no one to help? Or had she forgotten about Celene?

Stop, girl. Jace will come for me if she can. Now stop whining and get out of this damn bed before you kick your own ass.

In the kitchen, Celene wiped away her tears with the back of her hand, cracked an egg, and poured milk into the pancake flour. She set the table for one, cooked the thin batter on a griddle, and ate in silence, the only sound her fork clinking against the plate. After carrying her dirty dishes to the sink, she soaped the plate and flatware, rinsed and dried them. With the breakfast clean-up complete, she brewed a second cup of coffee, lit a fire, and grabbed *The Path,* opening to the next story, a tale from thousands of years ago. Or so the Cambion wrote.

Ohngel sat bare-footed and cross-legged on a rug, reciting his morning devotions, the daily routine of ablutions and sword practice completed.

His peace was disrupted by angry footsteps beating on the stone tiles as Gahya stormed into his quarters, stopping within a foot of him, her arms folded across her chest, pushing up her already ample breasts. "Did you see him last night?"

The warrior twisted his neck to gaze at her, his fiery wings tipped with razored blades, swooping out in a show of irritation. "Good day to you, Genitrix."

Hating the overcast skies with their dark clouds, Gahya rarely visited Angor where Ohngel chose to live near his fellow assassins among the unapologetic lawbreakers contained therein. They were the same detritus he and his brothers tracked, punished, and confined. But there was an honesty to their crimes which creatures in The Vast lacked, a place where the chosen ones marinated in false disguises.

"Yes. Good day." Gahya's foot tap-tap-tapped. "Well, did you see him last night?"

"Him being?"

"Gabriel."

"Yes." Ohngel's gaze fixed on her chest. He couldn't help himself. Damn lust was his go-to flaw. He cleared his throat, concentrating on lifting his eyes.

The goddess patted her blonde upswept hair, words spitting from her red lips. "He won."

"I heard."

Gahya's nostrils fluttered as she inhaled a slow breath. "He was lucky."

"Or allowed to win. Did you ever consider the OneCreator may control the outcome of Cee-lo?"

Her mouth fell open. Catching herself, she waved a dismissive hand through the air, continuing her rant. "Anyway, did Gabriel the prick tell you what he has done? It's outrageous."

"Yes. He created his own beings from the DNA of the OneCreator's Homo erectus. It's a good thing your demons didn't kill them all."

The Genitrix paced, vexed words emptying from her mouth like flotsam. "That's not all. He linked his species to mine by also using the blood of Aeternals to make what he calls his Homo sapiens."

She snarled, pacing from one side of his atrium to the other, the clack of her sandals loud on the tile. "The arrogance. Gabriel the prick says his beings are the greatest creation. Ludicrous. Mine are stronger, fiercer. Their desires drive them to survive. I made them in the perfect image of myself. They are pure and will outlive his weak, paltry humans. Another name he grants them." Her foot started its angry rhythm when she paused.

"The OneCreator seems unusually pleased with the prick and his Homo sapiens." Ohngel unfolded from

his position on the floor. When he stood toe-to-toe with the Genitrix, his fingers tickled along her arm.

She backed up, avoiding his touch. "Why do you think his humans are better than my creatures?"

Snapping out his wings, the warrior drew a sharp breath before he turned on his heel, crossing his living space, circumventing the pool in the center formed from rain that fell through the opening in the ceiling. "I don't believe they are better or worse."

From the portico behind his atrium, Ohngel gazed down on Earth, admiring it. It was vibrant with color. The blue of the oceans. The green of the forests. The white of snow-capped peaks. The energy of life unfolding, becoming.

Angor, his home, was often shrouded in fog and storm clouds, dim and colorless on most days, a palpable gloom ranging from shadow to darkness. Yet, the fickle weather could change in an instant—gale-like winds and tornadoes turning to gentle breezes, monsoon rains becoming light mists, or black skies heralding sunshine. The Vast, on the other hand, was relentless, everlasting light. But Earth was the best of both. Days filled with sun and nights of darkness. A time to grow. A time to shelter.

"How can his creations outshine my lovelies?" Gahya moved silently until she stood at his back, her hands caressing his shoulders.

"As I recollect, Gabriel spoke of their innocence."

She paused as if considering his words. "True."

"All this talk of innocence makes me hard." Ohngel slid black silk pants down his legs, freeing his aching cock as he turned to face her. "Come, Gahya, I have need of you."

She licked her lips, her throat bobbling with a swallow, his charm ample. Then she shook off his appeal.

"This first."

"As you wish. I'll start without you." Ohngel sank into pillows on the courtyard floor, spreading his knees wide. He fisted his member, stroking from crown to base. Through halting breaths, he rasped, "I like it better when your soft hand manipulates my flesh, but this will do. We can talk while I pleasure myself to the sweet cadence of your voice."

Gahya fell at his feet with her legs folded beneath her. She scooted between his thighs, fondling them, caressing his skin, her eyes locked on his hand as she stroked his huge erection.

"You know you want to do me," he said, a smile curving his lips.

"What is the OneCreator's plan for my Aeternals?" Gahya bit her lower lip.

Ohngel rocked his hips, increasing the speed and rhythm, adding to his pleasure. "I. Don't. Know." He snagged Gahya's hand, forcing it to ride his aroused flesh. "Harder, goddess." His fist clenched over hers, squeezing as his balls drew up and he exploded into the air.

After some moments, he spoke. "There now. I can concentrate."

"I can't." Bending her head, she reached out with her tongue to lick the head of his penis.

His partially flaccid member sprang to life. "Do it, Gahya."

"My gift to you." She wrapped her moist lips around the crown of his cock before she sucked him in deep. What was not in her mouth, she gripped, riding up and down his length, her slurping sounds pleasing to his ears.

Ohngel palmed the sides of her head, thrusting forward, fucking her mouth with a steady but quick cadence. "Yes. Take me to the back of your throat."

She reached down to cup his balls as she sucked harder.

The fire-winged warrior arched his back, pitched his hips, and restrained Gahya so she could not escape his plundering cock.

The assassin of the OneCreator, one of his Feared, erupted into her mouth, down her throat. He was a beast with insatiable appetites even he could not leash.

He pulled out inch by inch with a groan.

With a pat on her head, Ohngel sighed. "What were we discussing?"

"My creatures and Gabriel's Homo sapiens. Should I worry?" Gahya wiped a forearm across her lips, a very ungoddess-like gesture.

"The OneCreator and Gabriel were whispering about something."

"What?"

Ohngel shook his head. "Perhaps, they have another bet going."

"The OneCreator does not bet. He watches from the sidelines. I could seduce Gabriel into telling me."

"The prick would welcome your attention."

"Many do." She sniveled. "Are you not jealous?"

"Do you want me to be?"

"Yes. No. Jealousy bores me. Sex with the same male bores me."

"That's my little goddess. Self-absorbed to the core. You have no feelings for me or anyone besides yourself, Gahya."

"What does that matter?"

Ohngel stroked her cheek with a gentle hand. "It does not, but it should, my dear. I hope someday you find a male who says such things matter."

"No offense, Ohngel. Though I may be weaker in

strength than any of your gender, I am stronger in will, blacker of heart. That is how I control males."

"Ah. I feel you are correct, my lovely Genitrix, but do you never tire of the games?"

"They and desire are the only relief in this endless eternity. You have war. I have games."

"Seek meaning."

"Pfft. The search for meaning is a waste of time. Gabriel's creatures are innocent, you say?"

Ohngel shrugged. "His words."

"They need knowledge."

Her companion laughed. "The OneCreator is all knowledge."

"You give him too much credit. His fascination is with watching us best one another."

"Perhaps but be wary. Your hubris shows again like your rosy nipples through a transparent peplos."

"I believe I shall corrupt Gabriel's creatures with knowledge."

He shrugged. "How?"

She lifted her sultry eyes, dipping her chin, her smile coy. "By teaching them the pleasures of the flesh."

"All this villainous talk makes me hard again." Ohngel grabbed her wrist, whisking her beside him.

She leaned onto an elbow, her chin thrust forward. "I will seduce Gabriel for more information. Afterward, I will visit his creatures." Gahya rolled onto her back. "One more fuck, my love, before I am on my way."

He laughed. "While I satisfy you, why not consider leaving the prick's Homo sapiens alone? And granting your creatures a conscience?"

Ohngel had no idea why he cared, but he suspected he was more invested in both species than were Gahya or Gabriel. Another flaw? First, millennia of uncontrolled lust. Then, a niggling concern for lesser beings.

"Who needs a troublesome conscience, my love?" She spread her welcoming legs.

As a warrior, Ohngel favored experienced opponents, those who willingly took up arms, knowing what to expect on the battlefield. Aeternals and Homo sapiens, however, were unaware and ill-prepared. They were caught between the goddess's hubris and Gabriel's willfulness, pawns in a game of destiny. Both were chess pieces set adrift on the board of life to find their own way.

Thoughts for another time. His lust pushed aside any serious contemplation as Ohngel thrust into the eager but uncaring goddess.

Celene closed the book, sad that Gahya and Gabriel tossed aside their creations as if they were failed, forgotten experiments. The whole world was adrift. She was forgotten. Humans could benefit from more guidance. And from what she'd seen of Aeternals, they were in desperate need of a strong hand. Along with a boot to the jaw.

Though Lort did not allow her any outdoor time since Jace's escape, he provided workout equipment, books, and movies. But she missed the sun on her skin, its warmth, its caress. She missed the sound of another human voice. One day turned endlessly into another. Why keep going? She swung her legs onto the couch, leaned her head on the arm, and closed her eyes. To hell with her daily schedule. Celene deserved a pout-day.

Chapter Fifteen

Chiara's head swiveled from Dax to Thorn. The vampire explained it all. The demons and warlock who nearly killed him and removed a chip from his arm. The guys who came to her cabin. Their escape.

Fin followed along with the conversation, too, a possessive hand stroking Thorn's thigh.

"Chiara," the shifter said. *Wolf*? He looked like a wolf. It was his shaggy hair and amber eyes. He stirred more sugar into his coffee. "You're a witch?"

"That's what I'm told."

"You suspect Blood Coven?" he asked Dax.

"It makes the most sense. How, I don't know. She's never been on Scath. Says she's been this way for years." He combed nervous fingers through his midnight hair.

Chiara noticed Dax's eyes were warmer than they had been when she first found him. They were still dark, but rather than as cold as obsidian, they reminded her of black velvet.

"You don't know the latest theory?" Thorn sipped his coffee from a huge mug.

"No. What?" asked Dax.

The shifter's laugh was deep. "New info out of Alarik's office says descendants turn when they have a relationship with a Firebrand. A close relationship." He squeezed Fin's hand.

Chiara gave the shortened version of how Dax had rescued her from a burning car when she was a kid.

"Why were you close by?" Thorn grabbed Fin's hand, kissing it after she brushed his hair off his face.

"Two Incubutts escaped from the gaffers in the Cubes. I was skirting the woods in pursuit. Heard the crash."

Propping his scuffed cowboy boots up on the table, the shifter chuckled again. "You're her spark, vampire. If you can't beat 'em, join 'em." He shook his thumb in Fin's direction.

Chiara noticed her pale purple eyes. "You're a witch, too?"

"She is," said Thorn. "Gotta be Blood Coven variety cause her eyes weren't this way until … well … you know."

Fin's flawless deep bronze skin reddened.

He locked an arm around her neck, kissing the tight curls on her head. "See, Dax. I jumpstarted Fin. I'm loving it."

Dax bounded off his chair to pace the room. "I'm no damn catalyst for a Blood Coven descendant."

"Don't mind him," said Chiara. "He gets all hangry when he hasn't fed."

Thorn's brows arched while Dax stopped to glare. "Does everything you think have to cross your lips? Have you heard of filters?"

"Dax, man. She's been your meal on wheels?" The wolf's amber eyes locked on her. "Not your usual type." He broke contact to sip his coffee.

The vampire snarled while resuming his back and forth. "Look. I saved her life when she was ten years old. She's grateful. That's all."

Chiara laughed.

"What is so fucking funny all the time?" he asked. He paused to glare.

"You. You refuse to recognize we might have a connection. Head. Buried. Sand. Mean anything?"

"We have no connection. Let's cut the bullshit and get home. I've got serious news for Kole. Once we're there, the Firebrands will protect you both."

"I'll be the one protecting Fin." Thorn growled, moving the woman closer to his side, claws punching through his fingertips.

Chiara felt a stab of … not exactly jealousy … maybe sadness. Dax didn't swear he would protect her. He was handing her off to somebody else.

"Your biz. Here's what's happened." Dax continued his story of how an army gathered outside the Missoula portal, probably a site Dante shared with them. "Two officers snagged jumpers. I don't think they knew how to use them, but… Shit."

Dax stopped mid-stride.

"What?" asked Thorn.

"That's who I saw in the sports car talking to the drug dealers I was tailing. That's why they're on my ass. The male was Boden, the director of the Ministry of Compliance. He must be neck deep in Arisen Dawn. If his ministry is supplying jumpers to Cerberus's assholes, things just went from shitty to shittier to shittiest. Let Kole know."

"I'll report in. Guys are scouring the forest where they almost took Fin. They haven't headed this way yet, but they will when they expand their search. My plan was to leave tomorrow. I was going to go through the Bozeman portal."

Fin punched his shoulder. "You were? When were you going to tell me?"

"Later today. For your safety, Fin darlin', you have to come to Scath."

"Do I have a choice in this?"

"No," Thorn growled. "You know you're staying with the wolf."

She popped off the couch, grabbed the tray, and slammed empty cups onto it. "I'll be cleaning in the kitchen. If you were smart, you'll come in to explain yourself."

Thorn shot up to snatch the tray out of her hands. "I'm smart, darlin'. A genius. Let me lay out all the advantages for you." With one hand gripping the tray, the other slipped to her ass, rubbing it as they left the room.

Chiara watched the couple leave the room, Thorn groveling and Fin silent. Despite a spat, they cared for one another. "You know, Dax, I'm probably not in danger. They were after you. If you want to leave me, it's fine. I've disappeared before. I can do it again."

"Orders are clear. We bring in all Blood Coven descendants. It's likely you are one. You'll go to Scath where a healer will test you to find out for sure. If not, you can return. But if you are, you'll move into the stronghold. For your safety."

"Thanks for planning out my life. I must be such a burden."

He twisted his head toward her, seeming puzzled by her mood. "Stop with the self-pity. You saw what those males can do. Besides, you already agreed to go this route. What's wrong now?"

What was wrong? Dax was wrong. He didn't caress her thigh or pat her ass. Denying any connection between them, any spark of attraction, he treated her like a millstone he couldn't wait to pass on to someone else. Face it, he hurt her feelings without even knowing he was doing it. He chipped away at her memories of him as her hero, her ideal man. If he wasn't more careful, all his knightly armor would be tarnished.

But he was right. Besides, maybe on Scath she would also get answers about herself. Answers she needed. "Nothing. Just a momentary slip. Of course, I'm going."

****

Once inside, Jace yelled over the loud music.

"This is the famous Blood Shed?"

"Yep." While Galena strutted into the bar, wearing an ass-high skirt, Jace assessed her own figure along with her conservative wardrobe. The long-legged Amazon had it all. Beautiful face. No flab on a body that turned men's heads. And *beaucoup* personality.

The only thing Jace had going for her was long strawberry-blonde hair. It had highlights and shine if she soaked it in conditioner and brushed the hell out of it every night.

Celene used to do that.

To pass the time, the two captive women also gave each other manicures and pedicures, having negotiated with Lort to order stuff from a beauty supply catalogue. Her friend chose wild polish colors, as wild as her daredevil spirit. Orgasm Blue. First Kiss Red. Lickable Lavender.

Jace chose Sweet Coral. Pink Dreams. Mundane Mauve. *Boring.*

Together, they exercised, brushed each other's hair, read aloud, shared stories, and planned an escape. She had to find Celene. The Firebrands and Skyler were working on it, but no progress yet.

Her thoughts turned back to the Amazon Firebrand who smoothed out the lines of a tight sweater which called attention to her large breasts. Jace glanced down at her own meager chest. No wonder Tyr never looked at her as if she were a piece of candy. She was still too skinny, needing to put on more weight after her imprisonment and escape.

"This is where we usually sit." Galena pointed to three couches and a high table with stools off to the side where Chay, Margo, Rein, and Braelyn were chatting. Acknowledging the others, the Amazon lowered her shapely self onto one of the sofas, tugging Jace's arm.

She signaled for a waitress and held up two fingers. "I know just what you need, girl."

"I'm not much of a drinker." Jace crossed her legs, hoping they looked good with her full skirt. "When I do drink, I go for red wine. Something like a Pinot."

Galena had other plans, though. "Uh-huh. Not tonight."

The bar quieted. Heads turned. Ram swaggered through the door with a possessive arm looped over Denim's shoulder, his long caramel-streaked hair flowing down his back. Women heaved breathy sighs at the handsome, sexy satyr Firebrand. After he sank his gorgeous ass onto the opposite couch with his mate tucked against his side, talk in the Shed picked up again.

Jace wondered if it bothered Denim when everyone ogled her man. His eyes, however, were on his mate. His eyes, his hands, and his lips now that they were seated.

"Where's the kid, girlfriend?" asked Galena.

"It's date night." Denim broke from Ram's kiss. "Jonquil is with her grandpa."

The satyr didn't look happy to be interrupted. In fact, the minute Denim finished talking, he got back to business.

Another buzz disrupted the bar. Tyr and Brak strode in with two other males on their heels. All in black, they moved like storm clouds. The crowd, sensing danger, cleared a path as the males carved their way toward the Firebrands' section.

The warlock with a silver piercing through his brow, spiked black hair, and face tat took her breath. His don't-mess-with-me swagger screamed sex on a popsicle stick. But the man was totally wrong for her.

Tell that to her racing heart. It was currently doing a 100-meter sprint. *Thump, thump, thump*. She palmed her cheek. *Hot.* Her body also moistened in the most embarrassing place as she envisioned him throwing her onto a bed and pressing down on her with his solid weight.

"What's wrong?" Galena followed her line of sight. "Brak or Tyr? Surely not their tails, Sig or Bade. They're just too immature. Now Brak's a big guy. He acts young sometimes, but I hear he's a beast in bed. Carnal demon. If you get my drift. Tyr, rumor has it, is all wild warlock. He used to be kind of a naive kid, but then his life took a left turn. When he was a rookie Firebrand, he lost a friend. That's his story to tell, but around the same time, Rein's sister, Elisabeta, dumped him. The change was overnight. No more Mr. Nice Guy. The feral kill-em-with-a-dick-and-a-dagger vibe gets him lots of action."

"Oh. I'm not…"

"It's the warlock." Galena eyed Jace from head to toe. "You are so not his type, girl."

Jace picked up the glass of dark and dangerous the waitress delivered. "I agree, but when I see him my Hyde becomes Jekyll. I become another person. I like structure, predictability. I get up at the same time each morning and go to bed at the same time each night. I avoid taking risks and like men who wear suits, not bike leathers. When I see Tyr, I feel like I'm jumping out of a plane without a parachute." Taking a sip of the drink, she coughed.

Galena smacked a palm on her back. "Good stuff, huh? Demon Rum. Hell, girl, if we only went for what's right, sex would get old fast. Expand your horizons."

Leaning closer to Galena, Jace whispered in her ear. "If I wanted his attention, how would I get it?"

The Amazon twisted in her seat to unbutton Jace's sensible cardigan until the plump tops of her breasts and her lacy push-up bra showed. "Be aggressive. Lesson one, a male's eyes are connected to his penis." Leaning closer, Galena shared other pertinent info about men, the bar, and Aeternals in general.

When the four men reached the Firebrand section, Tyr and Brak took the remaining couch while Sig and Bade pulled over two stools.

Jezzi sauntered over to join the crowd. "Who wants to share a seat?"

When every arm except Tyr's shot into the air, Jace smiled.

The sleek black-haired panther shifter sank onto Brak's lap, wrapping an arm around his shoulder.

Oh, for that kind of confidence.

Jace nodded at the new arrivals.

"What's wrong with me?" Sig frowned at Jezzi. "I have a lap I'd gladly share."

"Nothing, honey. I just like my males old enough to shave."

"I shave." His brows drew into an angry slash as he stroked his cheek with the palm of his hand, probably feeling for whiskers.

The waitress dropped off four beers as Tyr pointed toward Galena and Jace. "Get 'em another of whatever they're having."

"What about the two lovebirds?" The waitress pointed at Ram and Denim.

"Why not? Maybe they'll unlock lips and come up for air soon."

To hell with it. Aggressive.

Jace leaned in, her sweater dangerously gaping open, and crooked her finger at Tyr. He tilted toward her. "Do you dance?"

"Yeah." He sat back. As if he finally caught on, he lurched forward, his eyes latching onto the swells of her breasts. "Let's do it."

The warlock Firebrand with hard, carved muscles stood, the light glinting off the silver through his brow.

****

Tyr clasped Jace's smaller hand, running his thumb along the delicate back of her fingers. The female was wearing black flats and a full skirt which touched her knees. *Sexy*. He had no explanation for the crazy thought. He preferred curvy, aggressive females with big boobs who wore short tight skirts and fucking high heels. This female was not in the same game. *Damn*. She wasn't even in the same ballpark. Nonetheless, she held his attention. Must be the unbuttoned sweater. Just one more pearl undone would be great. What he wouldn't do to see all her delectable flesh. To have his mouth on her.

When they hit the dance floor, the DJ switched to the slow and soft "First Time Ever I Saw Your Face." Tyr could dance to anything, but this was his preferred music, a tune where he could shuffle his feet while his body seduced his partner.

With an arm wrapped around Jace's waist, he let a hand on the other rove down to the curve above her ass. Skinny but nice. She needed a few pounds, but that didn't take away the rounded appeal of her buttocks.

In time to the sultry sounds of Roberta Flack, he swayed with Jace locked in his embrace. "Take out the ponytail. I like your hair loose."

When she reached behind her head to tear out the scarf, her breasts arched against his chest. Tyr moaned while he rubbed his cheek in her hair. *Silky*. She smelled like fresh lemons.

"Lace your arms around my neck. I want to feel you against me."

The female surprised him. Not only did she do as he commanded, but she ran her fingers through his spiked hair. He drew a deep breath, eyes closed, as she nibbled her way up his neck, her lips enticingly warm.

Tyr bent to capture her mouth in a hot, wet kiss which had his cock saluting. To show Jace what he wanted, he grasped her hips in both hands, pulling her against his arousal while he ground into her in time to the music.

She moaned into his mouth, her tongue dancing the tango with his.

Tyr wasn't one for a lot of foreplay. He broke off the kiss. "Why do you like me?"

"You make me feel safe. Why do you like me?"

"You make me feel protective." He grabbed her hand to lead her toward the exit.

Though the female brought out his uncharacteristic your-my-female-and-I'm-gonna-keep-you-safe genes, Tyr should have added how she made him horny as hell. In addition to his gorilla chest-pounding, having Jace in his arms ratcheted his lust up several notches until he had to have her horizontal. Right now.

She tugged back. "Galena said the rooms are that way." She waved her thumb toward the back of the Shed.

"They are. I'm looking for a little more privacy."

A quick fuck in a backroom was his MO, but Jace wasn't that kind of female. *No.* She was a knee-length-skirt female. *The worst.* They tied a male up in knots, cut off his balls, and trapped him into mating. But here he was, escorting her out the door, all rational thought sprinting from his brain. He hoped he'd draw the line long before she tied him down with a strong half-hitch.

Good plan. Fuck and forget.

Outside, he drew her in for another kiss, held her close, and whispered in her ear. "Is this what you want?"

Her smoky blue eyes fixed on him as she nodded.

They portaled to outside his place, arm-in-arm, their palavering easy. He escorted her to his studio apartment in Covenkirk. It was small, a couch which converted to a bed, a kitchen, a bathroom. He didn't have time to care for anything bigger, but he kinda regretted not being able to show off something more spectacular.

Hell.

He forgot to make the bed. The sheets were clean, though. The floor wasn't covered in discarded clothes.

With his tongue down Jace's throat, he backed her up until her legs ran into the mattress. He explored every sweet crevice of her mouth as he unbuttoned each tiny pearl. He slipped the sweater down her arms, letting it fall to the carpet.

Breaking from her lips, he gripped her shoulders, pushed her away, and admired the view. She might dress like the girl next door on the outside, but inside was a different story. She was all siren, luscious curves and soft flesh. No red bra today. She wore a see-through black one. Ripe nipples stood out behind the sexier-than-hell bit of lace. He dropped his head to suck a nub into his mouth. He nipped and licked until the fabric was wet and the bud peaked.

Jace arched into him as he reached behind her to unclasp her bra.

When he heard the snap, he slipped the straps off her shoulders. Tyr molded his hand to her firm mounds while gazing into her hooded eyes. He watched her reaction as he stroked, licked, and plumped. First one breast. Then the other. "Do you like that?"

Her voice was sexy, throaty. "Yes."

He ripped off his jacket, dropping it to the floor.

Grabbing the hem of his shirt, she yanked the whole thing over his head. Her roving hands warmed his bared skin.

Her eyes widened. Amazement? Thrill? Disgust? "You have rings through your nipples."

"Uh-huh." Tyr pulled her in, skin to skin, letting her feel his piercings up close and personal.

Jace dipped her head and tugged on a nipple ring with her teeth. "I like it." She licked around it.

That answered the question. The female was thrilled.

"Pull harder." Tyr pressed the back of Jace's head, his arousal biting into his zipper.

Damned if she didn't. She plucked at it until a delicious pain rode through his body. He shoved a knee between her legs and sent her falling to the bed. As he dropped onto her, he bunched her full skirt to the waist.

She helped him by wiggling out of her panties while he rolled to the side, watching. Skinny but perfect. Pale skin. Long legs and strawberry curls where her thighs met. "Bend your knees. I want to see you."

Her flesh turned a rosy pink, but she did as he asked. Tyr kneeled between her legs, pushing them wider. His eyes skimmed from her face to her pussy. "Delicious."

He kissed the inside of her thighs, heading toward her sweet spot.

Her hands fisted his hair. "Please."

"Please what? What do you want?"

"I can't."

"Sure you can." He flicked his tongue between her wet folds as she squirmed in his hold. He peeked into her half-lidded eyes. "Do you want that?"

"Yes."

He sucked on her clit. With a grin, he stopped. "How about that?"

"Uh-huh."

"Then I better get serious." Tyr ducked his head

between her legs to tease as she ground against his mouth.

"More." Jace's hips bounced off the bed.

Tyr's tongue invaded her. Fierce, wild, he plunged into her pussy as she cried out, an orgasm exploding through her, making her entire body quake.

He continued his attack until she fell back against the pillow with a sigh. He rolled off to shuck his leathers.

His pants gone, Jace's eyes locked on him, and his cock grew painfully hard.

She swallowed, her throat bobbling. "You're pierced there, too."

"You'll love it." He slid between her thighs, palmed her breast again, and rolled a nipple between his fingers.

Her fingers traveled to his cock. She gripped him, softly exploring.

"You can squeeze tighter." He groaned as her hand stroked from tip to base. "That's it. Harder." He pushed into her fist, feeling the tug on his piercing. He loved the pain and pleasure of it.

"Are you wet?" His fingers explored her sex as she continued to pump him. He thrust one in and then another as she arched into him. "You're so ready for me. Playtime's over."

He grabbed her wrists in one hand, holding them above her head, nudging her with his cock, taunting between her folds. "You want it? Ask me nice and I'll share."

Her heels dug into his ass. "I want you, Tyr."

He couldn't wait any longer. He thrust his hips forward, eager to feel her muscles tighten around his shaft. This conservative sweater girl with the hot pussy.

She muffled a groan as he buried himself balls deep in her tight sheath.

"Are you okay?" he asked. He released her hands.

"Give me a minute."

He waited until her hips began a slow undulation.

"Tyr, you feel so good." Her soft, warm hands caressed his shoulders and his back.

He picked up the rhythm, anxious to feel her come all over him. Faster, he rolled in and out. The friction nearly unbearable.

Jace matched him thrust for thrust. As he drew out and slammed back in, her nails scraped down his back, drawing blood. His female was wild. The things he was going to show her. Things she'd probably never done before.

"Come for me now," he ordered, holding back for her.

When her lips tugged on his nipple ring, his abs tightened. Frantically, he pounded into Jace, shoving them both toward ecstasy. She cried out, her hips slamming into him, her spasms rippling along his cock.

Once he was sure she'd reached her pleasure, he fucked her harder and faster until he erupted, his semen spilling into this female. Over and over. Again and again. Finally, he froze and raised onto stiff forearms, keeping his weight off her.

"Jace" was all he could mutter as he rolled to the side, taking her with him, wrapping her in his arms. Her head rested against his shoulder.

Damn.

That felt good. He made it a rule never to sleep over with a female. Once the deed was done, he would get up, slip into his duds, and saunter off. But this time was different. *How do you kick a female out of your own bed?* See, there was the problem with bringing one home. Why this time? Why Jace? He thought about the predicament as he closed his eyes. Just for a little bit. He wouldn't sleep. Next thing he knew, someone was calling his name, jiggling his shoulder while light streamed in the window.

"Tyr. Wake up. It's morning. I have to get back to the stronghold."

He fell asleep with a female in his bed. Jace was beside him with ruffled sex hair, swollen kissable lips, and a sheet barely covering her breasts.

He was fucked.

Little Miss Full-Skirt-To-The-Knees was hot. His gaze settled on her breasts. No hiding herself from him. No blush. He remembered those tasty things. Still groggy, he swung his legs over the mattress and stood up, turning to face the female in his bed as he stretched his arms high over his head and arched his back.

Her eyes locked on his dick as if she wanted it. He looked down, and it jumped to life on cue. "When you stare at my cock, I get all kinds of dirty thoughts."

She arched her brows, all innocent like. "So do I. Are you going to do anything about them?"

Tyr crawled back into bed, his palm landing between her thighs. "What's say we play around a little bit?"

Jace laughed but spread her legs wider, her nipples already tight peaks.

When he gazed into her eyes before taking her mouth, a grin tugged at his lips. He stared into smoky lavender irises like Scottish heather. No more dusty blues. "I think I jumpstarted your witch. Come give us a nice morning fuck."

Chapter Sixteen

Chiara perched on a stool in Thorn's kitchen following an early breakfast and clean-up. After two nights at the ranch, they readied to leave. Fin had just asked a question, though, and she hesitated to answer, drumming her fingers on the counter instead.

"Too personal? Sorry. I don't always have a filter." Fin stretched onto her toes, putting away cups in an upper cabinet. "Thorn loves my witch gift. It's pretty weak now, but he says it'll get stronger with use and training. I just wondered what yours was."

"I've had mine since Dax rescued me when I was a kid."

"Cool. What is it?" She pursed her lips. "Sorry. I asked again. Nosy me."

Chiara was reluctant to share. Obviously, Fin read her expression. No poker face for her. After all these years, she still wasn't at peace with what she could do. Too long she'd seen herself as unnatural. An abomination. A killer.

Yet here was a woman like her in many ways. The first Chiara had ever met. Thorn and Dax believed they both descended from the powerful ancients, the Blood Coven. Something straight out of a horror film.

With a deep sigh, Chiara said, "I can heal. The flip side is, I can also hurt people."

"Sounds like a good-news-bad-news kind of thing."

"It is."

Fin leaned against the counter, crossing her arms. "Does it happen accidentally? I mean without your wanting it to?"

"Sometimes. It's the reason I ran to the middle of

nowhere." Chiara rested an elbow on the table. "Years after Dax saved me, I … killed someone because I knew nothing about my power."

"Wait. You killed someone?"

"Yeah. He was scum, but he was a human being."

"You didn't know, honey." Fin pulled a stool beside her, running a hand down Chiara's arm.

"You said you weren't surprised to see Thorn turn into a wolf. Why?"

Fin talked over her shoulder while she searched through cabinets. "My mom. She was a paranoid schizophrenic who ranted about superhuman beings. Vampires, shifters, demons. I didn't believe her, of course. No one did. When I saw Thorn, things snapped into place. I was surprised but not shocked to find a man who could shift into a wolf. On top of it, there was something special about Thorn. I melt when he talks. If he touches me, I'm gooey. Sappy, huh? Just for him, though. Most guys have never turned me on. What about you and the vampire?" She waved a bag of trail mix in the air.

Chiara nodded as Fin tossed the snack into a cardboard box for the trip. "I've loved Dax in one way or another since he rescued me. For years, he was a superhero who fought off my nightmares. As I matured, he changed from savior to hot fantasy."

"So, the two of you are … an item?"

"No. Almost, a couple of times. And he feeds from me because he has no choice. I think he gets turned on when he does, but afterward the vampire's all pissy about it."

"You want him?"

Chiara sighed. "I do."

"You hang in there, honey. He sure looks at you like he's got the hots."

****

Thorn loaded supplies and duffels into the backend of the She Beast.

"Do you have weapons?" asked Dax.

"Do I have weapons? Am I hung like a stallion? Firepower and blades are in a duffel on the front passenger floor." He opened another bag, passing Dax a sheath, a short sword, and a Sig Sauer automatic.

The vampire strapped on the scabbard, sliding the blade into it. He jacked the gun into his waistband. "What did Kole say when you contacted him?"

Thorn ran fingers through his hair, brushing the long strands out of his eyes. The vampire seemed different. Clear-headed. Concerned. Usually Dax hid in a shadowy corner, keeping his mouth shut while the Firebrands discussed business. It was always hard to tell if he gave a shit or not about a sitch. He skirted the edge. Like all of them, the Phoenix called him to the cause. But today? Today, he acted as if he cared.

Thorn slammed the truck gate shut. "He's sending some guys to check out the Missoula jump point. I told them you said to be careful. Not to take the portal to Earth. They'll meet us when we come through from Bozeman. I'll call when we get close."

When Thorn jerked his head around, he sniffed the air. "Shit." He sniffed again. "We've got demons, satyrs, and a witch heading our way."

Dax sprinted toward the house. His boots hitting the porch, he burst through the door, shouting. "Females. The truck. Now."

Dax hustled Chiara along by her arm. Fin ran behind them, holding a small box.

"We've got company. Get your asses in the truck." Thorn grabbed the box, boosting Fin into the front of the cab.

Dax shoved Chiara through the backseat door. He crawled in after her.

Thorn charged around the She Beast, climbed into the driver's side, and started the engine, peeling out, churning gravel. Sticking his head out the window, he spied a squad of Arisen Dawn soldiers break from the surrounding forest. When shots pinged the truck, Dax threw his body across Chiara. Thorn's free hand cupped Fin's neck to push her to the floor.

A witch materialized in the middle of the road, blocking the She Beast.

"What the fuck?" Not hesitating, Thorn gunned it, heading straight for her.

She disappeared as the air around her shimmered, her molecules reforming in the truck bed.

"Teleportation spell. Get flat on the floor now," shouted Dax.

Thorn kept an eye on his rearview mirror as the powerful vampire crawled through his window. He flung himself into the backend.

As the mage came at him, Dax gripped the top of the truck and kicked his legs out, landing a strike to the female's jaw. She flew onto her back.

Snapping to her feet, she threw a spell at Dax, who didn't duck in time.

Damn. A boulder to the chin. Thorn thought that must hurt.

The female smiled. In slow motion, the arm at her side floated up, her wrist bent, and her hand shot out. She mouthed some mumbo-jumbo.

When Thorn swerved, he glanced back at the road to steady the She Beast. He returned his gaze to the rearview mirror to watch the show.

Dax was faster than her spell. He drew the Sig and fired. Dead center forehead. Witch brains all over the truck bed. Least stupid wins.

Removing the sword from the scabbard, Dax lobbed off her head. He tossed both body parts out the backend.

The vamp slid back inside through the open window. Once seated, he lifted Chiara from the floor, cradling her in his arms. “We’re okay for now.” He tapped Thorn on the shoulder. “Who do you think they were looking for? Chiara and me or you and Fin?”

“Since you escaped in a car, they couldn’t have followed you without scrying. Most likely, they tracked me to my ranch after I rescued Fin.”

“What do you mean by scrying?” asked Chiara.

Thorn met her gaze in the rearview mirror. “Some witches and warlocks use things like crystal balls, mirrors, water to find people. It’s a gift. Of course, it helps if they have a personal item.”

Fin braced a hand on the dashboard when the road got bumpy. “What happens now?”

Dax still cradled Chiara. He showed the signs of a possessive vampire.

Interesting.

Thorn patted Fin’s leg. “It’ll take them time to regroup. Hard to track a moving vehicle, but they gotta figure we’re headed to the closest portal. If we make Bozeman to cross first, we’ll be okay.”

Chiara’s lips squeezed tight. “If I’m the reason they found us, drop me off. They could have been at my cabin, grabbing a lot of personal stuff to do that scrying thing. I’m not getting the rest of you in trouble.”

Dax snarled. “Fuck no. You are with me. Wipe anything else from your little witch brain. Thorn, crank up the She Beast. Let’s see what she can do.”

Yep. Protective. Interesting.

****

"Been here. Done this." Dax poked an elbow out the front passenger window, the cool air refreshing. He and Fin had switched places.

Thorn parked the She Beast on the side of the road, tilting it into an embankment. "The portal is compromised?"

Dax eyed the barrier blocking the street. "Yep."

The wolf tapped his D-chip to let Kole in on the news. He thumped his wrist again to disconnect, sharing the conversation. "I told the commander we're shit out of luck in Bozeman. He asked us to scout it out tonight."

"A new motel. Another recon. I never thought I'd be happy to get home." Dax scrubbed a fist across his jaw. "This is Missoula all over again."

Thorn threw the truck into gear to take off, none of his usual squealing tires.

When they checked into a seedy motel, Thorn asked, "How do you want to divvy up the beds, Dax?"

"You and Fin in a room. Chiara and I'll take the other."

Thorn flashed a wide, wolfy grin at the vampire.

"Knock it off, shifter."

After a shower and a fast meal, he and Thorn parked near the barricade again. In response to the shifter, Dax smirked, raising his arm for a little show-and-tell when Thorn suggested they meet at the same spot in precisely an hour. "Does it look like I have a watch?"

"Oh, yeah. In that case, after the recon we'll connect in my room to share war stories. Whenever."

"Works for me."

Thorn opened the truck door, stripped, and laid his folded clothes onto the seat. After an explosion of color followed by loud pops, he stared at Dax through feral amber eyes as he padded toward the nearest barricade.

Dax shadowflashed to a dark spot further down the road beyond the barriers. After four more jumps, he hid near the parking garage with the portal. As in Missoula, American soldiers milled outside, some standing guard with rifles, some armed with M2 50s, and some behind muzzle-loading mortars aimed at the gateway.

Tents lined the street. He counted a company of men, no more than two hundred. His guesstimate included some who might be resting inside.

Sneaking from shadow to shadow, Dax staked out foot soldiers, officers, and sleeping quarters. Three helos parked like cars on the road. These men were here for the long haul. Aeternals exiting the portal in Bozeman would be walking into a trap.

After about forty-five minutes of flashing around, the vampire's blood supply was depleted. Not wanting to tap the little witch again, he planned to find a harmless female but go through with the bite this time. To hell with his promise. Lancing a Blood Coven descendant who claimed to love him was crazy. If his *frerons* were any indication, repeated sips from Chiara's neck could lead to the mating call. He would not do that to her. Even he wasn't that cruel.

So Dax waited outside a bar until a shapely blonde stepped out for a smoke. She grasped a cigarette between two fingers, lighting it. *Hiss*. Inhale. Exhale. He staggered toward her as if he was drunk on too many beers. When she saw him, she didn't react, but as he got closer, she recoiled, the cigarette falling from her lips. Natural human response to a predator. Like any of his breed, he calmed her. She relaxed against the old bricks, shooting him an enticing smile.

Standing toe-to-toe, he trailed fingers down her

arms, traced her breasts, and compelled her to sweep her hair away from her neck. She was cooperative, not too bad looking. But Dax didn't care. He was here for the plump vein. He pressed his chest against her boobs while licking her throbbing pulse. She arched into him.

When his erection swelled, he thought he might enjoy some action. Fangs shot from his gums, and he scraped them along the female's neck. With a quick stab, he pierced her flesh, letting blood flow into his mouth. Just as fast, he pulled out. Dazed, the female bobbled. Clasping her arm until she was steadier on her feet, Dax wiped her memory.

He flashed around the corner of the bar, hiding in the shadows. Disgusted with himself. His slip seemed like a betrayal of Chiara. He didn't want emotional ties.

The little witch has ruined me. I'll starve if I can't tap a vein. I want her on my tongue. Her nectar, pure, innocent, and scented with unique spices.

He returned to the motel room in a pissy, snarly mood. Once the meet with Thorn was behind him, he'd show Chiara what an aroused, thirsty vampire was like. No more holding back. Tonight, she would take all of him. She'd let him go once she realized she couldn't possibly love a monster, especially one who didn't save his mother or beloved sister.

The door opened and an unhappy Thorn stormed in. Dax rose onto his elbows, having stretched out on the bed. After the shifter relayed intel about two tanks with guns aimed on the portal, he shared his news.

Thorn tapped his wrist to phone Kole.

Dax swung his legs over the side. "Tell him they've got three Black Hawks, M2 50s, and muzzle-loading mortars."

"Got it." Thorn relayed Dax's intel before he disconnected. "I told Kole not to come through at

Bozeman." Running fingers through the straw-colored hair hanging in his face, Thorn threw himself into a chair. "Logan says to head up the road for thirty minutes to Livingston. It's a small town along the Yellowstone River. Less traveled portal. We'll take off at first light to give the ladies some rest."

Dax strode toward the door.

"You okay, *freron*? You're looking a little pale. Need to feed?"

"Yeah."

"Chiara?"

"Seems so."

Thorn shot him a knowing grin. "Watch it. You might get attached."

Dax's jaw snapped tight, his teeth grinding together. "Never. Attachment makes males weak."

A chuckle escaped Thorn's lips. "I'm interested to hear you share your misguided belief with Rein or Kole. Remind me to duck. Send my Fin over when you go next door to your Chiara."

"Not my Chiara."

"Whatever you say, bloodsucker."

****

Chiara was on the bed with Fin, watching a game show when she heard the snick of the lock.

Dax pushed through the door, brushing his long black hair over his shoulder. His mouth was a hard slash, his teeth gritted. The news wasn't good.

Fin turned off the TV to say her goodbyes, looking extremely excited to join Thorn.

Setting the book on a side table, Chiara swung her legs to the floor. "Bad day at the office? Home for dinner, dear?"

Dax aimed his cold, obsidian eyes shot with red at her, a sure sign he was hungry. Gone were the black velvet irises. She paused, almost frightened. *But no.* This was the man she loved. He was surly, dangerous, proud. Despite his denials, he was also protective and honorable. She didn't know why he couldn't see himself for who he was.

Chiara sashayed over to her vampire, sweeping the curly hair from her neck. "Dinner served."

Dax twisted an arm behind her. When he tangled his hand in her tresses, he push-walked her toward the bed. "No rules, little witch."

"When you put it so sweetly, how can…"

"Quiet. You're about to be fucked by over two-hundred-and-fifty pounds of thirsty vampire." He captured her lips in a rough kiss, shoving her onto the mattress.

When he climbed on top, Chiara curled her fingers around his neck to pull him in tighter. Tonight, he belonged to her.

Weighing her down, he used a knee to part her thighs while crumpling her gown to her waist. He ripped off her panties, thrusting his tongue into her mouth. His aggression was palpable, the air shimmering with his hungry savagery.

Chiara sucked, licked, and stroked his tongue. Maybe he didn't love her, but he would change. She would change him.

Her fingers delved between their bodies, searching for his zipper. She pulled it down, grasping his hard length. Setting her palm on fire, his cock pulsed, warm flesh over hot steel. She coiled her fist around its thickness, stroking him. Up. Down.

Dax moaned while he thrust into her hand. He shimmied his pants to his knees as she continued to pump his shaft, gliding from crown to root, using his sounds to guide her.

Dax broke from the kiss, leaving Chiara's lips cold. "Harder. Always harder."

She obliged. When his palm traveled to the cleft between her legs, she released him.

"So wet, little witch."

"Dax." Chiara moaned softly, rocking into his hand.

He teased her, stroking her engorged clit, dipping between her folds. A finger invaded her. In. Out. He removed it to plunge in with two, his rhythm faster. But he gave her no release.

Chiara arched into his strokes while her hands skimmed his muscled shoulders, his biceps. When she caressed his Phoenix brand, she imagined the feathers trembling at her touch. She moved on to his chest, avoiding the gruesome necklace of fangs hanging between them.

Dax removed his fingers, leaving her whimpering, empty. When he positioned himself at the entrance to her sex, she tightened her grip on his shoulders in anticipation. She was eager for Dax, this wild, nearly feral vampire who made fierce love to her.

He leveraged his hips forward, burying his cock deep with a single powerful stab.

Chiara cried out. She expected the pain, but still it hurt. Her eyes watered despite her agonized joy at finally having Dax inside her.

He jerked away, almost pulling out. "What the fuck? You're a virgin."

Her breaths were ragged as she struggled against the shock. This couldn't be what all the books talked about. There had to be more to it. She gripped Dax's face between her hands, tears wetting her cheeks. "Please don't stop. I want this. I want you."

His eyes glowed, no longer dead, no longer cold.

He nuzzled her neck, his warm lips pressing against her, his moans throaty. Sliding his shaft deep again, but more slowly, he waited, unmoving.

"Is that it?" she asked.

He flexed his arms when he rose above Chiara. His face gentled. The sharp angles of his jaw and cheeks softened. He smiled, looking pleased, maybe a bit humble. "No. There is much more, but you should have told me. I wouldn't have…"

"Please don't stop. I want my first time to be with you."

"Damn, little witch." Dax's biceps rippled as he balanced over her. He tossed the fang necklace over his shoulder, the teeth hidden from her view, now a solid wall of muscled chest. "It shouldn't be, but it is. Let me know when you're ready." His last words were a warm whisper in her ear.

Once the ache subsided, she felt only the marvelous fullness of Dax. Having adjusted to his thickness, she risked lifting her hips, pushing upward. She relaxed. "Oh, that's really good."

"More?"

Her voice trembled with need for only this man, this vampire she had dreamed of for a lifetime. "Yes."

After studying her eyes, he took over. Dax withdrew. He shifted forward. Retreated. Again. Again.

Chiara watched his cock slide into her body. It glided out until she felt only the tip. Then he shoved deep. Trying to hold him inside, she squeezed his thick flesh which was surrounded by hers.

Needing to touch him, she stroked Dax's back, loving the play of his muscles. His dark hair curtained her while his abdomen clenched tight and his hips worked up and down. His total attention was on her as he set a slow in-and-out pace.

When it wasn't enough, she latched onto his firm ass with her nails. He rode her harder.

"Wrap your legs around me." His voice was a raspy whisper.

She encircled his hips, locking her ankles, opening herself fully. He drove deeper, filling her more completely.

"You are so fucking tight, little witch. I'm trying to last. I want to make this right." He worked his fingers between their bodies to find her sensitive nub, playing his thumb over it while he plundered in and out, his rhythm faster but exquisite. He rubbed against her until she quivered.

Dax's midnight eyes fixed on her, his mouth opening, his fangs punching from his gums.

She begged, "Please." Chiara desired his bite along with his body. She wanted to possess him totally.

His beast rose to the surface as he bent forward.

"Do it, Dax."

When his sharp teeth slid into her skin, the sucking pulls erotic, Chiara lost control. He fed. Her blood saved him as he had saved her. Floating in a hazy fog, she bucked her hips until her flesh sizzled, and her heels clenched Dax's ass to pull him in closer.

A tidal wave struck Chiara. It ebbed. It swelled. She couldn't tell if she rode the crest higher and higher or if she drowned beneath the surge of water. Whichever, she didn't care if she ever breathed again as long as Dax was inside her. When the sea calmed, she floated. Weightless. Sated.

Yes. Yes. This is better than the books said.

While she still trembled, he withdrew his fangs and licked her neck, sealing the wound.

She slid her heavy lids up to study him. Poised above her, he was exquisite. A touch of blood stained his lips. His eyes rolled into his lids. His shoulders bunched. Fighting for his own release, he was frenzied, rough, pounding into her. But she didn't want tame. She wanted her vampire. After a last huge push, he stilled, his warmth spilling inside her.

Minutes passed before he fell onto Chiara, her body pinned beneath his heavy weight. Wrapping his arms around her, he twisted them both to the side.

"Why didn't you tell me?" he whispered, his heart beating rapidly.

"I didn't want it to be a factor."

"But it is." He shifted to his back, cradling her against his chest.

"Why?" Chiara struggled to steady her breathing.

"Because I shouldn't have been your first." He buried his nose in her hair.

"Why?"

"I wasn't gentle. Damn. I should have gone slower. I could have done other things to prepare you. We didn't even get naked. My pants are around my knees, and your gown is at your waist. We should have been flesh to flesh."

"I thought we were great, but what do I know."

He tucked her under his chin, his palm stroking her hair. "Your first should have been a male who loved you."

"I want you," she mumbled against his skin.

"You can't have me." His reluctant hand pressed her closer.

"Why not?"

"I'm ruined. Broken. I'll never be what you need. For Gahya's sake, I don't want to be what you need."

Breaking from his hold, Chiara wriggled her gown down her legs. She punched the pillow. "Don't tell me what I need. I wanted you to make love to me. You did."

Propping his head in a palm, his elbow on the bed, he laughed, his beautiful mouth drawn into a sneer. "Make love? Little witch, I didn't make love to you. I fucked you. And I fucked you hard." Leaving an icy chill between them, he grumbled, rolling over to give Chiara his back. "Go to sleep."

Really? He fucked me?

She drew her bent legs to her chest and with as much strength as she could gather, kicked her feet into Dax's ass. He shot to the floor, his stupid pants still around his knees.

From his disadvantaged position on the rug, he muttered something. His fangs gleamed white as he snarled, "Damn, female. What the hell was that for?"

"That's for being a fangwad. If you try to sneak into my bed, I'll turn you into a dead toad."

The vampire hoisted his pants into place, zipped up, and yanked off her blanket and top sheet to make a pallet on the floor. "Flip me a pillow," he growled.

"No."

She rose to get another cover from the closet, grinning when she saw Dax curled on the uncomfortable thin carpet, squirming, wiggling from side to side. *Let him suffer.* She crawled into bed, pulling up the blanket. A moment later, she tossed and turned. "Damn. Here." She lobbed a pillow at the arrogant vampire's head.

Chapter Seventeen

Thorn rubbed his fingers over the back of Fin's hand as they grinned at each other like lovesick idiots. The waitress interrupted with their breakfasts. Eggs over easy, potatoes, toast, and extra ham for Dax and him. Fin went with biscuits and gravy. *Good.* Lots of calories to keep up her strength. Chiara fiddled with some yogurt thing topped with fruit.

Dax growled as he lifted a forkful toward his mouth, more surly than usual. In response, Chiara popped a strawberry into her mouth, wrinkling her nose at the vampire. They'd been at each other all morning.

Snap. Crackle. Pop. Glare.

He and Fin, on the other hand, were all smiles, having made love until the sun peeked above the ridge.

With an awkward breakfast out of the way, the four of them piled into the She Beast. Thorn checked the NAV System before heading for Livingston. They'd been driving east on I-90 for ten minutes when Kole called. Thorn listened, nodding and grumbling. When he disconnected, he twisted the wheel, crossing the median to swing back toward Bozeman.

Fin and Chiara grabbed onto the doors in the backseat as the truck dipped, bumped, and spun.

"Damn. What's up, wolf?" Dax one-handed the dashboard.

He shot the vampire a furtive glance before returning his eyes to the road. "A shitstorm. Arisen Dawn is pouring through the Bozeman portal. The humans are defending the area on this side while Kole and the Firebrands are on Scath holding back crazy-ass Aeternals."

Dax punched the armrest, knocking it off the

door.

Thorn arched his brows. "You're gonna pay for that, my *freron*." The She Beast lunged forward as he floored the gas pedal.

"The females are our priority," said Dax.

"I agree. We'll just have a look-see." He changed lanes, gunning past a slower vehicle.

Either Dax was suddenly altruistic, or he cared for Chiara more than he admitted. Thorn was betting on the latter. The vampire didn't seem the type to go down easy, though. He had the brooding thing going for him, which was typical of his breed. Every vampire Thorn knew carried an unhealthy dose of guilt. Shifters on the other hand were… *Nope*. They were pretty fucked up, too. Lucky for him, Fin rolled past his flaws. Of course, since he whirl-winded her, she didn't have much time to see any.

Chiara tapped Dax's shoulder. "Don't worry about me. You are not my protector anymore. I release you from all responsibility. Besides, I can take care of myself. I don't need some inconsiderate bloodsucking fangtard to worry about my safety."

When Dax snarled, Thorn knew the female hit a sore spot. *Hell*. All Firebrands were protectors. The closer they were to danger, the greater their need to play hero.

"What about you, Fin? Do you need a male to fight for you?" Chiara crossed her arms to stare at her backseat companion.

Thorn's female caught his gaze in the rearview mirror, but instead of responding, she hung on tighter to the door as the truck flew down the interstate on its way to the city.

"You two have been chipping at each other all morning," said Thorn. "Love spat?"

At the same time, Dax and Chiara both said, "Shut up."

"To quote another famous shifter, you 'doth protest too much, methinks.'"

"Shakespeare was a shifter?" Fin wide-eyed him in the rearview mirror.

"Nope. Just messing with the bickering lovers."

When Fin smiled, his heart clenched. He'd park away from the skirmish, hide the females under a tarp on the floor, and hope Dax and he survived the recon mission. In case things went from fucked to royally fucked, he'd leave the keys in the She Beast. The Blood Coven descendants could skedaddle. How would they crossover to Scath? *Think. Think.*

Thorn tipped his head toward the duffel at the vampire's feet. "Weapons. Blades and guns. On the off-chance we get drawn into the fray."

Opening the bag, Dax snagged a Heckler and Koch MP7 for Thorn, the Sig again for himself, and four blades. He unlocked his seatbelt to strap on a chest harness, tucking in two knives. He loaded several extra magazines into pockets and secured the firearm in his waistband. He set Thorn's stuff onto the center console. Next, he removed two Berettas, clips, and a couple more blades, passing them into the back.

"What are we supposed to do with these?" asked Chiara.

"The shifter and I have to scout out Bozeman. Shoot anybody but us who tries to get into the truck."

"I've practiced at a gun range," said Fin. "But I've never fired at a person."

"I've shot critters," said Chiara. "But I've never targeted a person either."

Thorn whispered to Dax, "If something happens to us, we have to make sure they can get to Scath.

Suggestions?"

"An Alliance office."

"How do we know if the Americans have breached them?"

"We'll leave all the addresses. Chicago's main headquarters. New Orleans. New York. Seattle." Dax removed paper and pen from the glove compartment and started writing.

"I hope you have a good memory, vampire."

"Excellent."

****

Cerberus kept his mind's eye on several skirmishes happening now. But this interview was too important to delay. Disguised as a satyr, he sat across from a witch who it was said could trace ancestry from a taste of blood. First, he'd test her beliefs.

He crossed his legs at the knee. "Why have you joined a subversive group such as Arisen Dawn?"

The witch straightened her spine, obviously not expecting the question. Cerberus claimed he wanted to hire her to uncover his heritage. His query had nothing to do with her skills to perform the job.

She ran an assessing eye over his form, possibly guessing he was disguised. "Why do you ask?"

"Let's say I am the welcoming committee."

"How do I know? You could be here to trap me."

"I could also be here to make you a valuable member of a team."

"Let's stop waltzing around. Why are you here, satyr?" Her eyes narrowed, lit with suspicion.

Cerberus brushed a speck from his pants leg. "I am here to assess your loyalty."

She leaned back in her desk chair. "I am loyal to Aeternals and my breed. Too long we have been harnessed. Taught to control our powers. Taught moderation. I believe we were created to rule the world. It's time we started."

"Have you killed when you feed?"

"Killing while I channel power from another to cast a spell would be illegal on Scath." She tapped her well-manicured nails together.

"Now who is dancing?"

"I believe in all Arisen Dawn stands for. I believe we should stay strong, each breed pure. I believe we should rule over humans. I believe we should feed from them until we are full. I believe I was meant to feed my powers however I choose. I believe."

"Good. Now tell me, is it true you can trace ancestry through a taste of blood?"

She nodded.

"Then you shall hold a high office in Cerberus's Arisen Dawn. You are just what he needs."

****

When they left I-90, emptying onto Main and following it downtown, Dax twisted around in his seat. "Here are addresses of Alliance offices. If Thorn and I don't return, drive to one of these locations. If that place is shot to hell, go to the next one. Shifter, fork over all your cash."

Tossing his money clip into the back, Thorn pulled into an empty space on the side of the street, both Aeternals jumping out the doors when the She Beast came to a full stop.

"I'm not leaving you behind." Chiara leaped from the backseat, following Dax onto the sidewalk. "I'm pissed enough to kill you myself, but I won't let someone else."

"If we don't come back in an hour, you and Fin get to the Covenkirk stronghold on Scath. They'll keep you safe. Your only chance will be from an Alliance office. If that doesn't work, you hide out. Maybe forever."

Chiara tilted her chin into the air. "No."

"Damn it. If I don't come back, I'm dead. It's the only thing that could keep me away." He pinched her chin between his finger and thumb. "For once, do as I say. I can't do my job if I'm worried about you."

Thorn and Fin stood on the other the side of the truck, probably having the same argument. Dax hoped the shifter's female was more reasonable. *Wait.* Did he just give a nod to the little witch as his female?

Hell no.

His whiplashing emotions about Chiara were getting to him. He had to get a handle on them. He would when this was over. When she was safe on Scath. When he got his life back.

Chiara's head pivoted toward the sound of gunfire as she swiped a tear from her cheek. "You better come back for me, Dax." She poked him in the chest. Once. Twice. Three times.

He shoved her finger aside and touched her palm to his lips, kissing it. Realizing what he'd done, he dropped her hand and took two steps back. He resented caring for her. At the same time, he couldn't help it. "Time to go."

He pushed Chiara onto the floor of the backseat. Once Thorn did the same to Fin, he pulled a tarp over them.

"I love you." Thorn patted the lump under the canvas that was Fin.

Dax said nothing to Chiara. "Ready, shifter?" After he cast one last look toward where Chiara hid, he put on his warrior face.

Thorn shot him a wolfy grin. "Always ready. Let's do it."

The shifter's amber eyes shimmered with the same excitement which flowed through Dax. No matter what, a Firebrand was always up for a battle. The bloodier the better. It was in their DNA.

They took off toward the gunfire, their legs pumping and arms heaving.

A chaotic scene met them a few blocks away. Crazed Aeternals charged out of the rubble where a parking garage housed the portal. Though the brick building had collapsed, the gateway was still active.

Tanks continued to fire on invading Arisen Dawn soldiers. Military grunts, armed with Sig Sauer MCX assault rifles, took out targets. Not enough. Though bodies littered the road, the humans didn't seem to realize most Aeternals would heal and rise. They needed to lob off heads, cut out hearts, or incinerate them. Big mistake. Bullets didn't always kill his kind.

The Earth army's weapons weren't stopping Arisen Dawn. Witches and warlocks diverted their firepower with spells. Other Aeternals were so fast the bullets couldn't catch them. Older vampires avoided the waiting military by shadowflashing around them.

Faced with charging demons in beast mode and shifters in animal form, the American soldiers were forgetting their training. At this rate, Dax figured the Earthers might lose the skirmish. *Hell.* They'd be lucky to walk away with their lives. The most monstrous of his species would be loose on Earth, free to maim and kill, free to feed.

Dax swung toward an ear-piercing scream. A coyote shifter clamped his jaw onto a soldier's thigh, tearing flesh from bone. The guy's buddy looked on, frozen in shock, so paralyzed his rifle hung limply at his side. When the Aeternal dropped his dead catch, the stunned human didn't even try to run. He was dog meat, his eyes empty as he accepted his fate.

Dax glanced at Thorn. "We've got no choice."

He started off at a slow jog but kicked up the speed to attack a female Aeternal who jacked a soldier off the ground, her fingers curled around the guy's neck. Dax snaked an arm around her throat and squeezed. She dropped the human but released her poisoned claws. To avoid the sloth demon's deadly weapons, he pressed his free hand to the side of her head and snapped it off her shoulders, blood spurting through the air. One down.

Dax flashed to a satyr who was finishing off a human. When he slapped his hands to the Aeternal's ears and twisted, another head rolled.

Pop.

A glance told him a half-shifted Thorn held his own with a succubus, dancing out of her way so she couldn't plant a hand on his chest to steal his lifeforce. In a swift move, the wolf's jaws fixed on her throat.

Dax hefted his Sig to fire dead center between a demon's eyes. An exploding melon. The next shot tumbled a witch. With her down, he targeted an incubus and kept going. Once he emptied the magazine, he shadowflashed from one kill to another, using his blade to sever their heads. The air ripe with blood, Dax's fangs punched from his gums.

A shifter howled as he prepared to sink canines into a high-ranking officer. A colonel. Dax slapped a new clip into his Sig and fired.

With the attacker dead at his feet, the officer whipped his head toward the vampire, his brows drawn tight, puzzled at the assist.

Dax drew the edge of his palm across his neck, signaling a slicing motion. The human caught onto the message, grabbed a blade, and whacked it across the Aeternal's throat, severing flesh, ligaments, bone, the works. *Job done.* The officer nodded a thanks before moving on to another invader.

Ping. Thud.

Dax slapped a hand to his shoulder as he hung a one-eighty. Blood seeped through his fingers.

That's what I get for playing the hero.

He looked around for the gunman. *There.* Another vampire. A young one. He flashed to the female's side, disarming her with one swipe. A blade through the neck sent another head flying.

Dax glanced toward the portal. No more Arisen Dawn soldiers exited the portal, but the humans couldn't keep the loose ones in check. Aeternals were fighting their way through the army's defenses, leaving terror in their wake.

Dax's eye caught a big muther who was grinning like an asshole as he flung humans right and left. Though he wasn't killing his marks, he was incapacitating a shitload of them, bowling his way through the American soldiers as if they were pins and he was the ball rolling down the alley toward a strike. The guy was a shifter. Maybe. Hard to tell.

The Arisen Dawn soldier sensed Dax's stare. When he raised his head, his gaze locked onto Dax. Shooting a two-finger salute to his forehead, the guy with the asshole grin sprouted wings and took to the sky.

When Aeternals began rising from the ground, not dead after all, panic set in among the American soldiers. They ran. Officers yelled commands at their backs. Dax gave the humans kudos. Despite their fear, they heeded orders, returning to the fray. But a few Aeternals already used the retreat to scatter onto Bozeman streets.

Thorn tangled with a strung-out animus demon who was hitting him with electrical shocks. Probably on too much Gold Dust to do any damage to the experienced wolf. Thorn shook off the current, his lips curled back from his canines in a snarl. Bad idea to piss off a Firebrand shifter.

Oomph.

An Amazon crashed into Dax with a frontal assault while a satyr jumped him from behind. Sandwiched, he shook his head to stop the ringing bells. Together, they flung him onto his back. With both fists flying, he fought his way to his feet. The female landed a solid to his gut. The other attacker battered his jaw. Dax ducked, bobbed, and weaved, pulverizing first one and then the other.

He crouched. Before he could rush his opponents, the Amazon sailed overhead to face-plant on the street. Lights-out. *What the fuck?* No time to ponder the situation. The satyr landed an uppercut. Pissed-off, Dax pummeled the guy. Jab. Cross. Lead-hand hook. Back-hand hook. Uppercut. Duck. Put him away.

Slipping on the blood which saturated the streets of Bozeman, Dax righted himself. The heady scent shot to his nostrils. Battle blood was tainted. A likely trip to the bludfrenzy. *Fight it. Too late.* His beast snapped. His lips drew back, fangs sliced through his gums, and his eyes filled with crimson.

Dax's chest rose and fell with deep breaths. At his feet, a barely alive Arisen Dawn ylve lay, his blood soaking into the dirt. Dax stooped to dip his fingers into the male's wound. He brought them to his lips. His tongue flicked out. *Tangy.* Burying a hand between the male's ribs, he pulled out the heart. After he stole a lick, his lips curled into a savage smile.

A thirsty Dax zeroed in on a berserker. The sound of the behemoth fighter's pulsing carotid thumped in his ears. With blurring speed, he took the Arisen Dawn soldier into the crook of his elbow, knocked his legs out, and slid a blade along his throat. Sinking to the ground with his prey, Dax cradled the male in his arms. His blood lust in full swing, he fed from the wound.

His hair matted with the gore of battle, Dax drew a hand across his mouth. Half-wild, he looked for the next rabbit.

****

Armed with the knives and guns Dax had passed off, Chiara and Fin hopped out of the She Beast, refusing to desert the men they loved. They hid behind an old storefront with an around-the-corner view of the chaos. The scene was straight out of a horror movie starring monsters and the US Army.

When they arrived, Dax had been in trouble. Two on one. Chiara raised a hand while she mumbled words. Her spell sent a huge woman soaring above her vampire. She was okay with a one-on-one. He could handle those odds.

She glanced at Fin, who had a far-away look in her eye.

"What's wrong?" Chiara pulled her head back around the corner of the building.

"Nothing. I've been testing my gift since we left the truck. Like I said, it's new. Not perfected, but I think I just talked to a bunch of wolves. They're coming to help. Two bears caught the message also. It's weird, right? I'm telling them to hurry."

"No stranger than anything else we've seen." Chiara risked another peek around the corner. A large Aeternal was firing at soldiers. Lifting her hand, she dropped the guy to the ground. *No guilt.* These were not good people.

Spotting Chiara, an Arisen Dawn attacker raised his weapon to shoot. She flicked her wrist, slamming the gunman into a brick building. *Splat.*

After toppling three more Aeternals, she rested her hands on her knees, took a deep breath, and brushed escaping tendrils of hair from her face. Using magic was as tough as an hour of Zumba. She was weakening. Dax had told her she needed to learn to feed, to draw power from others to cast a spell. Now was not a good time.

Fin tapped her shoulder. "Listen."

Chiara straightened. Wild howling wolves raced into the battle, attacking only Arisen Dawn soldiers while humans retreated to safety.

She smiled at Fin as a grizzly reared onto its back legs and snatched a guy off the ground by his head.

Catching her breath, Chiara sensed her vampire. Down the street, he clasped a man in his arms. Dax twisted the guy's head off to send it rolling. He drew the back of his hand across his lips, blood dripping down his chin. With his canines bared, he charged another Aeternal, burying his fangs deep.

Dax's head snapped up. Cold, red-streaked eyes fixed on Chiara. In a blur, he flashed from the scene to stand in front of her, his blood-streaked hair whipping behind him, caught in a windstorm of his own making. One arm curled around her back to slam her against his chest. He threw back his head, his savage roar thundering through the air. Chiara let him press her cheek against his blood-stained tee.

When his mouth crushed her lips, his tongue lashed out, demanding entry.

Though revolted by the coppery taste of blood, Chiara allowed the kiss. Something was wrong. She smoothed her palms along his thickly muscled arms and stroked the feral beast. His need was so great, it rippled beneath his skin.

Dax's hand tangled in her hair. He growled,

unable to form words.

With his fist knotted in her dark curls, he ripped her head back. His eyes, wild from his fresh kills, locked onto hers. She should fear this man, this vampire. His control was broken. Every bone, every muscle in his body was a hard plane, carved in savagery. He could snap her neck with just two fingers. Yet, he would never harm her that way. Rather, he came to her for help.

Dax cupped her bottom, lifting her against his hard arousal. He growled, the sound primal. "Stop the madness." His voice was a raspy whisper.

She traced the wound on his shoulder. "You're hurt."

"Ignore it." His eyes narrowed.

Chiara took his hand and led him behind a building where they were out of sight.

He jammed her back to the wall hard enough to rattle her teeth, his fingers trailing along the throbbing vein in her neck. "A taste."

Dax didn't need blood. He'd taken more than enough on the battlefield, but she wouldn't deny him. She swept her hair aside and angled her neck.

When his fangs pierced her flesh, she soared, floated on the dark cloud who was her vampire. He took life, but she gave it. The perfect symbiosis. With each draw, her body hungered for his. She ground her hips against his swollen shaft. She could so easily give in to him despite his blood-soaked clothes, menacing sounds, and murderous eyes. *Hell.* The battle heightened her own desires. But not here. Not now.

Besides, what Dax needed wasn't frenetic sex brought on by the thrill of death and manic feeding. Chiara pulled back her hips. When he withdrew his fangs and licked the wounds, her hands stroked up and down his spine. Though nearly bereft of magic, she shot what little she had into her fingers.

His shoulders sank. His biceps relaxed. His hands loosened their painful hold on her. Dax bent forward, his nose rubbing through her hair. As he drew deep breaths, he calmed.

Her vampire held her close for some time, seemingly unwilling to release her. Then he stiffened and pushed her away. “What the hell are you doing? You were supposed to stay in the truck. I told you what to do if we didn’t return.”

She sighed, deciding the best way to meet Dax’s bossiness was snark. “I couldn’t remember it all. My little human brain doesn’t work as well as your big vampire brain.”

“Knock off that shit. When will you listen to me?”

“Let me think. How about never? Besides, I saved your life.”

His forehead wrinkled. “You downed the Amazon?”

“Yep.”

He scrubbed a hand across his jaw. “Don’t ever risk your life for me.”

“Or what?”

He took a threatening step forward, but she wiggled her fingers. “Spell coming and it’s a doozy.”

Dax snarled through his gritted teeth.

Chiara ignored him to peel up his shirt sleeve to examine the bullet wound. “We did a good thing, right? We won.”

“No. Maybe we kept Arisen Dawn from taking out all the human soldiers, but enough of their assholes escaped to do some real damage. It wasn’t a clear win.” Dax brushed off her fingers and rolled down his sleeve. “It’s already healing.”

When she brushed her thumb across a smudge of blood on his cheek, she winced. "Did you see the bears and wolves?"

"Yeah. What was that about?"

"Fin. She's Dr. Dolittle but with lipstick and boobs."

That's when she lost control of her body, her brain misfiring, her arms and legs jerking.

Chapter Eighteen

Jace curled into a chair, her feet tucked under her while her thumb held her place in *The Path: The Words of the Warrior Ohngel as Recorded by the Cambion.* Despite grumbling about the dust, smell, and cantankerous old bastard at the register, Tyr had rummaged through a Covenkirk bookstore to buy all five volumes. Rough Goth exterior aside, he was all heart, finding the time for her when he had so much going on.

Besides a trip to a bookstore, Tyr had squeezed in a couple rides with her on the back of his motorcycle after he presented Jace with her own bike leathers and boots. Surprising herself and the warlock, they were growing close fast. He was unlike anyone she had met, and his heart sang to hers.

Today he came to her place at the stronghold bloody and tired from fighting Arisen Dawn at some gateway to Earth. After a meal, a shower, pleasuring Jace, another shower, and a short nap, he prepared to leave again, but Kole ordered his warriors to rotate into on-off shifts. They were exhausted from skirmishes, training recruits around the clock, watching multiple portals for signs of rebel activity, and searching for Cerberus's hidden garrison.

Now her new warlock lover lazed on the couch in her apartment, watching a football game with Ram, enjoying a brief but well-deserved rest.

A shout drew her attention as Ram jumped up, a beer bottle in his hand. "Bad call, ref. Pass interference, idiot."

Tyr shrugged, peeling the label off his lager, a brew from the demon region of Knife's Edge Ram had brought along. Her warlock was probably okay with the call because he was rooting for a different team. He was a Seahawks fan while Ram went for the 49ers. Or was it the other way around? Didn't matter. They deserved to let off steam.

Jace rose to gather the sandwich plates. "More?"

The two men exchanged hungry glances. "We wouldn't turn down another." Tyr gave her his bad-boy grin which made her toes curl. Later he'd be getting more than sliced ham.

"Where are Denim and Jonquil?" she asked Ram.

Squinted eyes glued to the screen, he answered. "The mate's running a few recruits through hand-to-hand techniques. I feel sorry for them. She's merciless. Broke some guy's arm the other day. Lucky we heal fast. The pest is still with my father." Ram shuddered. "He's stuffing her with bad food and teaching her worse habits. It'll take a week to get her back in shape."

Once Jace stacked two more sandwiches thick with ham, roasted pork, onions, pickles, and Swiss cheese in front of the football fans, she snuggled into her chair.

With a mouth chock-full of food, Tyr garbled a question. "What did you call this?"

"A Cuban sandwich."

"S'great." As he moaned with pleasure, Ram nodded, chewing with his eyes closed in silent appreciation.

Tilting the light into a better position, Jace returned to her favorite parable in *The Path*, a smile tugging at her lips.

Be not bothered by those who would imprison your body. They can never shackle your mind. If you give it wing, it is forever free. Free to imagine. Free to travel the world. Free to learn. Free to determine its path.

Jace fingered the diamond pendant around her

neck, re-reading the same paragraph, wishing Celene could grow wings.

Her hand flew to her brow. She was lightheaded, and she felt as if her body floated above her comfy chair. The book slipped from her fingers when the living room disappeared. Jace was deep in soupy fog, plunging through it at a blurring speed.

Landing feet-first on a jungled mountain peak, she stumbled to the edge of a cliff atop a long, steep drop. To the right was a gigantic waterfall. Her chin dropped as she checked out her clothing. Boots. Coveralls. Pads. Gloves. She tapped her head. Helmet. Glasses.

Another step had her peering over the side with the strongest urge to jump. So, she hurtled into the air, flew alongside the water, and plummeted toward the ground. Crazy. She was a mad woman.

Somehow, she knew this was Caracas, Venezuela, where she'd come to base-jump Angel Falls.

At the last second, her chute snapped open. With its release, she bounced around while tilting her chin to spot the landing zone.

When she set down perfectly on the run, she spun to catch her parachute. As she was bunching it, from nowhere, two men dropped a bag over her head and tased her. She collapsed.

She drifted in and out of darkness but sensed motion, the passage of time, voices.

Then she awoke alone on a cold cement floor. She rolled over onto her stomach to push up off her knees. Shaking, she wobbled to her feet, spreading them apart, holding her head to ease the pain of an unbearable headache.

She was in a spartan cell. A cot with a blanket, a hole in the floor that passed for a toilet, and a water spigot. She approached iron bars and gripped them in her fists. While rattling them, she shouted, "Hey, anybody there?"

When she got no response, she shook the bars harder. "Hey, motherfuckers, somebody talk to me." Louder. "Motherfuckers."

"Kur, shut her up." A voice carried from outside her vision.

A beefy man with dirty-blond hair grinned from the other side of her cage. He drawled, "Get back." Then he snarled and flashed large canines.

A foggy darkness engulfed her again as she spun toward a white farmhouse. This place was familiar. She hovered above the yard, seeing a fence she recognized. Beyond it were thick woods.

She drifted through the front door and on to another room, plopping onto a bed she knew well. A huge man walked in and said to get her ass into the kitchen.

"Go fuck yourself," she replied.

He rushed her, his palm landing a solid to her cheek, which immediately welted as it turned cherry red. When the man yanked her to her feet, she pulled back.

As he dragged her from the bedroom, she stumbled to the floor. Rising, she bent to bite his hand. He whacked her again, shook her, and thrust her into a kitchen chair.

Her head snapped backward. Sweeping her stylish chin-length blonde hair behind her ears, she laughed at the behemoth. "Only a dick picks on women half his size." Picking up her fork, spearing a carrot, and chewing, she spoke with her mouth full. "Hi. I'm Celene Bailey. What's your name?"

Jace came out of the trance to find Tyr standing over her, a crease between his brows, his hand squeezing hers.

"Are you okay? What happened?" His fingers rubbed up and down her arm.

"I don't know." Jace shook the fog from her head. "I saw Celene's kidnapping."

Ram drew closer, no longer watching the game. "What?"

"I watched Celene jump Angel Falls. No. That's wrong. I was Celene." Jace bragged about her friend's courage. "She was like that. No fear. A self-described adrenaline junkie. Anyway, the guys captured her. Me, in this case. They put her in a cell, like mine but somewhere else. Next, I woke up on her bed in that house we shared."

Jace looked down at her necklace but avoided fingering it again. "I think it happened when I touched the pendant."

The two men exchanged glances.

"The necklace was Celene's. Does that mean something?" Jace looked into Tyr's neon purple eyes for the answer.

He lifted her from the chair, sat, and resettled her in his lap, continuing to caress her arms until she stopped shaking. "You found your gift, witch."

"Really? What am I?"

"A diviner. Some mages can read an object's history. Where it's been. Who owned it. Stuff like that."

"Is it a helpful gift?"

"For authenticators, scholars, crime-fighters. My uncle contracts out to museums all over the world. Guy's loaded and in demand. Here as well as on Earth. Of course, humans don't know he's a warlock. "

"Can I find Celene because it belonged to her? She gave it to me as a going-away gift."

Ram drew fingers through his caramel-streaked

hair. "No. You can see your friend's history only for the time it was in her possession. We already found the house where you escaped. It was deserted."

Jace's shoulders slumped. Then she squealed as she twisted in Tyr's lap. "How stupid of me. Damn. Skyler can use it to scry. She needs something personal. I forgot about the pendant." Jace threw her arms around Tyr's neck. "I'll keep my promise to bring Celene home."

****

Kole pounded the table, sparks shooting from his fist like fireworks. "We need to find Arisen Dawn's garrison and crack whatever spell they got going."

He, Rein, Nico, and Sabine rushed to Cadmon's meeting fresh from the battle at the portal. Not even a shower.

Nico, his face streaked with sweat and dirt, pushed aside the stray lock of hair which fell across his vision. "I'm telling you, we've been over every square foot of Scath. No Arisen Dawn fortress, garrison, barracks, or whatever-the-fuck. Their people ghost into nowhere once they access a portal. Maybe the expert warlock who Alarik sent us is defective. Or maybe Cerberus is just better than us. Whatever the case, we've done due diligence."

Sabine, the only one of Kole's warriors who still looked fresh in her unwrinkled tan cargo shorts and combat boots, patted her mate's leg. With the stroke of her hand, Nico took a calming breath, his shoulders relaxing.

"It makes no sense," said Rein, his torn shirt stained with the blood of Arisen Dawn soldiers. "How can you just lose track of them? Your D-chips should keep you glued to their asses through any portal."

Nico slammed back his chair when he jumped to

his feet. "Speaking of asses, why don't you get off your righteous vampire one and look for them if we're doing such a shitty job?"

Rein shot the warlock a fangy grin.

Kole bounced a ball of fire in his animus demon palm. "Sit down, Abello. We're all frustrated."

Tension was high among the Firebrands.

Despite the turmoil, Nace's second, a shifter called Mix, sat at the table cleaning his nails with the tip of a pocketknife. He seemed to pay little attention to the negative energy bouncing around the room. If he wasn't grooming his nails, he was flipping his blade into the air.

Maybe it was just an act. After all, protectiveness was built into Firebrand DNA. Without a solution or a big win, they would self-implode.

Nico wasn't helping the situation. Once a respected agent high in the ranks of Earth's Alliance, he tested positive as a Blood Coven descendant. Kole ordered Sabine and Tyr to bring him kicking and screaming to Scath. The male used bribery to land a spot with the Firebrands but hadn't enjoyed being one of the weakest members on the team. Too many years as top dog. Then he got his power. Even with it, he was still a hothead. Being mated to the nymph Firebrand Sabine should have calmed him. It did. Sometimes. Somewhat. But he was arrogant and aggressive. Like most of the warriors.

So Kole bounced a fireball, tempted to lob it at Nico. Most of his Firebrands had been on the receiving end of his hands-on discipline. He loved them, but they were an exasperating lot.

With a tug on Nico's arm, Sabine said, "We're as puzzled as you are. They just poof into air when we follow them through a portal. Damn strange. Alarik's warlock can't find them. Obviously, they are gathering somewhere."

"Fuck, Sabine," said Rein, leaning back in his chair, his arms across his chest.

"Watch how you talk to her." Nico shot to his feet again, his violent warlock eyes challenging Rein.

Cadmon, the normally calm ylve high commander, banged a fist on the table. "Take it down a notch. So, Kole, your Firebrands battled Arisen Dawn in this realm while American forces stood them off in a place called Bozeman, Montana. Is that correct?"

"Yes." He shifted in his seat, extinguishing the blazing ball in his fist. "Dax and Thorn lent an assist Earthside. The shifter buzzed in afterwards to say it was a nightmare when Arisen Dawn broke through. The human soldiers scattered, and Aeternals ran wild through their ranks until they re-organized. We don't have a body count, but it must be high."

"What's happening with your two warriors in Bozeman?" asked Jarek.

"They're on their way home through another portal with two likely Blood Coven witches."

Eyebrows arched around the room.

"We need a plant in the American forces." Nace clawed the table, his beast close to the surface. The shifter's pack occupied Central America fifteen hundred years ago when the Mayans saw the jaguars as gods. "Do we have any Aeternals currently serving?"

Cadmon jotted down a note. "I will check."

Jarek said, "If we have anybody Earthside in the military, they could request a transfer to this Montana unit. That way we will have eyes on the human soldiers."

With an unusual expression of weariness, Cadmon rested his chin in his knuckles. "In the meantime, Arisen Dawn numbers continue to multiply. I have requested to meet before a joint session of Temple justices and the lawgivers. It's time to take drastic measures. I recommend we round up or kill-on-contact all confirmed Arisen Dawn members. Suspected members will meet similar swift punishment unless they prove their loyalty."

Kole scrubbed a palm across his buzz-cut hair. He had no qualms about using deadly force to uphold order in a violent realm, but he usually killed only if he had a touch of proof. Suspected was a pretty loose standard.

"What about your informant?" Jarek looked no happier than Kole. The six-foot-eight djinn commander frowned as he pushed a war braid over his shoulder, his massive arms covered not only with his Scion Firebrand brand but with glyphs depicting his many battles. Like others of his breed, he survived by feeding on the energy of fighting.

"He does not know the location of the garrison. He gets in and out through portals but has no idea where he is. Even to its occupants, the fortress is cloaked. In the meantime, I have a list of all gateways on Scath. Each stronghold will check on those in their regions for any build-up of Arisen Dawn." Cadmon passed papers to each commander.

Darius, Jarek's second in command, ran the back of his hand along the scar on his cheek. "That's thousands."

Cadmon nodded. "I guess we're lucky so many recruits have joined the Firebrands and that insomnia plagues our sleep."

****

Roark leaned a lazy shoulder against an old brick building far from the army headquarters on the outskirts of Bozeman, Lort at his side. "That was fun."

The vampire general's gaze fixed on an escaping Aeternal who raced through the streets, scattering, heading for parts unknown. "I have instructed them to do damage and return by another portal. Most are crazed on Gold Dust. I doubt they can handle the freedom. Once the Earth army reorganizes, it will round up and kill our people but not until they've gorged on humans. They are disposable."

Roark cocked his head. "Disposable? That's harsh."

Crossing his arms, Lort closed his mouth around fangs which punched from his gums, likely from the smell of blood. "But they further our cause. Every soldier serves a purpose. These are our sacrificial lambs. We will see how long they last. Test the human response teams. Shifter, you impressed me today with your efficiency, coolness under fire. Next time, I want you to lead a unit, become one of my officers."

Roark flicked a nail. "Thanks for the confidence. Only if I train them. I don't lead anybody I haven't personally trained."

"That's doable. What is your assessment of today's incursion?"

"Arisen Dawn took the Earthers by surprise. This was their first skirmish against us. They won't be so easy the next time. They'll learn how to kill us permanently. What technology to use. Where to aim it. We can count this a win, but we weren't pretty. We were an angry mob, not a professional army. The humans have numbers and advanced weaponry on their side. We can't rely on brute strength and breed powers as long-term solutions."

Lort pinched his chin between thumb and forefinger, stroking. "True."

"When they meet us again, they will be primed. Better trained, more heavily armed, and less likely to break ranks and run."

"I count on it, but we will be more prepared, too.

Our army needed this taste of victory to draw more Aeternals to our side. Doesn't matter we were sloppy. Nothing sells allegiance like a win."

When Lort's cellphone rang, he snagged it from his pocket, glanced at the screen, and answered. He listened, finally speaking. "The mission was a success. I'll be there." He jammed the device back into place.

Roark elbowed off the wall. "I thought I'd find a plump human female who likes a big dick. Settle in for the night. Return to Scath tomorrow. What's on your list?"

"I have a meeting with Cerberus. Afterward, a celebration with a loved one on Scath."

"You don't strike me as love material."

A thin grin slid onto Lort's face. "I'm not."

Rumor said Lort kept a human male as a blood slave. Roark figured it fit his cruel nature to sink fang in an unwilling partner.

"Tomorrow, we gather at the Arisen Dawn garrison. I'll let you pick your unit and begin training them. In the afternoon, all officers will meet in my tent to plan the next operation. Since I have promoted you, your attendance is mandatory. We wasted quite a few resources coming through here in Bozeman, but the shock and awe were worth it. The humans will be quaking in their combat boots, especially after the escapees have their fun. But, as you observed, they will also judge us as disorganized, relying on savagery rather than strategy."

Lort shadowflashed his way to a portal.

The air around Roark shimmered with an explosion of color. When it settled, he had a beak, talons, and feathers. His raven took to the sky, feeling free as it flexed gigantic black wings. It soared high to catch a current. Riding from one to another, it passed over

Bozeman several times. With sharp eyes, it spotted Arisen Dawn invaders spreading through the streets of the city, looking for humans. When they found them, they fed, leaving bodies to rot.

But the American soldiers were fanning out through the Montana town, taking aim when they caught up with an Aeternal. They decapitated each kill, a valuable lesson already learned.

The raven screeched as it passed in front of the sun, using bright light to shield its presence.

Chapter Nineteen

Miller cradled the cellphone to his ear as he leaned against an old building in an alley in Kansas City, the latest stop as he kept one step ahead of Cerberus's men. Rein was right. Most likely, they were tracing him through his blood. How long could he last? Braelyn's muscle-bound bloke told him to come in, to have a mage spell him so the bad guys couldn't find him. He wasn't ready yet. Soon.

"Chiara Bianchi," he said. "Got her name from a tracker who just got back to me about a cold, cold case. I forgot about the girl. Her parents died in an auto accident. Afterward, she was in foster care where *Custodes Templii* kept an eye on her. Bianchi went missing from a group home over ten years ago when she was still in her teens. Do you think Cerberus has had her that long?"

Muffled sounds came from Braelyn's end as she obviously consulted with her egotistical mate. "Rein just told me a Firebrand stumbled across a woman in Idaho. Bad led to worse, and now she's on the run with him. Her first name is Chiara, not a common name, but the last name isn't right. This woman's last name is Flores."

"You're right. The first name is pretty distinctive. This one's personal, luv. My guy has never given up on the kid. The mother was *Custodes Templii*, a tracker when she died in the car crash. It was an accident, but the woman and the daughter belong to us. They're a special case."

"If Chiara changed her last name, you may be able to write her off your list. I'll get back to you once they get to Scath. Also, we have Finley Sage coming with her. Still no Celene, but we're looking for her. Jace is helping on that one. None of the other names of missing have surfaced yet."

Miller waited through a long pause. "Still there, luv?"

"Please let us protect you."

The song was getting old, but he knew it was time to leave Kansas City before the Aeternals got to him again. To the ex-British agent, his freedom meant everything. Going to Scath, a human among supes, was not his idea of a fun time. Was that vanity? Sure. So what? He didn't want to be the bloke on the bottom of the food chain. Soon, though. He was running out of choices.

"Luv?"

"Yes, Miller."

He liked the soft sound of Braelyn James's voice. It calmed him, helped him feel not so alone. Too bad His Nibs the vamp got to her first. She was a beautiful woman with her short spiky auburn hair and freckles which raced across her nose. "If they find me one more time, I'll come in. You can bury me on Scath, a nobody among somebodies."

"It's not so bad here. In fact, it's pretty great. New places to travel. Lots to see."

"Yeah? How out of place do you feel? You know, a human among nons."

"I'm not so human anymore, Miller. It's hard to admit, but I'm changing every day. I'm somehow more. Not less. It sounds frightening, but…"

"Not sure I want to give up my humanity, luv. It's the best thing I've got going for me. Nearly lost it in Iraq. Not eager to slip again. The next slide could be a long one into darkness."

"You won't be alone here, Miller. We all have that fear, but you know what?"

"What?"

"No one has become evil. The closest is Abello, but he was that way before." She chuckled.

It was a nice sound. Warm. Friendly. It almost made him change his mind.

"I worry about you," Braelyn said.

He nodded, knowing she couldn't see the gesture. Miller was tired. He'd seen the world many times over. Sometimes while working for British intelligence. Sometimes while tracking his charges. Recently, while running. Tired. Worn thin. He didn't fear dying at the end of Cerberus's blade. *Hell.* He wasn't even afraid of torture. He worried they could turn him into someone he wouldn't like. He had it in him. The cruel inhumanity. The sense of evil, eating at his insides. What if they uncovered it and used it? *Yes*. That was what he feared. He hadn't liked it when it had grown in him before.

A man stumbled into the alley where Miller talked on his cell. Something was strange about the guy. The Englishman switched off his phone, dropping it into his pocket as he bolted. He didn't sign off on the call. No time.

****

Chiara jerked awake cradled against Dax's warm chest, his arm flexed around her back. Her confused gaze met wintry midnight eyes framed by thick, dark lashes. "What happened to me?"

"Power blowback. Healers are very susceptible. You're casting spells without feeding." He wiped a thumb down her cheek.

She grabbed it to have a look-see. "Blood." Now that she thought about it, her skin was sticky, and a coppery scent stung her nose. She pushed away from Dax's shirt. "Yuck."

Her eyes rolled left. Right. She remembered. The

fight. So much death. "What's a healer?"

Thorn spoke from the front seat. "That's what we call Aeternals like you. A witch or warlock in the med field. Like a human nurse or doctor."

"I hope they have more control than I do. I'm as likely to kill someone as cure them." Chiara pressed two fingers to each temple where a drum-heavy band played a Sousa march.

Dax moved his legs, resettling her in his arms, finding a nearly-clean spot on his shirt to press her head. "When we get to Scath, you should have a sit-down with one of your kind."

With a sigh, Chiara mulled that thought over as she resigned herself to Dax's bloody shirt. "Others like me. I never thought about that before."

"A whole shitload of them. Pains me to say since I hate witches and warlocks."

After shooting Dax a WTF glare, she stared out the window when they pulled into Livingston. "You mentioned blowback. What's that?"

"All healers can kill, but it comes at a price sometimes. They call it blowback. Headaches. Fatigue. Unconsciousness. It varies."

Fin twisted in her seat. "Welcome back." She tapped Thorn's shoulder. "Do we have time to stop at the bistro over there? Fighting makes me hungry."

"No time to eat, darlin'." The shifter draped his arm over her shoulder, one hand on the wheel. "See the storefront with the blue awning? The portal's inside. We'll go around back to a roll-up door where the She Beast can go through."

Dax pointed ahead. "Take that street."

Thorn twisted the wheel, rounding the corner.

The vampire rolled down his window. "Let's circle a few times. Then pull into the alley for a little up-close scoping. We don't need to meet and greet the American army or Arisen Dawn."

Thorn eyed him in the rearview mirror. "I agree."

Dax set Chiara on the seat, buckling her seatbelt. "You okay here?"

"Just a little brain fuzz. I'm good to go, but I think doing a mile on the treadmill is out."

The vampire opened the door, stomping boots on the ground when the truck slowed. "I'll explore on foot."

Chiara caught Dax's wrist. "Be careful."

She thought he might have nodded. *Maybe not. Surly vampire.* When did he get the text saying he was bullet-proof?

"Okay." The truck lurched as Thorn stomped on the brake. "We'll meet you back here in a few."

After twice around the block, Thorn moseyed the She Beast behind a building while Chiara and Fin kept their noses pressed to glass. No movement.

A good sign.

The truck crept along the alley until Thorn spied Dax.

Flinging open the door, the vampire hopped into the truck. "It looks good. I don't think the gateway is being monitored. Let's go."

Thorn circled one more time before stopping behind the vacant store hiding the portal. When he touched his wrist, the garage door opened. Driving through, he tapped again. *Kole, we're on our way through at Livingston.*

The truck and four passengers headed into what Thorn called the Whorl.

"What the hell?" Chiara shrieked as her stomach flip-flopped like tossed salad.

Fin giggled, apparently crazy enough to enjoy the sensation. She heard Dax growl and Thorn shout,

"Yippee ki yay."

Her hand clasped to her abdomen, Chiara bounced against her tight seatbelt when the truck landed upright. "A little warning would have been nice."

While the words slipped from her lips, a lot of big men wearing black and armed with swords or knives surrounded the She Beast. Their expressions were grim as if they'd survived hell.

Not more trouble. They deserved a break.

Dax must have heard her *oh, shit* gasp because he secured her against his bloody T-shirt. "Relax. We know them. Firebrand escort."

Thorn tapped the button to roll down his window. He spoke to the most brutish but handsome man Chiara had ever seen. "Brak, good to see you. Hey. You look like shit."

If this was the guy looking like shit, she couldn't imagine what he looked like all cleaned up and dressed in his Sunday finest. He was huge with dark, thick hair bushed off a masculine face but curling at his neck. His olive skin and tight tee pegged him for a Greek god.

"You don't look so good yourself, shifter. We ran into a few Arisen Dawn crazies heading your way into Livingston. We sent their spirits to Angor, swept up the area, and still obliged Kole by providing you with extra muscle. Thank me later with a good Scotch and an easy female."

Dax stuck an elbow out the window on his side. "Let's compare war stories later. We need to secure the females."

Chiara leaned forward to get a better view of their escorts. Disheveled hair. Torn and blood-stained clothing. Wounds. Bony protrusions. Tired eyes.

Except for the big guy. He looked energized.

Brak poked his head in the window, a wide grin

revealing brilliant white teeth. His clothes were slightly wrinkled. His black hair was slicked back, curling on his neck, not a piece out of place. His olive skin, kissed by a Mediterranean sun, was unmarred. His only flaw was a slight crook in the bridge of his nose, but it could have been broken years ago. Not today. And it sure didn't detract from his looks. "Nice to see you all in one piece. We'll hop in the back. Your safe ticket to the stronghold."

When the men catapulted into the back end, metal clanged against the truck bed. Brak pounded the top of the cab twice, signaling a good-to-go.

Thorn stepped on the gas, and they sped through a city with tall buildings, noisy traffic, cars and buses, streetlights, road signs, and walkers going every which way.

Fin twisted around, eyes wide. "Just like home."

The shifter rested an arm on the back of her seat. "Covenkirk. Normally we would have taken the portal inside the stronghold but no can do with the truck. We're a little security conscious at headquarters. It's just a short spell down the road."

At top speed, Thorn wove through traffic.

When somebody honked, Dax flipped them off. "There it is." He signaled thumbs-up to the guys in the truck bed.

Chiara's mouth gaped when a huge brick building surrounded by a giant iron fence rose suddenly in front of them, materializing out of nothing.

Thorn tapped his wrist. An ornate gate decorated with a Phoenix emblem swung outward, and they sailed through toward an underground garage. Again, the shifter tapped his arm. A roll-up door opened silently as if well oiled.

Chiara angled around to watch it slide down once

they were clear. The men in the back leaped over the side after Thorn pulled into a space.

Dax dropped to the ground. Brak slapped her vampire's shoulder before pulling him into a man-hug. As big as Dax was, his friend topped him by at least five inches. "We couldn't find you. Thought you were doing your Lone Ranger routine. The commander and Tyr were pissed until they heard you were ass deep in trouble." Brak paused to offer Chiara a hand, his eyes surveying her with a slow head-to-toe crawl. "Lovely female. I'm all yours."

Dax growled.

Chiara smoothed her skirt and fluffed her dark curly hair. *I must look a mess.* But she accepted his help, bouncing from the backseat. "Thanks."

"No problem. You just stick with me, and you'll be fine."

Dax shouldered Brak aside. "She's already fine, carnal demon."

Chiara snapped her gaze toward the vampire, her brows drawn tight. Why was he behaving so strangely?

Putting a possessive hand on her lower back, Dax led her toward a door. "Let's go."

Brak raised both hands in the air. "Excuse the hell out of me. Didn't know she was taken."

Chiara tilted her chin up in defiance. "I'm not."

Dax snarled.

Swiveling his neck, Thorn checked the men following Brak. "Who are these meatheads?"

"Recruits," said the huge Firebrand, his long legs eating up the hallway. "They're coming out of our asses faster than we can wipe. You'll meet them all cuz you'll be helping to train them." Brak leaned in to whisper. "They need a lot of work along with some serious butt-kicking. Though I gotta say, they were awesome in the fight today."

The men followed behind Brak like puppies hoping for a pat on the head, a yummy treat, or directions to a warm shower and bed.

"Where are we going?" Chiara threw her chin up to look at Dax, her hand in his as they walked through the long concrete hall, their footsteps echoing off bare walls.

"To Kole's office. He's the commander. Afterward, someone will settle you and Fin into new quarters."

"Do you stay here?"

"No."

"Where do you stay?"

"Here and there."

"Could you be more specific?" Why was every conversation with Dax a struggle? As if he wanted all the toys and wasn't sharing.

"Doesn't matter. You don't know your way around Covenkirk. The other Blood Coven descendants will take care of you. Tell you what's what. The whole drill."

Chiara tugged on Dax's hand, pulling him to a stop. "Why can't I stay with you?"

His inky midnight glare stabbed her in the chest. "Why would you want to do that, female?"

"I trust you."

He fisted her upper arms. "Do not trust me, little witch. That would be a big mistake."

"Too late. I already do."

"Look. Ask anybody. I fuck shit up. I'm not an honorable male."

Chiara smacked his hands away, rolling her shoulders to erase his painful grip. "I don't care. I want to stay with you. I'm not comfortable with strangers."

Fin, Thorn, Brak, and the battle-weary recruits had gone ahead. Dax grabbed her hand again, stepped up the pace, and dragged her along. "Enough of this convo. Issue settled."

What a fangdick.

He was passing her off like a piece of worn clothing, a broken-down car, a chipped vase. She was stubborn, especially when she wanted something. She wanted Dax, but he dug his heels in. Pretty soon, she might tire of kicking and dragging.

****

When Lort arrived on the cliff overlooking the garrison, Cerberus was already standing there, hands clasped behind his back, a lord-of-the-kingdom expression plastered on his condescending face. Today the Arisen Dawn leader was again disguised as a satyr. He'd better reveal himself to his army soon because they would not follow a ghost much longer. Lort already heard whispers of dissent.

Cerberus turned his back on the view, tilting a haughty chin toward his general.

Did he know the Bozeman outcome? Lort suspected he was a powerful mage, capable of using a spell to watch the action or capable of snatching the memories from a mind. Could be a spy in Arisen Dawn who reported everything to Cerberus before Lort got the chance. If it was, he would suck the blood from the snitch's veins, pick his fangs with the squealer's bones, sever the spy's tongue with a serrated blade. But he doubted the existence of a snitch. Far more likely Cerberus was a warlock.

In the meantime, caution.

"The Battle for Bozeman went as planned, Cerberus. Our losses were many but as expected. We broke through their defenses and had the Earther army running scared. They regrouped but not in time."

"How many of ours are loose to plunder?"

"My guess is about twenty. They scrambled through the defenses. But the humans will round them up quickly. We'll keep an eye out to analyze the army's responses."

Cerberus squeezed Lort's shoulder. "The victory in Bozeman is already filtering through the Scath gossip grapevine. Aeternals are flocking to our cause, eager to enslave the weak humans. So many among us are tired of hiding, tired of not taking our rightful place as masters, tired of not sating our hungers on *Homo sapiens* flesh."

Lort brushed a hand through his hair, his gaze on his boots, while he listened to his leader's usual rant about the superiority of Aeternals, their destiny to rule the three realms. *Blah. Fucking. Blah.* Oh, Lort swallowed the rhetoric. But he preferred the concrete outcome. He wanted the ranch he had been promised where he would corral humans like cattle. He'd free his bludfrenzy, dine at will, fuck his food until they collapsed dead in his arms. He didn't want oratory. He wanted fresh meat.

Lort glanced up when the tirade ended. "Our damaged ones are loose on Earth this time. No use wasting valuable soldiers as fodder when we have so many strung out on Gold Dust."

"I hear the Firebrands attacked Arisen Dawn on this side of the portal."

"They did. Their warriors stopped some of our fighters from getting through to Earth. Our next battle will be more strategic. Our disposables were a good strategy this time, but eventually, we must send in a stronger invading force."

The faux satyr stroked his chin. "Have you identified capable officers?"

"Yes, sir. Quite a few. A clever shifter fell into our laps, along with others I have been grooming for leadership positions."

"We will win because Earthers are inferior."

Lort nodded. "Of course. But in the meantime, we analyze, plan, build, train. We keep our heads low, expand our army, get all Scath to our cause, and defeat the Firebrands. Our disposables will continue to vex the humans with small, unexpected incursions into out-of-the-way locales. The Americans will eliminate them but not before they have instilled fear in the populace. These minor raids by drug-addled Aeternals will make the Firebrands and humans think we are ineffective, incompetent, out-of-control, and few in number. When we show our true power and invade Earth, we will set the humans on their knees at our feet. Praise Gahya."

A smile teased Cerberus's lips. "Praise the Genitrix."

Chapter Twenty

Dax reported to Kole and shared how Boden, the director of the Ministry of Compliance, was ass-deep in Arisen Dawn. When Firebrands checked on the guy, he was in the wind. Following the meet with the commander, he chatted a few with his sister Bounty. Unfortunately, he couldn't erase the vision of Chiara when he deserted her, her eyes glittering with moisture, her usual laughing lips downturned.

Now he sprawled in his favorite chair at the O blud den, the scent of drug-tainted blood heady, his fangs eager to pop a vein. He waited for one of the place's whores, not caring which one.

This was where he belonged, proof he wasn't mate material. He was no hero. He was a selfish sonofabitch who saw to his own needs first. If he hadn't, Bounty would never have been… Fuck it. He didn't want to think about the past now. What was done was done. Anxious to get busy, Dax snapped an ankle over his knee, stared at the upper balcony, and willed a door to open.

At least he wasn't stupid enough to mainline the stuff as his mother had done. Highway to addiction. *No.* He was smart. He took the shit filtered through a female's veins. No addiction. Just the numb. The unfeeling zone. The dead end. Dax was screwed up, but unlike millions of other losers, he knew it. That made him the Jesus Fucking Christ of vampires. He leaned forward, resting his head in his palms, his long black hair shielding him like a curtain.

Bounty had been at her desk on the computer when he'd left Kole's office. The comm was lucky to have her. She had always been level-headed, wise, a happy kid despite her surroundings.

It was Bounty's eleventh birthday. He had used his last penny to buy a cake with chocolate frosting because no one else would have. She leaped onto a chair to get in the best position, her blonde hair, badly tied with a red ribbon, falling over her shoulders when she bent forward. The tips of her scuffed black shoes peeked from beneath her long skirt, wrinkled but clean. He saw to their laundry when he remembered. She blew out all the candles while their mother looked on from a chair at the end of the table, her eyes glazed as usual, not seeing what was happening. Not caring.

The female, once the proud mate of a Scion Firebrand who had been Dax's father, was now an O blud whore who worked for another male. The one who was Bounty's sire and Dax's stepfather.

"Good job. You got them all." Dax clapped at his half-sister's success and delight. She slipped down into her chair, holding her plate, a wide smile lighting up her innocent face.

Dax cut a large wedge of cake and plopped it onto a saucer, a rose on top of her slice. He cut one for himself, glancing toward their mother. She was unaware of what went on around her. So, he didn't give her any.

With her mouth full, Bounty questioned her brother. "Did you get me a present?" She wiped a few crumbs off her lips with the back of her hand.

"Let me think." A man leaning against the doorjamb drew away his attention. His stepfather and owner of the opiate whorehouse. The slime focused his gaze on Bounty who, despite her age, had begun to blossom into a well-developed female.

Dax watched the wheels grind in the male's disgusting brain. Despite being fifteen, the young vampire knew he would never allow this life to touch his sister. She would not become fodder as their mother had.

He was too young to protect or care for Bounty as a full-time job, but he did know a prize the perverted male would value more than his sister.

Dax shoved a brightly wrapped package toward the girl. She squealed as she tore off the ribbon along with the paper, too excited to take her time.

She ran child-like fingers tipped with jagged dirty nails along the gold-embossed cover of a diary. "Oh. How beautiful." It was bound in red leather, her favorite color. She opened it, exposing lined cream-colored pages. "I will write all my adventures into this book. I'll write about you, too, Dax. For you will be a great hero. One of the greatest Scath will ever see. You'll be a Firebrand like your father."

A snort of laughter erupted from the doorway, making Bounty squeeze her lips into a disapproving pout.

Dax glared in the direction of the hollow sound. "Don't bother about me, little sis. This book should be about you and all the wonderful things you'll do with your life." He knew with bright clarity it was up to him to give her that chance.

His pulse ticked up a notch. His breaths drew fast and shallow as he approached his stepfather. While Bounty showed their non-responsive mother the gift, he took the male by the elbow. "We have something to discuss. Follow me."

Long before his vampire Awakening, the ritual when he would assume his full powers, Dax was a force of nature. Stubborn, determined, strong. He looked and acted far older than his fifteen years.

The male followed his stepson into an office, closing the door. His demeanor colder and more calculated than it had been in the kitchen, the bastard took a chair behind the desk. "Sit."

Dax declined the invitation. "I can say what I came to say standing."

His eyes narrow slits, the O blud den owner shrugged. "Spit it out."

"I have a deal to offer. It's two-fold. First, I'll work for you. You've seen the females eye me. They want me, but nobody gets to stick fang or dick in me. I'll handle the males my own way. Second, Bounty will never set foot in one of your client rooms."

The male who was his stepfather grinned like he'd struck Darque's coveted phosphorescent gold.

Despite the lump in his throat which warned he was trading his future for Bounty's, Dax continued. "The day the deal is broken, I promise you I will no longer bring in business. And the loss of money will cut you like a Spriggan's blade." Dax leaned onto his stepfather's desk, his fingers splayed to hold his weight. "Here's what else I promise, and maybe this will make you think thrice. I will skin you alive, motherfucker. Alive. Cut your fangs from your gums. And then set you on fire."

His stepfather probably knew Dax already humped some of the females in the den. Who could blame a teen bloodsucker for liking pussy? He pretty much liked anything that fisted his dick. And that thing never got soft. Dax blamed it on being jacked up on extra libido.

Recognizing a good deal when he heard one, the slime agreed. He didn't even blink at the threat. Dax wasn't stupid, though. He knew a time would come when Bounty would be worth the male's betrayal. His stepfather would break the deal. But before then, Dax would be capable of supporting them, and he would take her and run.

When he walked out of the office, an excited, smiling Bounty met him at the foot of the stairs, her diary open. "Look. I already wrote about my birthday party.

The best one ever." She turned the pages toward him, flowing letters penning her first entry.

Her threw an arm over her shoulders. "There'll be lots more, little sis. You'll see."

From the start, Dax was a hot commodity. Loved by males and females for his youthful bod, bulging muscles, big dick, and inventive activities. Truth be told, he was a randy adolescent. He would have dipped his wick for free. He also got all the free veins he could sink his fangs into. He didn't need to hunt. Unless he was feeling particularly predatory. Or savagely hungry. Sometimes after a particularly violent or inventive session, he not only dined on a client, but later he over-sated himself with a bloody meal-on-two feet. He figured he was a natural at this whoring business.

He also learned he got off on pain. Giving it. Not so much taking it. But for the females, what little conscience he had made him save his unadulterated bite for those who got off on BDSM. He never released males from the hurt, always denying them the pain inhibitor he could secrete through his fangs. Yeah. Whimpers, screams, and struggles were aphrodisiacs. Strange though, his clients left satisfied, eager for more. Ah. The adolescent vampire. Erotic angst at its best.

Dax barely remembered his birth father, a longtime Firebrand. And the realm had been in bad shape back then. Some say he was a good male, but some claimed he was a cold-hearted bastard. At least he'd had an honest job. He died in battle. In a way, so did his mother that day. His stepdad had hooked her on O after he mated her. The why escaped Dax. She eventually died from grief or addiction. He didn't know or care. He didn't attend her Cede, the funeral ceremony, and he didn't tell his sister.

With his whoring, he eventually saved up enough

to run with Bounty. He just did it too late.

After their escape and his Awakening, the Firebrands called him to service. Why him, he couldn't imagine. He figured the Phoenix had pulled a real boner.

When a position opened in Kole's office, Dax slipped a word to his sister. The rest was Scath history. Showed how smart and talented she was. Traits he lacked.

He was skilled with the kill, though. Maybe he underestimated the street smarts of the Phoenix. The Firebrands needed murderers with no conscience. Talk about a good fit. Shoe. Foot. Perfect.

A door opened on the balcony above as meaningless laughter, devoid of real pleasure, rolled down the steps. The sound was nothing like the joy which came out of Chiara's mouth. Dax unfolded his bulk from the chair, lumbered through the hallway, and pushed open the door, banging it against the brick wall.

On the street, he took a deep breath, inhaling the fresh, cool scent of clean air. Today, he wouldn't feed from or fuck an O blud whore.

Today.

Tomorrow was an eternity away.

****

General "Lip" Lipton opened the note a sergeant had just delivered. He nodded before turning toward the command officers and staffers gathered in the tactical operation tent for the After-Action Review in the early morning. He folded the message, tucking it into his pocket. "No word on Colonel Garcia yet. The last information has him scuffling with one of those otherworlders. We have not found a body. Best guess, he's been captured."

Mateo Garcia, who commanded his Ranger battalions, had led a mop-up crew into the city to round up frenzied otherworlders. His men returned but not the colonel. Damn fine soldier. And friend. Lip swallowed the hard lump in his throat. Anger and loss were debilitating emotions. So he shoved them aside to make room for the cold reason he needed to command his unit.

Before the message about Matty, he had reviewed the *what-happened*, the description of the battle's events, KIA stats on both sides, number of wounded, captured otherworlders, weapons and equipment used, and comments on supplies. They had moved on to the *why, how-to-do-better,* and *what's-needed.* He was closing the AAR.

Lipton recognized his youngest lieutenant colonel, a tall, rangy officer with red hair who led one of the Ranger battalions assigned to SMO Left Bank. "Bozeman was a clusterfuck. We learned it takes fewer of them to overpower us than expected. Our soldiers faltered when they saw how alien our enemy is. Credit to them, they got back into the game quick. I count the fight as a learning experience. But it wasn't pretty."

"Did we get video?" Lipton rubbed his neck as he addressed an intel staffer.

"Yes. We've scheduled everyone to view the film. The next time, they'll know what to expect. Hell. They fed on us." He closed his eyes as if to erase ugly visions.

Lipton clasped his fingers behind his back. "A soldier reported a strange occurrence. He said a … um … vampire, he guessed, fought on our side. Savage man. Fed from the otherworlders he killed. And he killed a shitload. The vamp was with a second guy. Half man, half wolf. The soldier said they made his childhood nightmares seem like wet dreams. But they were on our side."

The red-headed officer pushed back from the

table, crossing an ankle over his knee. "What do you make of it?"

Lip shrugged. "Maybe they're not all the same. Maybe some are the good guys."

"How do we tell the difference?" asked his female lieutenant colonel, commander of the second Ranger battalion.

"We don't. If it's an otherworlder, kill it or capture it. No change to the goal. Okay. Let's talk. What don't we know?" Lip signaled a staffer to take notes on a whiteboard.

The oldest of his officers, who commanded Task Force Green, leaned forward onto an elbow. "Where they will invade. We are aware of some portal sites but not all. Probably very few." His temples may have been graying, but his analysis was as sharp as ever.

"Check." Lip nodded at his notetaker.

"We don't know their numbers. Leaders. What are we calling them? Their … powers?" The Task Force Blue commander pointed at the whiteboard. "What their world is like. Are they all savages? Are some normal folks with … strange appetites?"

"We don't know how to get through their portals to where they live." The female lieutenant colonel held herself stiff-spined, her posture as army as she was.

"What do we know?" Lip pushed off from his chair to stand. He paced, heavy brows hooding his eyes.

The woman officer leaned forward. "They're hard to kill. Bullets don't necessarily keep them down. I saw dead ones rise to fight again. Like a fucking zombie apocalypse. We need to kill them for real. Colonel Garcia told us to lob off their heads."

The redhead rested his hands on the table. "Some are vampires. There's something I never thought I'd say. Others I'd call werewolves. Hell. One had a lion's mane.

What's that? A werelion? Used claws to rip out a soldier's heart. Gruesome way to go. I saw a petite woman wave her arms through the air. Like a witch auditioning for a role in *Bedknobs and Broomsticks*?" A few chuckles made it around the room. "Hey. I got kids. I read bedtime stories."

"I'd go with *Hocus-Pocus*," said the Green Task Team colonel.

The woman officer said, "How about *The Witches of Eastwick*?"

Lipton held up a hand before the officers let off any more steam by listing movies about witches. "Continue, Red."

"Nothing, just we know they're different species or races."

"We know we need stronger firepower. The tranqs we acquired from Dante's Humans First group are effective if we can hit them." The Blue Task Force commander crossed his arms over his chest.

Lip stopped pacing to face his officers. "Zero in on our biggest problem?"

"Pinpointing where they're coming through so we can get soldiers there fast enough to stop them," said the Green Task Force colonel.

The redhead added, "Being able to kill them once we're there."

Lip turned to his notetaker. "Star those items. Staffers, we need solutions for these problems yesterday. Long-term picture, scientists are studying the devices we took off the otherworlders. Apparently, the tech is difficult to decipher. Once they figure out the damn things, we believe we can invade their homeland. Take the battle to them. Roll in with big guns, tanks, planes, bombs, the works. Comments? Questions?"

Lip searched the faces of his advisors. They had

volunteered for this mission. He hoped he was the leader they deserved. They stared back at him through expectant eyes, asking if he was the man to get the job done.

It was the same question he had asked himself every night since Joint Ops had created Operation Frankenstein and assigned him the Left Bank Special Mission Unit. His answer to his own question? *Hell yes.* He was the man for the job.

Now, how would he get Colonel Mateo Garcia back?

****

Chiara leaned into the pool table, one end of the cue resting on her thumb and index finger. She relaxed her knees, eyed the ball, and aimed for the sweet spot. Missing the pocket, she gripped the stick, resting the bumper on the floor.

Oops.

A grinning demon named Sig rubbed his chin, stepping up to the table while his friend Bade, a vampire, watched the eight-ball action from the sidelines, offering occasional advice.

Stronghold live-ins had gathered for an impromptu party, welcoming Fin and her into their fold. Tonight, forgetting about Arisen Dawn for a few hours, they vowed to eat, drink, and talk too much. The recruits had been assigned to check the portals while they celebrated.

Waiting for Sig to miss, Chiara grabbed a piece of pepperoni pizza with extra cheese.

Jace shook her head, caught up in an argument with Ram. "That's not the way to eat a slice, satyr. Use the fold hold." She flipped one section over the other lengthwise.

"What makes you such an expert?" asked Ram, looking to Denim for support.

His mate arched her brows. "Don't look at me. I don't eat the stuff. Requires extra gym time to burn off the calories."

Jace offered her deets. "Anyone from New York knows how to eat pizza. The rest of the world is screwed up."

Giving in, Ram folded his pizza as directed. "Where's your warlock tonight, Jace?"

When a loud cheer erupted from the TV area, Tyr sent an over-the-head wave toward Jace. She grinned. "That would be him with Chay, playing Red Dead. Their fav game."

"You're up, gorgeous," Sig said, interrupting Chiara's fascination with her newly acquired family.

A shout came from the corner. "Yes." Fin fisted the air, her dart centered in the bullseye. "Waiting tables in a bar for so many years paid off in victory." Thorn brushed the tight curls from her forehead where he planted a kiss.

When Chiara lifted the pool cue and aimed at a striped ball, Sig stepped behind her. "Here. You're holding the stick wrong." He leaned his body over her, guiding her hand, demonstrating correct form.

His groin pressed to her ass. She pushed him away. "I get the idea. Thanks."

A dartboard-defeated Thorn passed by the pool table. "Hey, recruit. You keep up that action, Dax will separate your head from your nuts."

"Mind your own biz, shifter." Sig's fingertips sizzled. Like Kole, he was an animus demon.

Chiara missed the pocket. "Dax has no control over me or who I talk to."

"Sure," said the shifter as he headed for the bar.

"Get me a beer, please." Fin leaned against the wall next to Chiara. "Why so sad?"

"I miss my dogs. My neighbor will take good care of them. But he's not me. Besides, they're all I've got."

Sig rested the handle of his pool cue on the floor. "Hey. You've got us."

Chiara smiled. Then a spark of heat shot up her spine, her legs weakening. When she turned, Dax shouldered the doorway, muscled arms crossed, a scowl on his lips shadowed by a hint of mustache and a goatee, his black hair falling like silk around his face.

How long has he been there?

His deadly gaze was locked on Sig.

Despite wanting to ignore the fanghead vampire, Chiara's heart thumped against her chest so hard she pounded a fist to her sternum.

Ignore him. Ignore him. He's irresistible with tons of sex appeal wafting out his pores, but you don't see him.

She leaned the pool cue against the wall while Sig pocketed two balls in a row. Chiara brushed away wisps of hair which had escaped her single, thick braid.

La, la, la. Oh, fuck it. The man is impossible to ignore.

She did what any star-struck idiot would. She stalked over to him, toe-to-toe. "Did you hear why my mom was so intense about my bug-out monkey?"

"No." His dark eyes continued to drill into Sig despite a relaxed pose.

"Braelyn told me my mother was a tracker for *Custodes Templii*. She found this out from Miller Nash, the guy who runs the group. So Mom knew we were descendants of the Blood Coven witch Eydris. Her job was to monitor the offspring in our line. Anyway, Nash's group kept track of me for years under my real last name Bianchi. They lost me when I ran from the foster home and changed my surname to Flores, one of the IDs in my bag."

"Didn't know." He continued to pin the demon at the pool table.

By this time, Sig had picked up on Dax's glare. He was uncomfortable. Sweat beads dotted the poor guy's forehead.

"Stop it." She stroked the vampire's forearm.

"He touched you." When his eyes shifted away from his prey, he ran a knuckle down her cheek.

Chiara sighed, melting into the caress, but Dax tensed as if he caught himself doing something bad. He jerked back his hand.

"Did you see me playing pool? Pretty sorry, huh?"

"Yeah. The worst." Dax resumed his unconcerned lean.

"You want to play a game with me when Sig and I are done?"

"No."

"Just no? Is there anything you want to do with me?"

Lightning fast, he snagged her wrist, his grip painful, his fingers marking her skin. "Don't ask for something you can't handle."

Chiara bristled, a chill breeze whipping around her bare feet.

"Shit." Dax flinched, dropping his grip. When he examined the blistered flesh on his palm, a bitter laugh tumbled out of his mouth. "Good one, witch."

"I'd think twice about hurting me, vampire. I've got game."

He pushed off from the doorjamb, growling as he stormed out of the room.

Rubbing where Dax had squeezed, Chiara

glanced around to see if anyone had noticed. But everybody was busy doing their own thing. Bade watched Sig rack balls for a new game. Jace chatted with Ram and Denim. Fin and Thorn argued over some rule about darts until he circled her waist to pull her in for a steaming hot kiss. End of argument when she melted against his body.

One person noticed. Braelyn parked herself beside Chiara. "Men. Well, at least, vampires. They're moody and temperamental on their best days. Are you sure he's what you want?"

Chiara toyed with her braid. "He can barely stand me. Why would I want someone who snarls at me all the time?"

Braelyn tapped her chin, appearing to consider the question. She pointed at Rein across the room. "See my vampire? Hot bod. Great sex. Loyal. A friend. My greatest love. But he buries his affection so deep it's sometimes hard to find. But it's there. And it's for me only and forever." The Blood Coven descendant wandered off, leaving Chiara alone with her desires.

She wanted the same. But her vampire, the man she had dreamed of all her life, couldn't care less about her. She had healed him when he was injured, fed him blood when he needed it, and given him the biggie. Her virginity. What was his problem?

Thorn whistled, catching the attention of the gathered guests. He announced he would be moving into the stronghold with Fin.

Sig found Chiara. "Your turn, witch. Don't make me look bad."

Chiara blinked to rid her eyes of moisture as she watched her new family. Denim ran fingers through Ram's hair, and Chay slung an arm over Margo's shoulders. Skyler perched on Kole's lap while she chatted with Jace, whose hand rested on Tyr's thigh. In a shadowy corner, Sabine and Nico danced, arms around each other's neck, feet shuffling. That's what love looked like. It didn't snarl and stomp off. Hot bod and great sex aside, Dax wasn't hers. Face facts. Move on.

Picking up her pool cue, she didn't push Sig away when he stepped forward to help her perfect her form. But she still wished for a vampire to press close, to wrap his arms around her and show her how to sink a striped ball into the corner pocket.

Chapter Twenty-One

Dax flashed from the stronghold to the O blud den, punching a fist to the door to slam into the waiting area.

A blonde slumped in a threadbare chair, her legs crossed, a short kimono flapping open. Her hair wasn't long, dark, and curly. Her skin wasn't kissed by the sun. She was perfect. Especially since she wasn't Chiara.

She'd wipe the little witch out of his system. Enough stalling. O blud along with a rough fuck would do the trick. He wouldn't back out this time.

Dax snapped his fingers, grabbing her hand to race for the stairs. "You'll do. Let's go."

She followed him, her feet stuttering to keep pace. He took the steps two to her one.

He led them to his favorite room. It had no bed. No chair. A free-standing bar, like a ballerina might use, was the only furniture. He chuckled. The blonde was no dancer. He hadn't seen a single female in the place who could do a *plié*. No. This bar had one purpose. Bend over and take it.

Once inside, she was naked in an instant. All she had to do was untie the sash of her skimpy robe and let it fall to the floor. She fingered herself as if that would make her more desirable to the vampire. The only thing he cared about was the high. The numb. The escape. She could stop with the finger motion.

With her other hand, she flipped her hair over her shoulder, running her fingers along the pulse in her neck.

His mouth watered. He already tasted the drug-laced blood. Smooth. Heady. Offering him everything he desired.

Let Chiara play pool with Sig. Or any male for

that matter. *Hell.* Let her take a lover. Maybe he had activated her Blood Coven genes, but he'd never mate her. She was chasing the wrong dream.

"Come on, baby," cooed the naked female. "You need some help? I can blow you."

When he snarled, shaking his head, she bent over the bar with her ass pointed at him, her fingers working herself hard.

The vampire Firebrand wondered what brought a succubus this low. What made her shoot opium to offer herself as fodder for males like him? Did she have a brother who cared about her? *Damn.* Erase. He didn't give a fuck how she got here. He wiped his mind of any concern for her sad existence. Everyone had a boo-hoo story. As Dax saw it, live the life you're dealt or get out.

He unzipped his pants, peeling them to his knees. His cock wasn't stiff, but he wanted to fuck the blonde while he fed from her. He wanted to banish the little witch from his mind. He wanted back where he was comfortable, buried fang and dick deep in an O blud whore. It's what he deserved.

He had allowed his mother to slip into a life of degradation. Sure, he had willingly offered himself to his stepfather as a substitute for Bounty. But had he done it to save her or to get his grind on? Did it matter? No. The result was the same. When the crunch came, he let his sister down.

He fisted his shaft and began to pump. It didn't take long to arouse it. Never did. He must be the horniest bastard around. Anything got him up and going.

He didn't need the little witch with the eyes like rare Darque orchids. All he needed was a hole and some hip action. His head lolled backward. Dax placed his hands on the blonde's waist, a smile curving his lips, his lids half-masted in anticipation.

****

Kole eyeballed the chaos in the chamber. Vampires bared fangs. Shifters got down and furry. Witches threatened spells while berserkers pounded their chests.

Known for a hot temper and no-shit tolerance, Kole wanted to fry at least twelve of the eighteen Scath leaders until crispy. A twist on the two-thirds majority rule favored by the lawgivers or the Temple of Justice. It was a fantasy. A good one.

Aras, the Temple's high justice, pounded a gavel. *Bang. Bang. Bang*. "Order." When his demand went unheeded, black wings punched from his back while he half-shifted into an eagle, his predatory sharp-pitched whistle rising above the noise. The rotunda stilled, attendees hesitant to piss off a beast with deadly talons.

Today was a rare meeting of Scath's two governing bodies along with the ministries. Alarik had offered the large high-domed chamber in his Ministry of Well Being.

The room was full of talking heads who cared more about winning elections than doing the right thing. Behind the community leaders sat clerks, interested dignitaries, and gofers. Taking the glaring spotlight were Cadmon and his commanders.

A blessed silent minute passed before the disputants jumped back onto their feet, yelling opinions, obscenities, and threats.

Justice Draven flashed pearly fangs at the djinn Roshan whose finger waved in response. Nymph Lawgiver Nerina slammed her notes on the table, pages fluttering onto the floor, while the demon Lawgiver Mara body-checked her, outweighing the smaller female by fifty pounds.

With the continued disorder, Aras took to the air,

his huge-ass wings sending cups flying, empty chairs toppling, documents scattering. The smart ones in the rotunda did a duck-and-cover.

Re-establishing silence, Aras settled back into his seat, naked, *sans* robe. An aide stepped forward to hand him a new one. "The Firebrands have come before us to explain recent events. Let them. We'll listen with civility. Afterward, we will provide informed direction. High Commander, please continue." He left out *or else.* But the room understood the implied threat. An angry eagle had an appetite for flesh.

"As I was saying, we are close to finding Cerberus and his Arisen Dawn garrison of fanatic followers, some strung out on Gold Dust, the drug distributed by shifter packs."

The high commander sank into his chair, white-knuckling the armrests. He nodded for his animus demon Firebrand to speak.

Kole tugged at the neck of his uncomfortable-but-required purple ceremonial robe while he prepared to face the bitchin' Nancies. He brushed a hand down the sleeve bearing the insignia of the fiery Phoenix. "The other day, Arisen Dawn trapped a couple of my males Earthside at a site now known as the Battle for Bozeman. My experienced warriors assisted the Earther army who was trying to defend their city against feral Aeternals high on this Gold Dust. At the same time, several squads of my Firebrands contained more of their crazies on the Scath side of the portal."

Justice Dolph glanced up from his notes. Or for all Kole knew, a solitaire game on his tablet. "What was the outcome?"

"Mixed." Kole cleared his throat. "The Earthers fought hard in this first major encounter but did a cut-and-run when faced with Arisen Dawn's savagery. To their credit, they regrouped quickly. Make no mistake, the future could be theirs because of superior numbers, advanced technology…"

"Big ass guns," interrupted Daire, the incubus lawgiver.

"Yes. Also home court advantage." Kole scrubbed a fist over his buzz-cut hair. "We estimate about twenty invaders broke loose. Polluted on drugs, they'll be a quick catch but not before they ravage humans throughout the city and countryside."

"How did your males come to fight alongside the Earthers?" asked Aras, resting on an elbow, trying to look relaxed while two wolf shifters went claw to tooth in the back of the chamber. "Excuse me." He rose, pounding a fist on the podium. "Somebody get them the fuck out of here. Sorry, Commander."

Kole shrugged. "Their participation was not by invite. They were on the way home but stopped when they figured the humans needed a hand."

Chaos erupted again. Obviously, everyone didn't agree with aiding Earthers. *Bang. Bang. Bang.* Aras's gavel pounded. "Commander Jarek. Comment?"

Jarek's deep voice thundered across the meeting room. "Let me remind you. This same Cerberus who heads Arisen Dawn could be the hound of prophecy who seeks Blood Coven descendants to jumpstart the destruction of the realms." Uncharacteristically, his djinn power slipped to the surface, surrounding his muscular body with smoke. Before he disappeared into it, though, he regained control.

Aras pointed the gavel at Cadmon. "Tell us, High Commander. What do you propose?"

The front of his robe covered with chest candy awarded after many successful battles, the ylve looked to Nace, Jarek, and Kole for confirmation. All three nodded. His mouth drew into a grim slash while he delivered the plan. "Martial law. Severe measures. Curfews. Identity checks. When we find the Arisen Dawn base, we terminate all present with extreme prejudice. We round up suspected associates. If they resist, assume the worst. Initiate a shoot-to-kill. No survivors. If they offer no resistance, send them to Outcast Keep on Darque."

An earthquake of sound met Cadmon's plan, the rotunda walls shaking with shouts of opposition or support. Fights broke out, Roshan and Daire drawing first blood.

Aras's eagle eyes narrowed to slits as he leaned forward in his seat, the gavel tightly clutched in his talons. "The next uncivil asshole in this chamber will be prey." To emphasize the point, he popped black feathers.

With steely warrior's arms crossed on his chest, Jarak waited for the rotunda to quiet, the combatants hoarse, exhausted, or terrified of Aras. "We also intend to contact the human army for a peace meet. Show them we want to work together."

Hands raised, the attendees taking the eagle shifter at his word.

"The podium recognizes Rike, the berserker lawgiver." Aras sipped water from a glass on the table, his wings snapping out, fanning the front row. "Speak."

"Consider this, Firebrands, if you destroy Arisen Dawn but the Earth armies are not in a compromise mood, you will have eliminated a vast number of able fighters. We may need them down the road."

Nerina pushed back her chair to stand, smoothing imaginary wrinkles in her red robe. Aras nodded his recognition. "Interesting. Strategic. Stupid. I agree with Jarek. I propose we see if this human army will meet. If they do, we try to reach a peaceful solution."

Kole had always found the nymph lawgiver to be rational, her research into voting issues complete, thoughtful.

"If I may, Aras," said Supreme Lawgiver Fera. She tapped her chin with a long, cherry-red nail. "Nerina is, of course, within her right to seek a weak position. Though I wonder. Perhaps we would be wise to consider Rike's observation and take it a step further. If Arisen Dawn defeats the humans, it may be time to resume our place on Earth."

With the female's sleek, muscled body and flawless face, she was reputed to be the most beautiful Aeternal on Scath. But only a suicidal male would bed her. Kole would rather fuck a poisonous scorpion. Of course, if he wet his dick even in a venomous insect, he was a dead demon. Skyler would deliver the killing blow. Never gonna happen anyway. He loved his mate too much.

Raucous shouts of *yes* or *never* followed her proposal. They stilled at Aras's cold-eyed threat.

Alarik unfolded from his chair, where he sat off to the side with the other directors of ministries, except the missing Boden. "We have no business ruling Earth. That's why the Blood Coven created Scath and Darque. Are we to go backwards?"

"As a nonvoting attendee, you have no business offering an opinion," said Rike. "If Arisen Dawn flexes its muscle, the humans will be more likely to negotiate. I say we adopt Fera's plan. Wait and see. If they succeed, perhaps our fate is to return to Earth."

Commander Nace, his golden jaguar eyes menacing, shouted above the melee. "There is no wait and see with Arisen Dawn. They are mercenaries, ferals who are hell bent on enslaving humans. The very worst of us. Will you free them to roam, kill, and feed? Is this what you want?"

"Of course not, Commander," said Fera, her brows arched, her expression a faked innocence. "But Arisen Dawn may make the Earther army more pliable. A good thing for us." She flipped her golden hair over a shoulder, looking at others for support.

Alarik jumped up. Director Jodran of the Ministry of Prosperity fisted his robe, trying to hold him in his seat. "Pliable, Fera? Good for us?" Alarik ripped the fabric out of his friend's hand, freeing himself to stand unimpeded. "Do you hear yourselves? You are condoning slaughter. Destruction. Feeding on humans. We are not about unwarranted savagery."

"You are warned, Director Alarik. Keep your opinions to yourself." Rike tossed a leg over the arm of his chair, curling his upper lip into a snarl. "If you want to vote so badly, run for office."

Kole surveyed the room, fire bouncing from one hand to the other as he fought to contain his rage. Cadmon rested a cool palm on his shoulder, urging calm.

"We cannot allow Earthers to find a way through our portals." Fera opened her robe to smooth her hands along the tight bodice of her low-cut black dress. "Can we?"

"No. We can't," said Cadmon. "They would bring superior firepower. We don't know whether the spell that prohibits our use of guns on Scath will work on their weapons." He looked to Alarik, who shrugged. "But wars should be fought only after all other measures fail. We first need to prove to them we have lived in peace beside them for centuries. Convince them we can continue to coexist, separated by the Whorl but connected commercially, emotionally."

Dolph the warlock justice stroked his chin. "Prove ourselves? When we are the older species, the superior species? An interesting approach, High Commander." He drummed his fingers on the table. "Of course, the humans may be understanding. Perhaps they will not invade our realm with their weapons of mass destruction. If we only knew."

"We have reports," said Jarek, the battle glyphs on his hands moving as if alive, "of drug-addicted Arisen Dawn invaders racing through Bozeman, destroying entire families in their sleep, feeding on them. Children and adults. Leaving behind empty husks. Is this the message we want to send to Earthers?" Again, he had to rein in the smoke threatening to obscure his body.

A lukewarm smile tugged at Dolph's lips. "No, Commander." He unfolded from his chair, throwing his arms high. He slowly spun around. "You know me, friends. I have little ambition for myself, a mild temperament. I am a warlock who prefers a smooth drink with a book by my side on a quiet evening while I relax in front of a fire. But in all good conscience, I must consider what is best for Scath. It seems unwise to destroy so many Arisen Dawn warriors before we ascertain our true enemy. I call for a vote of lawmakers and justices." He dropped into his seat, his spine straight, his eyes backlit with passion.

"Is there more discussion?" Aras's gaze swept the rotunda.

Viktor the lawgiver pressed his palms on the table in front of him, pushing up with the grace of an ancient vampire. "As you know, Humans First mercenaries kidnapped, tortured, and killed my son. I have every reason to seek vengeance. Yet, I do not wish other fathers to lose their children to unnecessary violence. I say we destroy Arisen Dawn along with this Cerberus. They dirty our species. We should never adopt their solutions. Instead, we should pursue peace between us and the Earthers. If that is not possible, we go to war with the Scion Firebrands leading the way rather than a band of Aeternal terrorists."

"Vote. Vote. Vote." Lawmakers and justices bounded to their feet, shouting.

When the room quieted, Aras picked up his tablet. "How many of you support the Scion Firebrand proposal to enact severe marshal law, eliminate Arisen Dawn as well as supporters, and approach the humans for a sit-down? Show by a raise of hands, please."

Too few arms shot into the air. Gilda. Aras. Eron. Miorise. Nerina. Daire. Viktor. Other lawgivers and justices glanced around the room, fingers laced together in their laps.

"How many are in favor of allowing Arisen Dawn to operate, to see where their actions take us?"

Eleven hands waved in the air amid a roar of victory from ministry directors and other audience members. Fera, Rike, and Dolph slapped the backs of neighbors to celebrate the outcome.

Aras banged his gavel until the noise faded. "High Commander, the Firebrands are hereby directed to keep peace on Scath but not to interfere with Arisen Dawn actions here or on Earth. No martial law. No severe measures."

"I am opposed to that order, Chief Justice." Cadmon's jaw clamped tight, his muscles flinching.

Aras inclined his head. "Nevertheless, it stands. The lawgivers and the Temple of Justice have voted as our rules dictate. To not follow the directive is treason."

Cadmon and the three commanders snapped their salutes, their boots a thunderous response to the order as they stormed from the meeting.

At the doors, Kole turned to face the congregation, his fire-gold eyes glowing with angry energy. As he prepared to tear the Scion Firebrand insignia from his sleeve, Nace stopped him, risking a severe burn. They spun, leaving the rotunda.

By the time he and the jaguar shifter bounded down the wide staircase to the lobby, Kole had to release the fire consuming his body. He created a hot ball of flame in his fist, rolled it around, and threw it onto a marble step, leaving behind a sooty stain.

Nace's skin sprouted golden fur, his beast flickering. He fisted his hands at his side, claws tearing into his palms. Jarek swept the thin braids at his temples onto his back. He leaned his head against the cool granite wall of the Ministry of Well Being, his breathing jagged, eyes closed as he struggled to contain his djinn fury.

Alarik and Aras raced down the steps, catching up with the Firebrands at the entry.

"This way," said Alarik, hustling them to an empty chamber. Gilda followed. In no time, Viktor, Daire, and Nerina slipped inside.

Aras locked the door. "Something is afoot. The vote should not have been so overwhelmingly in support of Arisen Dawn and its activities. Someone has laid the groundwork for a coup."

Kole bounced a ball of fire from one hand to the other. "I will not sit on my ass while others kill humans for sport and food."

"Allow me to finish, Commander." Aras held tight to Kole's shoulder. "I am suggesting as a first step we find out who is controlling so many votes. Let us investigate. See what we are up against. Change minds. Gather support. Seek a political solution."

Daire slapped Jarek on the back. "Your fellow djinn, Bahar, voted to give Arisen Dawn its head. He is a male of peace. Someone got his vote. Who?"

Cadmon looked each of his Scion Firebrand

commanders in the eye before giving Aras an answer. "I promise you I shall weigh your words. But if my conscience is tested by events I cannot condone, I shall act. Then you may arrest me for treason."

Kole stepped in front of Cadmon, shielding him from Aras. "Anyone who comes for this male will come through me. You might kill me, but I'll take a shitload of you bastards with me."

Jarek and Nace stood shoulder-to-shoulder beside their *freron.*

The growling jaguar shifter, fighting to hold back his beast, leveled two golden eyes on Aras. "What he said."

****

Rein clasped Darius's forearm in the traditional Firebrand greeting outside Kole's office. "Grim times, *freron.*"

"Yeah." Jarek's second inclined his head toward the conference room. "The big guys are gathered. We're the last two."

The three commanders sat near Cadmon, who elbowed the table, forehead in palms. The tension was sour enough to curdle Rein's vampire blood.

Darius nodded at Nace and his second, Mix, who as his name implied was a halfling, part wolf, part mountain lion. A rare, deadly sonofabitch since he retained the powers of both breeds. Rein always wondered how Nace's jaguar played nice with Mix. He'd love to watch the two spar.

Kole's gaze sizzled with enough volts to barbecue a questing beast. Rein took the spot beside his fiery commander.

Cadmon lifted his head, scrubbing a palm across weary eyes. "We just returned from a joint meeting with the Temple of Justice and lawgivers, where we shared what we knew about Cerberus and Arisen Dawn. We put forth a martial law proposal to contain the threat. We also shared our desire to initiate peace talks. Some supported the measures. Others disapproved."

The seconds around the table, not privy to the meeting results, eyed each other. "No one looks pleased with the outcome," observed Rein.

Nace pushed his chair back, crossing an ankle over his knee. "They voted. Weaklings."

Jarek pounded a fist on the table, his stoic demeanor slipping, his visible battle glyphs vibrating, smoke swirling around his head. "We didn't get their support."

"What do you mean?" asked Darius. The snake tat winding from his eye, across his cheek, and down his neck slithered when the muscles in his jaw twitched.

Kole's eyes sparked. "While maintaining they oppose killing humans, the majority voted against the extermination of Cerberus's forces. They want the Firebrands to adopt a wait-and-see as far as Cerberus's group."

Rein shifted in his seat, his heart gripped by a fist of ice. "Wait and see what?"

"See if Arisen Dawn conquers the human realm," said Cadmon. "Some want to return as rulers. Fera. Rike. Dolph. Others fear we shall need Cerberus's soldiers if the Earthers find a way through the portals and attack us."

"The Temple has commanded the Firebrands to stand down. We are to patrol Scath but ignore Arisen Dawn. We are to let the humans worry about themselves." Kole molded a ball of fire in his fist.

Rein unfolded to his full height, his upper lip curled back, his fangs long, sharp. "That's an order I won't obey."

Kole rose from his chair. "You espouse treason, vampire."

"I pledged an oath." He fisted his sleeve, pulling it up to uncover his brand while he pointed at the words beneath it. "*Natis in Igne. Probata est in Sanquinem.* Born in Fire. Tested in Blood. I will not dishonor Braelyn's ancestry. I will not dishonor my vow to protect."

The commander of the Covenkirk stronghold grasped Rein's forearm. "*Freron*, I take the same stand."

One by one, the Firebrands at the table rose to their feet, destroying a thousand years of obedience to those who governed Scath. They were not easy males. They weren't even good males. With personal demons nipping at their asses, they often walked the edge of right and wrong, fighting to maintain balance for the good of their realm. But the Phoenix called them for a purpose. And they were the fiery symbol's warriors first. Screw the Temple. Screw the lawgivers.

Cadmon sighed, nodding at all six Firebrands. "This is not a thing I would ask of you. I had already decided I would no longer submit to the rule of the Temple of Justice. But you … consider your actions with care."

"You didn't ask. But we're with you, ylve," said Kole. "For duty. For honor." He quoted the words above each stronghold's entry. "If our *frerons* join with us, we will no longer fight under the Temple's banner. To them we'll be traitors. If the Firebrands decide against joining us, we sever our ties. Stand alone. Each commander must meet with his warriors. Let them choose their own path."

Rein folded his arms. "Your stronghold's gonna follow you, Kole. We have never followed the Temple. You are our destiny. And we'll have your six through the gates of Angor, into its frozen pits, and back out again."

Chapter Twenty-Two

Skyler's thoughts were with Kole. He seemed distracted. Regardless of the problems facing him, he agreed to help her. She reached out a hand to accept the locket from Jace. "Personal objects like this are great." She turned it over, examining the piece of gold jewelry.

"I had forgotten all about it because it's been on my neck ever since Celene lent it to me."

Jace had told Skyler at the welcoming party she could see the history of an object by touching it. But she couldn't use her gift to find Celene's current location.

Each Blood Coven descendant proved to have a distinct talent. Braelyn manipulated minds. Margo influenced microwave energy. Denim controlled the elements. Lizette was a conjurer. Nico was a magnet. Chiara was a healer with a side ability to kill. Fin called wild animals. As a plus, she could talk to them.

"What's the next step?" asked Tyr.

"Kole is fixing up a room for me." Skyler pointed toward a closed door down hall. "He knows what I need to do my best work."

"Can we help?" Jace fingered the buttons on a pale yellow sweater which looked great with her straight-legged tan pants and matching flats. As Tyr often teased, she was a throwback to another time, quite a contrast to the pierced, bejeweled Goth-like Firebrand.

"I could do with a few more vanilla-scented candles. Braelyn usually has some. The ones I've been using are nearly kaput. I have all my other supplies. The mat, iTunes, my mate to set up the room."

"Tyr?" Jace aimed her arched brows over her shoulder.

He returned the gesture with a mock salute.

"Right. I'll run upstairs to see if Braelyn has candles."

Jace put her arm through Skyler's after the warlock disappeared in the stairwell. "I have to save Celene. I promised, and she's my best friend. I would never have survived without her."

Skyler patted her hand. "I'll do my best."

"May I watch you work?"

"No. I need complete concentration."

Just then, her huge, thickly muscled, and brutishly handsome demon opened the door. Seeing Skyler, Kole grinned, a crooked smile tugging at his lips. *Breathtaking*. "All ready to go, Frisca. Check it out."

"Where's…?"

"Last I saw, Kae was propped on Bounty's desk in her cradle, getting her nails done."

"You're starting to finish my sentences. That's scary, demon."

He laughed as she walked arm in arm with Jace into the arranged room.

Tyr ran in, carrying an armload of candles. "Got 'em."

Skyler plucked them one-by-one from the warlock, replacing the burned-out pillars. "Time to leave, everyone. This is a solo event." She gave her mate a peck on his stubbled jaw. He swatted her ass. The man had no shame.

Once the room was empty, Skyler sat cross-legged on a yoga mat. She started with a relaxation exercise to encourage visions. She rolled her head, stretching her neck. She raised her shoulders to her ears and lowered them. Straightening her legs, she bent at the waist, resting her head on one knee, grabbing her toes and pulling. She switched legs.

Enya's "Echoes in Rain" played softly on her cellphone as vanilla-scented candles flickered in the darkened room.

For this process, some mages used mirrors, glass, crystal balls, anything reflective. Skyler's medium was the ice inside her. That, along with her astral projection ability, made her unique.

When she closed her eyes, clouds floated in front of her, followed by the void of space. Stars brightened the dark sky. Rain fell. Freezing rain. She imagined herself encased in ice. She became the ice. When her frozen mind awoke, she skimmed over fields of green grass, rode air currents across desert sands, and flew above woods thick with trees and ferns.

Skyler clasped Celene's necklace to her heart. Though her lids opened, her pupils didn't see the stronghold chamber. They saw a house in North Shelters where she hovered high enough to recognize the area's mountain range.

While she waited for a door to open so she could slip inside, Skyler settled barefoot in lush grass, enjoying the moisture on the soles of her feet, the tickle of the blades as she curled her toes.

A trainer had explained that physical laws, no less real than Brownian Motion or Einstein's Mass-Energy Equation, governed the Scrying Principle, or more specifically in her case, Etheric Travel. Her body remained at Firebrand headquarters while her spirit roamed, existing in air and composed of the same gaseous substance. But in that form, she could not use already occupied space. No passing through objects and no grabbing them. She could feel a doorknob, but she couldn't turn it. When she asked for a clearer explanation, her trainer clapped hands to hips, frowned, and snapped, "Just accept it. You will never float through walls."

When a large man opened the door, Skyler

floated inside behind him. In the kitchen, a woman sat at a round oak table which had seen better days, head in hands. She appeared listless, sad shoulders slumped forward. The man who had unknowingly let Skyler inside leaned against the refrigerator, arms folded over his chest.

The vision crumbled, pixel by pixel. Skyler tried to hold on with her mind but had no choice in the matter. Her visions ended when they wanted. Her eyes focused on the candle-lit room in the stronghold, on Enya's ethereal sounds, and on the scent of vanilla. With shaky legs, she rose to her feet to cross to the door. When she struggled to open it, Kole pushed in to grab her around the waist. She leaned her head against his warm, comforting chest.

"I saw her. Get me a map. I can show you where the house is."

Tyr brushed a tear from Jace's cheek as they listened to Skyler.

****

Roark hid in an alley within sight of the portal where a band of Aeternals crossed to Earth. No army waited at this gateway, but the local police scrambled to it when chaos erupted, panicked humans having punched 911.

Squad cars, vans, and emergency vehicles arrived on the scene, sirens blaring. Uniforms and plainclothesmen took cover. Their firepower was not enough to stop the invaders from turning the streets into a killing field as they sped through, tossing bodies aside like yesterday's garbage.

When a news van parked nearby, a tall slender female wearing a blue suit and heels jumped down from the passenger seat. She and the driver rushed to the back end where she pulled out a microphone while he hefted a camera onto his shoulders.

Taking lipstick out of her pocket, she applied the bright red without using a mirror. Occupational skill, Roark guessed. She looked in a van window, fluffing her shoulder-length dark hair. Then her mouth guppied as she spoke a series of nonsense words. Probably preparing to babble eloquently as reporters do.

Breaking news.

The cameraman signaled the female. She smoothed her skirt, glanced over her shoulder at the chaotic scene, and held up the mic. The man gave her the countdown.

Roark's enhanced hearing, like all Aeternals, allowed him to filter out other sounds and listen to the reporter despite the distance.

"Thank you, Roger. Twenty minutes ago, creatures the police chief is calling mutants invaded Seattle. We are outside the Westlake Center Terminal where SPD is set up to contain them. These mutants are extremely dangerous. In the meantime, stay inside and lock your doors. Do not approach them."

She paused to glance at the mayhem behind her, the hand holding the mic quivering as the action moved closer. Taking a deep breath, as if steeling herself, she nodded at the cameraman, resuming her report.

"This station has received tips that citizens are arming to patrol the streets. Do not do this. These mutants are strong and fast. Though our own Seattle PD is struggling, the chief assures us the situation will be contained. Do not take matters into your own hands."

Roark crossed his arms, his attention moving from the newswoman to the vampire beside him. "So, do we pull them back or let them keep going until they're caught or killed?"

Lort shoved his hands into the pockets of his

Arisen Dawn uniform, his gaze fixed on his soldiers.

An incubus streaked by chasing a twenty-something male dressed in a pinstriped business suit. The Aeternal caught up with the guy, wrapping an arm around his neck. Tears streamed down the young man's cheeks as the incubus slapped a hand to the Earther's chest to feed on his lifeforce. After several moments, the drained human collapsed to the ground, an empty husk, trash in the gutter.

"The Gold Dusters are as good as dead anyway," said Lort. "Even if the Earthers don't eliminate them, they will eventually die from their addiction to the drug. But in the meantime, they are terrorizing the humans."

"We're bound to run into Firebrands again. Like at Bozeman."

Lort's forehead creased. "Possible, but the odds are with us. Too many portals for them to cover. If we keep the sorties small and quick, our successes increase. Besides, they are being removed from the action."

"What do you mean?" asked Roark.

"They've been ordered to cease and desist. Those assholes are being straight-jacketed."

A vampire lashed out at a policewoman, taking her to the ground, his fangs sinking into her neck, his throat bobbling with each draw. When he was done, he shook her like a rag doll, tossing her aside, blood dripping down his chin onto a once-white shirt. His irises streaked with red, he grabbed another victim.

A female wolf shifter jumped over the body of a dead Aeternal to catch an ambulance driver between her jaws. She shook him until he was limp. Plonking him onto the ground, she tore the flesh from his bones. A passing hedon demon, known as an eater when the rage took him, saw the fresh kill and moved in, snarling at the shifter. The female growled but backed away from her victim, leaving her prey for the larger, more dangerous demon.

The eater consumed what was left of the driver, picking his bones clean before he charged down the street, drunk on fresh meat and looking for more. The hedon demon wasn't picky. He stopped to feast on a vampire who had been shot by a policewoman.

Roark shrugged. *Oh well.* The vamp might have recovered. Not now.

A satyr rushed a policeman who had stepped away from the open door of his squad car to take a firing stance. *Bang. Bang. Bang.* Three to the chest. While the Arisen Dawn attacker was down, the officer approached to fire a couple rounds point blank to the head. The bullets shredded the Aeternal's skull. No coming back from that. Score another for the humans.

Roark angled his head toward Lort. "We still don't have an army. These Aeternals are in it just for the fill and kill. The short-term. Not the long-term victory."

Lort eyed the butchery taking place, gleeful satisfaction pasted on his face. "I know that, but Cerberus wants the humans terrified. Bone-deep scared. Once we have them tenderized with fear, we come in with our armies. They won't stand a chance. They'll be cowering in their homes, subjugating themselves to us for protection."

Roark wondered if Lort wasn't mistaken about the Earthers' reaction.

The vampire general reached out to grab the arm of a passing human. Her legs left the ground as he pulled her against his chest. When the female's fists pounded his shoulders, he bent his head, burying his fangs in her jugular. Finished, he released her, running a forearm along his lips to wipe off the blood. His eyes were streaked with crimson, a sure sign he was fighting bludfrenzy.

She staggered, clasped her throat, and stumbled toward the street. A satyr stepped from the shadows, tearing off her clothes, green-eyeing her, feeding from her arousal as he fucked her. She was dead by the time he searched for another victim.

"I think we're done here, Roark. Let them have some fun."

The raven shifter pushed off from the wall. "What's next?"

They passed the news van. The camera was on the ground, a coyote shifter dragging its operator down the sidewalk. The mic was shoved to the curb along with one navy blue high heel. *Where's the other shoe?* Tatters of a blue suit blew into a sewage drain.

"Sacramento. First another small incursion of Gold Dusters tonight. Want to join me?"

"Nah. I'm good. I'll go back to catch a few winks. Be ready for tomorrow's training."

"That's what I like about you, Roark. You're all business."

As the raven shifter strode toward the portal, the sounds of gunshots dwindled. The police were killing the Arisen Dawn soldiers or chasing remnants through the streets. He noted the devastation, cops and Aeternals littering the streets, while he strong-armed a rampaging animus demon out of his path. The female snarled but ran around him. She obviously had no desire to tangle with a beast deadlier than she was.

Not all business, but I know how to keep my eye on the goal.

****

Midday, with over four hundred pounds of wolfhound prancing at his side like show ponies, their nails clicking on the tile, Dax strode into the stronghold with a guilty conscience. Whenever they bounced, yapped, or howled, he flashed his predatory black eyes and they whimpered but settled. He had established who was alpha.

Ivan was his favorite. *Hell.* He knew why. The dog had appointed himself leader of the small pack. Since he was stronger than the others, he fought Dax's control the most. The vampire respected the challenge. It was a beast-to-beast admiration. Ivan, despite his need to test Dax's hold, liked him also, if licking the vampire's hand served as evidence.

Dax wiped another round of slobber off his pants. "You've got a bad drool thing going on, big guy. You'd make a more convincing alpha if you controlled it."

Ivan snarled but swept his tongue out to catch the blob of liquid before it fell.

"Now you've got it."

After his slip-up at the O blud den, Dax remembered what Chiara had said to Fin at the stronghold the night of the party. The wolfhounds were all she had. So with his conscience riding him hard, he had hit a portal and driven to Ernest's place, explaining how Chiara was vacationing but wanted the dogs with her.

He ticked off the reasons for his out-of-character kindness. One, the animals were better off with the little witch. Two, they would keep her focused on remaining at the stronghold where she belonged. Three, they were good protection. Four… It was too personal. So he dropped that one.

But the last reason clawed at his brain, eating away at it like a swarm of mange-mongers, Darque organ eaters the size of Texas mosquitoes. He did want Chiara to be happy. Her beasts made her happy. It was a bene if he could use them to assuage his guilt after a trip to the O blud den.

What the fuck did he have to feel guilty about? Pissed at the thought while he had driven away from Ernest's place in Idaho, he had nearly turned around with the dogs and returned them into the old man's keeping. Instead, he had kept driving, his fists white-knuckling the steering wheel.

As he was still examining his reasons, unfamiliar with pangs of conscience or a desire to make someone else happy, Chiara strolled through the kitchen's swinging door.

She was reading a book while walking. Stupid female. When she looked up, she stumbled. Her eyes flitted from Dax to the hounds and back again.

Her mouth gawped open as the arm holding the book fell to her side. "You brought my boys." The dogs charged her, tails wagging, bodies twisting, fur flying, nails clicking as they jumped.

When they nearly knocked her off her feet, Dax growled. The dogs snapped their eyes in his direction. It was a stare-down. Dax won. The wolfhounds calmed, sitting and waiting while she petted them one at a time. Though their tails still swished back and forth uncontrollably, the vamp figured she was okay. No danger from death-by-happy-tail.

Chiara's black hair hung to her waist in a thick braid. He preferred it loose, but she was an angel, outfitted in an off-the-shoulder peasant blouse and a long colorful skirt with her bare toes peeking underneath.

The smile which spread across her face made Dax's corrupt heart beat fast. He shrugged. "I thought…"

He didn't have a chance to finish before she plowed through the white and gray shaggy-haired dogs to throw her arms around his neck, her breasts rubbing against his chest. Dax allowed himself to enjoy the warmth of her embrace. He even dropped his head, nestling into her neck to catch the scent which was uniquely Chiara. The woods, rosemary, and mint. Coming to his senses, he trailed his hands to her shoulders, along her arms, and to her wrists where he disengaged her fingers.

Despite his snarl, she continued to grin like an idiot. Emptiness chilled him when her eyes swung to her dogs, forgetting him.

"Ivan, Boris, Victor, Peter. Hugs all around." She dropped to her knees as the wolfhounds bounced around her, no longer in Dax's control.

She flung her arms around all four animals, tears streaming freely down her cheeks. The vampire sent them a warning when they almost pushed her to the ground.

The skin around her eyes crinkled as her gaze sought Dax through all the happy fur. "Thanks," she mouthed, returning to burying her nose in dog.

One word. One look.

And her warmth poured into every fiber of Dax's being. He pushed back at the unwanted sensation.

A soft heart gets you killed.

****

Braelyn got off the phone with her father in Seattle. The offices of *Strange But True* were fine, having battened down the hatches while Arisen Dawn ran wild through the streets.

Heading to the common kitchen on the first floor, she halted at the top of the stairs. Dax turned over four humongous dogs to Chiara. The newcomer witch was on her knees, her arms wrapped around all four hounds, tears rolling down her cheeks. The animals took turns cleaning her face.

Dax shifted from foot to foot. The only thing

missing was an *aw, shucks, ma'am.* Then the vampire spun to leave.

Chiara ran after him, grabbing his shoulder. He stopped. She couldn't have stayed him unless he had allowed it. But when he spun around, he didn't look happy. Then again, Braelyn didn't know what happy Dax looked like.

She raced back to her apartment and punched numbers into her cellphone. Rein stepped from the bathroom, a towel around his hips, his muscled chest bare, a hip jutting against the doorjamb. Braelyn froze at the sight, her arm dropping to her side.

No time for that fine man right now. She raised the phone again. "Dax. It's Braelyn. Glad I caught you."

A *hmph* came from his end. *Friendly bastard.* But this was for Chiara. Who was she kidding? It was for love.

Rein arched a brow as he strode across the room to sprawl in a chair, spreading his legs wide and displaying his package. His thick, hard, erect package.

Braelyn licked her lips, her attention hijacked by the sight of her mate. The man was insatiable. *Back to the phone.* "Anyway, I arranged for Chiara to start with her skills coach today at the Thaumaturgy Institute outside Covenkirk. I was thinking it would be best to send a Firebrand with her. You know, for safety. Brak's a good choice. He's strong. Everybody likes him. Probably because he's a carnal demon and they're hot. He's also smitten with her, so I know he'll take great care of her. In fact, I think he plans to ask her on a date. He'll be taking her in the truck since the Firebrands are sending along some supplies and equipment. Just wanted to let you know since you were the one to bring her in. Makes you like a brother. You know?"

"I'm no fucking brother."

"Oh, I'm sorry. I didn't mean to imply you had an obligation to her. Just forget I called. Bye." She disconnected and faced Rein, a smile tugging at her lips. "Happy to see me?"

When he crossed an ankle over his knee and slouched back, her heart punched against her chest as she stalked toward her mate.

Rein had slept fitfully last night. Something was on his mind, something he said he couldn't share with her. Yet. He would, though. A promise.

"What are you up to, Brae? You can't possibly be baiting Dax." He cocked his head to the side, his icy blues turning hot cobalt. "Fuck. You are. Being a matchmaker for that vampire will not go well."

"Just a little nudge in the right direction never hurt anyone. Especially vamps. Your breed seems to wallow in guilt and too much angst for your own good. A push. What's the worst that could happen?"

"The worst? You could piss him off enough he'll try to make you suffer. Then I'll have to get in his face. He wouldn't like that. You've seen two vampires go at it."

"Remind me."

"It's ugly. Lots of fang, blood, and torn flesh. Then it gets violent."

"Hmm. Are you saying you can't take him?" One hand was on her hip. With the other, she stroked her chin.

His glare would topple weaker women. Fortunately, she wasn't weak. *Hell.* If she was, Rein would have her under his thumb begging for mercy. She only begged for one thing from her mate. The rest of the time, she stood her ground. Stubborn to a fault, he said.

"I'm taller. Beefier. Almost as mean. Definitely sneakier. Then I've got the added warlock-incubus thing going on. Yes. I could save your tempting ass. Thing is, do I want to because you decided to play matchmaker? Got me?"

"Cluck. Cluck. Cluck." She folded her hands into her armpits and flapped like a chicken.

He laughed. "I could be persuaded to protect you."

Braelyn's brows shot up.

Rein brushed aside the towel, fisting his very large cock. "But I'd expect a reward."

"Just for rescuing little ol' me?"

Stroke. Stroke. Gasp.

Her heart pounded in her ears, loud enough to echo off the walls downstairs.

The tips of Rein's fangs glistened in the light from the window. "That's right. Now come suck me off. Your hero's waiting."

"Yes, master, and thank you." Braelyn dropped to her knees and gripped his velvet-over-steel length. Her mischievous eyes locked onto her mate's glowing blues as she licked a bead of moisture off the tip. Her tongue stroked along his shaft. She took him into her mouth, a moan escaping as her nails dug into his muscular thighs. Her head bobbed up and down.

Rein spread his thighs wider, sinking into the chair, tossing his arms onto the back. If her mouth wasn't so busy, she'd smile at the king enjoying his reward.

His hands dropped on top of her head. "Faster, Brae." He pumped into her, his hips rolling up and down. "Yes. Damn."

Chapter Twenty-Three

Pissed, Dax disconnected from Braelyn. With an eye on his D-chip, he searched for Brak. *Demon, get the fuck out here now.*

Brak sauntered out the kitchen door, a sandwich in hand, his mouth full. "What's up, vamp?"

"Change in plans. I'll take Chiara to her witch training at the Thaumaturgy Institute."

Brak pulled his brows down in confusion. "No can do. Got things to deliver there followed by a meeting."

"Okay. You can come along. Chiara, leave the furry mutts alone and get over here. What time is your training today?"

She patted Boris's head, rising unsteadily as the dogs pushed at her legs. "In about an hour." She stumbled when Ivan nudged her but caught herself, giggling as the animals jumped up.

Dax growled while he sent a sharp look to the beasts. They plopped to their haunches, heads hanging, their droopy eyes pleading for mercy. He held his hand out level, the dogs dropping to rest on their bellies.

Chiara glanced from dogs to Dax. "Stop controlling my babies."

Dax squinted. "Not doing a thing."

"Yes, you are. You fixed your black beady eyes on them, and they behaved."

"You need to be strict. They're too big to let them run wild. Beasts need a firm hand."

"Maybe, but just look at them." She bent to stroke Boris's fur, making Dax jealous. "They're too sweet. Not everyone requires submission."

She was wrong. In the world where Dax lived,

you were either the conqueror or the conquered. No in between. At the top of the food chain or on the bottom. No doubt where he was. No doubt where he wanted Chiara to be. On the bottom, under him, his big body between her legs, his cock sliding in and out of her pussy, his fangs in her neck.

He shook his head to erase the picture. “Let’s go now.”

“What about my wolfhounds?”

“I’ll turn them loose outside. They can’t go past the stronghold’s boundaries. Brak, you drive. Chiara and I will be in the back.”

Chiara took off for the stairs. “I’ll be right down. I need a sweater.”

Chewing his last bite, Brak gazed at his empty hands. “Sure. Let me grab a snack for the road.”

Dax nodded, snapping his fingers for the animals to follow him through the outside door where he released them. He filled a huge bowl from the kitchen with water, setting it in the back where the dogs waited for him.

“You’ve got water and acres to roam. Avoid the firing range. If you try to go beyond the stronghold’s border, you’ll get a shock you won’t forget.” The dogs looked like they understood every word he said. *But who knows.* Ivan’s head bobbed up and down, his eyes clear and bright. *Okay. Alpha guy probably does.* “You’re in charge, big guy.” Taking a few treats from his pocket, he patted each wolfhound’s head while it ate from his hand. “That should hold you for now. I’ll get you more later.”

When he returned, Chiara said, “I don’t like you giving orders all the time.”

“I don’t care, little witch. Get used to it.”

“Don’t push me.” She wiggled her fingers. “I’ll melt your bones. If you keep pissing me off, you’ll be a puddle of vampire on the floor.”

Dax snarled. The conquered were supposed to be submissive. He had a lot to teach this female about their relationship.

Wait. What relationship?

****

At his desk, Cerberus studied a map on his computer showing raids in progress. He reviewed the statistics on victories and losses. The numbers of Arisen Dawn Gold Dusters sacrificed were well within the range of acceptability.

Conquering North America would have a priceless fear effect. Once he was victorious on this continent, the rest of the world would fall like teetering dominoes. A decisive win in the States would also bring nearly every Aeternal to his movement. Maybe even the high and mighty Firebrands would see reason. They thrived on aggression. Why not join the cause to give those desires free rein?

A knock interrupted his contemplation. Cerberus waved a hand in front of his body. Upon entering, Lort saw only a demon at work. "Your men have not brought the English Blood Coven warlock to me yet."

Lort tugged on the sleeve of his black uniform. The general's dress was as crisp as his demeanor. He was a confident male. Too confident at times.

The faux demon pointed to a chair in front of him.

Lort sat, his spine rigid. "Miller Nash is clever. His early training in British Intelligence makes him a slippery target. But our vampire who tasted him can track him like GPS."

Cerberus swept his arm across the desk, knocking papers and pens onto the floor. Though Lort did not flinch, the momentary flash in his eyes betrayed wariness. *Good.* "I want him."

Lort shifted, vinyl creaking under his weight. "I'll personally see to his capture."

"Do not let me down." Cerberus released his power.

Lort clawed his throat, slipping from the chair onto the floor, his feet kicking as he gasped for air.

The warlock watched the general squirm, his mouth gaping as he struggled to breathe. Cerberus fed from him, drawing energy to fuel his future spells. Soon an entire world would be at his feet, begging for his permission to live. Chuckling, he flicked his wrist to dissolve the spell. "As long as we understand each other. My plans are proceeding on schedule. We have Celene Bailey and others. You will bring in Miller Nash. I need only three more bloodlines. But I do enjoy ample back-ups."

Lort fingered his neck, reddened by a magic hand print as he crawled back to the chair a little less confident.

Cerberus laced his fingers together, resting them on the desk. "With the Blood Coven descendants, I will make the world whole again. We will assume our rightful place as rulers. We were the first species, the apex predators. We will conquer by the rule of might. Humans will be cattle while our numbers will flourish once again."

"It is time, sir, to make your followers aware of who you are. Rumors are spreading, murmurs saying you don't exist."

"Soon, my dear Lort. Soon. I will renounce my current position, reveal my identity, and take up the mantle as leader of Arisen Dawn. But know this, the realm will quake when they discover the source of my abilities. I am unbeatable."

****

Chiara lifted a foot to step onto the running board after Dax opened the door to the black SUV. She was about to leverage herself into the backseat when strong arms gripped her waist to raise her effortlessly. She slid across, stopping midway.

Dax edged her over to squeeze in beside her. Not deterred by his scowl, she rested her hand on his thigh, a natural move, proprietary.

He did not shrug off her touch. His leg beneath the dark fabric of his BDU's burned her palm like molten steel. He might not tell her how he felt in words, but his body didn't hide his response.

Brak threw an arm over the seat, twisting toward them. "I have a stop to make. We'll stick to surface roads until I pick up some equipment. Afterward, we'll drive through the closest portal."

Chiara didn't mind a longer ride since it would give her the opportunity to see more of Scath. Having stopped for the humongous demon and Dax to load up the SUV, they rode through Covenkirk's heavy city traffic, skirted suburbs filled with cloned houses and strip malls, and now rolled through green farmland on their way to a portal.

Chiara eyed the countryside. "What can I expect from my lessons?"

About to bite into his ride-along sandwich, Brak paused halfway to his mouth. "Witch school's a mystery to me."

"Dax?" she asked.

"I hate witches and warlocks. Never saw the need to find out how they train. I just know how to kill them."

Chiara rolled her eyes. "You don't have to be such a fanghole just because one got the best of you in Idaho." She folded her arms across her chest.

"I was fighting off two demons at the time. I may

have been distracted."

"Did you ride along just to irritate me?"

"No. Brak asked me to keep him company."

The demon glanced at Dax in the rearview mirror, his brows pulling on his forehead.

Though Chiara was certain they exchanged some secret guy signal, she relaxed her arms to cuddle against Dax. "You can't hate all witches. You liked me enough to pick up my babies."

"It was just good biz."

"How so?" She shifted, her breast brushing Dax's chest, her hand resting once more on his leg.

He flinched. "You'll stay put if the dogs are with you."

Chiara lifted his solid arm to loop it around her shoulders, snuggling deeper into his warmth, wisps of her dark hair tickling her cheek. "Still, it was terribly kind."

Despite Dax's general snarkiness, he did not change position. In fact, he rested his chin on her head.

"Will they make me kill things?"

Dax jerked away, putting them eye-to-eye. "Hell no. They'll probably work mostly on your healing shit."

She sighed while his gentle fingers stroked her hair. "I want to plant a garden at the stronghold. I'd enjoy growing a few herbs and things for my concoctions."

"I'm sure the institute will teach you to cast spells without potions. You won't need a garden."

"But I enjoy my plants. You could even take me foraging in the woods for some items."

"I'm not into that shit."

"You don't have to be. Just hold the bags, grumpy."

"Hey, you two. Stop arguing about veggies. Trouble ahead." Brak disturbed the moment by slamming on the brakes hard enough to fling everyone forward. "The portal."

Dax bolted upright, staring out the darkened window. "Damn."

She saw a man wearing what Chiara recognized as an insurgent's black uniform with a patch depicting two mountains and a rising sun between them. Before Brak pressed the gas pedal, the guy signaled his companions. They charged the vehicle, palms to the undercarriage, lifting it off its wheels. Though Brak gunned the engine, the tires spun uselessly while the males held nearly three tons of metal off the pavement.

Dax squeezed his *freron's* shoulder. "You know what to do. I'll distract them. Get her out of here."

Chiara grabbed Dax's upper arm with both hands. "No. We won't leave you."

The SUV rocked, nearly tipping over. Dax gripped her wrists so hard her fingers popped free. "Let go, little witch."

Chiara bristled, her chest heaving up and down. "You do not get to be a fucking hero again. You'll die. I'll never forgive you."

"Stay safe," Brak said from behind the wheel. "I'll send help."

"Please. Please, don't do this." Furious tears rolled down Chiara's cheeks. "I can help."

Dax cracked a smile as he leaned toward her, planting a goodbye kiss on her lips. "Now, *freron*."

Brak grabbed Chiara's arm, pulling her over the seat and into the front when Dax opened his door. He lunged out of the SUV to land on the ground with a thud, his long dark hair whipping behind him.

"Hold her tight," said Dax over his shoulder. "She'll spell you. The little witch has a mean streak."

"Turn me loose. I'll rip off your dick. Make you a

fucking eunuch." He was about to risk his life for her. Again. Chiara fought the demon's grasp as he floored the vehicle while her hero distracted the attackers.

****

Dax vaulted onto a vampire and a demon, an elbow locked around each breed's neck. He listened. The SUV squealed away with Chiara yelling obscenities. He chuckled, not envying his *freron*. His witch had a temper.

Taking both Arisen Dawn soldiers to the ground, he banged the bloodsucker's head into the dirt until the guy passed out. With one temporarily out of commission, Dax plunged a fist through the demon's flesh to rip out his heart. Returning to make sure the vampire never rose, he put one hand to the head and the other to the neck and twisted.

Pop. See you in Angor.

Mobbed by others, he was up to his ass in black uniforms. He bobbed, weaved, ducked, tossed an incubus over his shoulder and sent a shifter flying above the heads of the attackers.

With extra elbow room, Dax pulled both jungle bolos out of the crisscrossed sheaths on his back. Twisting the weapons in an intricate pattern, he beheaded two miscreants while keeping the others at bay. At least ten mutherfuckers surrounded him. His blades swooshed through the air to keep them at a cautious distance.

Though outnumbered, he only had to wait until the Firebrands arrived. Which would be more than a few minutes. Brak would have to D-chip Kole. After he clarified the situation, the Firebrands would need to muster.

When a fidiot incubus charged, his weighty blade pointed forward, Dax swept his bolo outward and lobbed off his head. Stupid. Two machetes wielded by an expert outclassed a badly handled sword any day. And Dax was talented.

As one of his bolos swung overhead, the other punched downward, the movements so swift as to be a blur. His weapons of choice required fast footwork and evasion, both skills he possessed.

With the blades in his grip, his maneuvers were second nature. He was a honed warrior, sharpened by his enhanced Firebrand speed and years of practice. His feet moved left or right, responding to his attacker. No thought. Only action-reaction. If a target went low, Dax bent his knees, his upper body straight, striking offensively to evade their move. He always protected his exposed hand and stepped toward his opponent.

Others came forward to challenge his skills. Once Dax reduced his opponents to half, he caught the thunder of boots on the ground. They didn't belong to his *frerons*. His blades still snapping overhead, his body performing an intricate dance of death, he prepped for more Arisen Dawn assholes.

The situation is going from hell no to fucking hell no.

He couldn't catch a break. Time to live up to his mantra. Wipe out as many mutherfuckers as possible before they get you.

It's a good day to die. Open the gates to Angor. I'm on my way.

Dax's enemies circled him, giving him the opportunity to lob off a few more heads.

Swish. Thud. Roll.

Despite being outnumbered, he resumed the deadly dance with his bolos, swinging high, swinging low. Spinning. Hacking limbs. Leveling the field. He sliced a berserker like a side of ham, diced a satyr as he would an onion, and minced a vampire for a clove of garlic in the stew.

Dax was in the zone, the killing zone. A place he knew well. A place where he excelled. No guilt here. No failures. No one to let down.

A mage's spell shoved him to a knee, but he rose, his weapons still whipping through the air. A nymph's blade caught his leg. A sword his chest. Fatigue sank into his bones.

Keep going. Just let me kill one more. Then another. As long as Chiara is safe, I've done something good for once.

A screech sounded. *Caw. Caw.* The crowd parted to let a male walk through. "Greetings, Firebrand."

Dax pushed onto unsteady feet to study the newcomer. "Shifter." Predator for sure. The male's aura was cloudy, though.

"Bunch of Nancies. I give you one job." He flicked his wrist, and a two-ton truck might as well have hit Dax. He flew into a tree, bending over as pain wrenched his gut, his jaw, his ribs. Blood gushed from his wounds, his twin bolos dropping from his broken fingers.

Fuck.

Dax snarled at the approaching male. "You're not a shifter. You're a goddamn warlock."

"Yeah. I might have fudged a bit. I'm a mix. A smidge of shifter with a dash of warlock. Nice, huh?"

"I fucking hate mages."

Dax's eyes slid shut. He considered a prayer to Gahya. But, what the hell, she had never answered him before. It didn't look as if today would be different.

****

Chiara kicked Brak's shins once he set her feet onto the office floor. "He's a brother, a *freron.* You deserted him."

Brak's jaw changed to stone. "He sacrificed

himself for you, Chiara. Don't sling mud on his action."

Her leg shot out again. Brak jumped back. Good thing. She was a venom-spitting Blood Coven witch.

"Bounty," he said. "A little help here? Where's Kole?"

"In the training room." The stacked blonde rose from her desk, her eyes slitted. "What about Dax?"

The stunning woman obviously knew the vampire well. Were they lovers? Why not? The floozie was a knock-out. Nothing like Chiara. Bounty was tall and mature to her short and imperfect. Sure, they both had big breasts, but this woman had everything else. She was regal, sophisticated in a way Chiara would never be. Her skin was flawless. Her hair was styled. Her manicure was fresh. Her makeup was faultless. Hell, Chiara would do the bitch if she were into women.

But she could use an ally. Even a Dax bimbo. Shaking her head to clear it, Chiara pointed at Brak. "The asshole left the vampire behind with a bunch of Arisen Dawn nasties. Deserted him."

Bounty stormed toward the demon, grabbing a fistful of shirt and dragging the giant down nose to nose. "What the hell is she talking about?"

Brak, three-hundred pounds of muscle, flinched. "Look. We ran into the assholes heading for Earth. They spotted us and overtook the truck with the witch in it. Dax did the right thing. He sacrificed himself to save her. Through and through Firebrand shit. Now, let me talk to Kole to see who he sent after the heroic bloodsucker."

In silence, the three stormed into the training room where Kole had his boot on a recruit's neck while other Firebrands watched the take-down lesson. The commander offered his palm to the female, helping her from the mat.

At Brak's sudden appearance, all Firebrand eyes

popped to him. “We’re safe. Who’s backing up Dax?”

Kole signaled the recruits to scatter. “Tyr’s leading the team. They should be boots-on-the-ground now.” As if on cue, he took a call on his D-chip and nodded before disconnecting to share the intel. “Our guys are at the portal. No Arisen Dawn. No vampire *freron*.”

“His body?” Chiara’s voice trembled.

When sparks shot from Kole’s fingers, he tented them to contain the fire. “Nothing.”

“I need to find his noble ass. I left him behind with a shitload of renegades.” Brak turned.

Kole fisted his arm. “You did the right thing. You got her out.” Kole shook his head at Chiara before she could talk. He tapped his wrist to make a call. “Jezzi, grab Ram. I need my two best trackers to find Dax. Report to Tyr’s unit.” When he disconnected, he turned to Brak. “Join them. Bring our vampire home.”

“The next time I see you, demon, my brother better be with you and alive.” Bounty had Brak against the wall, her long, sharp fingernail slicing across his throat. “He’s all I’ve got.”

“Brother?” Chiara and Kole called out their surprise in unison.

“That’s right. The best, kindest, most honorable brother a female can have.” She locked eyes with the commander. “Do not leave him alone out there.”

Chiara closed the distance to take Bounty’s hand in hers. Through her own tears, she looked up at the woman Dax had talked about in such loving terms. Facing Kole, she said, “Bring him home to the two women who love him.”

Kole glanced at Brak. “Brother? You don’t look surprised.”

“Yeah. I kinda knew, but it was their biz to share. I’m outta here.”

"Chiara and I will be waiting upstairs. There will be hell to pay if you come back without him. And I'll deliver it." Bounty gripped Chiara tighter as they strode out of the gym.

Chapter Twenty-Four

Without companionship, the outdoors, or hope, Celene fought each day to get out of bed. She had been a daredevil heiress with little thought to her own safety. The same willpower kept her going now. After a routine of push-ups, jogging in place, and fake sparring matches, she threw herself into a chair and opened *The Path*.

Ohngel hovered silent and unseen above a box canyon, a place of natural beauty such as only Earth offered. Odd-shaped spires of rock prevailed as towering devotions to the gods. Stark plays of light and shadow danced across the terrain. Blue skies stood in contrast to bright crimson soil.

But where there should have been serenity, there was only violence and pitiful cries for help.

Three vampires herded a small group of humans into a canyon. The bloodthirsty creatures, fangs bared, their savage howls reaching even Ohngel's ears, spread out to block the only exit.

Terrified mothers shooed children behind them, backing them toward the unrelenting rock walls of their prison. They fell to their knees, hugging their young in weak arms, saying their goodbyes in pitiful wails. Fathers threw their fragile bodies in front of their families to protect them from Gahya's beasts. All efforts were useless.

Ohngel watched the creatures strike, drinking their fill of the humans, leaving drained corpses for the circling buzzards. He was helpless to step in. Such was not the way of his kind. The OneCreator was most clear on that directive. No interference.

His wings a streak of fire across the skies, Ohngel jetted to another site where humans were dying, not from the bloodthirsty horrors of vampires but from an excess of pleasure. In a thick copse, a crowd of incubi and succubi fed upon humans, fucking them and sucking out their lifeforces. The entranced Homo sapiens cried out happily, moaning with pleasure even as they were dying. When finished, the Aeternals tossed the depleted bodies onto a heap to rot. The sight was macabre. Wrong.

Elsewhere demons staggered along streets, drunk from so many orgasms, the result of orgies with humans. Unwilling participants, the victims were raped.

All breeds had begun to eschew feeding from their own kind. Somehow Gahya's creatures preferred nourishment from Homo sapiens. Not content with a small taste, they feasted, gorged, killed the addictive humans.

But even as Ohngel despaired, he saw hope. Strigodierna cruors urged vampires to cease killing to feed. Such was not necessary, they said. Ylves urged reason, encouraging their breed to steal a breath of soul but leave behind enough for life. Satyrs and nymphs prayed in their temples for guidance on how to capture erotic pleasure but not kill. Other breeds, likewise, warned against deadly behavior. But as is oft the case, once savagery gains a foothold, it is difficult to root out.

Food, sex, and death became a sick triumvirate for the Aeternal species. And they had forever to carry out their serial feeding on the new humans, a sweeter taste. Or so they claimed.

The Aeternals who kept Celene prisoner were savage, uncaring, and brutal. She had a front-row seat to their actions. Kudos to the Cambion for putting their sins into writing.

****

Days later, Kole strode into the training center, his mouth drawn tight and his fingers shooting fire. What had been a stronghold of fifteen was now more than seventy-five. But his warriors were exhausted. The hunt for Dax. Too many hours on patrol. Too little sleep. Too many wounds which healed only to re-open in the next action. Not enough feeding. Worry over loved ones. Heavy weight of responsibility pressing on their shoulders. Skirmishes at portals. The search for the Arisen Dawn garrison and Cerberus.

But they came when Kole called. Dressed in everything from workout shorts or sweats to leather or combat fatigues, they sagged against walls, sprawled on training benches, or slumped on the floor half-asleep with their lids fluttering open and closed. Some chatted, their voices low. Some were clean. Some were bloodied.

Everyone snapped to attention when he entered with Rein pulling up on his left.

"Is it Dax?" someone shouted.

"No." Ram took Kole's right. "Jezzi, Brak, Tyr, and I have searched two days and nights. No sign of the vampire. Yet."

Even the satyr, the snappiest dresser in the crowd, showed wear, strands of his caramel-streaked hair escaping the leather strap which held it back. When Kole pointed at the tear in his black T-shirt, Ram shook his head. "We thought we had a lead. The asshole turned out to be a dead end. I got roughed up a little taking him down."

"Keep working the angles. This meet's about another issue." Kole scrubbed a fist over his buzz-cut hair before he shouted to his audience. "My stronghold is not a democracy. Brilliant or dumbass, the decisions rest on my shoulders. But this one thing must be decided by each of you. I will not bust an order."

Feet shuffled while eyeballs pinged around the room. Those who had been under Kole's command all these years were slack-jawed, guessing it pained him to even talk about Firebrands and democracy in the same clipped sentence. They looked concerned, and they hadn't even heard the breaking news yet.

The newbies just looked happy to be included in a meeting. Too bad their first one could earn them the death penalty.

"I'll get right to it. The other day, High Commander Cadmon, Nace, Jarek, and I met with lawgivers and the Temple of Justice. Our purpose was simple. We shared our plans to take down Arisen Dawn. We'd step up the heat, wipe out not only every Arisen Dawn soldier upon contact but also suspected sympathizers if they didn't capitulate and change their ways."

"Yeah," shouted Bade. "Right on. Kill the mutherfuckers."

Kole held up a hand, a weary smile curling his upper lip. He bent his head to stare at a sheet of paper. "They issued an order. I'll read it exactly as given. 'High Commander, you and your Firebrands are hereby directed to keep peace on Scath but not to interfere with Arisen Dawn actions here or on Earth. No martial law. No severe measures.' We were told refusal to follow the command would be treason."

The only sound in the room was shuffling feet until Sig spoke. "I don't get it, Commander. Our job is to keep peace on Scath and Darque. To prevent Aeternals from harming humans. Am I wrong?"

Thorn jacked a worn cowboy boot against the wall. "That's always been the mission. What's changed?"

Kole's lip curled with disgust. "The government wants us to adopt a wait-and-see. Maybe Arisen Dawn will soften up the Earthers, make them amenable to peace talks. If that plan goes to shit and we have a full-out war with humans, they want the renegades alive to help us fight. Some of them even support Arisen Dawn's goal to conquer Earth."

Ram shifted his legs farther apart, his hands clasped behind his back. "That's whacked. We should negotiate with the humans now. Show them we mean no harm. Convince them Arisen Dawn's the bad guys and we're taking them out."

Ram jumped up a few notches in Kole's eyes. After all, the guy had just been tortured by humans.

Sabine, who put her hand on Nico's shoulder, possibly before he could lip off, asked, "What would you have us do, Commander?"

"That will be each male and female's decision. I speak only for myself."

"Then speak," said Sig. "What's your path?"

"I will not follow the order. I choose to follow my conscience, to do what Firebrands have done for over a thousand years."

"What about your mate and kid?" asked a succubus recruit. Kole wished he could remember her name. She deserved that much.

"I hope to get her and Kae to safety. Wherever the hell that is nowadays or in the future. We're discussing the issue. Unfortunately, our talks are sounding more like a domestic dispute. My Frisca packs a mean wallop."

A few chuckles traveled through the crowd.

Rein clasped Kole's shoulder, the same concern about protecting loved ones icing his blue eyes. He shared his decision with his *frerons*. "Darius, Mix, and I will fight beside our commanders. I will not follow the Temple or the lawgivers. I follow my conscience."

Ram locked eyes with his mate Denim who was standing beside her Amazon friend in the crowd. She nodded. "My mate and I choose the same path."

Galena stepped forward, her spear banging her shield. "There is no honor in obeying an unjust order."

"You've chewed my ass so many times, Comm, it belongs to you," said Chay, shifting from foot to foot. "I'm in all the way."

Nico grabbed Sabine, planting a kiss on her lips while cheers went up. He gave the room his middle finger when he came up for air. "We're with you, Commander. When I commit, it's forever."

Kole ran his fire-gold eyes over every Firebrand in the gym. "Be aware, you are advocating treason."

"By who the fuck's definition?" Thorn growled. "My conscience is clean. If I did as they commanded, my wolf would be pissed. Nobody wants my beast in a lather." He took an unlit cigar from his pocket, scrunching it between his teeth.

Sig punched Bade's arm. "We didn't join up to let the bad guys win. Did we, vampire?"

"Hell, no."

Bounty sneaked into the room but leaned against the doorway, her skin-tight red skirt showing leg. Her eyes searched the crowd for Ram. When she found him, he shook his head.

"Bounty, as my secretary, you can walk away. No shame. No blame. Not your fight."

She straightened, folding her arms under ample breasts which had most Firebrands panting. "What the fuck makes you think I'd walk? And I'm not your damn secretary. I'm your fucking executive assistant."

One side of Kole's mouth quirked into a smile but quickly faded.

The room erupted in the Firebrands' war cry, echoing off the walls. *For duty. For honor.* Then a new shout. *Kole. Kole. Kole.*

Rein clasped the animus demon's arm. "You have your answer, Commander. Your *ferons* follow you, not some misguided order from assholes rotting in the stench of power."

"I hope I'm not leading them into Angor."

"If you are," Ram brushed dust off his black tactical pants, "it'll be a fucking fun ride because we'll own Angor. It'll be our bitch."

Kole raised a hand. "Our first mission is to locate Daxton, scion from the Bludclan Mortus, beloved brother of my executive assistant."

The room fell into stunned silence as Bounty daggered everyone in the gym with a glare, challenging them to say something stupid. Except for Brak and Ram, the warriors were shocked. He guessed the experienced Firebrands were slack-jawed because Dax, the most feral of the warriors, had a sister. The recruits were in shock because the leggy blonde executive assistant was too scary to have a brother. Even if it was the surly vampire they'd seen only a few times. They figured she would have squashed a sibling like a swatter with a fly.

"Here's the plan. Once Dax is home, we hunt the Arisen Dawn bastards and their sympathizers. And we stay out of the hands of the lawgivers and justices. From this moment on, we are renegades the likes of which Scath has never seen." Kole lit up his fingers, shooting flames to the ceiling like Roman candles.

Thunder erupted as the Firebrands stomped their boots and rattled blades against shields or walls.

Kole. Kole. Kole.

****

Dax landed mug first on the concrete. He'd been worked over, barely fed and rarely conscious. Had it been hours or days? He suspected days.

With his arms planted beneath his chest, he

pushed his broken fingers against the floor. Not happening. Too weak to get off the fucking ground, he flicked his tongue out, tasting blood from his busted lip. He groaned. *Holy Gahya.* A few cracked ribs. Leg and chest wounds.

He passed out again.

When his gritty lids finally dragged opened, he glanced around the sparse but clean cell. With a moan, he flopped onto his back, his hand wiggling his broken jaw. Two cots, a sink, and a hole for waste. A regular Covenkirk Hilton suite.

More surprising, however, was the occupant of the cot against the left wall. An American soldier in a torn uniform, sporting a black eye and bruises. A colonel, according to his decor. Familiar. But Dax didn't know more than a few humans.

The man was alert, watching every painful move of his cellmate but not afraid. Wary.

Kudos to the Earther with steel balls.

Dax ignored the guy. No threat. When he finally maneuvered off the floor, pain shooting through his neuro system, he faced outward to the open bars. Silver. He touched them because… *Yeah. I'm just that stupid. Fuck.* His flesh sizzled from the burn, blisters immediate. He wasn't breaking through those without frying his jewels.

Someone had excised the D-chip from his wrist. *Again.* At this rate, the Firebrands would start charging him for replacements. *Okay. I'll escape the old-fashioned way.* By shadowflashing. His bloody chest expanded with a painful breath as he concentrated power on the shady corner outside the cell.

Nothing. He tried again, his focus sharper, energy bristling through his body. Nothing.

"Wards. Fuck."

"What did you say?" The American colonel studied him with the cold stink eye.

I must be one scary-looking nightmare.

Hair a mess, fangs visible, body broken. But the guy didn't so much as cringe. "Wards. This place is locked down tight."

"What are wards?"

"Spells witches and warlocks use to bind us here. Otherwise, I'd shadowflash elsewhere. Somewhere less confining." He held up a hand as he stumbled toward the empty cot. "I come in peace. What are you doing here?"

"Right now? Pouting and figuring out how to save my sorry ass. What'd you do to get the presidential suite?"

Dax fell onto the mattress, his boots staying on the floor. "I was trying to snuff out about thirty Arisen Dawn rebels."

"I'd ask how that worked out, but I can see it didn't."

"How long have you been here?"

The human flipped his wrist. "Sonsabitches took my watch. Probably thought it was a GPS device, but it was a gift from my father. I'm guessing several days. Since the Battle for Bozeman. Why were you fighting them? You're their kind."

"Don't lump all us assholes together." Dax growled, his fangs still filling his mouth. But the guy didn't flinch. "I'm a Scion Firebrand. We're on the same team. I bet that warms your four-chambered heart."

The guy's forehead creased. "How can you be on team human? You're one of the otherworlders."

"Not otherworlder. Vampire, originally from the same place as you." Dax blew out a breath as his lids closed.

"Figured you for a vamp. The fangs are a

giveaway. Unless it's already Halloween and I'm out of costume."

Dax snorted. "To set the record straight, my kind was on the planet long before you."

"No shit. Speaking of fangs. Tell me you've already eaten."

Dax grunted, patting his stomach. "I'm not too hungry. But they haven't given me enough blood to heal fast."

"How often do you feed? And, just to be clear, I am not on the menu."

"You better hope they start wining and dining me in style, especially since I'm so fucked up. Otherwise, you're gonna be breakfast."

He pursed his lips. "Gotta say, I'll fight fucking hard to keep you away from my neck, and I fight mean."

"So do I. How'd they snag you?" Eyes open, Dax swung his feet onto the cot, stretching his legs, feeling pain from the gash along his calf.

"Near a Bozeman portal where a bunch of your mutherfuckers came through. I took some out, but they got me while my men and I were on a clean-up mission. The guy who brought me in was big." The colonel snapped his fingers. "That's where I've seen you. You crashed the party in Montana, signaled me to cut off my opponent's head. Why?"

"Told you. We're on the same team."

The colonel braced his elbows on his knees. "Why would you help humans against your own kind?"

"Remember, Scion Firebrand." Dax pointed a healed index finger at his Phoenix brand. "Our job is to keep order on Scath and Darque. When necessary, we protect human ass."

"So, you're in the protection biz?"

"Yep." He smiled, his fangs cutting his lower lip.

"When we lived together, we nearly ate all your kind. Tasty. We moved to Scath when the Blood Coven created the realms. After which, the Firebrands organized. Now this shit-storm threatens to cause all sorts of problems with the balance."

"Nice fairy tale."

"You want a fairy tale? I've got a good one about the big bad wolf. He huffs and puffs."

"Heard it." The human rose from his cot, hand out. "Colonel Garcia. Call me Matty. We might become best friends. That is, if you don't bite me."

Dax shook his head. "I'm not so fond of *Homo sapiens* as nourishment."

Except Chiara.

"So how do we escape?"

"I'm busy working on a plan." He got horizontal and crossed his arms under his head.

****

When a metal door clanged open and shut, Dax's eyeballs tracked three Aeternals who pounded toward the cell.

"The big fucker in the middle is the guy who captured my ass." Matty's voice was barely above a whisper.

"Busy male. He snagged me, too."

"Morning, fellas." The shifter-whatever fisted the silver bars. "We're gonna have a play date. You first, vampire."

"I've been to the party. No thanks. Besides, my previous date was prettier."

The asshole signaled the two demons beside him. They marched into the cell, but before Dax could charge, they shot him with electrodes from their tasers. Like a meteorite caught in Earth's atmosphere, he went down.

Spasms jerked his body across the floor, his boots

tapping an erratic rhythm. Then lights out.

Feet shuffled across the concrete. A door crashed. Open or shut? He didn't know. His lids were heavy sheets of sandpaper, but he scraped them open. Trussed and naked, he was in a cold concrete room chained to a chair sitting atop a drain. *Not good.* He didn't think he was here for a shower.

When he tilted his chin up, he saw hooks hanging from the ceiling. Behind him, chains dangled from the wall. *Sweet.* A torture chamber. His stepfather would have been amused to see Dax here.

Pushed open with a muscled shove, the door slammed into the wall. The smiling asshole shifter-whatever walked in, his face contorted with malicious glee. Dax had to admire a guy who enjoyed his work.

A demon carried a stool into the cell, dragging it across the concrete, taking it to the soon-to-be torturer. "What's your name, vampire? I'm Roark."

"Go to hell."

The male waved a hand in the air. "Look around. We're already there."

Dax rattled the chains which kept his arms locked behind his back. Solid. Silver. Burning like a sonofabitch.

"Name? Come on. That's the easy stuff."

Dax glowered, opening his mouth when his fangs pierced his gums. He remembered a time when he had pissed off his stepfather. The sadistic bastard was so angry he had two males hold him down while stepdaddy beat him bloody with fists and claws. Of course, the guy had made sure Dax healed before he reported to work. After all, he was the favorite boy toy of the clientele. That was before the night when everything changed.

Roark sighed. "Are you choosing the hard way?"

A laugh started deep in Dax's chest and rumbled

to the surface. “That’s how I roll. I’m my own worst enemy.”

“Until now. As of today, I have the honored role.” The shifter mix vaulted onto his feet to pound Dax with a fist to his jaw.

Dax spit out blood. “My sister hits harder than that.”

A gut punch followed a strike to the temple. He shook his head, expecting bells to ring. *Not yet.* But the day was young.

“Your name.”

Dax hawked another mouthful of blood onto the interrogator’s boots.

Roark kicked out, his heel connecting with the vampire’s groin, knocking the chair over in the process. *Okay. That hurt.* Dax’s eyes watered from the pain in his balls. He hoped they still functioned after this. He was fond of them.

“Name?”

“Mary Poppins.”

A smile quirked Roark’s lips. “Superfuckingfragilisticexpialidocious.”

Circling behind, he righted the toppled vampire. Roark pulled down the ceiling hook and attached it to the chains on Dax’s hands. “When I hoist you, it’s gonna hurt like a bitch. Your arms will probably snap out of the joints, depending on how long you can hold yourself up. Can’t be too long.”

Dax locked his elbows, his shoulders stiff. As they began to tremble, he felt like an Olympic gymnast going for a perfect ten on the rings. When he was about to lose control, a satyr rushed in and leaned toward Roark’s ear. The mixed breed Arisen Dawn soldier growled, lowering Dax to the concrete.

“I have a treat for you, vampire.” A warlock

walked through the door, long robes, stringy hair, and a snarly expression on his face. The only thing he was missing was the pointy hat.

I hate warlocks.

While he waited for the mage to settle in, the shifter-whatever softened up Dax with a few cracked ribs and a broken jaw. Then came the invasion. The mage ripped into his head with a mind spell meant to pull out memories.

Dax's lips moved as he muttered softly. "Hickory, dickory, dock/The mouse ran up the clock…"

The nursery rhyme recitation did not work long. Eventually, Dax's screams echoed off the walls while Roark leaned against the concrete blocks, grinning. The asshole warlock not only extracted the vampire Firebrand's name but a shitload more.

Good news. Bad news. Pain meant Dax was still alive. He could handle that. Someone rummaging around in his brain, burrowing in like a Darque pincer beetle, was unacceptable. The vampire didn't know how, but he would break free and kill the mutherfucking mixed breed and his sidekick mage. Their days were numbered.

One and counting.

Dax was barely conscious when two demons dragged him back to the cell, the tops of his feet scraping along the ground, his blood drizzling on the concrete the entire journey. His head lolled side to side as he watched the crimson blobs fall.

Drip. Drip. Drip.

A door clanged open, and he landed on the floor in a heap, falling into a wake-sleep state where painful memories bubbled to the surface.

Chapter Twenty-Five

"Ladies," Braelyn shouted at the women gathered in her stronghold apartment. When no one paid attention, her eyes pleaded with Denim, who stuck a finger and thumb in her mouth and whistled.

The chit-chat stopped.

Braelyn nodded at the satyr's mate. "Always wanted to be able to do that."

"All present and accounted for," said Denim. "Except for Nico. He's busy with Firebrand stuff. Besides, you said this was a gals-only event."

"Why aren't you with the Firebrands?" Margo followed the question with a sip of wine from her goblet.

"You are my peeps. So, I told Kole and Ram I had a female problem. It's surprising, but when you say that to guys, they never ask questions. They just wag their chins and let you do whatever you want."

"So true." Lizette snorted, very unlike her usual polished, professional demeanor.

Braelyn stroked a hand down Chiara's arm. "Thank you for coming, but you don't need to be here. We know you're worried about Dax. We all understand if you give this a miss."

Chiara stared at Braelyn, her eyes reddened by tears and lined with puffy dark circles. "I don't have the right to worry about him. Dax and I aren't involved."

"Of course not. Cause he's an ass." Margo's red curls bounced with an angry shake of her head.

Chiara blinked but then shrugged. "He's not. He's just…"

Braelyn interrupted. "Yeah. A misunderstood asshole vamp."

She nodded. "Maybe, but you're right. I care

about him. I'll stay, though. The distraction is good."

Margo nibbled on a piece of Gruyere from the tray on the coffee table. "Sorry about calling the vampire a glute. All the guys have attitude. The kind with a capital A."

"You got that straight. Let's get to business then. Here's the latest about Jace's friend Celene. Skyler?" Braelyn scooped fingers through her spiked hair.

"I located her in North Shelters, the shifter region. My vision didn't last long, but she's in a farmhouse under guard." Skyler stopped talking when the door creaked. "Hush, everybody."

All eyes turned as a gorgeous quirky woman bounced into the room, wearing her signature long skirt, tinkling bracelets, and unlaced combat boots. "Hey. Blood bitches. I'm here for the fun. Somebody pour me a big glass of red."

Shocked looks swung to Braelyn. "Most of you know Rein's aunt. Chiara, Fin, and Jace, you may not. Let me introduce Indigo. She's a witch with amazing powers."

Indigo walked around the room, high-fiving all the women. "You forgot *femme fatale*, conjuress *extraordinaire*, jet-setting slut, and finder of all things lost." She threw herself onto the floor at Margo's feet and accepted the full glass of pinot noir shoved into her hand. With a nod of thanks, she continued. "I'm here to help. Hey, Red, I hope you appreciated my heads-up on adding all those extra beds to the barracks."

Margo nodded.

Indigo gave her a thumbs-up. "Please, continue, niece-in-law."

"Do you know what we're planning?" asked Denim.

"Of course. A big gryphon whispered in my ear.

For those who don't know, Oskar's my pet. He knows all. Sees all. Blabs all. Don't ever tell him a secret. He has loose lips."

Braelyn winked at Indigo. "Or I invited her."

The witch tapped her chin. "You're right. I get confused sometimes." She patted Margo's knee. "Don't I, Red?"

Margo smiled as people do when they listen to a crazy person. Braelyn, however, suspected Indigo was saner than she let on. Every once in a while, her violet eyes sparked with hyper-awareness, observant of every action around her. But sometimes playing crazy got better results.

"Anyway, carry on. Don't mind me." Indigo took a drink of wine. "Yum. Pass the cheese and crackers."

Braelyn handed the platter of snacks to Margo, who started them around the room again. "After Jace and Skyler came to me with information about Celene's whereabouts, I called each of you. You all wanted in on the rescue gig. The Firebrands have a lot on their plates, and Jace's ex-roomie is our biz anyway since she's one of us. To get the ball rolling, I contacted Denim since she has military and police training. She drew up the broad strokes of a plan for us to fine-tune. Skyler's done her thing. Now, it's up to the rest of us. How many guards are we looking at, Jace?"

"When I was there, we had only one or two at a time. I'm guessing three or four now. Skyler, how many did you see?"

"Only one. Like I said, my vision was brief. I have no control over it when it decides to pull me out."

Denim opened her tablet. "As Brae said, plans are still rough. Speak up with ideas or refinements. We want you to be comfortable with your roles. *Capiche*?"

Jace brushed her palms together. "Tyr had Logan

search for a building plan of the house where Celene is being kept. Neither guy knows why I wanted it. Anyway, the computer wiz came through."

Denim continued reading the plan. "I used it to come up with this step-by-step. Here we go. First, since I manipulate weather, I'll lay down a thick fog around the house. Second, Margo will take out communications. That's her gig. Third, we attack. Brae will be first through the front, using mind control if she spots a guard. I'll come in behind her and next Chiara. At the same time Brae hits the door, Indigo, you'll take the rear. That should be the kitchen. Smack down the first guard you see. Lizette follows you with her Bengal tiger. Margo, you come in behind them to keep eyes on the situation. Shout out a warning if necessary."

Indigo punched the air with her fist.

Denim clasped her ponytail, pulling it tighter. "Chiara, how's your training going? We know you haven't worked long with your witch, but you were already strong. Thing is, you've got shit going on that could dull your abilities."

"I've only worked a few times with my trainer, but I've gained a lot of control. You're right. Dax is on my mind day and night. But this is a chance for me to do good. If I can't save him, I want to help someone else. I'm good to go. I'll be spot on when the time comes."

Braelyn's glass clinked when she set it on the table. "Okay, Chiara. When you come in the front, go after any guard still standing. Jace, you'll be last in the main door. Your sole mission is to locate Celene and get her to my SUV. Skyler, same job as Jace, but you'll go in the rear. Fin, you're in charge of the outside. The first thing you'll do when we get to the site is to call in your wild animals to stand guard. Nobody sneaks in behind us."

Braelyn tapped her wrist. “Most of us have D-chips thanks to our mates. Jace, since you don’t have one yet, ride in my SUV to the operation staging area. Stick with me if things go to shit. I’m your way home. Chiara, same deal. Since you don’t have a device, glue yourself to Denim, who’ll drive the second vehicle.”

“Got it,” said both women in unison.

Braelyn held out her glass for Margo to pour more wine. “When we hit the guards, we go at them fast and heavy. We cannot engage in a prolonged hand-to-hand. We’d lose. Clear?”

Everyone nodded.

Braelyn checked her watch. “Let’s give this some thought until tomorrow. Bring questions and ideas about your role in the action. Our target rescue date is in three days. Between now and then, work with your trainers to perfect your gifts. We need to be at peak performance.”

Jace stood. “I have something to say.” She ran a finger around the edge of her wine goblet. “You don’t really know me or Celene, but you’re willing to risk your lives for us. No words can tell you how I feel. Thank you is too mild. But thanks anyway. I’ve had friends before, but none like you. Raise your glasses, ladies. ‘Some ships are wooden ships, but those ships may sink. The best ships are friendships and to those ships, we drink.’”

Glass clinked to glass.

“We are coven.” Braelyn moved to the center of the room, motioning the women to stand close. “We are strong and will prevail.” When they looped arms over each other’s shoulders, the floor buckled, the walls shook, and the room spun.

“Hot damn,” said Indigo, her lips curving into a smile, her eyes sparking with that hyper-awareness Braelyn had seen before. “Rock my world.”

Braelyn took a deep breath, sensing the spirit of

the Blood Coven, each woman's individual gift, and their solidarity.

When they broke, Indigo pumped her fist in the air. "Now, let's smoke 'em. Kill 'em. Suck their hearts out. Rip their heads off."

When everyone gasped, the witch flipped her long curly black hair over her shoulder and scrunched her brows. "What? You know you're thinking it."

Denim tapped her wrist. "Three days, ladies. Practice. Plan. Perform."

****

Later, Dax couldn't figure out if he was awake and remembering or comatose and dreaming. Either way, his memories were disturbing but true.

Dax laced up his leather breeches, tugged up new boots bought from his earnings at the O blud den, and slipped a white linen shirt over his head, leaving it untucked. A smile curled his lips. He was what he was meant to be.

The eighteen-year-old had taken an unprecedented action. He had approached a Scion Firebrand from his dead father's stronghold to offer a proposition—coin earned from his whoring if the male arranged a guide for an Awakening ceremony. The warrior argued Dax was too young. Most Aeternals celebrated the rite between the ages of twenty-two and twenty-five. Too young and he could die. But Dax would wait no longer. He had seen his stepfather ogling Bounty in a way that gave him dark chills. The time for them to run was now.

His father's old friend came through on his promise. Dax reported to the cave as directed, fed from a female vampire while he fucked her, and opened his mind to his guide. The experience nearly killed him as powers exploded into him, sending him flying into the cavern wall, his heart stopping, crimson fluid leaking from his ears and nose, his lungs devoid of air. He passed out for days. But he awoke, his life forever changed, his powers those of a mature vamp.

Proving his strength had multiplied tenfold, he shadowflashed from one dark spot to another in the cavern. His speed was blurring, and he already communicated telepathically. His skills had the guide's mouth agape and his eyes wide. He claimed never to have seen such power in a male so young.

When thirst gripped him again, his guide brought in a new donor. Dax took her pussy and her vein with his pants around his ankles. No use taking off all his clothes. He was likely to repeat this action frequently in the coming year. Hell. He probably shouldn't wear clothes at all.

His thirst quenched and his sex drive momentarily satisfied, Dax sneaked into the O blud den, not revealing he had completed his Awakening. He would save the news for a surprise. In the meantime, he had to resolve how to care for Bounty and himself once they ran.

In his room, Dax flung himself onto his bed. Though the Awakening had been grueling, his wounds had closed. He showered, washing off the blood which caked his flesh and clothing.

Once he toweled off, he flung his head forward to shake the water from his hair. He slipped into a pair of skin-tight leathers the females loved. He didn't bother with a shirt because it wouldn't stay on too long once the night's activities began. Off to work. His dick got hard just thinking about the succubus who would be waiting for him. She liked the sex rough. And right now, he was feeling sadistic.

When he rounded a corner in the hallway, he

heard sobs. Bounty. He quickened his pace. Her door was cracked. He pushed it open. On the bed, his thirteen-year-old sister huddled in a tight ball, her knees to her chin and her fingers clutching the hem of her dirty dress around her feet.

Hearing Dax, she bolted upright, her hands covering her face. "Get out."

"It's me, little sis."

"No. Leave. I don't want you to see me like this."

A growl rumbled up from Dax's gut. He grabbed his sister's wrists, pulling them away from her dress. He scanned her body. The mattress. Blood. A small drop of blood. Her innocence. Her childhood. Gone.

"You're hurting me." Tears streaked her cheeks.

Dax had gripped her tight, but he loosened his hold. "I'm sorry. Who did this to you?"

"What are you talking about?" She sniffed.

A brother knew when a sister was hiding something. Besides, he was staring at the evidence on the bed. The bed creaked with his weight as he sat, giving her a little shove to make space for his large frame. "Tell me what happened, Bounty. I'm not leaving till you do."

She turned on him, her eyes on fire. He had never seen her so angry. "No. You think I don't know what you do for me? I'm young. Not stupid."

"I don't do anything for you."

Her hand reached out to cup his chin. Calm returned to her. "Yes, you do, brother. You protect me from my father. The same male who killed our mother." She swallowed. "I know. He didn't murder her outright, but he hooked her on O and that killed her."

"Bounty, you are a child. My job is to protect you. I failed. Now tell me who raped you."

He said it. He gave words to the horrible event. She broke into gasping sobs.

Dax had tried to keep her from the sordid side of their lives. The beatings. The sex. But he had been off going through his Awakening, enjoying his new powers, while his stepfather offered up Bounty as fodder in his whorehouse.

She rolled over, her back to Dax. "No."

"You will or I will ask him."

She flipped around, her fingers clutching his arm. "No. Don't fight with him. He'll kill you one of these times."

Dax laughed. "He can't. I'm too strong for him and too valuable."

"You're not too strong. You haven't had your Awakening yet. He's a mature vampire with power."

"Little sis, trust me. He cannot hurt me."

Even before his Awakening, Dax had worked out every day with Firebrands at the North Shelters stronghold where his real father had been a warrior. They had taken him under their wings after he had approached one of them, puffing out his chest and proclaiming he would be a Firebrand someday.

"Your father's an arrogant SOB who bullies females and weak males. Now tell me, or I swear I'm never moving."

Bounty's lids hung low, making her look younger than her years. "Sagen."

Dax's fangs punched from his gums, crimson fury rushed to his eyes, and shallow breaths pumped in and out of his chest. Bounty drew away in fear, shuddering.

Dax clenched his jaw tight. "You will shower and pack immediately. Do you understand?" He clenched her upper arm, imprinting it with bruises.

"You're hurting me, Dax."

"Sorry." He relaxed his grip.

"Are you angry with me because I let the male

take me?"

He brushed the back of his hand across her cheek, wiping away the moisture. "Never. You are perfect. Pure. All of this is my fault. Blame me. I failed you."

Her lips quivered into a shaky smile. "Where are we going?"

"I don't know yet but someplace safe. Stay here. Do not leave this room until I return. Let only me in."

She slouched into a ball again, squeezing a gray stuffed wolf in her arms. "Please be careful. You're all I've got. I love you."

"Shower, dress, pack," Dax reminded. He wanted to storm out, but he would not. He leashed the beast he had created during his Awakening and prowled toward his stepfather's office, his mind clear, his mission set. He brushed the door open and stepped inside, his shiny black boots sinking into the thick carpet. The bastard was reading ledgers. Before he looked up, Dax was upon him, the crook of his elbow locked around the predator's neck. Flinging Bounty's shitty father away from the desk, he slammed him against the wall, the plaster cracking from his newfound strength. "What did I promise to do if you ever broke our deal?"

The asshole had the good sense to be scared. His lids popped wide while his mouth fluttered with pleas. He smelled as if he had pissed his pants, and his skin carried a deathly pallor.

With fingers curling into claws, Dax struck. Blood splattered the carpet, his own chest, his dark leathers, his new boots. The male gurgled, hands to throat.

Locked eye to eye, the Awakened young vampire severed his stepfather's head. Opening the scum's mouth, he cut out his fangs, holding them up high. Trophies. A reminder of the evil in the world.

Next stop, he found Bounty's rapist in one of the rooms, grunting and rutting atop a nymph.

Sagen looked up at the intrusion and rolled off the female. Dax motioned her to leave. She scurried off the bed, looking happy to desert the flabby vampire and leave him to his fate.

"What the hell do you think you're doing? I paid for her, young whelp." He reached out a hand for the female, but she was gone.

Dax bent his head, his long black hair falling like a shroud over his face. When he lifted his chin, he was in full vampire mode. His canines massive and pointed, his gaze crimson, his cheeks and jaws granite, a hungry, thirsty growl crossing his lips.

Sagen scuttled back on the bed, throwing the sheet across his naked body. Dax curled his clawed hand around the covers and tossed them back, exposing his sister's rapist. "I will start with your cock."

Screams fell like music on Dax's ears. He hoped Bounty could hear.

Finished with Sagen and the blood-soaked walls, bedding, and floor, he showered, added the rapist's fangs to his new necklace, and packed what few belongings he had. He found his sister dressed and waiting, her scuffed boots tapping the floor, her hands folded in her lap. Her eyes were dull. It was his fault. But he would find the light again and give it back to her. They left from a side door so she would see no bodies.

With his own suitcase and hers under his arms, they left the O blud whorehouse forever. He became Bounty's caretaker until she was able to provide for herself. But when the Phoenix called him, even the creature who had arisen from the flames to start life anew could not burn away Dax's guilt. He had let down the only person in the world who loved him.

****

Roark had taken Matty out of the cell hours ago. Dax worried. It was a long time for him to be tortured. The guy had guts, but human was human.

Clang. Clink. Clink. Clink. Shuffle. Shuffle.

Chains. The American stumbled along the concrete, demons carrying him between them, each locked onto an armpit. A guard dropped Dax to his knees with one taser load, just enough juice to knock him on his ass. They tossed Matty into the cell where he crumpled onto the hard floor.

When Dax finally pushed himself up, still wobbly from the electric jolt, he limped to his cellmate. The human's pulse said he was alive. Barely. The vampire Firebrand wiped off blood and checked for the worst wounds, doing what he could to stop the bleeding. Since his thirst was rising, Dax had to concentrate on the task. Otherwise, he would be licking his cellmate's injuries, a reminder he needed to feed soon.

Stooping to lift Matty into his arms, Dax carried him to a cot. All he could do was wait. Hope for the best.

Meanwhile, he explored every inch of the cage. The window was high, near the ceiling. Even if he could reach it, it was too small to slip through. The enclosure's walls were solid blocks of concrete. The bars were silver. As a vampire, he couldn't touch them without severe burns. Despite his willingness to endure the pain, his breed could not bend the metal anyway. Since the guards pressed a remote twice before entering, he guessed the cell had a forcefield ward as well as a locked door, both operated by the handheld device. A warlock or witch had activated wards that controlled Dax's powers. No shadowflashing. No speed. Sapped energy. He wasn't even as thirsty as he should be. Lucky for the colonel.

Dax stopped his survey of the cell when he heard a moan. His bunkmate was waking, eyes open but heavy-lidded. "How are you doing?"

"Never better. Sissies can't hit worth a damn, *mi amigo*." Matty fingered his jaw.

"Yeah? You look pretty beat up to me."

"I tripped over my own feet. Never could dance."

"What did they want?"

"The usual crap. Which portals are guarded. Troop movements. Size."

"What did you give up?"

Matty took a sharp breath as he swung his feet to the floor, sitting up. "Do I seem like the kind of guy who would talk? I'll have you know I got an *A plus* in dumber-than-shit and will-never-confess-no-matter-what-you-do."

Dax respected this male. And he respected very few beings, including his *frerons*. Rein, Kole, and Ram numbered among them, but he would never release that newsflash. "Watch out, human. I could end up liking you."

"I don't swing that way, but if we're in here too long, I might change my mind."

Dax chuckled. "Don't worry. I have another human I want for that activity." Now where did such a dumbass statement come from?

Clang.

"Here comes fun," said Matty, lying back on the cot with a quiet moan.

A guard clicked the remote once and shoved a tray through a trap in the cell. "Eat up, girls. You're gonna need your strength for round two."

Dax didn't answer. He watched as the jailer tapped the handheld device again. *Yep. Forcefield. Damn.* This place was looking impregnable. The interrogation room might be the only way out. Fat chance. Still. He wasn't about to go toes up in this shithole. His stepdad, more Aeternals than he could count, and *beaucoup* wildings hadn't killed him. He would not give the honor to these misfit bastards. Until he saw an opportunity, he'd hold out for the Firebrands. In the meantime, stay alive. Stay strong.

He lifted the tray, sniffing. Handing a bowl to Matty, he grabbed the other for himself. "It's safe to eat." Dax passed out the bread and a spoon, planted his ass on his cot, and tucked into the prison food, drinking the glass of blood first.

Chapter Twenty-Six

Dax perched on the edge of his cot, slurping down a mug of barely-fresh blood while rubbing his temple where a fireworks display exploded. He had returned from another bout of questions accompanied by fists where they must have given up when he slipped into unconsciousness.

Once he finished the breakfast drink, he lifted his shirt to watch a nasty wound close. In another two or three hours when he'd be completely healed, Roark had promised a torture instant replay.

Maybe they'd kill him next round. Good news was if they did, Chiara was better off. No more mooning over him, calling him a hero. *Hah.* He was nothing but a degenerate vampire who hadn't protected his mother or sister. Bounty would shed a few tears. Then she'd get on with her life. He would be free from finding inventive, degrading ways to punish himself for his shortcomings. The Firebrands wouldn't have to debate whether it was time to off him.

Yeah. My death is a plus all around.

"You are one tough bastard." Matty swilled what passed for oatmeal from a bowl. "When they dropped you off from your date, you looked like a slab of ground meat. Now you're almost pretty enough to catch my eye."

"Good genes." Dax raised the empty glass. "Great blood."

"Not my choice, but…"

The colonel was cut off when a noise like Thor's legendary hammer sounded. Dax bounded off the bed, spreading his legs wide to maintain balance while the walls and floor trembled. The guards scrambled, boots thudding when they raced for cover.

"Under the cot," Dax yelled when iron struts in the ceiling crumpled aluminum-foil style. The cell filled with dust while the quake continued. Tucking his head under his arms, the vampire fell in beside Matty to wait out the disaster. With the roof destroyed, they heard loud screams joined by a bestial roar which came from the outside.

When the rear wall caved in as if a wrecking ball had struck, Dax grabbed Matty's arm, pulling him out from under the bed. He leaped for the opening with the human in tow.

Though both males were barefoot, they scrambled across iron girders and fallen blocks to escape. They halted abruptly when they saw what awaited them outside the prison. The center of the garrison was in chaos, Arisen Dawn soldiers running in all directions in various stages of dress. Of course, that wasn't the shocker.

"Holy shit." Matty pointed with his free hand. "What the fuck?"

Dax, who teetered on a girder, dropped the colonel's arm to steady himself. He swiped a fist across his vision. "A dragon."

"Is that…?"

"Yep. A guard between its teeth."

The beast shook the Aeternal and tossed him into the air. Opening its mouth wide, it caught the guy and swallowed, a big bulge making its way down its neck, a claw swiping across its satisfied lips. Finished with the snack, it swiveled its head toward the escapees, a puff of black smoke snorting from its nostrils. Red eyes locked onto them, its lips pulling into a reptilian grin to reveal rows of knife-like teeth.

"I think he likes you, *amigo*." Matty's voice was

shaky.

Whipping its monstrous neck toward two running Arisen Dawn soldiers, the dragon fried them instantly with one shot of its deadly breath. At the same time, it snatched another victim in its long black claws, using him like a pincushion. Sun glinted off blue-green scales while its forked tail swished back and forth. Under its skin, slabs of muscle rippled with each movement.

With the latest victim still in its grasp, the dragon crouched to spring onto a roof. The structure collapsed beneath the beast's weight. Soldiers scattered, fleeing every building. Standing atop the rubble, the creature opened its mouth. Out came a stream of fire, torching its clasped prey until he was extra crispy. It popped the fried morsel into its maw. *Straight up.*

Dax grabbed the American's elbow. "Let's move while we can." He bent to snatch boots off two dead assholes, tossing the smaller pair to the colonel. "Here. These are better than bare feet."

Matty slipped them on as he did a combo hop-run. They dodged a large group of their captors who huddled in an open field gawking at the flame-breathing beast, their mouths agape, eyes wide.

Alongside others, the two escaping males sprinted toward the tree line, glancing behind occasionally to see if their asses were on fire. No one in Arisen Dawn stopped them. To be honest, however, they were otherwise occupied by a dragon who preferred them as appetizers. Talk about the hand of Gahya. Though Dax wasn't much of a believer, he was reconsidering his lack of faith.

At a fast clip, they raced through the woods until the sun was high in the sky. When Matty fell behind, Dax slowed.

The human caught up, bending forward with both

hands on his knees. "I gotta rest for a bit. You go on."

The Firebrand nodded when he slumped to the ground, flopping onto his ass. "I could use a break, too."

"What did you make of the dragon thing?" Matty's chest bounced with rapid short breaths as he stretched out.

"I have no idea. I thought they were extinct. Shows what I know."

Matty scrubbed a weary fist across his hair. "Dragons. Damn."

Dax opened his mouth to take in more oxygen. "I have bad news, though."

"You mean worse news. Can't wait to hear it." Matty, still drawing deep breaths, curled an arm under his head.

"We're not on Scath. We're on a realm called Darque."

"Why do you make it sound bad?" Matty twisted toward Dax to stare.

"Cause it's populated with feral beasts. We put them here fifteen hundred years ago."

"Tell me we have a plan."

"I always have a plan."

"What is it?"

"To stay alive and get to the Firebrand stronghold."

"Does your plan have details?"

"No. Details only muck you up." Dax stretched before propping himself up on both elbows.

"Since this is your battlefield, I'll go with your plan. Just give me my orders."

"Okay. Offer yourself as meat to any attackers so I can get away."

"You'll forgive me if I don't like my assignment. I'm fondly attached to my ass." Matty's breath steadied though his eyes narrowed.

Dax pushed off the ground, did a three-sixty, and eyed the landmarks. “Time to boogie.”

Brushing off his pants, Matty stood. “Is there a good news part to this shitstorm?”

“Yep. We’re close to my commander’s hidey-hole. Food, drink, and communication devices are stored there since he and his mate were once marooned there.”

“You could have led with the info.”

“We’re not there yet.”

“You’re a cup-half-empty kind of guy, aren’t you?”

“Yep.” Dax slowed his pace for the next few miles of the jaunt as he explained how Skyler and Kole had been stranded on Darque when the warlock Uwrick blocked the commander’s D-chip. After a hunting party of gagan nearly killed him, they made it to a cave. Now, Kole always kept it stocked as a just-in-case place for the Firebrands.

When they arrived on the banks of a wide, turbulent river, the vampire pointed to the other side. “I hope you’re a strong swimmer, cuz we need to be over there.”

“I’ll make it. Don’t make me have to drag your pansy ass to safety, though. My lifeguard skills are not the greatest.”

Dax dived in, rose to the top, and shook out his hair. “Hey, human. Come on in. The water’s fine.”

After tying his boots onto his belt hooks by the laces, Matty pushed off from the bank, jackknifing into the deep water. When he bobbed to the surface, he swam toward the other side with long, powerful strokes. “Race ya, vampire.”

Dax laughed and hand-over-headed it to catch the human.

Competitive bastard.

Matty reached the other bank first, but Dax grabbed his arm before he could emerge. "Get down now. Stay under."

They both submerged, struggling against the current but coming up for quick breaths several times. Finally, Dax punched Matty's shoulder.

Water spewing from his mouth, the American colonel gasped for air. "What was that all about?"

"Harpies. Overhead. We don't want to tangle with them."

Matty spied the back end of a flying wedge of black-winged creatures in the distance. "I feel like I got dropped into a *Jurassic Park* sequel."

"Don't know what you mean."

"Vampire, you have some serious cultural deficiencies. When we get out of this hellhole, we'll have a sleepover, rent some classics, and paint each other's toenails."

Dax hauled onto shore, offering an assist to Matty, dragging him up by an arm. "Sounds like something I'd enjoy. Pink's my favorite color." The vampire pointed at the mountain. "Kole's place is a cave behind the waterfall. We need to reach it before nightfall. I'll be able to see no matter what, but I'm guessing you can't."

Matty eyed the long rise which grew sheerer near the top. "Don't worry about me, gumdrop. I always make it."

As he slipped his boots back onto his wet feet, Dax spoke. "Several Firebrands would actually like you. They're smartasses, too."

"Everybody likes me."

"Nobody likes me." Dax shrugged, a side of his mouth curling into a smirk.

"Hard to believe. You have such a cheery disposition. Is there a woman in your life?"

"No. Kind of. I don't know."

I want a specific female. A little witch in a gypsy skirt who I don't deserve. "You?"

"Yeah. Ex-wife. Thinking she'll be really pissed if I die out here. She may be the only person who doesn't like me, but she loves my alimony checks. They'll stop if I croak. But she'll chase me into hell." Matty slipped, sending loose rock scattering below him. He gripped a thick-leafed plant for stability. "How about family?"

"A sister."

"She like you?"

"Fuck no. She's smart, beautiful, has a good sense of humor."

"So, total opposites."

Dax chuckled. "You could say."

Struggling alongside the river, they finally hit the base of the waterfall. The vampire stared uphill. "It gets hard from here."

"Yeah. Cause the rest was so easy."

"We'll be scaling the rock wall. Get good grips because the terrain is difficult. Near the top is a ledge that leads into the cave. Follow me."

"In all honesty, I have to tell you. I flunked mountain climbing. Not my proudest moment."

"In that case, I'll race you to the top, gumdrop."

"Did you make a joke, vampire? Cause if it was, you need to work on your sense of humor. For a first attempt, though, it's damn good."

Dax jumped and gained a handhold on the cliff. Digging in his foot, he started the climb. He glanced back to see Matty keeping pace. The guy owned balls the size of boulders and wasn't a waste of good oxygen. First, Chiara. Now the colonel.

What's wrong with me? I never liked Earthers before.

When he heard rocks tumble, Dax looked below. Matty was further behind but still climbing. He was tiring but saved himself from a slip. "Keep coming. I'll wait. You can do it."

"You sound like my ex." Matty paused before he resumed the struggle up the steep face.

When he pulled alongside Dax, the vampire tilted his head. "There's the ledge. Hug the cliff wall. One jump and then we're in the cave."

Dax made the entrance first. As Matty faced the mountain and tightened his body against it, he shuffled along the edge. His foot slipped. Dax let out a growl. Shoving out a hand toward the human, he met nothing but air. He couldn't latch onto Matty.

The colonel caught himself, though, and kept toeing the ledge. When he finally grasped the vampire's arm, he swung inside on wobbly legs, collapsing to the dirt floor.

"Crawl further into the cavern. I'll get drinks," said Dax.

"No blood for me, *amigo*. Water will do fine." Matty squeezed his hands together, working the muscles in his arms and fingers.

"Don't worry. I wouldn't waste the good stuff on you." Dax disappeared into the darkness at the back of the cave. He returned, drinking from one bottle and handing the other off to Matty.

"I contacted the stronghold while in there. We need to wait."

Matty gulped the water. "Didn't you say something in the cell about not being able to shadowflash because of wards? After we escaped prison, could you have used the power to get home?"

"Kind of, but vampires can't flash to another realm. For that, I need my D-chip." He wiggled his wrist at Matty. "All gone."

"But you could have gotten here faster?"

"Yeah."

"Why didn't you?"

"And leave your cheerful ass behind? I would have missed your bad jokes."

"I owe you. Twice now you've watched out for me. I don't forget good deeds." Matty stretched out on the ground, his eyes shut.

"You owe me nothing."

"Not to worry. I didn't say I would pay you back. Only that I owed you."

Dax was about to respond, but Matty had fallen asleep.

After nodding off several times, Dax heard noise over the roar of the waterfall. Ram, Sabine, and Nico dropped through the cave entrance.

The satyr Firebrand smiled. "Damn, vampire, you look like shit."

Matty shot to his feet, wide awake.

Ram's grin vanished when he locked onto the human. "What the fuck is he doing here?" He pulled his Scottish dirk from its sheath and rushed the colonel.

As Matty moved into a defensive stance, his legs spread wide, Dax threw himself between the two males, stiff-arming it to hold them apart. "You know each other?"

The human snorted. "You could say we're old friends."

****

Matty listened to the Firebrands from a chair in front of Kole's desk, feeling lucky Ram hadn't carved him up like a holiday turkey. Though the guy had tried, the other warriors stopped him, arguing it was the commander's decision.

Dax leaned against the wall, his body tilting slightly forward while he objected to having his sanity questioned. "I know a fucking dragon when I see one. I'm telling you, a fire-breathing beast crashed our prison party, tearing the place apart. He gave us time to escape."

Sitting military straight, Matty stared at a collection of weapons which decorated the wall behind the commander's desk.

"Dragons are extinct." Kole brushed a meaty fist over his hair.

Dax played with his scary-ass fang necklace. "Obviously not. If it hadn't been for that creature, we'd still be doing time at the Arisen Dawn garrison on Darque."

Shifting his gaze from the wall to Kole, Matty defended his new vampire friend. Correction. Only vampire friend. "It was a dragon. I've seen *Eragon*. Are those weapons all yours?"

"No. Belonged to fallen Firebrands."

Matty nodded. "Good tribute. Though I've never seen a live dragon, this thing was green, had scales, and breathed fire. It was bigger than the proverbial brick shithouse."

Ram glared at Matty from the sidelines, Thorn on one side of him. Sabine and Nico were on the other. Obviously, they expected him to cut loose again.

Finally, the satyr rushed Matty, grabbing his shirt. He snatched him from the chair and shoved into his chest. "No more convo about dragons. This male was in the room while Dante tortured me. I want justice."

Matty elbowed Ram, trying to nudge the male backward. The guy didn't budge. "True, but I didn't lay a finger on you. If it's any consolation, I celebrated when those Arisen Dawn guys ripped out Mars's heart during the Battle for Bozeman. Dante's so-called general was a sadistic SOB. Got what he deserved. Sorry I wasn't the one to deliver it."

Ram kept a fist tangled in Matty's shirt while he paused. "Good to hear he's dead. For the record, I would have torn out his organ to eat it." Obviously satisfied with the news, the satyr returned to beast mode. "While I was in Dante's torture chamber, you watched my entrails spill onto the floor. You may not have had a hand in my misery, but you didn't stop anything either."

"True. Today, I would handle the situation differently." He was sincere. Dante was a sadistic man, as bad as his general Mars. The whole scene had never sat right with Matty, even though the specimens on the tables had been otherworlders.

Ram persisted. "Yeah? Mind you, I don't give a shit about your army killing Arisen Dawn invaders, but what's happening to the innocents you guys have captured? Can you tell me they aren't being tortured right now?"

"No. I can't." Matty scrubbed a fist along his jaw.

Dropping his hold, Ram gave him some breathing room. "I remember every scalpel cut, each cracked rib, my chest being pried open while I was on the table. I even coded several times. They tortured a young female vampire. They murdered her male. He was the son of a lawgiver, a vamp just out of his Awakening who had done nothing but sneak off to Earth to party. Do you feel for them?"

Matty refused to look away from Ram. He owed him that much. "I do. I own my role. I was wrong and your anger is righteous."

"I'm going to slice your balls off and shove them down your throat. I didn't do it at the cave, but it's reckoning time."

Shit happened fast. Ram prepped to drive his blade forward. Dax threw himself between Matty and the satyr. Thorn and Nico rushed him. Kole shot from his desk, sending a blast of fire to Ram's dagger.

The satyr dropped it, his fingers sizzling. "Damn, Comm. That fucking hurts." He blew on his singed palm.

"You have a right to this human." When Dax opened his mouth, Kole raised a hand. "Think, Ram. We need to get the Earthers to the negotiation table. This sadistic asshole may be our way in."

"I take offense…" Dax shook his head, a warning before Matty could finish. "I was about to say, I take offense at being called sadistic. I accept asshole."

Ram gritted his teeth but stood down. "I'd be happy to torture him for information about his troops."

"Good luck. The perverted A-hole Roark failed. I don't have high expectations for you." When Matty bent to retrieve Ram's sword from the floor, weapons flew from sheaths, holsters, and ankle straps. Grinning, he passed it off to the satyr by the blade. "Paranoid bastards."

"Good reason." Ram slid his weapon home.

Dax piped up, obviously not knowing enough to keep his mouth shut. "This guy's not half bad, satyr. Aside from his silent complicity in your torture."

Mateo Garcia straightened the collar on his shirt. "Thanks for the high praise, vampire."

"Okay. I believe he's a good male. We should trust him. If he says he'll work on getting us a sit-down, he'll do it."

"You trust him, Dax? You? The vampire who doesn't trust anybody?" Ram adjusted the strap on the sheath across his chest.

Matty slapped a palm to Dax's shoulder. "Hey.

Don't bust on *mi amigo*. He's working on his issues. I've been counseling him."

"You're not well." Ram puzzled his brows while Thorn and Rein bit back chuckles.

"True. What I am, though, is a high-ranking officer in Operation Frankenstein, West Bank. No offense. I didn't create the title. I can work on getting you a meet. I say Dax comes as your rep since he seems more reasonable than the rest of you."

"Now I know he's not well," said Ram. "Let me just kill him. He's delusional."

Kole cocked his head, studying the human. "You're on, Colonel. I'm warning you, though. If you betray us, the Arisen Dawn maniacs will seem like kittens. Humanity could not survive unleashed Firebrands."

"We share the same goal, Commander. A peaceful coexistence between our species. I vow to you I'll work toward the goal. Like you, though, I'm a soldier first. If talks fail, I fight for my people."

Kole, his lopsided grin spreading, zinged the human's cheek with a blast of fire. "I expect nothing less from you, warrior."

"Holy hell. Why the burn?" Matty fingered his singed skin.

"Because I can. Besides, I find a visual drives home the point. The point being, you better keep your vow. Dax, is the plan okay with you?"

The vampire nodded.

"What do you need from us?" Kole lowered into his chair, his fingers tapping together as sparks jumped between them.

"A secure link to my command post, a private conversation, and safe passage home," said Matty.

Kole nodded. "He's with you, Dax. I'll contact

Cadmon to set up the convo with your people for tomorrow morning."

Dax shoved Matty's shoulder. "Don't make me look like a jackass, human."

"Too late, buddy. You already look like one."

As they prepared to leave Kole's office, Thorn called out to Dax. "Fin and I are having a mating celebration at the stronghold later tonight. We postponed it for this meeting. Everyone else knows. Now you have an invite. I guess you'll have to bring the human."

Ram piled shit onto his *freron*. "Does she know you shed? Dog fur everywhere. Gotta be a bitch to clean. And you're not housebroken."

"I make up for it in things a satyr lacks. Like brains along with a really big dick."

"Get out the tape measure," Matty said, interrupting the exchange. "I'm thinking I've got you both beat. Mexican-American. Second generation. I have the goods to please the *damas encantadoras*."

All eyes pinged to the human.

"What? I thought we were doing locker room natter. The lovely ladies do admire me."

Ram shook his head. "This guy is seriously disturbed, and we're hanging our destiny on him."

The door flew open as Chiara barged inside. She threw herself at Dax, jumping up, encircling his neck with her arms and wrapping her legs around his hips.

Matty's brows arched. "Is this the no-kind-of-I-don't-know woman you mentioned?"

Dax snarled, easing Chiara to the floor. "Get ahold of yourself, female."

She tossed her long, dark braid onto her back. "Get ahold of myself? That's what you want to say after nearly being killed trying to save my life? You idiot." She punched his shoulder.

Ram's brows arched. "My whole world is tilting. Dax is not Dax. Here's a female who actually cares about him alongside a human who'll next be telling us they're friends."

Matty cocked his head to the side. "Watch how you talk, man. The vampire and I have a bromance going."

Chapter Twenty-Seven

In the outside training area behind the stronghold, Dax whispered the gist of the shifter mating ceremony to Matty while Commander Kole presided over the rite. He read from a tome written in an ancient breed dialect.

Dax leaned forward. "We're at the best part. The challenge. Thorn must prove he's strong enough to protect Fin. *Frerons* are lining up to take him on."

Rein shoved guests out of the way. "Stay outside the circle." He pointed to a bright yellow ring drawn in the grass.

"Might be better to step back a few. Don't want any fancy duds splattered with gore," added Chay.

Sig barged into the center, the first to take on the wolf shifter. He cracked his knuckles, a wide grin spreading across his face.

Thorn shook the challenger's hand, using the gesture to pull his opponent in where he whispered in his ear. "I hope you have medical insurance, baby demon."

Dax's sharp hearing allowed him to make out the words. With a grin, he passed them on to Matty. "Thorn's an expert at psych warfare."

Throwing the first punch, Sig missed when Thorn dodged to the right. With fast footwork, the shifter continued to dance around the younger Firebrand. When the demon hurled another wild swing, Thorn sighed, moving in close enough for Sig to land a fist to his gut.

"Finally," said the wolf shifter as he launched his first blow, knocking his opponent out cold. "Rein, remove the body. Next up? Get your Goth ass in here, warlock."

Tyr made a show of removing his earrings and the silver rod through his brow, handing them off to Jace.

"Hold these. If I return toes up, just stick them in my pocket." He lumbered into the circle, beckoning for Thorn. "Bring it on. The things I do for my *frerons*. Watch the face. It's my best feature."

"That's not saying much," barely left the shifter's lips when Tyr sent a solid to his jaw. As he shook it off, Thorn came out fighting, taking the warlock down with a one-two punch.

Though Jace booed from the sidelines before rushing to Tyr's aid, Brak let out a loud whoop. "Two down. My turn."

Despite the carnal demon having a few inches on him and a lot more bulk, Thorn didn't wait for Brak to get into position. He charged, ramming a shoulder into the big guy's gut, taking him to the ground.

Thud.

They rolled. Thorn on top. Then Brak. Fists flew, blood splattered, flesh pounded flesh.

Braelyn jumped away too late, a drop of fresh crimson staining her white silk blouse. "Men," she muttered.

Despite shredded knuckles, purplish bruises, and nasty cuts, Thorn got his demon *freron* in a headlock. When he rolled, he pinned him to the grass. "Concede, you big mutherfucker."

Brak pounded the lawn with the palm of his hand.

While blood dripped down his left eye from a gash through his brow, Thorn bolted to his feet, brushing his hair away from his face. "Any more takers?"

"One more." A guy Dax recognized stepped through the crowd. Lobo had been with Kole's stronghold before personal reasons had him transferring to North Shelters. Both wolf shifters, he and Thorn were close.

"You can't challenge. You're mated." Thorn

shoved his shaggy straw-colored hair off his face.

"Nothin' in the rules say that's a problem. Payback's a bitch, Thorn."

Thorn had challenged Lobo at his mating not that long ago.

As the big mutherfucker strode into the circle, a tall blonde ylve, her straight hair falling to her waist, sidled up to Fin. "You need to call for bets. First blood and the win."

"Why would I do that?"

"Cause the Firebrands are pulling out the cash now. I made a haul at my mating to Lobo." The blonde yelled, "We're taking all bets against Thorn here. Get out your cash, honey."

Dax pulled out bills, betting Lobo would draw first blood. It was for a good cause.

Matty patted his pockets. "Empty. Arisen Dawn wiped me out."

The two contestants shifted to four legs, fur flying, teeth bared. Thorn came out the winner, and Fin raked in the dough.

"That's cold," said Matty. "What if Thorn lost?"

"Fin would end up with a strange bedfellow. No worry, though. During the ceremony, a wolf's pheromones are so high he can't be defeated. Besides, I don't think our *frerons* were giving their peak performance. Especially Brak and Lobo."

"I'm almost in tears." Matty drew a sleeve across his face, wiping away moisture which wasn't there. "Weddings make me cry. Course, I didn't weep at my own, but I water-logged the carpet during my divorce. All that alimony. And to a conniving ex who cheated on me."

"Wolves don't divorce. They don't cheat either. Thorn's in it for life." Dax grabbed a whiskey from a tray. “Thanks, Margo.”

“You’re welcome, Dax.”

“A life sentence, you say. Ouch.” Matty nodded a thanks as he snatched a beer from the same tray.

“You have a very negative outlook on life, human.”

“But you’re a cheerful sod. What’s coming up?”

“Ceremony over. Thorn wins. The end.” Dax downed his whiskey.

With his beer in hand, Matty surveyed the crowd. “Now, there’s a beauty who could make me forget my vow never to marry again.”

“Who?” Dax followed the American’s gaze. “That’s my sister. Off limits.”

“That’s her? Somehow, I pictured her as ugly. Like you. Your *hermana* is hot.”

“Yeah? One wrong move will get you knocked on your ass. If not by her, then by me. Life has been hard enough on Bounty with a worthless brother. She doesn’t need a human to break her heart.”

“Looks to me she’d break my heart. Along with a few other body parts.” Matty pushed off from the wall. “Here she comes. Be sure to talk me up as if you like me. Lie.”

Bounty sashayed toward them on four-inch heels and too few clothes, in Dax’s estimation. She threw her arms around him. “Brother, come on. Take a risk. Hug me.”

As he pried her fingers from his neck, he whispered, “Damn, shush. Everyone will hear you.”

“Too late. I already outed us. I’m tired of all this secret shit.”

He glanced at the guests. No one was watching. They were enjoying their private convos.

“Who is your friend?” Bounty batted her

mascara-heavy eyelashes at Matty, licking her too-red lips.

"Fellow prisoner. A human. Ignore him. I do."

When Matty lifted her hand to his mouth for a kiss, she smiled. "Impossible. I would never ignore someone so handsome."

"I was just telling your bro I saw the most beautiful woman at the party."

"Who was it?" Bounty blinked with feigned innocence.

Dax poked a finger in Matty's chest. "I warned you."

Bounty tugged on her brother's arm. "Really? I've been meeting males on my own for over a century. Oops. Does that make me too old for you, handsome?"

"Definitely not. I love an older, experienced woman."

Dax snarled. "Not only is he a human, but he's with an Earther army. They're trying to kill us."

Matty tilted his head toward Bounty. "Everybody has faults, *mi amada*. I could never kill you, though. Except with kindness."

"You could charm the panties right off me if I'm not careful."

"Please, Gahya. I'm standing right here." Dax's eyes flitted from Bounty to Matty. From Matty to Bounty. "This will not turn out well."

"Brother, we are two consenting adults."

Dax held up a hand to quiet his sister before he slammed Matty against the wall, forearm to the human's neck, prepared to give him some friendly advice. When someone tapped his shoulder, he cocked his head and looked down.

Chiara.

"You're making a scene, Dax. Release the nice

man and get me a drink. Hi, Bounty. Nice to see you. Is your brother pissing you off?"

Dax's eyes bounced around again, looking for eavesdroppers. "What the fuck, Bounty. You did tell everyone about us. Are you crazy?"

"Yes. I told everyone. Your female. Your friends."

"I don't have a female or friends."

"What am I? Chopped taco meat?" asked Matty. "I'm insulted."

Chiara slipped her arm through Dax's.

Instead of pulling away from the little witch, he made the mistake of eye-wandering over her curves. She was in a short, almost indecent skirt rather than one of her usual long ones. Tall-ass heels showed off her shapely legs. He paused at her cleavage, showcased by a pale silk blouse with too many buttons undone. After long seconds, he shook his head to erase the tempting vision.

"Stop being rude." Chiara brushed back an errant strand of long dark hair which curled atop a plump breast.

"You're as crazy as my sister. I mean … Bounty. Damn. This is a major fuck-up." Dax felt the veins in his neck throb.

"I'm still waiting for my drink. Bounty, do you want one?" asked Chiara.

"That would be great. Make mine white wine. Would you like another beer, Matty?"

He tipped his bottle, checking to see if it was empty. "The same."

"I am not getting drinks." Dax growled, the tips of his fangs protruding.

"I'll get them," said Matty, "but I could use some help, beautiful. Four drinks are a lot for a weak human to carry."

"I'm right on your ass. Such a nice ass." Bounty swatted him before she locked a hand into the crook of his elbow.

As Dax watched his sister walk away with the human, an unwanted memory popped into his head. She was huddled against the headboard at his stepfather's blud den with the hem of her soiled skirt squeezed tight around her feet after a male had…

Chiara's smooth voice drifted into his consciousness, interrupting unbidden thoughts. She was saying something about the dogs. Her arm was still locked in the crook of his elbow. His heart pounded against his chest as he fought for breath. He needed to get away before he did something stupid. "Stop." He untangled himself from the little witch. "I'm poison. Get me? We've had this talk. Now walk away before you're hurt."

"You're the only person who can hurt me, Dax." She tilted her head, her innocent eyes focused on him, waiting for… What? Something he couldn't give?

Surely, she saw his darkness, his cocked-up life. "That's what I'm trying to tell you. I'll end up hurting you. It's what I do. If you won't walk, I will."

With Chiara's gaze stabbing him in the back, he strode away. When he passed Bounty, he bent to whisper in her ear. "Take care of the little witch." He jerked his chin toward the stronghold. "You coming, human?"

For once, the guy was speechless as he looked at Bounty for the answer.

She rested a hand on Matty's shoulder. "No. He'll stick around. He's next on my dance card, but I will deliver him here tomorrow morning. None the worse."

"Will I be smiling?" Matty asked.

"From ear to ear."

"This is so fucked up." Dax stormed into the stronghold through the rear entrance, his leather coat flaring, his long hair whipping across his shoulders, his failures echoing with every loud step on the tile.

****

Chiara's heels clicked on the floor when she chased after the stubborn vampire. Seducing him was harder than she expected, but she struggled to stay upbeat even in the face of his repeated rejections.

She was determined to show Dax the man she saw, a gruff savior who risked his life for others, who expected nothing in return. Though he pushed her away, she couldn't fight her feelings. She was in love with the man. The vampire. He was difficult. He was flawed. But he was so much more than the sum of his mistakes. If she couldn't force him to accept that, they stood no chance of being together. He would sabotage the situation every time.

After she trailed him into the library, she shut the door.

Dax spun toward her, his obsidian eyes furious. He snagged her elbow. "Why the fuck are you following me?"

Backing her against the wall, he locked an arm around her waist, pulling her tight against him. The hard ridge of his erection thrust against her belly. At a sudden loss for words, Chiara shook her head. "I wanted to talk to you. To tell you how I feel."

"How do you feel?"

"I love you, Dax."

He laughed. Not a pleasant sound. Rather, it was derisive, harsh, uncaring. "I feel bad for you, little witch. I thought I was fucked up. You're worse. What's it like to want a male who doesn't want you? Who won't or can't love you?"

"Knock off your crap. You care about me."

He rolled his hips, confirming how aroused he was. "Is this what you call caring?"

"Yes." Her hand squeezed between their bodies so she could stroke his cock through the soft leather of his pants.

Dax seized her fingers, tightening her hold. "If you're going to do me, little witch, learn what I like."

"What do you like?"

"Nothing you can give me."

"I must have something which appeals to you. You've used me as a feed and fuck. You saved my life. You brought my dogs here."

"You were a body, a ready supply of nutrients." Still grinding into her hand, Dax yanked her blouse off her shoulder and slipped her bra strap down, baring a breast. He took her nipple into his mouth, tasting it until it was a hard nub. Then he nicked her with his fangs.

Chiara threw her head back, moaning, her knees weak.

He jerked away, licking blood from his lips and dislodging her grip on him. "Your hand's not doing it for me, little witch." He unzipped his pants, his rigid cock jutting free. "Your mouth is much more skilled. Get on your knees."

His voice was harsh, guttural, without feeling. Chiara recoiled at his snapped demand as she adjusted her bra and blouse. She refused to cry because he was trying too hard to offend her.

"Never mind, female. I'm not in the mood for anything you can offer." Dax zipped up his tight leathers on his way to the liquor cabinet. "Drink?"

"No."

"Whatever. I'll have one." He poured a full tumbler of whiskey.

"Maybe I don't know what you want. Why don't you tell me?"

"Great idea." Glass in hand, Dax grabbed her elbow, his grip bruising her pale skin. He led her to a high-backed chair, flinging her into it. After he took the seat on the other side of a round table, he tossed back his drink, slamming the empty glass down. "You want to know why I brought your dogs to the stronghold?"

"Yes."

His eyes were cold obsidian. "Guilt."

"What do you have to be guilty about, Dax?" Fearing his answer, she wrung her hands in her lap.

Dax snarled, his teeth grinding together. "I made a trip to my favorite haunt. The O blud den."

"What's that?"

"It's a place vampires go to drink opium-enhanced blood."

"You're saying you're addicted to opium?"

"No. Only those who mainline the stuff are. I drink from Aeternals who shoot up. The buzz is brief but intense."

"Okay. You've got a problem. I'll do whatever I can to help." Her eyes pleaded with him.

Dax scraped fingers through his hair. "I don't want to stop, Chiara. I don't intend to stop. That's not why you shouldn't be with me, though."

"Oh?"

"I walked into the den to latch onto the first O blud whore I spotted. She was a blonde with a firm ass who was strung out just how I like. After I took her hand, I led her upstairs to my favorite room. She removed her robe. I bent her over a bar…"

Chiara clapped her hands over her ears.

Dax shot out of his chair to lean over her and snag her wrists. "You'll listen to what I have to say.

Understand what I want in a partner."

Chiara struggled, but Dax wouldn't let her block his message.

"I dropped my pants and fucked her. Before I came, I bit into her neck, swallowing the sweet O blud. Then I zipped up, relaxing in a chair to ride the high."

"Why?"

"Why do I crave O blud?"

"No. Why are you telling me?"

"So you see who I am rather than who you want me to be. I don't need some female clinging to me, changing me."

A steady stream of tears rolled down Chiara's cheeks. *To hell with it.* She'd cry if she wanted. Besides, she had neither the strength nor desire to wipe them away. "You want a woman who shoots up with opium?"

"That's it."

After Dax released Chiara's wrists, he strode to the liquor cabinet. "I need another drink."

She stared at his back, his broad, uncaring back. "You've been harsh. You've been aggressive. You've been cold and cruel, but you've never destroyed me. Until now."

Still turned away from her, he poured a whiskey. *Glug. Glug. Glug.* "Yes, I have. You've just refused to see me. You're still a ten-year-old girl who thinks a hero saved her. Wake up, Chiara. A monster dragged you from that burning car. So, unless you plan on shooting up to become my O blud bitch, I suggest you get out of my life. Agreed?"

After one thundering beat, her heart felt as if it ripped from her chest, leaving a black hole filled with rage. She fought against calling him all the bitter names which popped into her head. Instead, Chiara drew up her shoulders and, on trembling legs, rose from the chair.

She strode from the library with all the dignity she could muster.

"Bastard."

Dax mumbled at her disappearing figure, "I'll take that as a yes."

****

"This is Colonel Mateo Garcia, Sergeant. Put General Lipton on the line."

Matty glanced around a conference room, his ear to the phone. A more morose than usual Dax, who was a full-blooded vampire and, *hell yes*, a friend, perched on the edge of a table. Rein, a vamp mix and huge sonofabitch, sprawled in a chair, boots propped on the same table. Ram, a satyr who had been the Englishman Dante's torture-target, leaned against the wall, his arms crossed, a scowl on his otherwise pretty face. Commander Kole, a rugged demon, stared out of fire-gold eyes. And an imposing ylve dude they said was the Scion Firebrand high commander sat stiffly, his fingers laced together.

Never had Matty imagined this scene.

Never had he pictured phoning his general to urge peace talks the morning after he had met a gorgeous, fanged woman at a wolf shifter's mating ceremony. Magnificent figure. Big boobs. Long blonde hair, the sweetest smile, a passionate nature, with the added benefit of brains. Wrong time to think about her. He shook his head.

Back in the game, Matty reminded himself he was a duty-first kind of guy. If his people said the talks were a no-go, a day might come when he would face these warriors while holding the trigger end of his gun. Not happily, but he would.

"General. I'm with representatives of a group on Scath which calls itself the Scion Firebrands. Think of them as special forces big-ass mutherfuckers. I'm putting us on speaker. Then I'll explain the rest."

Kole tapped a button on the conference phone.

"Matty, what the fuck are you talking about?" asked Lipton. "Where the hell are you?"

"During the Battle for Bozeman, I was captured by what I now know is a rebel unit called Arisen Dawn. In a nutshell, they're the bad guys. They put me into a cell with one of these Firebrands. A vampire. We were both tortured by these subversive assholes, but we escaped. You'll never guess how. A dragon. That's another story. Dax got us to a safe location where he contacted his people. I'm with them now."

"I'm listening."

Muffled sounds in the background caught his attention. Matty asked, "Are others there?"

"Yes. Go on."

"I trust these guys, General. What we have here is another realm, populated with what we've labeled otherworlders. Strange, though, they were born and bred on Earth like us. Technically not otherworlders. They call themselves Aeternals. They say they are another species created before we were."

Matty heard whispers on General Lipton's side. "On to the bad guys. A fellow named Cerberus organized Arisen Dawn, the assholes who are making sorties onto Earth with an eye to the kill. The Firebrands don't know this guy's identity or how to find him yet, but they believe his goal is to open all portals so they can invade *en masse.* Maybe we can defeat them with our technology or numbers, but a fifty-fifty chance for a win is dodgy. They have superior strength, speed, and astounding powers. Unfortunately, large numbers of Aeternals are joining this rebel group."

"So, who are these Firebrands?"

"Sorry, let me introduce the men in the room with me. High Commander Cadmon, Commander Kole, Firebrands Rein and a guy you might remember from our visit to Dante, Ram. Dax, who was in prison with me, is also present."

Lipton grunted an acknowledgment.

"As I said, the good guys. Though they're trying to stop the insurgents, sadly, they may be on the short end of the stick. Their government isn't being helpful."

"What do these Firebrands want?"

Leaning toward the microphone, Cadmon identified himself. "We want an alliance with you, General. For the good of both our realms. We fight Arisen Dawn on Scath. You battle them on your side. We'll cross over to help when needed. I speak for all three of my strongholds. We'd like to meet with you to discuss actions against our common enemy."

"What do you propose?"

Kole scrubbed a fist along his jaw. "A contingent of Firebrands will meet with you on Earth after we complete an important task here. Because of new intel and a powerful warlock's unmasking spell, we know where your colonel and our Dax were held. We're going immediately after this convo to destroy the Arisen Dawn garrison. With any luck, we will not only decimate their numbers but also capture Cerberus. If our raid nets good results, our meet and greet may not be necessary."

"Who's talking?" asked General Lipton.

"Sorry, Commander Kole."

Lip cleared his throat. "We set the meeting place and rules."

"Understood," said Matty after a nod from Cadmon.

"When can I expect you back, Colonel?" asked the general.

"I'd like to lend a hand on their mission. Later today, I expect the Firebrands will shuttle me home through a portal. So don't shoot me."

Chapter Twenty-Eight

Leading the infiltration team, Dax stomped over the fallen steel gate which led into the Arisen Dawn garrison. Only the sound of their own boots greeted the Firebrands as they trod into the site where he and Matty had been imprisoned. The base was abandoned.

With a disappointed snarl, he nodded at the warlock beside him, the male who had cast the spell to unmask the garrison. The mage had done it by tapping into Matty and Dax's memories.

As team leader for the mission, he signaled the rest of the Firebrands who waited at a distance, ready to spring into action. *All clear. The fortress is empty. They must have moved on rather than rebuild.*

Dax needed his head in the game. Instead, his thoughts meandered to Chiara. He had destroyed any chance of a relationship. But how else could he protect her? Matty's voice drifted to him as if it were a far-off echo. How long had the guy been talking to him?

Yep. Head. In. Game.

"Vampire, what the hell's wrong with you?" Matty propped a boot on top of concrete rubble, staring at the silent and morose Dax.

Kole, Ram, Galena, Rein, and Chay joined them at the site of the demolition derby.

"Each of us will recon a sector. Look for clues as to where they might have gone." Kole ground his molars, his jaw like stone.

"Matty and I will take that building." Dax pointed toward a still standing facility. "Stick close to me, Colonel. We don't want any surprises."

"You do love me."

Dax snorted.

As the two males entered through an open metal door, Dax raised a jungle bolo, expecting trouble. In his estimation, shit always happened when he least expected it.

Like running into Chiara. What were the odds? Crossing onto Earth near her cabin. The female being a Blood Coven descendant. His forming a bond with her. *No. Damn.* This was not the time to be thinking of the little witch.

Dax felt the weight of Matty's hand on his shoulder. "What?" he grumbled. When he turned around to glare at the human, he knew the guy had been trying to get his attention again.

"For the third time, what are we looking for?"

"Let's check out these rooms. Kole said to look for evidence of where Arisen Dawn might have fled. An added bene would be finding out who Cerberus is."

Matty walked through an inside doorway. "This is a big-ass bedroom."

Dax strolled into an adjoining room, kicking at rubble to see if anything of value was beneath it. "Office in here. I'd say whoever had these quarters was high up on the food chain. Luxury." It was a suite with a kitchen and a sitting area. These were not foot-soldier quarters.

When Matty entered the office, he rifled through the desk drawers. "Jackpot." He scooped out some papers, handing them off to the vampire Firebrand.

Dax shuffled through a few sheets. "Looks like Boden stayed here."

"Who's he?"

"Director of the Ministry of Compliance. They control the manufacturing and distribution of portal jumpers."

When Matty's brows nearly met his hairline, Dax said, "Yeah. That's how the assholes are crossing to

Earth."

"Good to know he's helping the bad guys."

"These are hard copies of some of the files from his ministry. Looks like he was in a hurry to vacate. Course, he likely had a dragon breathing fire up his ass." Dax handed back the paperwork. "Hold these. Let's explore the other rooms."

"I'm with you."

From the hall, they entered another suite. "This makes the other place look low-rent. Somebody higher up than Boden." Dax did a three-sixty, fists on hips.

They swept through the kitchen, sleeping quarters, office, living room, and outdoor garden. The dragon had missed this area. No papers to give away the occupant either. The apartment was pristine. Hardly looked lived in.

Two other quarters were in the same building, but they were in rubble. No evidence.

Dax brushed concrete dust off his pants before he lumbered out into the mid-afternoon light.

****

While he read e-mail on his laptop, Cerberus tapped the fingers of one hand on an antique horseshoe-shaped mahogany desktop, furniture befitting a male of his importance. The accommodations in the new garrison were acceptable.

Beneath his desk, his soft-booted feet sank into the thick pile of a dark blue, decadent wool carpet. Floor-to-ceiling bookshelves, filled with volumes he had never read, lined one entire wall. Original paintings decorated the walls. He had given Lort a list of famous artists to hand over to a decorator. Most were Earthers. Picasso. Chagall. Miro. Some were Aeternals. Acryl. Parch. He could not recall all the names. Frankly, he didn't know one from the other. And a few of the works looked like a child's scribbling to him.

The windowless room suited his desire for safety. Of course, no one was aware of the escape tunnel which ran beneath his quarters. He had wiped the minds of the construction team.

The living room, dining room, and bedroom also reflected a lush, warm richness which spoke of wealth and success while his kitchen gleamed with cold polished stainless-steel appliances. Of course, he would not be cooking for himself. Someone else was assigned the task.

The quarters, while lavish, were temporary. Soon he would have his pick of any place on Earth. He envisioned a modern glass and concrete house perched on a cliff overlooking the Mediterranean Sea. Spain? France? Italy? If not one of those places, maybe he would reside in a Covenkirk mansion built on the rocky shores of the Aleam Ocean.

But this apartment would do in the interim. He was a patient male.

A knock.

Cerberus flicked his wrist to see who stood outside seeking entry to his chambers. His general. A male as cruel as his thin-lipped sneer.

"Enter, Lort." With another wave of his hand, Cerberus unlocked the door.

The haughty vampire pushed into the room. He hesitated, his eyes widening with recognition, before he resumed his soldierly walk forward.

Cerberus leaned an elbow onto the desk with his chin planted in his palm. "General, you seem startled."

"I am, sir. You are not disguised."

"You know me?"

"Of course. Who wouldn't? Do you prefer…?"

"I prefer to be called Cerberus. It is my designation in the prophecy. My destiny."

Appearing to recover from the surprise, a rigid Lort walked to a chair and sat, spine stiff. Cerberus admired the vampire's severe bearing.

Lort's chin lifted before he spoke. Another sign of confidence.

"Traitorous Aeternals are gathering outside strongholds to seek refuge. We will attack all three Firebrand locations simultaneously. Though unlikely we will gain entrance, we will cause havoc to those who seek refuge. It might make those cowardly Aeternals think twice about going to the warriors for protection. Some may reconsider joining our cause."

"The attack is a wise strategy."

"I have let it be known most lawgivers and justices support us. In fact, today, they declared the Firebrands traitors for continuing to move against us. But, of course, you already know this."

Cerberus nodded. "With more Aeternals joining us, both those whom we have conscripted and those we know are loyal, do we have enough space at this garrison?"

"Space can be created. When this fortress reaches capacity, we have other sites. Since the Firebrands are declared traitors, we can risk more exposure, live in plain sight. Some of our loyalists opted to stay with their families, joining us for training and operations only. That saves space."

"I understand the Firebrands found our abandoned base this afternoon." Cerberus buried a smile.

"They did, destroying what was not already in rubble."

"Any information on the dragon which attacked the garrison?"

"None, sir. I was unaware dragons still existed. In fact, everyone I have spoken to thought they were extinct."

Cerberus pinched his chin between a thumb and forefinger. "They are. It makes no sense."

"I am not the only one to see it. Hundreds of males and females witnessed the same event. All agree. It was a dragon."

Cerberus waved a dismissive hand. "It will remain a mystery until it isn't."

"The mage you found who can trace bloodlines tells me we are closer to having all the descendants we need. I am concerned none have shown powers yet. You said…"

"Do you question me?" Cerberus unfolded from his chair, his fingers tingling with the desire to cast a spell that would hurt Lort, teach him to have faith.

The general swallowed, the lump in his throat a visible quiver. "No, sir."

The warlock returned to his seat with a sigh. "I said my plan is proceeding as it should. Each piece will be in place when it is needed. Bring Boden to the office."

"Yes, sir."

As Lort's ramrod straight shoulders disappeared out the door, Cerberus closed his eyes to visualize all the moving parts of his strategy. *Yes*. The plan was in play.

Cerberus's mother Echidna, daughter of Seraphine, daughter of Blood Coven witch Niviane, died centuries ago, but she had raised him on a daily ration of destiny. While other young warlocks played or practiced their skills on silly matters, Cerberus eschewed childhood games. His mother had not waited until his Awakening to teach him deadly spells. He killed small animals with childish mutterings, ripped into weak minds, and controlled others before he reached maturity. Any failure was met with punishment. A dank cellar, smashed fingers, no food for days. Pain was a strong motivator. So, he learned. Eventually, he never failed. He was the perfect, powerful warlock his mother created.

The door creaked open. Cerberus made a mental note to have it oiled. Lort escorted Boden into the office. The director of the Ministry of Compliance was as shocked to see the real Cerberus as Lort had been.

"Sit. Sit." He gestured toward two chairs. "Boden, my dear friend, we must solve this portal jumper problem. It is cumbersome to send our soldiers through in small groups. Why can't we have D-chips as the Firebrands do?"

Boden squirmed in his seat. Wise man since Cerberus did not suffer incompetence. But he needed the director. No one knew more about travel through the portals.

"My department neither created nor manufactured the Firebrands' implant chips. Their own tech Logan oversees its production, and they guard its secret well."

Cerberus narrowed his eyes in thought. "Where are they manufactured?"

"I do not know."

Cerberus tapped his index finger on his desk but stopped himself, realizing the habit showed nervousness. He would display no weakness. Alarik's Ministry of Well Being was key to much on Scath. His witches and warlocks maintained the portals, controlled gun use, and probably knew the science behind the D-chips. "Is there a way to breach Director Alarik's ministry, Lort?"

"I doubt it is possible. He is too powerful. When you add in the combined strengths of those who work for him, his building is impregnable. The lawgivers could remove him from office."

"Hmm. They could but would he leave gracefully? We have made limited progress on guns."

"Yes, we can use them in certain areas on

Darque. No mage has been capable of undoing the explosive weapons ban on Scath."

Boden interrupted the conversation. "I did have someone alter our portal jumpers to allow larger groups to travel to Earth."

Cerberus's severe gaze flipped to the director. "Yes, Boden, but ten at a time is still a small number." The warlock rubbed his temples. The male sitting in front of him was irritating at times. As the papers on Cerberus's desk funneled upward in a small windstorm, both males in front of him shot up from their chairs. "General, carry on with the attacks on the strongholds. Leave me. I must think."

****

Bounty slapped Dax's face. Her brother had shown up at her office after the disappointing raid on Arisen Dawn's abandoned garrison. As usual, his head was up his ass.

"What the fuck?" He rubbed his cheek.

"That's for talking smack about yourself."

He opened his mouth to say something else stupid, but she held up a hand. "Before you lay out all your faults, let me tell you about you. You were the male who cleaned up Mom when she wallowed in her own vomit, too sick to get out of bed. You are the one who picked her up when she stumbled, high on O injections. You are the one who bandaged her wounds when my asshole father beat her."

Dax grumbled.

Bounty arched a brow, daring him to speak. "Shut it. There's more. Every birthday, you made sure I had a special gift and a cake. On my fifth birthday, you gave me a rag doll."

"I found it in someone's trash."

"On my seventh birthday you gave me a copy of

Alice in Wonderland."

"Used." His eyes rolled away from her pinned gaze.

Bounty tapped her chin. "Let me think. On my tenth, a gold necklace. It was a heart. I still have it."

"Stolen and not gold."

"Shut the fuck up. When nobody else took care of me, you did. You made sure I had a supply of blood. You guarded my door on dangerous nights to make sure I was safe. Don't think I was unaware you slept in the hallway on the cold floor. When nobody else noticed if I had a clean dress, you did. When nobody else stepped up to save me from monsters, you did. You sacrificed your soul to control the man who donated his sperm to my creation. And you did all this while barely more than a kid yourself."

Bounty reached behind her brother's neck to untie the leather band of the necklace Dax had worn since the day he had killed her father and her rapist. A string of their fangs. "It's time to lose this." She dropped it into his hand.

Dax squeezed his fingers around the grim reminder. "I fucked everything that moved at the O blud den."

Crack. Another smack to his jaw. "Did you enjoy yourself?"

"Yes. I loved every minute of it."

Before she could smack him again, Dax grabbed her wrist. His nostrils flared. "I did enjoy it, Bounty. It was what it was. I'll make no excuses."

"How noble."

"Yeah. That's me. I didn't save our dam, and I didn't save you. But I had a good time feeding and fucking."

"You couldn't save Mother. Nobody could. She

was bent on self-destruction after your father died. I agree, you're a vampire with an active libido. You walk a fine line between aggression and control. Sometimes you slip onto the wrong side. So what? From what I can tell, that makes you just another Firebrand. You saved me, Dax. Protection is hardwired into your DNA. That's why you are a warrior. Problem is, who saves you?"

"Forgive me, sis."

"Nothing to forgive. I've never blamed you. If I had only known you…"

"I need the words. You were a little girl, and I didn't protect you from the monsters." Dax's fingers raked through his long, black hair. "Without your forgiveness, I can't move on. I'm stuck in your father's O blud den watching you cower in that bed after…"

She threw her arms around his neck, sobbing into his shirt, crying for a mother who never cared about her, a father who was evil, and a brother who carried too much responsibility on his shoulders. "Then I forgive you. I forgive you."

Dax held her until she ran out of tears.

Drawing away, she cradled his jaw with both hands. "Now, shut the fuck up and move on. Stay out of the O blud den. Tell Chiara you love her."

"I don't…"

"Am I going to have to smack you again? Why can't you be honest with yourself?"

"I am."

"Tell it to somebody who doesn't know you. I see you make puppy eyes at her." Bounty glided toward her desk where she pulled out her office chair, wiped a Kleenex across her eyes, sat, and crossed her legs.

Dax growled. "I couldn't make puppy eyes if I tried."

"You're right. It was a stretch. She's a little

crazy, you know, but maybe you need crazy. Someone to balance your brooding moods." Bounty rested an elbow on her desk.

"I don't know how to be what she needs, sis."

"She needs you. Flaws and all. Someone who loves her and will protect her. Nothing more."

Dax lowered his chin, his gaze cast toward the floor. "I'm a sonofabitch. I have no friends."

"So? Smile more. As for friends, open your eyes. You have the Firebrands. Your *frerons*. You will never desert them, and they will always stand by you."

"I've never been down this road." Dax clasped his hands behind his back.

"You think Rein had? How about Kole?"

"They're different. They're good men."

"Here we go again. I'm going to get up and slap you. If that doesn't work, then I'm kicking your ass."

"Hold on. Let me think."

There went his fingers, brushing across his sinister barely-there mustache and goatee.

Bounty leaned back in her chair, crossing her arms on her chest. "No. You think too much. Before you snarl something stupid, listen to me. You deserve happiness."

"What if I can't be what Chiara wants?"

Bounty rose from the desk, walked to her brother, laughed, and mussed his hair. "Silly male. You already are what she wants."

"The last time I saw her, I destroyed any chance to be with her. I told her about my trip to the O blud den. I lied to her, saying I fucked an O blud whore. I didn't. I almost did, but I couldn't. Didn't want to."

Dax threw his fang necklace into the trash as Bounty strolled to the fridge to snag a bottle of blood. She tossed it to Dax. "You need this."

"It's cold. I don't like it cold."

"Whine. Whine. Whine. Then find Chiara and take it from the neck. At the same time, you might want to own up to the falsehood."

Dax popped the top and chugged. "Ew."

"Not as good as the little witch, huh? It's time for you to ball-up and do something for yourself. I could use a sister-in-law, someone with a sense of humor. You're dour most of the time. All that noble angst which haunts most of the Firebrands. And some of you have it worse than others. You're one."

Dax raised his brows. "You gonna expect me to laugh more, tell jokes?"

Bounty kissed his cheek. "No. I expect you to be you. The brother I love. What I do expect, though, is for you to grovel at Chiara's bare feet." She looked at her hot-red nails as she sank into her chair. "Enough about you. How's my Matty?"

"You know you can't keep him, don't you?"

"Why not?" She squeezed her brows tight.

"Because he'll age and die. Fast."

"I think Matty with a sprinkling of gray hair at his temples will be strikingly handsome."

"I think he's a borderline ass."

"No, you don't. You like him. He considers you a friend."

Dax opened his mouth to say something stupid again, but Bounty held up a hand. "Don't."

"Seriously, sis. A long-time relationship with the human will only hurt you."

"Here's a tip. It's easy to be miserable, bro. Happy? Not so easy. So, when you find it, grab on with both hands. Maybe it won't last long, but what a great ride while it does."

"How did you grow up to be smart? Good?"

"I had an excellent role model. Don't change the subject. Back to my lover."

"Is that what Matty is?"

"Yes." Bounty checked out her nail polish. About time for a change, especially if she snagged a hot date with the human. "He's tasty."

"Your eyes say he's more."

"Is this the new you? All in touch with emotion?"

"Yeah. I'm about to gag." Dax threw himself into a chair across from his sister's desk.

She leaned her elbows on the desk. "You never answered my question. How's Matty?"

"We sent him through the portal back to Bozeman, but before he left, he asked about you. Pretty soon, you two will be using me to pass notes in class."

"He asked about me?" Bounty examined her nails again. "Of course he did. What did you say?"

Chapter Twenty-Nine

Chiara dragged herself into bed early. After the raid on the abandoned Arisen Dawn garrison, a bunch of pissed-off warriors showed up at headquarters, hungry for dinner with a side-order of bitchiness. During the clean-up, she, Margo, and Fin discussed hiring kitchen and house management staff, a task dumped on them by Kole. Afterward, the Blood Coven females sneaked in a brief confab to solidify plans to rescue Celene. Cooking, cleaning, and sneaking around were exhausting.

When the doorbell rang, Chiara kicked off the Afghan with a sigh, crawling out of bed to eye the visitor through the peephole.

Shit. Dax.

She rested her forehead against the closed door. No way was she letting him inside. She had taken all she would from the vampire. "What do you want?"

"To talk."

"You said enough last night." Was it really only late last night Dax had broken her heart?

When she didn't answer, he blabbed through the door. "I don't deserve it, but just give me a couple minutes."

She checked out her nightgown. It was flannel and boring. With her hand circling the knob, Chiara stiffened her spine, swung the door open, and moved aside to let him into the apartment.

The vampire swept past, heading straight for the couch where he flopped onto the cushions, legs spread wide, arms flung along the back.

Chiara couldn't help but stare. Dax was all man, the massive wall of his chest pushing against a fitted black tee, his bulky thighs straining his leather pants, his broad shoulders taking up most of the sofa. He raised one bulging arm to finger-comb his long hair back from his face.

She blinked, taking a stiff-backed, uncomfortable chair. Its advantage? It was far from the vampire's tempting body. Chiara put ice in her voice when she asked, "Do you want a drink? I have soda or water. I could make tea. I'm all out of O blood."

"I deserved that. No thanks."

His fingers tapped on the cushions where his arms rested. He was nervous. Strange for a man whose every move, just like his words, was all about economy. Cold. Planned.

"What can I do for you? It's been a long day and I'm tired." Chiara arched her brows, urging Dax to talk.

Silence. Awkward.

"I don't know where to begin." The sofa creaked under his shifting weight.

"The beginning's a good place."

Dax cleared his throat. "Humor. That's one of the things I like about you."

"Really? I could have sworn it irritated you."

"Maybe sometimes. Mostly I like it. You set people at ease. I don't."

"No. You don't." Chiara glanced at her watch. "Get to the point or leave."

"Gotcha." He leaned forward, elbows on his knees. "I'm not a good catch."

"No. You're not." Chiara stared, tired, unsure where Dax was going. Uncertain she cared at the moment.

Dax flinched as if he had expected her to argue, but she was too tired to play games.

"Damn, female. You're not making this easy."

"Making what easy? I have no idea what you're

trying to say."

"I didn't fuck the O blud whore. I went to the den but lied about what happened. Actually, I went twice. The first time I sat in a chair a few secs and left. The second time I got as far as inside a room. Nothing happened on either occasion."

He had her attention. Chiara inched forward in her seat, her weariness swept aside.

"Except for you, I have been celibate since the day in your woods."

Her brain fizzled. He had not betrayed her. "Why did you tell me you had?" She took a deep breath, cautious of sinking into the black hole which was her go-to place with Dax. Truth or lie, he had intentionally hurt her. The result was the same.

"It's a sad story."

Chiara crossed her legs. "I'm listening."

"The past is past."

"Profound." Chiara checked her watch again. "Goodbye."

Dax jerked his brows down, looking puzzled. But then he opened his mouth and words flowed. "My father was a Firebrand. When he died on the job, my mother turned to O blud. That's how she met a den owner. We moved in with the asshole after she got pregnant with Bounty. She flew straight for a while. But with my sister's birth, Mom slipped, mainlining the stuff so males and females could enjoy a high from sampling her blood. Her fate was sealed. I probably could have helped more, but it was all I could do to watch out for Bounty. Since I feared what her asshole daddy would do with her, I made a deal with him. I traded myself for her. I failed there, too. Anyway, shit went down, and I beheaded him along with another asshole. It wasn't enough. It will never be enough. I am still angry. But I am so tired of carrying that load."

He fingered his neck where his fang necklace once hung. The ugly thing was missing.

"Then let it go, Dax. Or accept a little help carrying it. You still haven't said anything to explain why you lied to me. I won't be a doormat, even for you."

"I don't want a doormat, but I lied to make you see me. The worst of me. The angry failure." He crossed an ankle over his opposite knee, one arm thrown onto the sofa back.

"You're not a failure. Look around. Bounty is a fabulous woman. You're a fucking Firebrand. You kill bad guys for a living."

"I'm not a hero."

"I'm not shopping for a hero. Maybe I was. Don't misunderstand me, the man who saved me from the burning car when I was a kid will always be my hero. He risked his life for a stranger, for a little girl who has loved him one way or another for most of her life. But I know the fantasies I created around him are not you. Now, why are you here?"

"I want to give us a chance. You know, try."

"Hmm. Not good enough."

Dax's chest expanded, pushed against his snug shirt as he took a deep breath. He exhaled, slow and steady, once more sitting straighter. "I … uh … need you, Chiara. I love you."

Oh, damn.

"You deserve better."

His dark, soulful eyes outlined by thick lashes bore into her. To hell with caution. It was overrated. Chiara rose from her chair, rushed to Dax, and plopped onto his lap, her hands tangling in his beautiful hair. "You're real. You're mine, Dax. You've always been mine."

"I don't understand what I did to deserve you, little witch. But I'm through analyzing it. I can't guarantee I'll ever be a good male, but I will be a better one."

Her lips touched his, parting, inviting his tongue inside. He groaned as he took charge of the kiss, exploring her mouth, taking his time.

Chiara broke the kiss to get off Dax's lap. Stepping away from him, she bit the tip of her thumb before she reached for the hem of her gown. She pulled it slowly up her legs and over her head, hoping her striptease looked sexy. She stood before her vampire in nothing but white lace panties. "Your turn."

He grinned, shot to his feet, and yanked his T-shirt off. She stared at the hard planes of his chest and took in his tight abs. Warm black velvet eyes fixed on her as he unzipped his pants and stepped out of them, already gloriously erect. All blood raced from her brain.

Dax's chin bobbed up as he sat down and leaned back. "Your panties?"

Chiara tucked her thumbs into the waistband and wiggled them down her hips.

When Dax drew a deep breath, her nipples hardened. He sprang from the couch. The naked man looming over her, his thick, erect cock prodding her belly, was delicious. Dark, deadly, spicy. Sleek, hard muscled. Huge, hungry, fanged. All hers. Real.

****

Dax snaked an arm around Chiara's waist, crushing her to his chest while his lips found hers again, his tongue teasing her mouth. With sure steps, he backed her against the wall.

When he cradled Chiara's ass in his palms, he lifted her, nudging her with his aching shaft. She opened herself, wrapped her legs around his hips.

"I'm going to go slow this time, Chiara. You're gonna enjoy every minute of my making love to you."

He recaptured her lips and nibbled his way down her neck to the swells of her breast.

With a delicate but eager hand stroking his length, she guided him to her warm pussy. Inch by inch, he claimed Chiara. A leisurely glide. *Ecstasy.* Dax threw back his head, savoring the feel of her silken passage as it swallowed him.

"Oh, Dax." She tilted her hips forward, urging him deeper, her fingers clamped to his shoulders.

He obliged, burying himself to the hilt with one long, slow thrust. His mouth latched onto a plump breast. He gorged on a nipple until it was a hard pebble. Moving to the other, he suckled, nibbled, flicked his tongue over it, delighting in the little witch's groans as she arched into him, begging for more.

Unable to hold still, he rocked his hips, stroking in and out of her. This was making love to his female. There was a time for fucking and a time for this.

She clung to him, her breathing shallow pants. "Please, Dax."

When he released her breast, he trailed kisses along her neck, grazing her throbbing pulse. Her vein resisted for a moment before it popped beneath his fangs, her delicious blood flowing down his throat. With the euphoric of his bite in her system, Chiara moaned and clamped her teeth onto his earlobe. Biting hard, she drew blood, sending a jolt directly to his groin.

With his control slipping, Dax growled. Nothing could be better, his cock deep inside his female, his fangs buried in her, her blood delivering life to his starving existence. She belonged to him whether he deserved her or not. He was never giving up Chiara.

While his rhythm increased to a steady roll back

and forth, her ass pounded against the wall. The repeated *thump, thump, thump* like music.

Her nails clawed his back, marking him, swamping him with emotion. Chiara's flesh quivered around his shaft, caressing him, begging him to go faster, deeper. When he did, he felt her orgasm build. She rocked against him, her muscles squeezing his length as she exploded, her back bowing. She cried out his name.

Withdrawing from her neck, he licked her wounds closed.

But he wasn't ready to end the experience. He latched onto a breast and once again his sharp fangs glided through her flesh.

Her hips flexed against him as she shuddered with another orgasm. He withdrew and licked the puncture marks. When she milked his shaft this time, he surged over the top. Slamming deep inside her, he fucked hard and fast until his body seized, his balls drew up, and his seed shot into her. He filled Chiara with all he was, all he would be. For her. For his mate. His eternal love.

Though he felt like crashing to the floor, he held onto Chiara, walking her into the bedroom and laying her on top the covers. He crawled beside her, taking her into his arms while he waited for their heartbeats to slow. Burying his face in her hair, he rolled around in the scent of his female.

Wait.

Something had happened. Dax recoiled. "You bit me."

"Tit for tat. Goose. Gander. Weren't those your fangs in my neck, vampire?"

"You don't get it." He slipped out of her warm, wet core and set Chiara on her feet, worrying fingers through his hair.

"Dax, you look scared."

"Terrified, little witch."

Her hand brushed across his chest, making his cock spring to life again. "Why?"

"Oh, shit." Dax doubled over, clutching his gut. The pain. Way to lose an erection fast. *Damn.* It started. The compulsion to mate, to complete the Bludhunt, was overwhelming. Too bad it could kill Chiara. He had to figure out a way to keep her safe.

Dax flung his head back, biting off a scream so he wouldn't frighten Chiara.

Larissa, the Bludhunt priestess, was an older, powerful vampire. Like Dax, she could communicate telepathically. He closed his eyes to connect with her mind, a vast repository of his breed's culture and history.

Larissa, you bitch.

Tsk. Tsk. How endearing. What's wrong, Daxton, Bludclan Mortus? What did you think would happen when you let the human bite you?

It was an accident.

Rein tried that one, too. If you Firebrands don't want to mate humans, stop fucking them while you exchange blood. The weakling is now yours. Come to the Bludhunt or face a lifetime of pain.

She can't handle the rite.

You should have thought of that before. Rein's human mate handled it. Maybe yours will, too.

I'm not willing to risk her.

You have no choice.

In case you haven't noticed, the Firebrands are a little busy right now. I need time.

No answer.

Did you hear me?

Of course I did. I grant you time, but the first lull, you get your ass over here along with your mate.

Understood.

Fat chance that was happening. He'd find a way out.

Chiara gripped his jaw between two hands, her eyes wide, fearful. "Dax. What's wrong? Talk to me."

He placed his palms over hers. "We've been called to the Bludhunt. I've asked for time. Larissa granted my request."

"Larissa? The what?"

"It's vampire drama. You bit me. I bit you. We fucked. Now we're called to the mating rite."

"Okay."

"No."

"You don't want to mate me?"

"I do, but you could die in the ceremony."

"Obviously Braelyn survived it."

"True. We'll talk to her and Rein."

Dax tangled his fingers in her hair, the silkiness of its curls stirring his arousal once again. "It's a savage ritual, Chiara, left over from a time when only the fittest vampires were meant to survive. It culled the weakest from our breed."

"What happens if we don't do it?"

"We won't be true mates in the eyes of the vampire conclave." He pressed his lips to the pulse in her neck, breathing in the scent of his female.

"What aren't you telling me, Dax? Let's not start off our lives with lies."

She had a right to the truth. "I'll be in pain, but I can handle it."

"No. We'll do the ceremony."

"I'll take any agony to keep you safe."

"I'm tougher than I look."

An ear-shattering alarm sounded, driving all thoughts of the Bludhunt or another bout of lovemaking from Dax's mind. He gave Chiara a little push. "Get dressed. Now."

She raced for the bedroom as he snatched his clothes off the floor. Both dressed, he dragged her out the door and down the hallway to whatever new disaster arrived at the stronghold.

****

The klaxon blared.

Kole hadn't heard the ear-jarring noise for nearly 200 years. During their rebellion, Amazons and berserkers attacked the stronghold, the alarm calling the Firebrands to arms.

Back then, Kole was a young warrior with Wynnfrith fighting by his side, the witch casting deadly spells while he hit the traitorous bastards with fireballs. When the assault ended, the Firebrands mopped up the dead and the healing began. Eventually, the two rebel breeds rejoined the fold where they became good citizens again.

Now, the combat boot was on the other foot. Lawgivers and the Temple of Justice had declared the Firebrands as the traitors.

He charged through Bounty's office, to the hall, and into the tech room next door. Logan was seated in front of the monitors, staring at the chaos outside their stronghold. Uniformed Arisen Dawn soldiers were getting their jollies by cutting down innocents who'd probably done nothing wrong other than oppose Cerberus and run to the stronghold for sanctuary, despite the Firebrands' new label as *persona non-grata*.

He had no choice but to drop the masking spell, fight off Arisen Dawn attackers, and bring the refugees inside. "We'll assemble at the garage doors. When I signal, make us visible. After we gather the civilians, activate the cloak again."

Logan nodded, keeping an eye on the outdoor

action. "Affirmative."

The sound of boots thundered across the lower-level stone floor as Kole's males and females raced for the armory. He joined them, barking orders. "Ram, assign your newbies to stay inside to defend the stronghold against any Arisen Dawn soldiers who might slip through us. Only experienced warriors outside. Dax, zip up your fucking pants. Skyler, get the mates to the safe room."

When Nico and Denim opened their mouths to give him flack, he added, "Except you two."

Skyler snatched his elbow. "The rest of us won't tuck tail and hide in the safe room, demon. We'll welcome the civilians as you send them inside. Don't bother to argue."

Stubborn female.

"Okay. Into the garage. We'll shoo them to you."

Once armed, the warriors took position. Thorn hit the wall switch to open the doors as Kole contacted Logan to drop the masking spell. The Firebrands streamed out.

When Kole signaled Sabine and Nico to herd the frightened citizens inside, the nymph took off into the crowd like an avenging angel come to save the righteous. Her blonde braids whipped around her head, and her double-bladed staff sliced and diced assholes while she gentled innocents inside, some adults and some children, all wide-eyed with fear.

Nico sheathed his haladie, the same type of blade Kole's parents had used, to employ his gift. As an electro-magnetic field shimmered around him, metal weapons flew out of the hands of the attackers near him, clattering to the ground. The disarmed cowards ran from the Blood Coven warlock.

Arrows streamed in rapid succession from Chay's

chu-ko-nu as he danced from side to side, taking aim, his long, dark hair whipping around, whoops popping out of his mouth each time he struck the enemy.

Rein was buried fangs-deep in the neck of a demon Arisen Dawn soldier.

Thorn, partially shifted for the fight, slashed long, sharp claws into the chest of a satyr who had made the bad decision to take on the wolf Firebrand.

Denim and Ram worked back-to-back, dead bodies at their feet. The Blood Coven witch parted a demon from his head with a swipe of her gladius. Her satyr mate smiled at her success before he sank his dirk into an Amazon's chest.

Dax swung his bolos in a deadly figure eight, slicing through necks with cold precision. He battled with a passion Kole had never seen from the vampire.

When Sabine signaled the refugees were safe, Kole whistled retreat for his Firebrands. They would fight Arisen Dawn another day. Today, they had innocents to protect.

Once the last warrior stepped into the garage, Kole rushed through the roll-up door. He slammed a fist on the button on the wall, cutting a hunger demon in half when he attempted to slip inside. He tapped his wrist, calling Logan. *Put the spell back in place.* The stronghold disappeared and was impregnable again.

Leaning against the wall, his ax still in his fist but hanging at his side, Kole took a call on his D-chip. He grounded the zap of electricity flowing from his free hand. As the air around him sizzled with deadly energy, Rein and Thorn jumped aside in the nick of time.

The wolf shifter shook out his shaggy mane, most of it standing on end from the charge. "Comm, your eyes are on fire. Literally."

"Bad news?" Rein licked a drop of blood from his

lower lip as he sheathed his knives.

"That was Jarek. His stronghold and Nace's were just hit. Similar circumstance. Refugees at the gate. Arisen Dawn assholes attacking. It's a shit storm out there."

Firebrands surrounded Kole, waiting for orders. He took a deep breath before he scrubbed a hand across his military-shorn hair and stared at the crowd huddled in the back of the garage where Skyler and other mates were calming them. "Dax, confab with Margo. She knows every inch of the stronghold since the remodel. She'll know where to tuck people into beds. Thorn, since Fin was a caterer, get her ideas on food and shit."

"On it," said the shifter.

"Brak, contact Director Alarik. I want stronger wards around this place. Galena, you're still in charge of the day-to-day operations. Pass out assignments. Tyr and Sabine are at your disposal. Consult with Ram on the recruits since he's training them, but if you need them, use them. Chay, I want constant contact with Cadmon, Jarak, and Nace. Rein, my office."

Chapter Thirty

Dax felt like a concierge at a fancy hotel as he went bunk-to-bunk with a clipboard. Margo had assigned each refugee to a bed in the second barracks since the first was filled with recruits.

His task was to check off names after verifying the guests were in their proper place and to see about their must-haves. With the latest newbies along with the refugees, they were filling fast.

Dax had grumbled and snarled about his task. Truth? It wasn't so bad. The frightened sanctuary-seekers were grateful. Healers had been called in to see to those with wounds. When he passed by occupied bunks, females patted his hand, males shook, and kids high-fived.

He sauntered toward the bunk Margo had labeled number forty-nine. There, a satyr pillowed his head on his arms, eyes closed.

Dax poised the pen above the list on his clipboard. "Name?"

The male jerked upright, swinging his feet to the floor. "Arne."

Dax checked him off the list. "Need anything?"

"Food would be great, though I'm not complaining. I'd like to earn my keep. I could be an extra hand in the kitchen? I know my way around one, though I'm a vintner by trade. Also a damn good amateur chef."

Fin was managing the food biz. She and Jace were slapping sandwiches together while recruits legged the stuff to the refugees. Dax was no expert, but the stronghold needed more supplies, bagged blood, and a way to nourish a variety of breeds unless they had brought along their own sources. Help in the kitchen would be good, too. Maybe the evacuees could fill positions.

"Sounds like a plan. I'll get back to you." Dax wrote a note beside the satyr's name while he moved to the next bunk.

His last stop was the area where Chiara was tending to a young demon in a bed. Having shed his covers, she rested a palm on his knee, likely sending healing energy to his wounds. Finished, she glanced at Dax, a smile lighting her face. Then she blushed. Apparently, she was remembering their activity before the klaxon interrupted.

Recovering, she pulled him aside. "Dax," she whispered in his ear, her breath a warm tickle. "That boy is hurting. I'm fixing him a little at a time. If I go too fast, I could cause more problems. Anyway, I think you need to listen to their story."

He set his clipboard on a side table, nodding to the mother and father. "I'm Dax." The demon stuck out a hand. Unaccustomed to gratitude, the Firebrand stared for a few seconds before he gripped it.

"Harm. This is my mate, Lucia, and son, Bale."

"Chiara tells me I should hear your story."

"Yep. Those assholes in the black uniforms are going door to door in the Knife's Edge area where we live, talking to families."

"What are they selling?"

"World domination. An invasion of Earth. I may not be a Firebrand, but I'm an honorable male. I know history. My great-grandfather came to Scath after the Karmic Schism to save ourselves and humans. He was proud of the Blood Coven's solution. Overall, life has been good. Why stir up trouble?"

"Is that what you told them?"

Harm glanced at his mate. "I wasn't home when

they canvassed our neighborhood the first time. Lucia just listened. We talked later. When they returned, I explained we wanted no part of their plans. That's when they grabbed Bale."

When his mate started to cry, Harm threw an arm around her shoulders and pulled her into his side. "They broke his leg good. Afterward, they gut stabbed him." He pointed at Chiara. "This kind female is helping him. Anyway, I killed both of the A-hole cowards, picked up Bale, and we ran here. Who hurts a kid?"

Lucia swiped at her tears. "Most of our neighbors are scared. When my mate was younger, he did some cage fighting. I know they don't buy into all the crap, but they're not as strong as Harm."

"So some are joining?"

Despite the pain showing in the harsh slash of his mouth, the boy answered. "Soldiers in black uniforms dragged my friend's dad out of his house. He was told he had to live in some garrison. They haven't seen him since."

"It gets worse." Lucia dug into her purse for a tissue, using it to dab her eyes. "The neighbor I had coffee with most mornings was mated to a carnal demon. She was an Amazon. Soldiers came one afternoon and dragged them both out into the street where they decapitated them. Afterward, the bastards pinned a sign to their chests." When her voice broke, Harm drew her in, patting her hair, trying to soothe her. "It said, 'No mixes.'"

The demon growled. "They were good neighbors. Are the Firebrands prepared to fight those bastards?"

"Damn straight," said Dax.

The demon glanced at his mate while he shook off her restraining hand. "I want in. Show me a weapon and where to practice. Though I'm not one of you, I'm determined, skilled, and pissed as hell."

The male's vow gave Dax an idea he wanted to run by Kole. He picked up his clipboard to make a note. "I'll get back to you, Harm. Let you know how you can help."

He looked for Chiara. She was in the adjoining mess hall, huddling with Braelyn and Denim. When they saw him, their whispers stopped. The females scattered like conspirators caught in the act. He heard Braelyn say, "We're postponing a day."

"What was that about?" he asked.

Chiara rolled her orchid irises from side to side, avoiding his gaze. "Girl stuff. Thanks for listening to my family. They've been through a lot."

Dax stared at Braelyn and Denim's retreating backs. Something was up, but he had no time to think about it. "You're doing a great job in there, little witch."

Moisture gathered in her eyes. "Thank you." She rose onto her toes, skimming her lips across his. "I love you."

His mouth curled into a stupid-ass grin. "I love you, too. Do you think I might room with you for a while? If not, I'll catch a bed in the barracks."

She locked an arm through his. "Just try to stay somewhere else, vampire. I'll turn you into a toad with warts."

Then, because he was beyond all help, he patted her backside to send her on her way, smiling once again, unconcerned someone might see him.

Once the sparks brought on by the briefest kiss from Chiara dissipated, he found Fin and Margo. He shared his thought about hiring kitchen and household crews from among the refugees. They loved the idea. After his success with them, he headed to tell Kole he was willing to train qualified evacuees to help in the fight against Arisen Dawn.

****

Celene shuffled from the bedroom, foregoing a robe, not bothering to wash her face, brush her teeth, or comb the hair which fell in tangles around her shoulders. In the kitchen, she plonked a wood bowl onto the table. After she dug out a spoon, milk, and a box of unknown cereal, she slumped into a chair to eat. Once the utensil had made the trip to her mouth twice, she dropped it with a clunk, pushing the barely eaten breakfast aside.

With her chin in her palm, she glanced around the kitchen. Last night's dishes sat in the sink, encrusted with dried food. Cans and wrappers littered the counter. A layer of grime coated the unswept floor. Why bother? Nobody was coming. Jace hadn't made it. So said a sneering Lort. He was right.

With a deep sigh, she ambled into the sitting area. Instead of lighting a fire to read on the sofa, she picked up The Path from the coffee table, returning to the comfort of bed, her drab unwashed sheets, and a warm blanket.

Celene opened the volume to the next story told by the OneCreator's assassin to the Cambion from Wales. If the fire-winged guy was so hell-bent on saving the Aeternals, maybe he would rescue her. *Hah!*

Inside Gahya's airy abode in The Vast, between Angor and the Evermore where immortals frittered away their time with betting, fucking, and court politics, Ohngel stood, arms crossed over his chest, legs splayed in a warrior's stance, uneasy in this realm where everyone glowed equally in the eternal sunlight, both the good and the bad.

Ohngel felt the heavy tug of his wings. He was soul-weary.

He watched Earth below where the Genitrix's

Aeternals suffered. A demon had been aging for nearly a year. Now, he lay abed alongside a fire which warmed the chamber but not his bones. His leathery face was lined with wrinkles, his hair grey, his hands trembling while they clutched the homespun blanket which hid his decaying flesh. His body rejected his mate's attempt to feed him from her orgasms, an act necessary for his breed's survival.

Impossibly, he was dying.

And he wasn't the only ill Aeternal. In another region, a female vampire languished despite a mate who offered her his wrist, his blood a stain on her pinched lips. Yet, she did not swallow.

Gahya's creatures were no longer immortal.

"No tears, Genitrix?" The fire-winged assassin of the OneCreator spun away from the view to observe Gahya, who primped at her vanity.

Her eyes caught his gaze in the mirror. With the haughty smile of a female accustomed to adoration, she reached over her shoulder, offering a brush for her golden hair. "Please, love. It is impossible to reach the snarls in the back."

He accepted her weapon of seduction, stroking her silken locks. The Genitrix was a beauty, but her heart was empty, devoid of warmth.

Gods. He was so tired. Though of late, he had been occupied with cutting off the heads of evil ones who had streamed from Angor to fight their way through to the Evermore. Their blood had coated his blade along with his razor-edged wings. And their blackened souls disturbed not one of his dreams because this brutal job was his sole pleasure, giving him a sense of ... what? Justice? Morality? Order? Yes. Thus, it was not his gruesome tasks which wearied him. No. He enjoyed those. It was his irritating flirtation with a conscience.

"You look so forlorn, Ohngel. If it is my creatures who concern you, remember, they have brought on their own ills. Besides, the OneCreator proposes a new bet."

"Explain." His jaw tightened.

She pivoted in her seat, her robe falling open to reveal the long expanse of creamy skin that was her leg. "Gabriel and I are to pit our creatures against one another in a wager."

"What?" When his wings snapped out, Gahya wisely flinched at the sight of his power.

"It will be fun, my love. The OneCreator will be in court on his throne to watch the game. Everyone is expected to be in attendance."

"You are like a bee gathering honey from a poisonous flower."

"You blaspheme when you say he is poisonous." Gahya resumed primping, glancing at the warrior in the mirror.

"To you he is. You have no defenses. Before a new game, finish the one you began. Do you not owe your creatures?"

"Are we back to them again, Ohngel? You grow wearisome, my dear."

A deep laugh rolled up from his chest. "So I have heard. There." He returned her brush. "Your hair is smooth, untangled. Unlike the webs you spin."

She turned on her seat. "You compare me to a spider? I thought you enjoyed my diversions."

"Yes. Your intrigues, along with your body, enthrall me. But I am a willful, weak male."

When she stood toe-to-toe with Ohngel, she feathered her fingertips along his bare chest.

As always, his heart pounded harder with her caresses. He loved a female's hand stroking his flesh. The warmth of her touch. The tingling sensations brushing across his skin. The bone-deep contentment of body-against-body. What would it be like from someone whose soft hands spoke to him of love?

He chuckled. The assassin was beyond such useless emotion. Instead, he would wallow in Gahya's carnal delights as she offered him a new experience each visit. "They age. They die. Your creatures are no longer immortal."

"I am aware. They still live long, however. Are you ever bored, Ohngel?" She clasped the back of his head, pulling him toward her luscious breasts.

He resisted suckling her to answer her unexpected question. "Sometimes I suffer from melancholia, but I'm sure your pussy can cure me of it. If not, I can kill something."

As further temptation, Gahya unhooked a shoulder of her peplos, baring a nipple.

Despite the aching arousal pushing against his breeches, he fought the urge to take her in his mouth. "You created Aeternals from a sliver of your soul. You gave them carnal knowledge. One of your demons killed a forbidden Homo erectus. Now, your creatures kill humans to feed. Well and truly pissed, the OneCreator has sent a virus to destroy their immortality. He levels the field for Gabriel's Homo sapiens."

"It matters little."

"Your ignorance is staggering." Ohngel yanked her gown back into place. Gahya gaped at him, no doubt shocked by his rejection of her plump charms. "Why do your Aeternals prefer feeding from Gabriel's creatures rather than from their own kind?"

"Human blood, soul, and emotion are apparently sweeter. Addictive, I hear."

"Still, you offer no guidance."

"My beings are adrift in weaknesses of their own

making. I shouldn't have to teach them everything."

Ohngel drew his brows tight, his wings snapping out to block the everlasting sun of the Vast, his blaze brighter, hotter than the glowing orb. "So, you plan to pit them against humans? May the best species win. The OneCreator challenged you to create sentient beings. You did, but they are flawed and adrift. In punishment, he steals their immortality. Now, he lures you into another bet when he could just kill them with a moment's thought."

"Such is not his way. Besides, if I win this new wager, my creatures will prevail."

"He is playing with you while, at the same time, he taunts Gabriel."

"I will win. Whose side are you on, Ohngel?"

"I do not take sides. Nor am I his flunky as Gabriel is, but I will not be yours either. I will never favor the slaughter of these new humans despite my partiality for your creatures. Perhaps I will draw up a stratagem of my own."

"Beware. In that direction lies danger. The OneCreator will not be pleased with your interference. Heed my advice. Learn when to let go."

"Letting go is not my strength. I am a stubborn bastard with a strong libido who also has a problem with authority."

"I have entertainment planned for tonight."

At the mention of sexual fun, his cock ached. He was easily distracted, and it had proved useless to convince Gahya of her duty to her dying creations. So be it.

"Rota the Norn and Zephyrus the Boread will join us in a diversion."

"Your never-ending creativity intrigues me, Gahya."

"Our proclivities must be kept fresh."

"Where are your guests?"

"In the spare chamber."

Ohngel took her hand and flashed them into the lavish bedroom decorated in heavy red and black brocades, a boudoir designed for sensual pleasures. His gaze focused on what awaited in the bed, but his attention was divided, an incipient plan forming in his mind.

Rota and Zeph lay naked, enjoying each other, their hands stroking willing flesh, their lustful sighs filling the room. Ohngel's nostrils flared with the scent of erotic pleasures as his tongue swept across his lower lip. He raised Gahya's hand, pressing a kiss to her knuckles. "Such a treat."

The Genitrix's eyes lit with passion's fire. She truly was a creature who thrived on carnal games, almost childlike, without compassion, without love, and without a conscience. He stroked her cheek.

Stripped of her robe, her flesh a creamy glow, Gahya crawled onto the bed where she caressed Rota's breast with the palm of her hand. Pinching a nipple between her fingers, she lowered her head to draw it into her mouth. The Norn moaned, her arched back pleading for more.

Ohngel approached the bed, his palm caressing Zeph's thigh. "So lovely." Suddenly, he stepped away. "But I think tonight I will decline."

Gahya made a popping sound as she released Rota's breast. "What?"

Disappointment shadowed the Norn and Boread's faces, legs untwisting as they pushed upright. Ohngel spun away from the bed, his blazing wings snapping wide to take him soaring through the open ceiling, his plan already solidifying.

Celene snapped the book shut. The story was interesting, but she was tired. Flinging her arms out, palms up, she closed her eyes, her spirit as soul-weary as Ohngel.

Her mental clock ticked off minutes. More minutes.

Her eyelids flicked open. “Fuck this shit.” Celene bounced out of bed, rushing to the kitchen to get a knife. In front of the bathroom mirror, she chopped off hunks of her long, tangled blonde hair. She donned shorts, a sports bra, and sneakers before striding toward the exercise equipment where she snatched two ten-pound weights. With one in each hand, she curled her arms.

Today ten, next week twenty.

I'm gonna beat those bastards at their own game. Bring it on.

****

From the shelter of a tree, Jace peeked across an overgrown lawn toward a shabby house. Though it wasn't the place where she had been imprisoned with Celene, it gave off the same evil vibes, making her knees weak and her stomach fluttery. Bad memories. Her kidnapping, her imprisonment, the cruel guards, Lort, her escape, days running. But she straightened her spine while she jutted out her chin. She would deal to rescue a friend.

Braelyn pulled alongside, pocketing the keys to the borrowed SUV. She was joined by the rest of the descendants and Indigo.

Though a day late because of the flood of refugees, the plan was a go. The timing was perfect. With the stronghold bustling, no one would miss the women. In fact, some of the mates were meeting with the American army. Other Firebrands were busy with their many duties, including her Tyr.

Denim, the ex-military, ex-Alliance agent, and current Firebrand, lifted her hand. She closed her eyes. The air chilled. When she flicked her wrist, a misty cloud rolled over the house and yard. In no time, it thickened to pea-soup fog. "You're on deck, Margo. Make it good."

The redhead stepped behind a tree trunk, slowly blinking while she wiggled her fingers. She smiled, freckles stippling her face. "Communications dead."

"Fin," said Denim, "time to call your animals. Have them patrol the perimeter."

Thorn's mate brushed back the dark springy curls of her short, stylish hairdo. "On their way."

"Good job, *cher*." Denim, her Cajun accent barely noticeable, clasped Fin's shoulder. "It's going to be hard seeing until I lift the cloud. I'll do that once we're all in place. The sound of the front door crashing in will be our go signal. Kill the guards if you have to. Don't let your conscience get in the way. Any questions?"

Heads shook.

"Indigo, you lead into the backyard. Brae will go first into the front. The rest of you hold onto another woman's shirt or belt so you don't get lost in the fog." Denim started toward the house, the women daisy-chaining as they moved forward.

Denim waited, her head bobbing as if she were ticking off minutes until everyone was in place. With a wave of her hand, the thick fog lifted. She signaled Braelyn who drew up a knee, kicked out, and booted down the door just like in the movies.

Jace slapped a hand to her chest, trying to still her sledgehammering heart.

Oh, shit. Here we go.

In the living room, a guard stared at a computer screen. With the crash of the door, he leaped over the desk, landing on two feet. Suddenly, he froze, one foot poised to run, his other stuck in place. He was like a granite-carved statue, except his legs twitched and snarls burbled from his chest while Braelyn took control of his mind.

Before the other guard, who was watching television, could spring over the couch, Chiara flicked her wrist. He crumpled to the floor. She leaned over, putting her fingers to the pulse on his neck. "Alive. I feel a beat." But his body spasmed, jerking as if he were a marionette whose controller had a nervous tic. "I think he's convulsing, though. Oh well."

A loud crash sounded from the back of the house. Indigo shouted, "All's good. We've got two runners. Oskar and Lizzy's tiger are on their heels." Boots thudded across the floor.

Jace flew inside, flinging open the doors off the living room. The rooms were empty. "She has to be here." Frantic, her gaze pinged around, looking for likely spots to keep a prisoner.

Skyler called from the kitchen. "Hey. Got a locked door. I tried kicking, but it's solid."

Jace sprinted out of the living room. "Keys. Does anybody see keys?"

Braelyn checked cabinets while Skyler raced to search the downed guards' pockets.

"Celene, are you in there?" Jace yelled through the thick door. No answer.

Lizette bumped open the kitchen screen door with her hip while clamping a hand to her upper arm, blood oozing between her fingers. She twisted to look over her shoulder at Indigo. "I'm just saying, your gryphon Oskar is very cool. Much bigger than my tiger."

"I'll tell him you said so. He's a sucker for a compliment." When Indigo saw the others raiding the kitchen, she arched her brows. "What's up?"

"We need keys. Check your guards' pockets." Jace pounded fists on the steel door.

"I hope Oskar didn't eat them," said Indigo. "He has a thing for shiny metal."

She and Lizette took off for the yard again, the screen banging on its hinges.

Jace paused to listen to the shouts outside.

"Found 'em. Let go, Oskar. Give 'em back. Do not swallow them. I'm warning you. I conjured you. I can un-conjure you. Think about it. Poof. No more gryphon."

Jace heard a couple snorts, followed by a cough. "Good boy," said Indigo.

When she returned, the dark-haired witch's clothes were askew, her cheeks smudged with dirt, and her boots unlaced. "Oskar didn't want to let go. Stubborn beast." Tossing the keys to Jace, she grabbed for Lizette—whose knees gave out, nearly sending her to the floor. "Not to worry. In the ruckus earlier, the guard stabbed her. I got her." With the injured woman settled in a chair, Indigo ripped a swath of fabric from the bottom of her shirt. With the makeshift bandage, she stemmed the flow of Lizette's blood. "Better?"

"Hardly a scratch," replied Jarek's mate.

Jace fumbled with the keys. Finally, one fit. The door opened with a groan. She switched on a dim overhead light in the stairwell. When she proceeded down the steps, the worn timber creaked under her weight.

The cellar floor was packed dirt, the smell earthy, musty. A good home for mushrooms. Not for Celene. More doors. Two were unlocked, the rooms empty. The third required a key.

Jace held her breath as she twisted it in the door

and crept inside. When she heard the rustle of fabric against fabric, she twisted her head toward the whisper of noise.

Flattened against the wall, with a thick book clasped overhead, Celene was about to crown her friend. When she saw Jace, though, her mouth fell open while the reading material crashed to the ground.

Tears streamed down Celene's cheeks as she yelped, racing into her friend's welcoming arms. "What took you so long, roomie? I thought I was going to have to break out on my own."

Chapter Thirty-One

As a good-faith effort, the Firebrands released Matty Garcia two days ago, sending him back to his command post to prepare for the peace talks. Now, Dax tumbled through the Whorl and exited the portal to find his friend waiting in Missoula along with thirty armed soldiers.

The vampire's mouth cracked into a grin. *Friend? Yeah.* How shocking was that admission? "You didn't tell me I'd be met by a welcoming committee."

"What can I say. You're a popular guy." Matty motioned for Dax to follow him out of the parking garage. "Let us through, men. He's with me. I'll take it from here."

His weapon locked on Dax, an officer stepped forward. "We've been ordered to secure the otherworlders at all times. Sorry, sir."

"Understood. Come on, vampire. You aren't gonna let a few humans with guns trained on your black heart stop you, are you?"

"Hell no. Those pop pistols will do nothing but piss me off. Have you told them it would take more than AK-47s and an entire battalion to stop me?"

Matty smiled. "No. I wanted to surprise them. Lead the way, soldiers."

Half of the Americans stayed behind at the portal to wait for the other arrivals.

After Dax followed the colonel into a large warehouse, he surveyed the locale. All looked legit. He addressed General Lipton. "In another few minutes, four more males are going to pop out of the gateway. For fuck's sake, don't shoot them."

The general said, "As long as they're the men we

agreed to in our conversation."

Dax dipped his chin as he tapped his D-chip.

"Okay," said Lipton into a mouthpiece. "Stand alert but don't fire."

Moments later, Kole lumbered into the warehouse with an armed escort, the air around him charged with electricity. Dax chuckled, enjoying the general's expression when he spotted the mountain of intimidating muscle with fire sparking off his digits.

Cadmon was right behind him in a crisp dress uniform.

Nace dropped into a crouch when he saw the soldiers lined up in the warehouse, a growl rumbling from his gut before he straightened. "If they keep pointing those pistols at me, I may have to shove them up their tiny asses."

Jarek strolled in, his face a stoic canvas as he looked around the room. "Gentlemen."

His throat bobbling when he swallowed, General Lipton motioned the newly arrived males to seats.

The soldiers retreated to positions around the edge of the room, their weapons remaining at the ready. Nace grinned, undoubtedly at so many humans about to shit their pants, as he pulled out the chair beside Kole.

Seated across from General Lipton, High Commander Cadmon cleared his throat. "Gentlemen, introductions first, I think."

The warrior ylve identified his Firebrands. Afterward, General Lipton introduced the Joint Op's Operation Frankenstein command, first his West Bank Special Mission leaders followed by his counterparts in the Central and East Bank Special Mission Units. Each leader was a decorated general.

Formalities over and important protocols reviewed, the two sides got down to business with

Cadmon jumping into the deep water first. "We have a common enemy."

Everyone's attention focused on Kole as sparks flared from his fingertips. "Sorry. Side effect of being an animus demon."

Lipton's gaze flitted from Kole and his scary-as-shit ability to Cadmon. "And who is the enemy? And why do we need your help? We have the big guns. The technology."

Jarek placed both elbows on the table, fingers laced together, his braids hanging down his chest almost to his waist. The many battle glyphs visible on his massive arms and neck outshone the medals weighing down General Lipton's uniform. "You may have big weapons, but you can't defeat an onslaught of Arisen Dawn soldiers. If they find a way to bring large numbers through the portals as we can, your time is up. Prepare to bend over and take it in your skivvies."

"We were told you can't bring through an entire army," said one of Lipton's officers, looking at him for validation.

Kole touched his fingers together. "Who said that? Dante? He told you what he thought was true. The Firebrands can bring every Aeternal on Scath through the portals. But right now, only we have that ability. The fear is, Cerberus is working to get it."

"We'll turn to a nuclear solution," said the East Bank general.

Dax shook his head. "You'd destroy your own homeland by employing weapons of mass destruction? Not a wise move. Also, how will you know where to set up? We have hundreds of thousands of portals."

Looking as if he had chewed on a sour pickle, the Central Special Mission commander said, "If you're really concerned for our safety, close them down."

Cadmon smoothed the lapel of his uniform. “That sounds easy, but the spells which have created them do not work that way.”

“I still think we can win with technology,” said the East Bank general.

“Bring it on. As far as technology, hell, we’ve got it, too. Fact is, we’ve shared some with you. GPS, for example. But it’s not our technology you should worry about. If Arisen Dawn can transport masses through the portals, they’ll have strength, speed, and what you’d call magic on their side. Face it,” Dax let his fangs drop, “you’re just table scraps for my breed.”

Cadmon rested an arm on the table. “Arisen Dawn is led by a powerful male who has no conscience when it comes to killing humans. I fear we have not yet felt the full force of his abilities. He figures ruling Earth is his manifest destiny.”

“His destiny? Explain.” Lipton tilted his body toward the ylve high commander.

Kole’s fire-gold eyes targeted each participant at the table. “History lesson. You were not the first sentient creatures on the planet. We were, but we grew too violent, killing you to feed. The Cambion from Wales viewed a doom-and-gloom prophecy. To counter it, he and twelve other witches and warlocks divided the world into three realms. We went to Scath. The wildings went to Darque. You stayed safely on Earth. As Firebrands, our duty is to prevent crazy Aeternals from escaping to Earth. If one slips through, we pursue them and drag them home to face judgment.”

Cadmon continued the story. “Over the centuries, both our species have advanced. But understand this, Aeternals have walked among you since your first days. Fact is, our lives and the threads of our civilizations are a tapestry of rich, colorful strands woven together. Most often, our symbiotic relationship is positive. We mix with you, trading goods and services, working together to solve problems, vacationing at the same hot spots, attending the same art exhibits and concerts. But now Cerberus has popped up. He professes to be Hades's hound from the Prophecy of Karma. As such, he will open the portals and allow Aeternals to feed on humans again. But this relationship will be parasitic. While he may be insane, he has support."

Matty scrubbed his jaw. "Long story short, even if we stop this Cerberus … and I do mean if … it'll be bloody. The Firebrands are honorable men. I've seen them up close and personal. With their help, we stand a chance of victory."

Lipton's sigh was so loud it echoed through the warehouse.

"General, they are stronger and faster than us. If you need a demo, Dax here will arm wrestle the entire battalion and come out the victor," said Matty.

Cadmon chuckled. "While I would love to watch, I don't think such a demonstration will be necessary. General Lipton, our lawgivers and Temple of Justice ordered us to stand down, to wait and see what Arisen Dawn can do. You should know, every Firebrand voted to disobey the order. They voted to fight for humans because it is the right path. By saving you, we save ourselves. For our decision, the powers-that-be branded us traitors. But we follow the mark of our birthright, the Phoenix. We'll stand against Arisen Dawn even if you reject our offer to work together. It would be better, however, if we shared intel and cooperated. Both of our chances would improve."

"Can we take a minute to talk, gentlemen?" General Lipton indicated the other high-ranking officers who sat at the table beside him.

Dax leaned back in his chair, just for the hell of it letting his fangs elongate again. “You better leave the warehouse for your chit-chat. We have excellent hearing.”

When the general scrunched his brows, questioning the vampire’s statement, Dax said, “For example, the soldier over there has change in his pocket. It jingles when he moves. That man in the corner has an erratic heartbeat. I’d get him to a healer after our meet.”

“Damn. That’s good.” Matty rose and leaned toward Dax to whisper. “You are so sexy, I want to kiss you. But your sister’s a jealous woman.” He turned to follow the retreating generals and staff.

Dax’s laughter followed the army representatives out of the warehouse.

After a wait, Kole back-and-forthed it in the warehouse, making an entire line of soldiers nervous. To stay awake, Dax thrummed his fingers on the table. The rhythmic thud of his commander’s boots hitting the concrete was a lullaby. Nace prowled the perimeter of their space, his caged jaguar growling, anxious to get out. Only Jarek and Cadmon waited patiently.

Finally, the outer door swung open. Lipton returned, leading the officers and staff back to the meeting. He lifted his fingertips, tapping his forehead in a salute. “Welcome to our war, High Commander Cadmon. We’d be proud to fight alongside any of your men and women. We know real soldiers when we see them.”

****

Back in his office after four hours ironing out details with the American army, Kole listened to reports from his Firebrands. Holding up a hand, he interrupted Thorn—who sat splattered in blood, shirt in tatters, hair matted—with a story about his dust-up with Arisen

Dawn. "It's Cadmon." He tapped his wrist and scrubbed his fist across his head while he listened. "How many beds left, Chay?"

"Last count, Red said we have about twenty bunks but can add more. We also have seven rooms on the third floor."

Kole relayed the info to Cadmon before he disconnected. He suppressed a jolt of electricity shooting up his spine. "Ram, Chay, with me to our portal. We're greeting incoming justices and lawgivers who are requesting sanctuary. Nace and Jarek are taking their share. Ylve, reach out to your mate. We'll hand them off to Margo. Tell her to notify the new household manager she hired from among the refugees. Thorn, you could do with a shower. Afterward, let Fin and the new guy … uh … Arne know to expect more for dinner. Galena, you've got my stamp of approval on the modified rotation assignments. After you assess their skills, Dax, get me your list of civilian refugees who want to fight. We don't want to send out anyone who doesn't stand a chance to survive. They are yours to train."

He yelled, "Bounty, Cadmon wants a get-together here. Me, Rein, Dax, the other commanders, and the arriving justices and lawgivers. Arrange it for tomorrow."

She leaned against the doorjamb, her arms crossed under her breasts. "Yes, O loud one."

Before following his two Firebrands to the stronghold's portal, he snatched his double-edged dagger. No sense being too good a host. In the outer office near Bounty's desk, Kae slept atop blankets on the floor. "Why do you have my daughter?"

"Don't know. Skyler dropped her off early this morning with a sh … boatload of toys."

With a shrug, Kole hurried into the hallway and

to the stronghold's portal.

At the gateway, Ram waited splay-legged, his Scottish dirk in his fist. Chay, alongside him, clutched a war hammer.

Some welcoming committee.

First through the portal was Aras. In his arms, he cradled an infant eagle shifter. Behind him were his female and a juvenile who positioned his body in front of his mother.

Kole lowered his blade, admiring the youth's protective instincts.

"Thanks, Commander," said the chief justice. "Our aerie is no longer safe."

Next through was Viktor, bowing slightly at the waist, still favoring the formalities. Though Dante had killed the lawgiver's offspring in a lab, the vampire didn't blame all humans for the evil of one. He chose forgiveness rather than vengeance. "You remember Dania, my mate. Arisen Dawn has been outside our door in Bludhaven for days. It was time to slip away." He stepped aside to reveal Norah. "This is the brave female who suffered at Dante's hands along with my son. Ossar and Licia, her parents, are behind her. You've met them."

"Welcome, Lawgiver," said Kole. He nodded at the group Viktor led into the stronghold. "Chay, take these guests to Margo. We'll talk later. Get settled in first."

Viktor clapped a hand on Kole's shoulder. "I cannot thank you enough. My family has seen enough tragedy."

Nerina, another supportive lawgiver, greeted Kole as Ram stood guard, his back to the wall, his eyes on the arrivals. A stream of family members followed her. "This is my beloved mate. We will fight, Kole. Though not Firebrands, we are trained and not expecting a free ride in your stronghold. Behind him are my daughter, her satyr mate, and son." She pointed at a voluptuous nymph with strawberry-blonde hair like her mother's who held hands with an adult male on one side and a boy of about five on the other.

Ram sheathed his weapon before he hoisted the young satyr onto his shoulders, rewarded by the boy's giggles. "Let's worry about fighting once you have a safe place to bed down."

After the guests were off to their unfamiliar quarters, Kole returned to his office where he allowed himself a moment to rest his head in his palms, elbows on his desk. This future was not what he wanted for his realm or Skyler and Kae.

As if on cue, his mate's voice drifted in from the outer office. Despite dark thoughts of the future, a smile tugged his lips as he opened the door to herd his infant and Skyler inside. When the now awake child saw her father, her chubby hands clapped together. Her mouth opened with giggles, and her little feet bicycled. He scooped Kae out of her mother's arms.

Kole's gaze traveled up and down Skyler. Usually in heels and with every hair in place, today she wore khakis, boots, and a cotton shirt. All slightly askew. Icy-blonde tendrils escaped a messy ponytail.

When she caught him eyeing her, she said, "Just came from a workout."

"In the gym?" He arched his brows, staring at her scuffed Dr. Martens.

"Uh. No. On the obstacle course outside. I figured I could use the practice."

Kae distracted him by pinching his nose. He returned the favor with a tickle to the belly. "A visit is what I needed."

"We won't stay. You have a busy day ahead with

more refugees. I have to check in at the Alliance even though I took the day off."

Kole tossed his daughter into the air while Skyler closed her eyes, wincing despite the girl's loud tee-hees.

Shifting Kae to the crook of his arm, he pulled his mate to his side with his free hand. "Have I told you how happy you make me, Frisca?"

"You have, but I can always hear it again."

"If things go south, I want you and Kae to resettle on Earth. I've set up a condo in Chicago along with a bank account." He reached into his desk drawer to retrieve a folder. "It's all in here."

Instead of taking it, Skyler snatched the girl from him, her mouth turning down into a frown, her words frosty enough to freeze his balls. "Don't be ridiculous, demon. We will never abandon you. Just try to make us leave." She spun on her heel and marched out, calling over her shoulder, "This subject is closed."

He returned to his desk, determined to open the closed subject again and again until his mate agreed with him.

After a few hours of tedious paperwork, Kole answered a D-chip call. He tapped. He listened, his erratic breathing threatening to bring on his demon beast.

Sonofabitch.

When fire streamed from his hands, he shouted out to Bounty, "Get the fucking mates and the new female they're hiding to the gathering room. Now!" As he pushed away, his chair clattered to the floor, and he stormed out his door. In his executive assistant's office, Indigo perched on the corner of her desk, her brows arched, a fuck-no expression on her face. With a snarly grin, Kole locked eyes with her. "Join us, witch."

"Oh, shit." Indigo jumped up. To Bounty, she said, "I think our chat's over. I'll be in touch."

****

Chiara tapped a bare foot on the floor while one Firebrand after another took a turn at berating the Blood Coven witches.

"What the fuck were you thinking?" shouted Tyr, the tat under his eye twitching, his metal piercing at a slant when he dragged his brows down. "While we're fighting out there to protect our asses, you're trying to get yours blown off."

Still wearing her leather pants and boots from the rescue, Jace shrugged, keeping a tight clasp on Celene's hand while they sat on a couch in the gathering area at the stronghold. Scattered about in chairs and three huge sofas was the rest of the rescue team, all on the proverbial carpet.

Dax leaned against the wall, his muscles taut, his jaw set hard enough to crack teeth. "They weren't thinking. Were you, little witch? Not a brain in the entire group." His fingers worried through his hair.

That did it. Bristling, Chiara rose, glancing at her friends. "Let me handle this. The stupid just rolls out of my man's mouth."

Dax, though sweet to worry about her, needed to acknowledge her abilities and the gifts of the rest of the coven. They weren't ornaments. They were partners in this fight.

The vampire stiffened, his lips snapping shut, his chest expanding with a deep breath, almost as if he recognized he was in shit up to his fangs.

Chiara smoothed her long skirt, brushed wild tendrils of hair off her face, and prepared for battle. "There is too much fucking testosterone in this room. Here's what we were thinking, baby. The Firebrands have enough on your plates saving the world and all. We were confident of our skills, planned the rescue with care, and implemented it successfully. Thank you." She bowed to the women who clapped at the conclusion of her remarks.

Tyr poked Dax's shoulder. "Did she just call you baby?"

The vampire's lip curled. "Shut the fuck up. She can call me anything she wants."

Brows lifted on every Firebrand, but Dax's growl stopped the snickers.

Jarek sighed, his eyes glinting like cold steel. "My mate is injured. The guard could have killed her."

"Didn't." Lizette high-fived Indigo, who sat beside her. "And don't you dare get all smoky and disappear."

Chiara smiled at the unlikely friendship which had developed between the two women since the rescue. It was a bond between the unpredictable Aeternal witch and the rational psychologist, once a radio talk show hostess, now mate of a powerful djinn commander.

Rein's arms crossed over his chest, his blue eyes crackling with ice. "Auntie, Brae, of all the damn dumb…"

Braelyn jumped up. "I wouldn't finish that sentence, big guy."

Indigo waved a thumb at her nephew's mate. "I'm with her, boyo."

Chiara had to give it to the on-edge-but-controlled Firebrand. When the two women challenged him, he swallowed his words.

Watching the commotion, Ram leaned against the doorjamb. "Denim, you're ex-military, for Gahya's sake. You must have known the danger of taking female civilians into a hot zone."

"I know my soldiers. Are you guys questioning the ability of women in tough situations?"

"Yes." Ram's eyes rolled left, right as if he reconsidered his answer. "No. Definitely not."

Sabine, who had not been part of the rescue, glared at the satyr. "I hope not." When Nico opened his mouth, she wagged a finger at him. "We don't need your two cents. I know you. Nothing good will cross your lips."

Her mate shrugged, relaxing his shoulders, smiling with his eyes. "Maybe I was going to support the coven kittens."

"Doubtful," said Sabine. "Your MO is to talk first and think second, your brain being in your cock."

"You like my appendage, nymph." His hand stroked her thigh.

Kole opened his mouth to speak, shook his head, and sputtered. Then he released a burst of fire that Chiara had to duck to avoid.

"Fuck, Kole. Watch it." Dax took a threatening step toward his commander.

Kole spread his legs. "Bring it on, vampire. I feel the urge to wipe the floor with somebody. You'll do."

Chiara signaled Skyler. "Let's stop the idiots." The women moved between their mates, who had the good sense to retreat.

Dax gripped Chiara's arm, leading her away from the confrontation. He bent to whisper in her ear. "Don't call me baby in front of everyone."

She whispered back, glancing around the room to make sure no one eavesdropped. "Don't call me little witch."

"Not happening."

"Ditto, vampire baby." Chiara broke from his grasp, flopping onto the couch where Braelyn patted her knee.

Thorn cleared his throat. "Fin, you can't let these

females lead you into danger."

"Lead? You're implying I don't think for myself?"

"Um. No. Of course not." A confused wolf paced behind Thorn's amber eyes. "Shit."

"Good, because you'd be sleeping alone on the floor tonight."

Dax's jaw clenched. "This will never happen again. No more forays into battle for you or your coven." He paused, his grin wicked. "Little witch."

"Now that just pisses me off, baby." Chiara rose, blinked, and flicked her wrist.

When a chill settled in the room, the males crumpled to the cold tile. Mouths dropped open, the women turning worried eyes to Chiara.

"They're only in a light coma. I couldn't listen to the inane babble any longer." Chiara brushed her hands together.

With a frown tugging her lips, Sabine fronted the spellcaster. "Nico wasn't part of the problem. He's Blood Coven, too. Why did you face plant him?"

"Collateral damage. Sorry."

Sabine sighed. "Shit happens. My mate's been a little triggered of late. He can use the rest."

Jace rose from the couch, pulling her rescued friend up with her. "I told you, Celene. You love them, right? Drinks, ladies? I could use one. Let's make some for the guys. They'll need straight shots when they come to."

"Great idea." Chiara, barefooted and with her skirt sweeping the floor, strolled behind the bar. "They're gonna be pissed, aren't they?"

Feeling for his pulse, Fin kneeled beside Thorn. "You better believe it. Maybe the men will have a little respect for our gifts, though."

All heads swung toward the sound of boots thudding on the tile as Nace strode into the gathering area. He halted. His eyes took in the bodies on the floor and then swept toward the women crowding the bar. "Anything you want to explain?"

"The guys were tired. I think you know everybody here except our new guest." Chiara, reaching for an offered glass of red wine, pointed to Jace's friend, the newly rescued Blood Coven descendant. "Celene, this is Commander Nace from the North Shelters stronghold."

A smile widened on the jaguar shifter's face as he stepped over Dax. "Lovely, where have you been my whole life?"

Celene tucked her blonde hair behind her ears. "Oh, here and there." She offered her hand to the newcomer.

Instead of shaking, the commander touched his lips to the back of her fingers.

While Celene clasped a kissed fist to her heart, every woman in the room *oohed* and *aahed.*

Chiara sipped her wine, peering over the rim of the glass. "So, Commander, what do you think of women going into battle?"

"Is this a trick question?" Nace accepted a whiskey from Sabine.

"Yes." The nymph Firebrand glanced at Nico still asleep on the floor.

Nace looped an arm across Celene's shoulders. "In that case, I think females make sneaky warriors."

The women raised their glasses.

"A gentleman and a politician." Chiara twisted around to stare at Dax as he shoved off the floor, rubbing his head. "Battle stations, ladies."

Chapter Thirty-Two

Kole glanced around the breakfast table at the stronghold. Arne had set out a fantastic buffet for the mates. Obviously he'd heard rumblings about last night.

With a plate stacked high with scrambled eggs, bacon, sausage, hash browns, and buttered toast, he took the seat next to Skyler, patting her hand. Though she still refused to leave him if things got hot, they had made up after the harsh words following Celene's rescue. Their apologies were loud. Demon style.

All the couples seemed calmer this morning. No hot tempers or accusations flying.

Rein finished off his coffee before he pushed away from the table. "Comm, it's time."

"Sure." Kole rose, bending to kiss the top of Skyler's head. "Frisca, take care." He brought his palm near his mouth and blew across it, returning Kae's kiss. She giggled. He said his goodbyes to the rest of his Firebrands and their mates.

In his conference room, the leather in Kole's chair creaked as he settled at the head of the table. Alarik arrived with Indigo, who smiled sheepishly before giving him a snarky finger wave. He doubted she was worried about last night's events. The witch was too powerful to be cowered. A little crazy, but a force to be reckoned with. Others followed them in, taking seats.

"Are you two joining us at the stronghold?" asked Kole.

"You must be kidding." Indigo sat beside her brother. "I get the willies being near so many bigwigs. No offense, makers and shakers." She nodded at Viktor, Aras, and Nerina, popping her gum, kicking her booted feet onto the table where her long skirt wrapped around her ankles.

Alarik, as always, made no move to control her behavior. He'd probably given up. "Elisabeta and Castia have moved into my ministry as have my employees. We are fine where we are."

"I have a question for Indigo," said Viktor, his arm braced over the back of his chair.

"Ask away, vampire. I might answer. I might not." The witch twirled a piece of hair around her finger.

"What have you observed in the River Am?"

She slammed her hands onto the tabletop. "Excellent question. Winged creatures. Dragons. The Phoenix. Ravens. Blood Coven descendants. Newcomers I don't recognize."

Viktor leaned forward in his seat. "What does it mean?"

"How the hell do I know? Big stuff poppin'. Things will get clearer as the future flows toward the present."

Everyone's attention turned to the door when Cadmon strode into the room with Nace and Jarek. Rein kicked out an empty chair for the high commander. He pointed at the empty seats for the others.

Glancing around the room, Kole said, "I don't think intros are necessary."

"No, I am acquainted with everyone here." Cadmon nodded as he took a chair. He propped elbows on the table and tented his fingers. "I received important intel yesterday."

Kole didn't share with the group that the high commander had a deep-cover operative in Arisen Dawn.

"What's up?" Rein spoke from Kole's left.

"The insurgents are gathering for a big incursion onto Earth."

Claws sprang from Nace's fingers. "Anyone else

here feel like shit's moving too fast? Coming at us at Mach speed? The scenery is starting to blur. Where? When?"

"Two days out. They plan to go through North Shelters to Sacramento. This will be their biggest invasion to date. I'm told they can transport slightly larger groups through the portals."

"Do I have a traitor I need to worry about?" asked Alarik.

While Boden oversaw the production and distribution of portal jumpers, Alarik's scientists and Logan guarded the D-chip technology which allowed Firebrands to pass through the gates in large numbers.

"Very doubtful. It's more likely Boden amped up the juice in their devices."

"That's possible, High Commander," said Alarik, "but they won't handle much."

"How many can they send through?" Jarek's brows knitted into a frown.

"According to my source, maybe ten at a time," said Cadmon.

"Dax," said Kole, "contact your human. Tell him to get his army to Sacramento for the big event. We'll attack on the Scath side. They'll be squeezed between us."

The vampire Firebrand nodded. "Any more details, High Commander?"

"They'll be coming into Sacramento through the warehouse portal near Tower Bridge," said Cadmon.

Nerina sat upright, her chin jutting forward. "As I offered before, Commander Kole. My satyr and I will fight alongside your Firebrands."

Viktor's fangs punched from his gums. "As will I."

"No strings are attached to your sanctuary here,"

said Kole.

"We know, Commander, and are grateful, but our honor requires us to stand with you." Aras's eagle flickered near the surface as he spoke, his eyes pale yellow, his gaze sharp, his tone allowing no contradiction.

Indigo threw a fist into the air. "I'm in. My bag's packed, my gryphon's fed, and I'm ready to rock."

Cadmon nodded. "So be it."

Dax slid a piece of paper across the table. "Comm, here's the list of refugees who want to fight and have some skills. They'll be training alongside Ram's recruits. He already has plans in place. I'll assist, rotating in off-duty Firebrands as additional instructors. Aras, Viktor, and Nerina, you are welcome to join us. Indigo, I don't think you require training."

Jarek leaned into his chair, seemingly at ease. "We'll meet tomorrow at my stronghold with our seconds to draw up a battle strategy. For now, think on it."

Cadmon rose. "I will leave the specific plans to my commanders then. Stay safe."

****

At the staging area before the Firebrands and allies faced Arisen Dawn, Dax draped an arm around Chiara's waist in a casual-but-possessive hold. She had forgiven him for not respecting her skills, for letting his mouth run faster than his brain. He had forgiven her for knocking him out cold. Afterward, he preened because he was learning the ins and outs of the relationship biz. Best part, they'd had lots of makeup sex.

His attention shifted to Kole, who reiterated the high points of the mission. Intel predicted Arisen Dawn would pass through to Earth at the remote North Shelters portal. With mountain ranges bracketing the valley on all sides, the place was perfect for an incursion.

Kole was answering a question posed by a recruit. “Jarek will flank our left. Nace will be on our right. They’ll be doing their own thing.”

Chiara traded her gypsy skirt for snug leather pants, a flak jacket over a long-sleeved T-shirt, and boots. With a short sword at her back, two knives strapped to her hips, and her unruly hair tied at her nape, she was hot. Seeing her dressed for battle, Dax fought the urge to strip her naked, thrust into her, and bury his fangs in her luscious neck.

As if she understood exactly what he was thinking, she shook her head. He shrugged and arched a brow.

Next to Dax, Thorn tapped his wrist, disconnecting from a call. “That was Luka with news. His old pack decamped with Karth. He thinks they’re heading out to join Arisen Dawn. My brother and his mate are on their way to help us.”

Dax gave the shifter a thumbs up.

Kole raised a fist, stopping all chatter. “We’re waiting to hear from our scouts at the portal. At their go-ahead, we charge in.” Though the commander had not refused the assist from the Blood Coven descendants who possessed deadly skills, he attached stipulations. “Chiara, when you tire from casting spells, get the hell out. No second guessing. Braelyn, the same advice applies. Nico and Denim, you’re one of us, but…”

Nico interrupted. “Fuck you very much, Kole. I don’t leave my mate’s side unless I’m dead.”

Sabine grinned. “He’s an irreverent bastard, but he’s all mine, Comm. I apologize for any disrespect.”

Nico pressed a kiss to her forehead.

Rein dropped his icy blue gaze to his mate. “We’ve discussed this with the females. They know to stay would hinder us."

Kole's arm shot into the air, high above his head, sparks shooting from his fingers. "For duty. For honor." He slammed a fist down, a signal to charge into battle.

The Eastern Stronghold stormed into the valley at the same time as Jarek and Nace's Firebrands. At the portal, Arisen Dawn soldiers outnumbered them, but as an experienced fighter, Dax knew victory was achieved one dead body at a time. It was bad *juju* to take in the whole field. So he looked for a single victim.

When a bolt zipped by his ear, it struck a berserker who had been about to attack him from behind. The guy was draped in a lion shifter's pelt and probably in a frenzy after the ceremony where he had drunk animal blood laced with *amanita muscaria*. The behemoth fisted the projectile lodged in his chest, but Dax lobbed off his head before he could yank it out. Chay acknowledged the shot with a grin, doing the Mohammed Ali thing with his feet.

Dax nodded his thanks and swept his eyes over the battlefield. Unable to dodge a warlock's spell, a newbie Firebrand went down, the bones in his legs snapping. Though Galena rushed to his side, short spear in her fist, she was too late to save him.

Whipping his jungle bolos through the air, Dax beheaded a satyr before the guy could swing a blade.

Near him, Tyr faced a berserker whose shield prevented the warlock from using his spells. Dax decapitated the Arisen Dawn soldier with a flourish of his blades, saving his *freron* the effort.

Chiara's arm was stiff in front of her, palm out toward a succubus, now crumpled on the ground. Distracted watching his mate, Dax took a bear claw to the jaw, blood spurting down his chin. Recovering, he whisked his blades in a figure eight, a little showy, maybe, but scary as hell. He sliced through the shifter's neck. Kicking the furry remains out of his way, he sought his next victim. With his fangs cutting into his lower lip, his eyes turned crimson with excitement.

Eleven dead opponents later and spitting out the bad taste of tainted battle blood, he checked on his lover. She swayed, narrowly missing an Amazon's blade. With Chiara weakened, the female Aeternal raised her weapon to swing again. Dax charged vampire fast to his little witch's side, a bolo clanging against the attacker's sword before she could strike. His lips curled into a feral snarl as their weapons locked in battle. The Amazon, however, was no match for his strength. He pushed her off and, in a smooth motion, lobbed off her head.

His attention back on Chiara, he caught her before she collapsed to the ground. "It's time," he said, steadying her on her feet. "You waited too long."

"Thanks." She gave him no argument. He shivered when Chiara's lips feathered across his ear before she retreated from the field of battle. "Return to me, vampire."

Dax charged an incubus who ducked under his blades, locking arms around his hips, taking him face down into the dirt. The male tried to flip him and steal his lifeforce, but with his biceps and thighs quivering, the vampire muscled himself to his feet.

Figure-eighting his jungle bolos in an intricate dance of death, he forced a retreat. When the incubus twisted on his heels to run, Dax shouted, "Oh, no you don't." Sharp steel to his neck, the vampire made a clean slice.

Kole was all fire now. One blast from his right hand incinerated an Arisen Dawn soldier while his left struck down another. Dax shook his head. *Ambidextrous sonofabitch.*

Near the commander, Sabine and Nico held their own. The Blood Coven warlock's magnetic force drew weapons from opponents' hands while his nymph mate lobbed off their heads. *Teamwork.*

Braelyn retired from the field, obviously drained by her mind control spells. That left Rein to his battle rage. Blood dripping down his chin, his huge ass fangs on display, his arctic blue eyes feral, he tore through the neck of a djinn who tried to smoke out.

Dax barreled toward an Amazon jacked up on Gold Dust, her eyes rolling around like pinballs while drool clung to her lips. Despite the drug, she was dangerous, lacking any concern for her own safety. She lunged, her short spear nicking Dax's shoulder. Close to his neck but no points. He pushed her back with fancy sword work.

The Amazon charged again, straight-arming her weapon, aiming for Dax's heart. He fell into a low crouch, his blades taking her out at the knees. Slice. Slice. Gruesome. Effective. The crazy-eyed bitch died, her pupils still dancing as Dax swung again to decapitate.

Thorn, all claws and canines, was in a savage fight with Karth, who had defeated his brother Luka in a challenge for alpha of the pack. The wolf Arisen Dawn soldier raised his blade. Before he could drive it home, Thorn dropped, rolled, and bounced to his feet. From a low squat, he attacked, flinging the pack's alpha to the ground. Blood, fur, and chunks of flesh splattered the air. Once Thorn trapped Karth beneath his massive weight, he wrapped his teeth around the traitor's throat. Legs kicking, hands flailing, the other shifter struggled until his howls of defeat echoed across the field. Then Karth's body hung limp, the Firebrand's jaws locked tight on his neck.

Dax almost took out Ram when they bumped into

one another.

"Oops," said the satyr, returning to his fight with a vampire. With the bloodsucker tiring, Denim whipped up a dust storm which had the guy swiping at his eyes. With his attacker blinded by his mate's elemental spell, Ram's dirk hacked through the guy's bone and tendons, leaving the body headless.

His black T-shirt stiff with blood but few wounds himself, Dax finished off five more Arisen Dawn soldiers, his blades singing as they sliced and diced through flesh. The ground beneath his feet was a quagmire of entrails and blood. His vision obscured by gore, he swiped a hand across his eyes.

Jezzi was in trouble, but Kole moved to the panther shifter's side, blasting her opponent with enough voltage to fry his brain.

Arisen Dawn soldiers beat retreat. The roars, the howls, the battle cries, the blade-on-blade clashes, the scuffling of feet in the dirt, the raucous sound of chaos dissipated bit by bit until the field grew silent except for heavy breathing and groans from the injured.

That's when Bade screamed, a sound which broke the eerie quiet. "No." The young vampire's boots ate up the dirt as he raced over littered body parts toward his friend. Sig lay in the grass, his neck nearly severed, his legs folded at an odd angle, and a blade hilt sticking out of his chest. He was too young to survive such injuries. Galena kneeled at his side, her shield abandoned, her fingers closing his lids. Chiara would cry for him, the young demon who had flirted with her in the game room while they played pool.

Tyr stood vigil over a female, a recruit he had helped train. The valley was strewn with bodies, some belonging to Firebrands, mostly warriors dead before song or legend would remember their exploits. Heroes all. *Frerons* would carry them home, shoulder-high, forever youthful, their souls undamaged by the darkness which comes with time or disappointment. *Hell.* Except for Sig, Dax didn't even know their names.

Bade stood tall beside his friend, a fist to his heart, tears streaming down his cheeks.

Amid green grass which was stained crimson with blood, Kole tapped his wrist. When he disconnected from a call, he reported to his Firebrands. "The human army routed the insurgents who slipped through us to Earth." His fire-gold eyes surveyed the battlefield, his arm limp at his side, his ax still clutched. "Incinerate the dead Arisen Dawn traitors."

While warlocks and animus demons carried out the order, the commander lumbered toward Sig. He rested a beefy hand on Bade's shoulder. "Our *freron* was brave. We will remember him along with all our fallen." Kole bent to retrieve the demon Firebrand's sword. For his wall, no doubt.

With the bodies of their enemy torched, the injured Firebrands carried off by healers, and their own dead on the way home, Kole sent his warriors from the bloody field. He would be the last to leave the valley. It was a duty, a tribute Dax had seen too many times before. Jarek and Nace would be doing the same in their sectors.

He offered a shoulder to Thorn, whose side gushed blood. "You need a healer."

The shifter accepted the assist. "I need my mate. Have you seen my brother?"

"Yeah. Luka held his own. Musta been tough to put down his own pack, but he did it."

Hearing the caws of a raven, Dax craned his neck to look overhead at a gigantic beast who winged its way toward a distant tree-barren hillside. It landed beside a male whose long black coat whipped around his boots. *Lort.* The vampire Arisen Dawn general had watched the battle from a safe, lofty perch. Dax wondered if he mourned the loss of his soldiers or if he had sacrificed them to study how the Firebrands operated.

Fin, along with others, waited at the stronghold's portal, tears in her eyes, a hand smothering a cry when she rushed toward Thorn. Dax released him to her care, glancing around at the crowd.

There. Chiara.

Once she was in his arms, he rubbed a thumb across the smudges of dirt on her face, tucking a wayward strand of curly black hair behind her ear. No wounds. When her hands stroked his jaw, he leaned into her warm touch. Nobody had ever waited for him. Usually after a fight, he beelined it to the nearest O blud den. This was better. So much better. Someone cared. He mattered to Chiara.

A slight chill settling over his aching body, he welcomed her spell, one which calmed a troubled mind and mended flesh. An odd feeling struck Dax. The little witch was his, but he belonged to her, too.

He cleared a throat raw with unexpected emotion. "It's over for now. I'd call it a draw. Not a win. Tomorrow…"

"Tomorrow, I'll cradle you in my arms, vampire. That's all I want."

He pinched her chin between a thumb and forefinger, lifting it. "What did I do to deserve you?"

"You saved me."

"No. You saved me."

Chiara gave him a cocky wink. "We saved each other. Now home. I have plans to fuck you silly."

He perked up, his wounds no longer painful. "Give me the deets."

Chiara lifted onto her toes, her hot breath whispering across his ear. "First, I'll get on my knees, unzip your pants, take you into…"

That's when his fangs punched from his gums, his cock nearly popped through the fabric of his jeans, and he tossed a giggling Chiara over his shoulder. Next stop, their bed. If he made it that far.

Chapter Thirty-Three

Roark widened his stance to withstand the rolling motion, the ground at the garrison tilting beneath his feet as Cerberus stood in the epicenter of an earthquake, his hair whipping around his face, his cloak stirring at his feet, his eyes mad with power.

So much drama.

The warlock certainly loved himself, being the narcissistic, charismatic, almost unkillable sonofabitch he was. Nasty combo for those on the other side.

Lort tossed from side to side as Arisen Dawn soldiers rushed from the barracks. When they saw Cerberus at the center of the phenomenon, they stopped, staring in awe when they realized who their leader was, stunned by the presence of someone so powerful.

The warlock's voice thundered through the air. "Hear me, Aeternals, and know who I am. Be not dismayed. We lost a skirmish but will win the war when I tip the scales in the final battle. My destiny is victory." The quake stilled with a wave of his hand. "Bow down."

Really?

Roark added delusions of godhood to the list of Cerberus's qualities. But the Arisen Dawn soldiers dropped to their knees, their heads angled, their eyes on the ground.

The warlock frowned at the males by his side. Wiping a sweaty brow, Boden immediately fell to the dirt. Roark shrugged, looking at Lort, who squared his shoulders. Both males took a knee but kept their chins up, their expressions looking as if they had swallowed a bitter dram.

After proper adoration from the crowd, the warlock gripped his black robe in a fist. "Dismissed."

The soldiers scuttled back to wherever they had come from, devotion to their leader written on their faces.

Lort, apparently as unmoved as Roark by the warlock's megalomaniacal show of force, spoke once the area was clear. "Defeat may be a bitter flavor, but I watched and learned."

"What did you learn, General?" asked Cerberus.

"This was not our battle to win. We were too few. Too inexperienced. But I learned how the Firebrands fight." Lort took a breath. "We rebuild. Add to our army. Train harder. Learn to counter the warriors' style of battle. Punish those who fail to live up to standards. We will continue to batter the humans with small incursions, keep them on high alert, ramp up their fears."

"Yes. This fits with my ultimate strategy. Once we have filled our stable of Blood Coven descendants, we will be ready."

"Care to share that ultimate strategy?" Roark examined his nails. "The more we know, the more we can help."

"No. I do not care to share my strategy."

The cruel slash that was Lort's mouth twitched. "I have a human male waiting in my bed. I need to replenish myself with drink and cock."

The sadistic bastard kept a human for pleasure and food, his own sex-slave-slash-dinner. He had probably used up several donors by this time.

"I have a bottle of whiskey to empty, a female to fill, and a straggling unit to train harder. All good plans," said Roark.

Cerberus flipped the hem of his cloak through the dirt.

More drama.

Roark was waiting for the guy to dance around

the garrison to a zippy musical number like *Fame.* The shifter was a little disappointed when it didn't happen.

Minister Boden was about to crack, though, words stuttering across his lips. "I'll see to the progress on getting more out of our portal jumpers. My hopes, however, are not high."

More sweat on the director's forehead. Couldn't the guy grow bigger balls? After all, he was the right hand of evil. Maybe villains weren't as tough as Roark expected.

****

With Skyler tucked against one side and Kae wiggling in his arm, Kole entered the gym. He paused to take in the room, revamped for the glammed-up event, part remembrance of those fallen, part celebration for those who lived. "Unbelievable."

With a possessive hand on his mate's bare back, he guided them through the crowd.

Skyler's frosty lilac eyes brightened at the scene. "Arne is a miracle worker. I hope we can keep him when all this blows over. The man recruited other refugees to help with the menu. Fin provided advice about food prep for a large group. And here's a surprise. Nico is an expert with meatballs. I guess he made hundreds for this event."

Kae, wiggling harder, babbled undecipherable words.

"I'll let you down in a minute, baby. You'll get stomped on. Wait until we're at our table." When the toddler held out her arms for her mother, Kole passed her off.

"Nice job with the decor, Frisca." Though he couldn't see the point of putting fancy cloths, flowers, and other shit on the tables when everyone was here to eat and talk, he'd never say that to Skyler. Besides, she could outfit the gym in pink flamingos and unicorns for all he cared, as long as she wore a curve-hugging white dress which swept the floor and revealed the sexy-as-hell expanse of skin from her shoulders to just above her ass. Males openly stared, but he had promised to be on his best behavior. He assumed his promise included not setting any of his mate's admirers on fire.

With Skyler in front of him, Kole continued to appreciate the wintery dress as her hips swayed side to side. Still, he preferred her without it, clothed only in her own pale, glowing flesh, surrounded by thick icy blonde hair spread out across a pillow.

Somehow, his mate read his thoughts. Then she double-tasked it. While taking the thumb out of Kae's mouth, she managed to admonish both demon and child with one squint-eyed scolding glare.

Skyler tempered the warning with a sexy grin tugging at her cherry-red lips. *Oh, yeah.* She had read his mind.

How long was this shindig supposed to last?

Kole, his fingers tugging on the stiff collar of his dress uniform, nodded at Firebrands and visitors as he followed his females toward the head table.

Skyler gave Kae back to her father. "I see the Alliance. I'm going to shake some hands."

When she pulled her mate's head down for a breath-stealing kiss, Kole got in a little tongue action before she walked away fanning her scarlet cheeks.

Somebody tugged on Kole's pant leg. He looked down and down until he saw Nerina's grandson. The Firebrand commander bent onto one knee, eye to eye with the five-year-old, his daughter in one arm. "What do you want, lad?"

"Whass her name?"

"Kae."

"Can Kae play?"

Kole searched for Nerina. When he found her, she was looking his way, pointing to the back of the room where young refugee children were chasing each other while older kids chatted in small groups. In a nearby corner, toddlers played on the floor.

He took a deep breath. With hundreds of people crowded into the gym, his protective demon nature screamed *hell no*, finding a million reasons why he should hold tight to his daughter. But he would never cripple her.

“Can I trust you, lad? She’s awful little.” An eager Kae squirmed, her legs kicking into his gut as she reached across his chest toward the boy.

“I’m gonna be a Firebrand like you when I grow up. I’ll keep her safe.”

A reluctant father set the extremely precocious toddler on her feet, smoothed out her party dress, and watched her waddle off hand in hand with a would-be warrior.

Ram pulled alongside. “First date?”

“If you treasure your pearlies, satyr, you’ll shut the fuck up.” Kole glanced at Jonquil. “Sorry, kid.”

“Pu-leeze. I’ve heard worse. Don’t worry, sir, I’ll watch over her,” said Ram’s daughter.

Before her stepdaughter took off on her mission, Denim relieved her of a sequined evening bag and yellow sweater. “You look beautiful tonight, *cher*. Don’t break too many hearts. BTW, cute guy on the horizon, parked against the wall. About your age.”

It was Ram’s turn to snarl.

“Fathers.” Denim chuckled as she waved at the Alliance table. She lifted the hem of her flowing black evening dress, muttering, “Damn high heels. Whose idea was it to play dress up?” Wobbling a bit, she headed off to see old friends.

"Our daughters are fine," said Ram. "Right? Not like we can stick them in a cage or give every boy who winks at them a knife between the ribs."

Tyr, the silver bar through his brow and his numerous earrings glinting in the overhead lights, called out to the satyr while he indicated two empty seats at their table. Jace sat in his lap, chatting with Celene.

Ram leaned toward Kole. "Did you hear? The punk warlock mated the Blood Coven witch. I didn't think he'd ever get hitched, certainly not to someone so different from himself, so normal."

"Yeah. They've got the opposite thing going."

Like Skyler and me. Different but the same where it matters.

Ram smacked Kole on the shoulder. "Gotta go. By the way, it only gets worse." He pointed toward Jonquil and Kae.

As a growly Kole thought about the satyr's words, he powered up to his table.

"Good turn out," said Cadmon.

The high commander was right. Firebrands and their families crowded the makeshift dining room, along with refugees and Alliance members. Aras, Viktor, and Nerina were with their broods. The guest list also included Alarik and his people.

The group was a mix of species and breeds, strange bed fellows, Cerberus's worst nightmare. An impure world. But to Kole, demon mate of a Blood Coven witch more human than Aeternal and father to an astounding mixling, it was the old world made new, energized with hope.

The doors opened, two Firebrands escorting Matty, General Lipton, and several American officers toward the head table. To make travel safe as well as efficient for their allies, Alarik enabled a secure portal between the Covenkirk stronghold and the American army's headquarters.

Cadmon, Aras, Viktor, and Nerina rose as Kole introduced the newcomers. The vampire lawgiver's jaw clenched when he saw the uniforms. Here were the Americans who had witnessed the captured and tortured Aeternals in Dante's lab. His mate Dania remained seated, her breathing on pause.

Standing in front of Viktor, General Lipton clasped the lawgiver's hand in both of his. "I understand your son died in the Englishman's lab. I have two sons of my own and can only imagine what you have gone through. My apologies are not enough, but they are all I can offer."

Viktor angled his head, studying the American as if he pondered what to do. "Can you assure me no other innocent will die?"

Isaac's gaze did not waver. "If I did, I'd be lying. War is a harsh mistress. Innocents are her first victims. I can tell you I will no longer treat all Aeternals as the enemy. Arisen Dawn is my target. My role, however slight in the Englishman's game, is much regretted, as is my ignorance."

Viktor nodded. "It is all I can ask. Please, allow me to introduce my mate, Dania."

"Ma'am."

Dania managed a dignified, slight nod, forgiveness not reaching her eyes.

Having chatted up the Aeternals at the table, Matty returned to Kole. "Seen your secretary in this crowd?"

"My executive assistant is at that table." He pointed toward the voluptuous, long-legged vampire who kept his office smoothly operating while somehow managing the aggressive, often difficult Firebrands.

Numerous admirers surrounded her. "You better hurry. Those are all unmated males."

Matty grinned. "She only has eyes for me." As he strode across the gym, sure enough, Bounty tracked his every move, her blood-red lips curved in a sultry smile.

Dax was sharp in his dress uniform with his black hair tied back, but his mouth was still a viperous slash between the sinister hint of his mustache and goatee. Chiara clutched his arm. "I just thought you should know, Kole…"

"No need to finish the sentence. Word is you two plan to mate. Congrats." Kole slapped the vampire's shoulder. "You were in a dark pit, son. No one's happier than I am to see you climb out." The commander lifted his drink. "May blood bind your souls."

When Chiara arched a brow, Dax explained, "It's an ancient vampire toast. It means good things for us."

She nodded. "Thanks, Commander."

"I don't know how we got so damn lucky, son. I try not to question it. I advise you to do the same."

When a tiny hand tugged on the commander's pants, he tipped his head in its direction.

"Kae stinks really bad." With his message delivered, Nerina's grandson rushed off to play.

Kole looked around for help. When he found Skyler, she was deep in conversation, chatting with human invitees, some who currently resided at strongholds for their safety. The job was his. He snagged the diaper bag from the head table and found Kae playing on the floor with other toddlers. *Yep*. She was stinky. He lifted her into the crook of his arm.

"Come on, baby, Daddy will take care of you."

She pulled Kole's nose as they left the room.

He banged on the men's room door, growling orders. "Everybody out now."

Two Firebrands exited zipping up pants, scowling, but when they saw the commander with Kae, their expressions changed rapidly to smiles.

"All clear," announced the last male.

Kole marched his daughter inside. He cleared off a small table, put her on it, lifted her frilly dress, and unfastened her diaper. He bit back a curse as he wiped her bottom and rolled up the mess, stuffing it into a container in the shoulder bag.

When they returned to the table, Skyler was waiting. "Fin said it's time for your speech. Everyone wants to eat."

Kole settled his small cargo into a chair between them. "I'm not giving a fu…" He glanced at his little girl. "…fricking speech."

Skyler smirked and arched her brows. "Okay. Just welcome everyone to the stronghold. Remember, good behavior gets rewarded." She rubbed a hand up and down his arm.

Kole's lips tilted into the lopsided grin he saved for her, thinking about where else he wanted her hand. "I can be very good, Frisca."

A loud whistle from Chay shut down all conversation while people stampeded to their seats.

Kole raised a tumbler of demon rum to his lips. After a hearty gulp, he cleared his throat and spread his legs apart, as if prepared to fight. "Last week was about sacrifice, death, and enemies routed. Since then, we have honored our fallen warriors at their Cede where a guide led their souls to the Evermore. Tonight, while we remember them, we also look ahead with hope, celebrating life with our *ferons*, our newly forged bonds, and those we love."

His gaze swept the room. "Here, Aeternals sit alongside humans. Species and breeds mix, growing more powerful, not weaker as Arisen Dawn preaches."

"To unity," shouted someone in the crowd. Glasses clinked together, and Kole returned the toast with his drink held high.

"We may stumble. Hell. We may fall flat on our asses. Um. I mean, faces. Now, I'm not a pretty boy like Ram." Hoots rang out from the Firebrands. "My mug can handle a few more scars. But stumble or fall, we will rise again because together we are stronger."

The ground shook as Firebrands and mates rose to their feet, stomping the floor once. "Oo ray," they shouted, their glasses raised.

When the noise died out, Kole set his empty tumbler down. Tucking into his pocket, he dug out a folded piece of paper, glancing at it before crumpling and tossing it onto the table. He didn't need the reminder. Each male and female's name was etched in his mind. One by one, he called out the fallen, beginning with Sig whom he knew best. "These *frerons* go before us to build a campfire. When it is our time to join them in the Evermore, their light will guide us. In the meantime, I swear on their blood I will shine light into every shadowed corner of the world to expose evil. Like you, I have heard of the dark prophecy and Cerberus's role in it. But prophecies written on scrolls are not destiny."

Kole gathered a fireball in his hand and bounced it up and down. He formed a second in his other hand. His eyes blazing red-gold, he tossed both orbs into the air. Near the ceiling, the two balls exploded, re-forming in different patterns, colors, and sizes. Bright-hued stars. Crackling sparks. Luminescent streams. Rainbows of startling tints. A spectacular aerial showstopper which shimmered to the floor, a gentle rain of light.

His audience gasped. An amazed General Lipton slapped a fist to his mouth as Matty laughed, his arm resting on Bounty's shoulders.

The commander dusted his hands. "Fuck prophecies. Our destiny is written in fire. It's an inferno fueled by the richness and power of mixed voices, by the Phoenix itself. Our blaze will light up the darkness so evil cannot thrive." He paused, his stare settling on Skyler and Kae before he spoke again. "Welcome to my stronghold. Welcome to victory." He raised his goblet. "A toast. May the tears for our dead be the blood of our enemies."

Kole sat, the room around him silent.

Maybe I went overboard. Yeah. Too much.

Snagging the neck of a nearby bottle of demon rum, he filled his glass.

Just as he was about to take a drink, General Lipton unfolded from his chair, slapping his hands together. Again and again. Skyler stood, Kae in her arms, her cheeks wet. Soon every chair in the room scraped the floor as humans and Aeternals rose, applauding the Scion Firebrand commander.

Kole waved them back into their seats, but they ignored him.

Skyler whispered in her mate's ear. "I am so proud of you. Tonight, you get a special reward, not for being good but for being spectacular. Forever, my demon."

Kole wondered if the guests assumed his grin was a reaction to their claps and hoots. His mate knew better.

Chapter Thirty-Four

Fin walked through the woods beside her wolf shifter, stroking her hand through his thick chestnut-brown fur, rewarded with a pleased growl. Thorn had parked his truck under a tree where he shrugged out of his clothes, folded them, and shifted before leading her toward Luka's den.

After about thirty minutes they arrived outside the cave where Thorn returned to two legs, baring a tight ass, narrow waist, and muscled shoulders.

Wowza.

"I can't believe you're gonna walk in there naked as the day you were born. Or is it whelped if you're a wolf shifter?"

He flung a heavy arm over Fin's shoulder. "I was born. Besides, it's my brother and sister-in-law. No need for clothes. You're the only one bothered."

"Hot and bothered."

Thorn chuckled, guiding them into the cave before calling out for Luka.

"Over here. Welcome, brother."

A large man prowled toward them. Thankfully, he was clothed. The shifter was a shorter, leaner version of Thorn, clearly her mate's sibling, both men marked by the same amber eyes, similar coloring, sexy smile. They did the male hug-pound-on-the-back thing.

"Luka, this is Fin. My mate."

The brother arched his eyebrows. "Really? You found someone to take a mutt like you?"

"Funny, brother."

When Fin stuck out a hand, Luka flicked it aside to clasp beefy arms around her, squeezing hard. "Sati, come meet Fin."

Before Thorn's sister-in-law could join them, Luka spun, shoving Fin behind him. "Wolves coming. About nine of them."

Thorn nodded, also facing the opening, crouched, his claws out, preparing to fight.

A shaky voice called from outside the cave. "Luka, it's Mori along with my mate and a few friends. We want to talk."

"Come in one at a time but keep your distance." A loud growl erupted from deep in Luka's chest.

Fin peeked around his wide shoulders to watch a stocky man enter, a red-headed female behind him with her hand on his back. Seven others, including an adolescent boy, crowded near the entrance.

"What do you want, Mori?" asked Luka.

The intruding wolf nodded at Thorn, obviously acquainted with him. "We've come to beg your forgiveness, to ask you to be our alpha again though we aren't as many as we once were."

"Why now?" Thorn curled his lip in a snarl.

Mori took a step back. "Me. My family. We are not strong wolves like you. We never wanted Karth for a leader but were unable to stand up to him. We need you."

Luka scrubbed a hand across his stubbled beard.

A woman, Fin assumed Sati, walked with deliberate, slow steps from another chamber of the cave, arriving in time to hear the request. She touched her mate's arm. "You sided against my Luka. You don't deserve him."

Fin thought she saw an angry beast stirring just beneath the surface of Sati's skin.

But Luka calmed her when he took her hand before he spoke to Mori. "Forgiveness is needed on both sides. I wasn't a good alpha. I chose to ignore what was going on in my own pack. If I return, all must give vows.

I vow to be better. You must vow to stay away from drugs, to be loyal to Scath."

Mori glanced at his followers. "We have already pledged to a better life, but we will do it again in blood to our alpha."

Luka angled his much larger body toward Sati. "Mate, this is up to you, too."

Her eyes softened as she caressed his arm. "Luka, welcome our pack into our home. Tonight, we celebrate beginnings. Our renewed pack. The mating of our beloved brother Thorn to Fin."

When Mori's mate broke down in tears, Sati rushed to her side, taking her into her arms.

Fin didn't understand the emotion behind what was happening, only the smile on Thorn's lips as the stiffness in his shoulders melted away. He had worried about his younger brother. Now, he could hope.

****

The chase was on again. What a cock-up. Miller had run to Las Vegas to check on one of his charges before he turned her and all his responsibilities over to his second. His replacement was ready to assume the load, probably thinking with a clear head. Too bad he couldn't say the same about himself.

Since he hadn't picked up the tail until he shoved off from his assignment's neighborhood, he hadn't led the supes to her, but it was just a matter of time.

Miller checked his cellphone, which was almost out of oomph. When Braelyn didn't answer, he left a message. "Hey, luv. Your favorite Brit here being chased by some non-human blokes. The same blood-seeking missile vampire is on my arse again. Anyway, I'm ready for a pickup. Tired of this shite. Call with the where and when. Gotta lose these guys. Out."

He was fast-footing it down the Strip, dodging

tourists who wore ugly shorts and sipped on tall drinks while they hurried off to lose money.

Miller had parked his rental car in the garage at the TI. On the way to his room in the Palazzo, he picked up his shadows. Now, he glanced over his shoulder as he crossed against the light, spying the two big guys hustling after him, one of them his nemesis vamp. Shoving between a man and woman, knocking another couple aside, he sprinted. Not toward his hotel but toward the Venetian. Across the bridge. Through the archways. Into the Grand Canal Shoppes.

Damn. They were still with him.

Miller dropped all pretense of being a nice guy while he bowled his way through the crowd. This was life-death stuff now. He raced into what passed for St. Mark's Square as he headed toward the parking garage where he had a spare auto. Lessons learned in British intel stuck with him. Don't park where you bed down and always have a second way out.

Not bothering to check his pursuers, Miller jumped into the Corvette, showy but fast, definitely not a banger. He needed speed. The garage was empty, allowing him to zoom out to Sands Avenue. Once he crossed the Strip, he took a right onto Paradise, grabbing 215 before he opened up on 15 Southbound.

Whizzing past cars, Miller full-throttled it, determined to lose the supes. Still barreling at top velocity, he neared Halloran Springs, weaving in and out of slower cars that obeyed the speed limit.

Then, in the distance, strung across the interstate were three SUV's. Rather than stop, Miller swung left to cross the median. The Corvette nose-dived into the ditch. Tires spun. Forward. Backward. He was going nowhere.

The sports car was built for speed, not off-roading. Hindsight being what it was, the TI transport would have been better.

Miller unbuckled his seatbelt. Dodging traffic in the middle of the busy highway, he flagged tourists heading the other way into Vegas, but they were in too much of a hurry. Tits, ass, all-you-could-eat buffets, and bottomless glasses of booze were waiting down the road. No one stopped.

Six big guys were coming at him fast from the direction of the roadblock. His favorite vampire was knees up, legs churning toward him from the other direction.

Convinced only plonkers were captured, Miller spurted off into the desert. Abandoned gas station. Diner. Lots of sand.

All in all, a terrific spot to be on foot and running for my life. Not even a big cactus to hide behind.

His cellphone buzzed. Braelyn. Great timing. "Not now, luv. I'm on the lam. They're gonna get me. You and your muscle-bound mate better put together a search-and-rescue."

Disconnecting, he raced across the desert, removing the cellphone battery and sim card. He paused long enough to crush his last connection to hope under foot, making it juiceless but untraceable.

****

Chiara lay on her stomach atop their bed, her head resting on folded arms, while Dax growled, bandaging the open wounds on her back. "It's not your fault. Shit happens to everyone during the Bludhunt. Normally, you wouldn't drag me by my ankles across a rocky ground for a sex session. Besides, look at my new tat after our mating ceremony."

Chiara lifted an arm to show Dax the underside of her wrist where the Bludclan Mortus's skull with fangs was emblazoned, a match to her vampire's marking. "It's a little grim. Still, it proves I'm yours. Live with it."

"I hurt you."

"Braelyn and Rein told us what to expect. All vampires become raging maniacs during the ceremony. You know, I put a doozy of a lump on your noggin when I knocked you out. You've also got lots of scratches. You don't see me snarling about the damage I inflicted."

"Say what you will. I should have controlled myself."

"While millions can't, you should. Stop being so damn hard on yourself."

"I could have killed you."

"You didn't. I held my own. Isn't that the purpose of the Bludhunt? To make certain we weaklings are deserving of your precious vampire sperm. After all, can't have your breed hooking up with a lame-ass human female who would pollute your pure vampire blood. Like Braelyn, I proved I'm strong enough to mate you. Give me the kudos I earned."

He patted her ass. "Done."

She pushed to her knees, flipped over, and rested against the headboard. "Come here. Let me heal you."

"No. I deserve every fucking pain I have."

"You love to suffer. Here's the thing. You were aggressive. More than a little scary. I give you that. But I must be wacky because I kinda liked you scary and doling out the wild sex. A repeat performance would be most welcome. Not all the time. Occasionally. You don't regret we are mated, do you?"

After the banquet, Dax had dragged Chiara to their bedroom, sex on his mind and an obvious boner chafing against his zipper. Unfortunately, he hadn't been able to carry out any of his wicked plans before he collapsed onto the floor, holding his stomach, writhing. The last thing she heard was him shouting "Larissa."

Then poof. Her molecules scattered.

She materialized in a barren cave alongside the high priestess of the Bludhunt, a nightmare cloaked in red, her bearing regal, her eyes cold.

Dax popped in snarling, about to jump out of his skin, his muscles bulkier, his build bigger. That wasn't his only upgrade for the situation. His dumb-ass fangs were longer and sharper. The bones in his cheeks were knife-sharp, and his crimson-streaked irises were like poison darts.

Larissa, living up to her rep as the stately bitch in charge of making sure the vampire breed stayed strong, had highlighted what was about to happen before she spoke a few words in a language Chiara didn't understand. Then Dax attacked, his goal being to subdue her. Her goal was to survive. She fought back, proving she was made of the right stuff. After countless bumps, scrapes, and spells, they had amazing but rough sex while they exchanged blood. More than once. By the end of the rite, Chiara was limp from numerous orgasms, branded, and happy.

Grunting, Dax rested his head in her lap, his long black hair fanning out across her thighs. Guilt shadowed his midnight eyes while he sawed his molars back and forth.

Chiara put her fingers to his temples. Pressing, she rubbed in small circles, channeling healing through her touch. Dax's wounds were not all on the outside. They festered inside, making him sometimes cruel and self-destructive. "I asked you a question."

He closed his eyes, his thick lashes laying in lacy arches on his cheeks. His snarls turned to moans as the muscles in his jaws loosened and his breathing relaxed. He looked at peace.

Chiara's magic touch soothed him, calming his

angry beast. Years ago, when he had saved her from a burning car, he'd unknowingly activated a Blood Coven descendant's power which she used to survive a perilous childhood. Now she repaid him by healing his mind, by loving him. She had found this extraordinary man, this vampire, and she was never giving him back.

Dax remained silent for so long, she thought he was asleep or had forgotten her question. Finally, his lids flicked open, his black eyes soft rather than sinister. "Little witch, I will never regret mating you. If all the terrible things I have done or experienced have led me to this moment, I would live them all again to be here with you."

Chiara swallowed tears as she continued to trace light circles on her man's temples. Four giant wolfhounds chose that moment to jump on their bedroom door, wanting inside.

Dax pushed off the bed, striding naked toward the noise, his black hair swishing across his back, his muscles flexing with each step. "I'll get them."

Softie.

****

Indigo strolled the banks of the River Am. Arisen Dawn was licking its wounds. For now.

Her job allowed no respite, though. So, here she was, steeling her nerves, preparing to gaze into the turbulent river upstream where she saw all possible futures before one roiled into the present. Some good. Some bad. All overloading her mind, driving her closer to a breakdown.

She flopped onto the grass, drew up her knees, and gathered her flowing skirt around her ankles. Not ready for the task yet, she pressed her palm to a heart which sat in her chest like a heavy coffin. She pushed against the ache, the ache for peace.

Removing cowgirl boots, Indigo wiggled her toes. *Aah.* If only her mind could be freed the same way. Grab a heel. Tug. Slide. Release. *Nope.* The burden still weighed on her heart.

Why me?

She angled her gaze toward the sky. High above, Oskar drifted on an air current, squawking to get her attention. "Naughty gryphon," she shouted, motioning the conjured beast to sit beside her, his sharp eyes not missing the gesture.

Her gryphon was unique. His head and wings were an eagle, his neck and torso a dragon's neon green scales, his haunches and feet a lion. When he swooped beside her, his massive head butted her shoulder. "You are so needy." She petted the creature, her warrior, her confidant, her alter ego.

He purred. If a gryphon could be said to do that.

Indigo looped an arm over his neck, not able to go halfway around it. "You've been with me since I was a wee witchling, Oskar. You know me best. Will the river drive me mad?"

She gazed into his darting eagle eyes. "What's that you say? I already am?"

His head whipped up. Down.

"Of course, you'd say that. But crazy can be freeing, my wild thoughts a dance. A tango of delusion. A waltz of fantasies. A foxtrot to a little number called paranoia." Leaping up, Indigo dug her naked toes into moisture-rich grass blades, her freshly painted nails a bright contrast. "Enough. Time to work."

She focused upstream. Gasping, she clenched her fists at her side, countless possible futures absorbed through her dark pupils, seared into her brain. A tear slid down her cheek.

So much to remember.

Oskar's tongue lashed out, long, sticky, to lick it off the drop of moisture.

"Yuck."

Indigo grabbed the hem of her T-shirt, yanking it overhead. Her hands went behind her back to unsnap her bra, slipping it off her shoulders, letting it fall to the ground. Her thumbs hooked into the waistband of her skirt as she shimmied it down her legs along with new red lace panties. While she steadied herself against Oskar's thigh, she stepped out of her clothes.

Comfortable naked, Indigo raised her arms to stretch right. Overhead. Then left. "I'm going in for a cold dip, Oskar. Don't let me drown."

Her feet slurped through the damp grass on her way to the river's edge. At the last minute, she pulled the tie from her hair, letting it fall free to tickle her ass, free from the weight of her heavy locks.

A voice.

She jerked to a halt.

A male voice. A loud, laughing male voice.

Indigo spun toward a still pool in the river, formed by boulders and fallen trees. "What the fuck?"

****

Matty chuckled as the crowd parted for four scary ass men who lumbered into the bar. Tough soldiers stepped away from the lethal predators who sucked the air right out of the room.

"I think they're here," said General Lip Lipton. "They are big mutherfuckers. I'd never stand a chance against that demon Kole." He pushed back his chair to stand. "Gentlemen. We saved seats."

Cadmon glanced around. "Is this a safe place to talk?"

Matty greeted the arrivals with a nod and a smile. "Sure. The soldiers are all ours. The place has the added bene of serving great local brews. What's your pleasure? The general's buying."

"What?" said Lip.

"In that case," said Nace, "I'd like dark and strong. You pick it, Matty."

"Give me the Hoppin Good Times ale." Jarek chuckled. "You do know ylves make that brew on Scath?"

"You're kidding," said General Lipton.

Cadmon pulled out his chair while he studied the chalkboard menu. "Get me the KBS. A distant relative of mine owns the brewery. Hope he hasn't had any trouble with Arisen Dawn."

Matty placed their orders with the waiter. "Those Arisen Dawn idiots have to be messing with the economy."

Kole tapped his fingers on the table, containing the fire. "They are. Commerce is suffering. More families, fearing for their lives, close their shops daily to report to the strongholds. We've become damn hotels for the displaced. Of course they have no place else to go. Kids being hurt. Unacceptable."

"We routed them this time," said the general. "A few losses on our side, but we know you turned back most of the sonsabitches before they reached us. We are grateful. I suppose it's too much to hope this is the end of Arisen Dawn."

After a tall soldier delivered the drinks, Cadmon took a big swig of KBS. "Aah. A fine stout. We figure the insurgents are regrouping, rebuilding, preparing for a bigger battle. Cerberus has a plan which will include the Blood Coven descendants. Most likely, since their ancestors created the realms and portals, he'll use their offspring to undo them. And, gentlemen, if the portals go, the bloodshed will be unimaginable. The destiny of our planet may be in the hands of a madman."

Lip set his glass on the table. "I was afraid you would say that. How many casualties did you suffer?"

"Five," said Jarek. "All newbies, not ready for battle. Nace?"

"Eleven, two of them experienced warriors. Others recruits. Not enough time to train. Sad."

Matty watched as bursts of fire shot from Kole's red-gold eyes. He admired the demon's power, glad the guy was on his side.

"Seven," the Covenkirk commander said. "One a young demon, not new but not dry behind the ears. The other Firebrands were green."

The table of human soldiers and Firebrand warriors sat in silent memory.

Matty raised his glass, fearing the salute would not be the last. "Muscles of steel, nerves of iron, tongues of silver, hearts of gold. Soldiers all."

The men held their mugs high. After taking a drink, Cadmon patted his pants pocket and dug out his ringing phone. He listened, the color draining from his face. Disconnecting, he paused before talking, his hands fisted, his eyelids heavy. "That was my informant. We know the identity of Cerberus."

The End

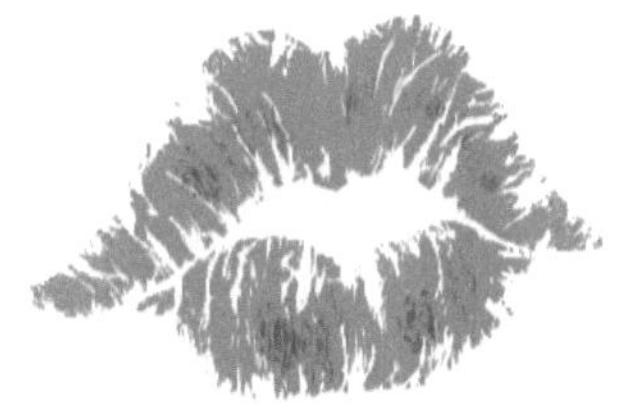

EVERNIGHT PUBLISHING ®

www.evernightpublishing.com

www.ingramcontent.com/pod-product-compliance
Lightning Source LLC
Chambersburg PA
CBHW020459020726
47493CB00001B/99

* 9 7 8 0 3 6 9 5 0 8 9 0 4 *